Lone Pine

by Ken Waxlax

Reader Praise for **Lone Pine** by Ken Waxlax

Spent an hour walking my dog, thinking about this book. It captivated me while reading it and stayed with me all day. Marie R

Hard to put down, paints pictures with words. Amazing book. Jacquelyn B

Just finished Lone Pine. Loved it! Felt like I was right there. Dianna B

This is an excellent story with characters that have depth. Good enough that I will re-read it in the future. Darth K

One of the best I've read in a while, couldn't put it down but didn't want it to end. Dianne C

A movie should be made from this book and filmed in that small town. Catherine D

The story line was well written and kept me interested to the last page. I felt that I was right there, and would recommend this read to anyone! Nita

This story captured my attention from the very beginning; the descriptions were spot on. It quickly becomes a page turner and the characters (especially those Thomson women!) engage you as the mystery unfolds. MJM

Tight, literary prose, quirky, well-drawn characters. A prize. Amy L

This is a work of fiction. Names, characters, businesses, places, events and incidents are either the products of the author's imagination or used in a fictitious manner. Any resemblance to actual persons, living or dead, or actual events or places is purely coincidental.

Second Edition

ISBN-13: 978-1530691616
ISBN-10: 1530691613

K Waxlax Enterprises Publishing
43630 Pisces Court La Quinta, CA 92253

Sincere and humble thanks

To my family and friends

You inspire and uplift me

And in my mind I still need a place to go

All my changes were there.

Helpless by Neil Young

Chapter One

September 16, 2003

David Chapman Los Angeles, CA

That 4am phone call still haunted him. He'd jumped out of bed, annoyed, thinking Dani had lost her purse or house key again, but that night, it was her life. October 20, 2001 and David Chapman was forever changed. Standing at her grave today, in Forest Lawn Cemetery, he remembered her happy dance when she was only six, smiling with her arms in the air, cutting circles to music only she could hear, a born dancer. They had named her Danielle, after a goddess of love.

He didn't cry every time anymore, but he felt it rising today. "I sold the house, Dani. It wasn't a home anymore . . . I'm going to Grandma's place in Lone Pine, Minnesota. Wolfe wrote a whole novel on why that's stupid."

It's ok Daddy

He could still hear her valley girl twang.

"It might not be a home either, but I'll check it out, like when you were a kid—check it out. I'll be back for you."

I know you will Daddy

"Bye my daughter. I love you." He turned and shuffled away. His pretentious douche-bag Range Rover was packed full. He popped an Adderall found in Dani's room while he was cleaning it out after the accident. Drunk Rich-Twerp had wrapped his BMW around a tree, dodging a deer. Twerp had lived. No cure for that except murder, which had received due consideration. He cruised down Forest Lawn Drive, past the last plots, and blasted off the onramp at eighty.

Three days later, he took the Highway 169 exit ramp off Highway 53 and shuddered at the familiarity. The two-lane road of old had been expanded and modernized. The steak house on the corner was gone. The place he'd taken Angie Thomson for their Junior Prom dinner. It came back so clearly, his first love.

Lone Pine was close now. He flashed on a line from a McCarthy novel about going home, the quote escaped him but the meaning remained lodged in his memory—the things you cherished would be gone and the things you loathed would remain.

Maybe Cormac was mistaken . . .

Chapter Two

September 19, 2003

Angie Thomson

Angie Thomson sat on her dock, and watched the thin wisps of breeze wrinkle the glass surface of Lone Pine Lake. Late September in northern Minnesota and the sun was out, the bugs gone, and it felt like it might hit sixty-five degrees today. All of which should have made for a nice day, except daughter Clarissa had called and said she ran into Olson, the contractor, who told her David had left LA. Clarissa had been her blessing and curse since birth thirty-two years ago. She knew exactly where to stick the knife.

Three weeks ago, she'd called to say Olson pulled a permit on the Chapman remodel, and she loved David's books but why would he come back to this sewer? Why indeed, Angie thought.

Clarissa said she would welcome him anyway. Angie thought about what "welcome" might mean to her daughter. Probably wasn't milk and cookies. Hell, he might be coming via the Arctic route and anyway she was forty minutes of bad road from town, so what did she care. He could and would be avoided. She jumped up, shook her head. "Ok, change these toxic thoughts. Beautiful day for canoeing," and pulled it down to the water. "Are you 18 or 50 for God sake? Grow up. That's thirty-three years gone and good riddance." She slung the life-vest over her shoulders and pushed off. A few strong J-strokes and she flowed into the cove. Smooth hard paddling, a smart course over a smooth lake toward the Bald Eagle's nest. "Thirty-two years and 233 days. But who's counting."

Chapter Three

Minnesota Highway 169 was straight and deserted. The hours alone on the road left David's mind quavering in on itself, never a signpost of sanity. Yet, this vacant road and the sheer distance between the life he'd left and the new one he was about to start seemed like grace notes floating above a dour backbeat. The lack of LA chaos lent a certain stoic pleasure. It seemed almost romantic, and he allowed a slight smile. What could be wrong with a little deluded romance in a fifty-year-old?

The road caught his attention again, curving sporadically around ancient township boundaries, inside which no towns had grown, marking sections of boreal forests, swamps, godless glacial deposits, all inhabited by black flies and mosquitoes and scant few humans. He would need to banish his demons, maybe try to recapture something simple and uncomplicated like enjoyment if that still existed. The thought of uncomplicated and enjoyment together gave him pause, but he let it go in favor of driving. The scenery blurred at eighty miles an hour, scents and sights so familiar that time melted into the forest tapestry. A world murdered in winter, reborn in spring, year after year.

He took the slight bend onto the long straightaway and touched the Rover up to eighty-five. The trees grew well away from the road. He could watch for deer. With luck he'd see one close. Instead, he saw the parked cruiser, but too late.

It came out, lights spinning. Shit. He slowed and pulled over, heart hammering. "It's speeding," he muttered. "Relax." But he knew damn well this had nothing to do with speeding and everything to do with thirty-two years and 233 days ago, when Officer Stark planted a pound of pot in his parent's car and he was shipped off to oblivion. This officer took the license and insurance, made a smart-ass remark about California, and inexplicably told him to get out of the vehicle. And waited for him do it.

The cop ambled away and stood at the cruiser door, talking on the box. David could almost hear him. Then a breeze blew words to him, "Yeah, it's him. Doing 85. What da ya want me to do?" The air went calm and all he heard was static. Then the officer was back, asking him if it was okay to look around inside the truck and David said, "Why?" The cop gave him a dirty look, handed him the ticket, and walked back to the cruiser.

He watched the cruiser pull away and turn right at Four Corners. He spun dirt and hit the highway hard, jamming the brakes at the stop sign, then cranked it up to eighty again before backing off the gas as the road passed through swampland. Black water surrounding tiny islands of weed, rust-needled tamarack trees sprinkled throughout the quagmire stretching on for miles, vast and empty. The smell of rot and decay assaulted him, with it a vision of his ex-wife Sandy wrinkling her nose. He'd quit smoking because she hated the smell of that, too. She was an Oregon girl with spunk, Hollywood looks, and mega-brains. So smart she scared him sometimes. Seventeen years of work had gone into their relationship, but in the end, they couldn't get past the death of a child. Although at sixteen, Dani was hardly a child, more like an adolescent trapped inside a woman's body. He reached for the pack of cigarettes he'd bought in Albuquerque and lit one up. Maybe out of spite. It made him light-headed, evidently not a smoker, yet.

Dead Man's Curve came up too fast. He braked hard. An old pickup flashed past going the other way, paint gone, bumpers rusted. First vehicle he'd seen in miles except the fucking cop. His laden Range Rover hunkered into the banked turn at forty, accelerated, swept around and shot out onto the straight stretch where rolls of green grass shimmered behind a single row of jack pines guarding the golf course to his right. He'd played only once since Dani passed and all that had done was remind him of wasted time he could have spent with her. He'd donated his clubs.

Ahead to the left, a deer appeared in cutover pulp. It ambled toward the highway. His chance. Mind raging, he stomped on the gas and roared straight at it. Its tail flashed. It leaped across the ditch, barely dodging the Rover bumping off the road, down the shallow embankment, close past a stump, dirt flying, tires skidding up the other side, and back onto the blacktop. His eyes flashed, heart pounded. He still wanted to kill Rich-Twerp, but a deer would do in a pinch. He'd spotted three others on this trip up north, but all too far from the road. Place is thick with them, he thought. Probably should get this under control. Wait a couple months for the season to open. He could almost hear her saying, *"I'm lonely,"* with a pained sadness that cut him.

Ahead he saw the water tower that every town up here had and knew the block letters said LONE PINE. He felt it coming, an amalgamation twisting into another meltdown, tears this time, the beauty and serenity overwhelming. The clouds parted and the sky opened into a shade of blue so deep and rich it seemed unnatural, like a paint-by-numbers mistake.

A black truck came up fast behind. The passing swoosh startled him. He glanced at his speedometer, a level sixty, the road rail straight now, and watched the truck disappear into a distant dot.

David passed the "Welcome to Lone Pine" sign, then old city hall with its two-cell jail remembered well and not fondly. He'd been raped there. That same building had housed the tiny library. He doubted any allocation for his own titles, doubted anyone here read his books. Critical acclaim meant nothing here, nor did unrealized potential.

Things here were basic, solid, and for that, he was grateful. He needed simpler, slower, and safer. No more traffic jams, country clubs, man-made lakes or breasts. He would work in quiet contemplation, without eighteen-wheelers rumbling by or airplanes thundering overhead, only the faint click of the keyboard to break the silence, to break the drought. What he needed was inspiration. And a new book damn quick.

He glanced at the little houses without fences, built in the fifties on curving boulevards, trees grown tall, old. Real homes filled with real people unknown to him. The lonely hollow returned. He saw a gray-haired woman struggling to hitch a boat to her truck and stopped. "Need some help?" The code evidently inbred.

She wiped sweat from her forehead and eyed him. "Can't seem to get the trailer over the ball hitch." She was breathing hard, tugging on the trailer fork. It was a small aluminum fishing boat with oars and a trolling motor. "Heavier than I remembered. It's my annual fishing day. Hubby and I talk. He loved his fishing, rest his soul."

David walked to the trailer and lifted the fork, easily centered the hitch over the ball, dropped it gently, and attached the safety chain. "How you going to get it back on the trailer?"

"Hell, that's the easy part," she said. "Cleaning all them walleyes is what takes time." She shook his hand, asked his name. He tried to smile, told her, returned the question. Mabel Ottoman said she'd lived in her little house for nearly fifty years. It was just like the one he'd inherited.

"Thanks," she said. "Missed you at your Mom's funeral." Her voice was compassionate, lacking judgment. She looked at the trailer apparently not expecting an answer.

"I couldn't," he said and figured she could hear his sadness. Officer Stark's threat had been easy to understand: "I see you here and you're going to prison." David should have known better as he aged, but if you were set-up once, it could happen again. So could rape. He should have ignored the threat and come anyway, but life got away from him even before the shit storm started.

Mabel climbed into the truck and started it. "We only do what we can." She waved and pulled away.

He did the same. A church slid by him unnoticed, then the high school, parking lot empty, the school from which he should have graduated, but didn't and thought, Dani never had that chance. His eyes drifted heavenward, then back to the road, the street sign, and all those miles were down to a few blocks. The house, the home maybe, was coming into view. His neck was knotted, head ached, and he was thankful that last Adderall was mostly worn off.

He stopped in front and eyed the place, the entry door was new, roof looked okay, but the whole place needed paint. He had the key on his ring, but he wasn't going in, not today. The basketball hoop still hung from the garage, the paint chipped and faded, the rim rusted. The Wolfe book rang in his ears, *'Do you think you can really go home again?'*

He touched the gas pedal, turned left on Main heading back toward the motel, hungry, wishing the remodel was finished, the kitchen, the confines of cozy rooms, in a safe and quiet town, with questionable restaurants reserved for people too tired or lazy to cook. Tired the operative word, lazy lived somewhere else.

At the stop sign on the edge of town, a late model Subaru rolled into the intersection, the driver's face turned toward him. Their eyes met. A woman. Her eyes grew wide. Her lips formed an O, shocked as if she'd seen a ghost. He certainly had. Angie Thomson's head snapped away and her car lurched forward. He saw the flat plane of her cheek that radiated an olive glow as it had all those years ago, her hair still falling in soft dark curls. A girl sat in the passenger seat that could have been Dani's twin. "God, not that too." His legs felt numb. Her car fled out of sight. An ancient dream dropped like a bomb, exploding inside his head and his heart.

He clenched the steering wheel, remembering their pure and desperate love. The night with her in his parents' station wagon remained sacred. His exile had ended all they had shared, if it had ended at all. The way his heart beat now, maybe it hadn't. Maybe they had both led parallel lives in their separate universes. Who was the girl, her daughter?

A car approached from behind him and he flexed his knees and stepped on the gas, turning to the roadside, narrowly missing the ditch. He flashed on meeting Angie's family, her mother, her younger sister Bunny, who were the two most attractive women in town, and thinking he was dating the most gorgeous ugly duckling in creation. He'd liked them, chatted, took an interest in their lives. The necessary work of small town relationships in 1970, and he wondered if that quaint tradition still existed up here. In his daughter's world, he was lucky if he got a quick handshake at the door. A sit down dinner was out of the question. Maybe if he'd demanded quaint, Dani would still be alive. But second guessing fate was a fool's fantasy and he knew that at every level.

He drove out to the lake noticing nothing but forests and the fading light and wondered what it would be like when the inevitable happened and he came face to face with Angie again. He'd heard parts of her story. The tragedy had unfolded while he sat in that jail cell, and it dwarfed young lovers. Her mother murdered, her father arrested for the crime, her beautiful sister found the body and lapsed off into herself and into an institution where for all he knew, she remained. Being back here and seeing her again reminded him of his unconditional adoration, a part of his past to hold tightly. A lucky gift—not a loss as he'd seen it then. But she had a life of her own, evidenced by the teenage girl in the car.

If she was still here, who else remained? Randy Stark, the crooked cop that framed and fucked him? David had little idea what he might say to Angie, and wondered if he could control himself if he ran into Stark.

Chapter Four

The black F-150 parked on the wrong side of the street, cop style. The Municipal Building was a ruddy brick structure two blocks long, one story high, a converted elementary school with two flagpoles and a long, wide sidewalk that Randy Stark leaped onto and, in spite of his sixty-one years, rushed up in his US Marines double-time walk.

Mayor Harry Barnet sat in the old Principal's office, now the mayor's office with windows facing the street. He watched Stark coming toward the building. The mayor frowned at a document in his hands, a permit for a remodeling job, an ordinary paper on an ordinary day in an ordinary little town, and still the name on the paper made him nervous. Randy Stark burst through his office door and stood before his desk.

"He's back," Stark said. "I told him to stay out."

"I doubt Chapman will create any problems, Randy."

"He's a problem just being here. Things could get dredged up."

"He didn't know anything Randy. You forget that? Hell, he's just another guy. Leave it alone. It will all go away."

"He had an attitude."

"He had your girl."

Stark blushed. "That ain't the point. This could be trouble. There's a million places he could go, why here?"

"Maybe he misses the place."

"That's bullshit and you know it."

"I called Clarissa. She'll find out. Take it easy. Go fishing." Harry's patience wore thin.

"I should take Chapman and throw the fucker overboard."

"Let's not have another murder, Randy."

Stark glared. "So send Pandora to open the box. Come on, Harry. There's no statute of limitations on murder."

"Cut the panic, Randy. Shove off."

Randy Stark grunted and walked out. When he was Chief of Police, he would have handled this his own way, like he always had. Everybody had dirt, stains on the fabric of their lives. He found it, and solved the problem. But he was retired now and whiling away his time on the lakes and in the woods, stripped of his authority right down to the privileged parking spot at the Municipal Building.

The town had not replaced him in the last year, just gave Policeman Pete a miniscule raise and contracted for more time from the Sheriff's Department.

The town was happy, except for Randy. He had relished the sanctity of police power since his stint as an MP in the Marines, stationed in Saigon and raking in graft. Next stop was in the rural St. Louis County Sheriff's Department where financial opportunities diminished, but so had the cost of living and the lack of supervision made up for the money in many ways, most notably the inherent ability to be judge, jury and executioner in a sparsely populated region replete with people like Randy who thought the country was going to hell. Laws were in place so the middle class knew in which direction to march, not to bring down a righteous President like Nixon, who had turned the country in the right direction. There was talk of a local Klan chapter, but in the end, they didn't need it. They had Randy Stark. He was their man, took care of business without the expense of lawyers and courts and that damn untidy media and those inconvenient constitutional rights.

He got in his truck, still fuming, tires squealed as he pulled onto the deserted street and headed back to his new country home to get his boat, a bucket of minnows, and get out to the lake before dusk where he could enjoy the solitude and think about the hope he had for the future now that George W. Bush was President and the country finally had a chance again. He had handled things before and he would again, his way, the right way.

Chapter Five

Angie Thomson ignored the rearview mirror. David's face looked rugged, a weathered patina pasted over that boyishness she remembered and she stepped on the gas and shuddered again, hardly believing it was David Chapman. She knew he was coming back to town, but she didn't know when and nothing prepared her for it today. Her chin elevated slightly and her face updated its haughty shield in spite of her grubby attire. Missing were her expensive clothes, part of an image she'd crafted over the years, though after early morning fishing and afternoon shopping, she was not up for the full make up, hair, and costume, opting instead for an old U of M sweatshirt and raggedy jeans. She had planned to drop granddaughter Elsa at home without extraneous stops. Then he showed up. Seeing him again ignited twitches in her leg, the car lurching slightly with each, eliciting glances.

"What is it, Grandma?" Elsa asked in her familiar tone that always sounded like a nun. Angie ignored it for the umpteenth time knowing it came from her father and his ilk and hoping she'd outgrow it eventually.

They passed Birch Boulevard, the teen still watching her, waiting for an answer. With nothing forthcoming, the adolescent urge to fill silence got the better of her. "You're different in town."

"Nonsense," Angie said, adding a slight smile to soften the defensive tone.

"No, grandma really. Think about it. In the canoe yesterday you're all laughing, splashing me, cold by the way, and all passionate about finding those loon babies, worried they were already late leaving. Today you're watching eagles instead of fishing. It's like the Holy Spirit enters you out there." Elsa smiled. "Right? And look at you now. All frozen lake. It's like that even without the man in the strange truck around."

Angie looked over at her, knowing the girl was right, but not about the man. So, yes, it was today. He's here, big deal. "You've worn me out, okay." Angie's face softened. "Give me your hand," she said and reached across the seat.

Elsa touched it and smiled, a bit teasing. "My girlfriends get that 'look' over boy problems."

Angie felt the squeeze, the girl's thumb rubbing softly. "It was two lifetimes ago, baby." That seemed all that was necessary, as if a crumb of truth was all the girl had waited for, a validation of her perception, and now the teen squirmed and faced forward, watching Main Street. Maybe the subject had faded into boredom. With Elsa it was hard to tell. She spent so much time cloistered in that Baptist church that separating the teen from the bible thumper took a fair degree of insight and sometimes Angie missed. But not often and not today. David Chapman or no, she needed to stay attentive and deliver a message to the girl's father, Bobby, one of the deacons of the church, that a couple things required addressing. It was *her* granddaughter and that made it her business regardless of what Bobby thought.

Today's two issues, seemingly minor to Elsa obviously, were just plain wrong. Angie's exasperation had started early this morning. A man who seemed bent on fixing up his sixteen-year-old son with Elsa for the past couple of years had invited them fishing. They'd awoke a bit late, scrambling to get ready. Angie had entered the bathroom where Elsa was washing her face and noticed the bra straps cutting at the girl's back and shoulders. She knew that damn fundamentalist father had a hand in it someway. Whether he tortured the girl on purpose or out of stupidity was immaterial. Angie had asked how old that thing was and was shocked to find out it was only a couple months old, and that father had given her three, all identical. "Doesn't it hurt to wear them?" Angie had asked. "A little sometimes," the girl said. Angie asked why she didn't buy her own undergarments at age fifteen? She said she didn't have money and dad had always done it for her. "Do you have a bank account?" The answer was no. Her father had sole custody, another Clarissa hiccup, but this was unconscionable regardless.

They'd finished fishing about noon, cleaned two nice sized walleyes, and Angie took the girl into the nearby town to shop. "Doesn't that feel better?" Angie had asked after they found the right size, and the girl said sure but they seemed so, uh, huge, which reminded Angie of her daughter who had said the same thing but with pride instead of something near shame.

They pulled to a stop in front of Elsa's house on Hemlock Drive and Bobby appeared in the doorway, leaning against the frame, waiting. "Thanks Grandma. Let's do it again. Call me, okay?"

Angie hugged the girl. "Maybe next weekend. We can burn your old bras."

She asked her to have dad come to the car for a word. It was a short word. Quit tormenting my granddaughter immediately, treat her like the young woman she is, and I'll be picking her up at lunch on Monday so we can open a bank account for her, which you may not touch. Understand? He started to argue, but the ice glare shut him up. "I'll be checking on you, Bobby. Your repression didn't work on my daughter and I'll make damn sure it doesn't come down on my granddaughter." She didn't raise her voice even the slightest. He stood away from the window, a dull expression that said he hadn't expected this and didn't have a biblical quote ready, and she put her Subaru in gear and pulled away.

Alone in the car, the image of David's face came back, his obvious shock, the bleached streaks in his hair, shoulders more thick than she remembered, and she turned onto Cedar Drive and coasted slowly past her old house and remembered kissing him parked in that driveway all those years ago, the day before she never saw him again.

Damn it, he was back. It seemed like days had passed, not years, but she would never let him know that. When she heard he was coming back the façade held but seeing him left a knot in her stomach. And pissed her off. How could he intrude on her space after all these years? She'd made a life here. Maybe it was a bit delusional in some ways but isn't that what orphans do? Create something out of nothing. Get by in whatever way can be conjured, make a new truth out of an old lie. She'd managed to finance it with compromises most women would never make. The men who'd inflicted it all on her were still right here in little Lone Pine, walking around, running the town. Her animosity remained thinly veiled.

She had her daughter here, her granddaughter, that was her life, and she was proud of it and them. But David's face in that Range Rover forced her to circle back, and it made her angrier and more determined. She had risen above the gossip, the innuendo, the judgmental rituals rampant in any small town, and had gained the respect she deserved, no matter how she'd done it, a little faux arrogance, a lot of patience and her Lady of the Lake persona which was accepted finally. David Chapman could not contaminate that. He'd had his chance with her. He'd failed.

She drove the forty-five minutes back her cabin where she'd lived for most of the last fifteen years since the skirmish with Clarissa over dating Bobby. She was Elsa's age then. He was a hockey player like David, though older and not as skilled, leaving a sour taste in her mouth and a vision of apples and trees, culminating in the highest insult of Clarissa moving in with her dad, Mayor Harry Barnet. It didn't last long and reconciliation occurred but those were stories for another time, Angie's mind was already overloaded as she pulled into her long driveway.

Daylight was gone and she wasn't hungry anymore, thank you David, but she had a case of good Californian Chardonnay that cost a small fortune from last month. Not that money mattered, it came with her divorce from Mayor Barnet, whom she had despised since age seventeen. She had married him purely for Clarissa's legitimacy and for his bankroll. The trust funds were properly and inalterably set up for her and Clarissa with another added when Elsa came along. All long after David. She poured a glass of wine and sat on her porch, listening to the silence, which usually calmed her. Tonight though, there was an odd, alien sensation. She wished Clarissa was here or Elsa, or maybe it was time to get a dog. She decided this was what long banished loneliness felt like. Why was it back, now? She blamed David. That was easy. He wasn't there to defend himself, although in her experience, easy usually meant paving over things that should be unearthed and confronted.

Owning forty acres of land made for an endless supply of work which she used against sullen and useless emotions like tonight's, and taking a second glass of wine, she thought it unfair to blame David solely, for she had a part in it too. It went back to her mother, to that day she found out what kind of compromises could be forced upon women. She remembered the August day before her senior year, before she had carnal knowledge of any kind, when mother had escorted her down a trail to the lakeshore while dad and the

Barnet's had cocktails in the remote cabin. Mom told her about the partner swapping, about her sexual intimacies with Harry and his wife, and about Stark finding out. He was coming tonight to either join the party or blow the lid off the whole thing. Her protests met harsh reality. It was already too late. Everyone, including Angie, would be badly damaged, jobs lost, reputations ruined, a different place to live would be essential. Unless. Unless what? Unless Angie gave it up to Officer Stark, that night. The fear she felt, the shame, the anger, all of it accomplished nothing and in the end she gave in. Stark had raped her and she'd suffered in silence. What else could she do? Turn them all in? To who? The cops? It could have left her and sister Bunny alone, without parents, orphans. Who could have known it would happen anyway? So she had swallowed two big glasses of vodka in orange juice, smoked a joint Stark provided, and in the blank delirium she'd let it happen. In spite of her love for David.

Angie had lied to David by omission all those years ago. Omission was the same as any other lie and she'd thought avoidance was the only answer, like the rest of that tragic time, but she still couldn't shake it completely. It floated around the edges of her life, pecking at her when she expected it least, and today it was back full bore. She had lost her mother, father, sister, and David on the same day. If only she didn't have to face him. Yet, here he was, on their home turf and a future conversation seemed inevitable. Damn him.

What could she say to him? Their love had been a figment of his boyhood imagination. That her own parents pimped her out to Randy Stark in exchange for his silence? How was that believable? That Friday night orgies were sacred to her religion, which was none of his business? Maybe that Clarissa was a love-child from Christ, not from now-mayor Harry Barnet? Lie or truth, truth or lie. None of it seems right or believable, like it was a bad novel from another life. She was always a horrible liar and wondered how she did it back then. Some black magic maybe.

She walked down to her dock where the night sky reflected off an obsidian lake. A shooting star crossed, then another, but she knew them for what they were, hunks of debris harnessed and burned, nothing new. It happened all the time. Like her story, nothing new. But to her it was personal, laden with emotions like space chunks laden with some combustible element, like ancient light just now arriving as had David Chapman, begetting the sadness of unoriginal repetition. God, how does it keep happening? Her great-grandmother, grandmother, mother, and herself, all victims. No wonder she lived in the wilderness, another woman sacrificed and for what? She couldn't pin that one on David. But he hadn't rescued her either.

Chapter Six

In a daze, David turned the final corner in the shadow of the water tower and parked in the small lot outside the motel. He shook his head. Cobwebs lingered. His hands tingled. The effects of that last Adderall all but gone. He opened the rear gate and stretched, looked around. Images flooded him. The years vanished in the face of memories vivid and real. He saw his buddies as kids again, thin, rock hard, with hair. And the girl, Angie, her face smiling, tan smooth skin, hair free on the breeze. So much good had happened here, before it turned bad, and he wondered what life would be like here after the passage of so much time, so much pollution under so many bridges. Could he make it here? A rhetorical question since he had only one other option. Viable but certainly final.

The motel desk clerk collected for all three days in advance. *Asshole,* David thought, as he dragged his suitcase to the room. The room was stuffy. He opened a window above the bed and slouched under it, tired and hungry and numb. The cool air felt good. He nodded off. Another dream came on him: Dani a zombie this time, dead and alive. He woke trembling, sweating. As usual. It was dark. He wanted a drink, maybe many.

In the bathroom, he threw off the stinky t-shirt, grabbed a quick shower, and looked in the mirror. God, frightening. His face gaunt, sunken cheeks, dark circles for eyes. His hair sun streaked from daily runs on the beach to escape his pain, shoulders and chest thickened from weightlifting, two-day beard. Grief may have made him crazy, but it kept him in pretty good shape for a fifty year old guy, something else to be thankful for. He dried his face and brushed his teeth, which looked bright white thanks to time spent with Dentist Feelgood who made sure to prescribe plenty of Vicoden.

David had no end to pain, but had lost patience with drugs, though a dozen or so were packed away in his suitcase just in case. He pulled on a chamois shirt and jeans. It would have to do.

He had abandoned one Byzantine web of social behavior in LA for this northern version, some of it he'd forgotten, some recalled, some obviously inbred. He didn't know one from another anymore but it couldn't be helped. Across the street a bar hid in a nondescript building also housing a bowling alley. A building moralistically camouflaged behind brown tin siding, faded and rain streaked. A twenty-year-old Miller High Life sign flashed neon yellow to the eternal consternation of the devout parishioners of the five local churches announcing the amoral part of town where the questionable citizenry gathered. A parking lot abutted the entrance. It was full.

He crossed the street, still feeling the pull of the dream and very alone. The sign said Tiny's Bar. He remembered Tiny from high school. He liked those thoughts better, a popular sports star that had never left and now put on a party every night, for friends and enemies alike. David wondered which camp he inhabited. Neon lit his face as he pulled open the heavy wooden door. Inside, the grungy carpet led to a dark room with a low ceiling. Cheap booze promotional signs with broken clocks stopped time at irregular intervals and fans spinning in the corners blew curly-cues of cigarette smoke.

Men with stained work shirts crouched over the bar, talking with accents he recognized, some sipping beer, some guzzling. The tables packed with Saturday's warriors, amalgamated voices cranked the noise louder with each additional drink, augmented by a layer of music. The old Wurlitzer flashed and belched. David gazed around. He felt invisible, surrounded by people that he probably knew at one time. Searching from face to face, he couldn't place a single one. A circuit disconnected after years without use. None of the memories matched, yet. A few people noticed him. Their faces seemed to flash recognition, which made him feel at a distinct disadvantage, like an outcast everyone knew but wouldn't talk to or even give more than a glance. He couldn't help but wonder why.

At the corner of the bar, a Vietnam vet in a field jacket still bearing the 7th Cavalry insignia hunched over a drink, greasy shoulder-length hair hiding his face, ignoring the patrons, the noise, the world, staring at the half-empty glass, glaring at any disturbance.

David ambled closer to bar. The bartender glanced and turned away. David frowned. The man didn't look that busy and it felt like an obvious slight, like a drink wasn't deserved. Like maybe he should leave not only the bar, but the town. Uncomfortable was an understatement. He walked to the jukebox and flipped through the offerings. The theme was no theme, like everyone in town made a request and all were honored. Hendrix, Hank, Blind Faith, Waylon, Manilow, the Four Tops, the BeeGees. He pulled out his only quarters, still reading song titles. Three versions of *Crazy,* he played the Ronstadt cover, and *Mississippi Queen,* and four other tunes he hadn't heard in years. David saw a man leaving a stool at the far end of the bar, away from the vet. He slipped toward the empty seat, plopped down and swiveled, gazing out over the smoky crowd wondering what they were thinking. He was thinking, *why am I here*? The choice was simple, alone with ghosts in a motel room or strangers in a throw-back bar? At least the strangers appeared real.

He felt a nudge on his shoulder. A redhead wearing tight jeans and a plunging spaghetti-strap top stood beside him, smiling, hair in huge curls, a silky complexion.

"New in town?" she said, green eyes somehow welcoming.

She had to be a hallucination. No food since the burnt bacon club in Hinckley, and the endless miles alone in his truck since LA left him confused. This woman would have been right at home in any seaside bar from Malibu to San Diego. She had to be an apparition He looked again, wiggled and bumped her arm. She raised her eyebrows, coy. Nope, real. *And now the word "nope"?* "Not that new."

She snaked a naked arm over his head and snapped her fingers. "Hey, Jerry. What the hell?"

The bartender scowled and shuffled toward them, threw down battered Budweiser coasters, and waited, wordless.

David turned to the her. "What're you drinking?"

"Champagne. Little homecoming celebration, eh." Her lips curled, plump, perfect. Brilliant white teeth, the front two askew, overlapped. It made the smile somehow more alluring.

The barkeep rolled his eyes, impatient. "Make it a bottle," David said and to the young woman, "Homecoming?"

She twirled her hair, slender fingers, no ring. "Sure. Minute Olson filed your remodel permit, the whole town knew."

He glanced at her. Said nothing. Privacy, another lost privilege.

She waited. Still nothing. "Sorry about your Mom."

"Thanks." Maybe the whole story of Sandy and Dani hadn't reached this far north. If so, he was grateful. He looked away. "Did you know her?"

"Not much."

Me either, he thought, and that's damn sad in itself. He slid off the barstool. "Have a seat," he said. He stood and worked his cramped shoulders. The champagne arrived, cheap Brut with two Miller High Life pilsner glasses.

She hopped onto the stool. Flashed teeth. "Gentleman, eh?" She poured the wine, handed him a glass, and swiveled her back to the guy beside her, creating the illusion of a private corner. "To happiness."

He put a foot on the rail and raised his glass. "To hope."

She leaned on the bar. He glanced at her curves, another bad habit. She caught it, the corners of her lips turned up just slightly, demure. "So, what are your plans?"

He studied her face, looking for a clue. Took a sip, buying time. Awful wine. He gulped. "Normally, I'm invisible to women like you. How old are you?"

"Learned nothing over the years, eh?"

He looked down, sheepish. Come on, he thought, use your head. Have you never talked to a young woman before? "That was a bit hapless."

She let him off with a graceful smirk. "How old you think I am?"

There was no way out. "You play rough."

She nodded. "When necessary."

He scanned her face. "Twenty-five, tops."

"Close enough," she said and looked up at him, then across the bar. She said nothing more. Her eyes made contact with half the patrons. Reactions ranged from amiable to flirtatious, a few winks, a couple nods, and a number of outright scowls. He noticed people at tables stealing glances at him now, same at the bar. Some rolled their eyes. Was it him, was it her, was it the two of them sitting together? It felt dangerous. Men shook their heads in plain sight. Was this someone's wife? "So why me?"

"Okay. Look, I know you're David Chapman. I've read your books. They're good. You, on the other hand, are not too popular."

"Really." He said it flat.

She sipped. He waited. "It's a small town. They remember."

Something stuttered inside. He felt adolescent again and took a drink to avoid her eyes, which seemed piercing. "Of course," he said. Did he think they'd forget? Did he think this wouldn't come with a price? They don't know what happened in California, only what drove him from town long ago. How could he blame them?

She leaned in. "So, what are you running from?"

He sighed. She doesn't know either. "Who wants to know?"

She looked down at her glass, up at him. He thought he caught a glimpse of guilt or pain. Had he jabbed too hard? She didn't come off as fragile. It seemed some bottled-up truth was ready to tumble out. Secret? Conspiracy? Then this nameless stranger young enough to be his daughter reverted to a woman so damn comfortable in her skin that a bar full of defiant people had no affect on her, like she owned the place and just didn't care what anyone else thought.

"Me," she said. She paused, looked around, made a miniature sweep of slender fingers encompassing the entire room. "I got nothing in common with these boys." Then her eyes flashed, almost a wink. "So, I'm hitting on you."

He hesitated. Then couldn't resist and laughed. "You come with a name?"

"Clarissa." She gave him the once-over. "I was picturing a bald guy with a beer belly, eh."

"A one-namer, huh." He chuckled. "And no you weren't. You saw the book jackets." He poured the last of the champagne into their glasses, head a little light now, almost relaxed.

"Helig. I hate it and don't need it." She nodded and gulped, made a sour-lemon face. "So, it's a tiny town. Everybody knows everything. Except why you're here."

He didn't answer. She brought forth a flirty grin, puffed her chest. Was it a distraction, or maybe a weapon she manipulated. He refused the influence. "Why are you still here?" he asked.

She touched his arm. He felt a jolt, saw another coy smirk. "Nobody wants my job. Third generation harlot, eh."

"Honorable work," he said.

"Damn noble. Every town needs one."

He felt a twinge of compassion. "Mighty neighborly."

"Get by on being Daddy's little girl. He's the mayor. Can we get a real drink now?"

He squirmed and switched legs on the rail, glanced up at the popcorn ceiling, inset dim bulbs coated with cigarette smoke film. "So, what's with all the staring?"

"Jack on the rocks, please," she said to the bartender, and turned back to David. "Two black sheep. Could be trouble brewing."

"Come on."

She nodded, the look in her eyes said: What-you-forget-everything? "Or might just be envy. I mean, you write books, how hard could that be? You got money. Come and go as you please. Probably don't have a care in the world. Envy's a natural reaction."

He heard the opening line of *Crazy*. "Dysfunctional bunch. I might just fit in."

"Depends on what you're really doing here?"

The thought of spilling his guts had a sudden attraction, but he recognized it as foolish. He was being taken in. Time to get out. "Just trying to survive." He paused, looked her over once more for emphasis. "And you? I mean, look at you."

"Look at this," she said, holding up her middle finger. "It's a damn good story, though." She batted her eyelashes. It was a weapon.

"I'm listening."

She averted them now. "I hardly know you."

He didn't know her and didn't know if he dared. The town was too small. She was too young. Apparently, he'd have enough problems without her. He came to disappear, to hide alone in his misery. Misery does not love company no matter the cliché. And this conversation was going nowhere now. "So, who's the vet?"

A man cruised to a halt in front of Clarissa's bar stool, squinted through red eyes, half smiled. "David Chapman?"

David searched the face. Nothing. Too many years gone, too many changes. "Yeah."

"I'm Brad Sterling. We had an art class in high school together." He broke into a broad grin. "Good seeing ya."

"Uh . . . thanks." He put out his hand to shake. Brad shook it. It felt good, strong, finally a friendly gesture.

"I'm the guide around here." He handed David a card. "Call me. I'll take you fishing. First time's on the house." He slapped David on the shoulder and wheeled away, out the door.

"Nicest guy in town," Clarissa said. "No squabbles, never takes sides. Catches fish when no one else does. He'll take you. His word means something."

David raised his hand for another drink. Jerry came right over. "And the vet?"

"Tough one there," Clarissa said. "Foulke, Nick Foulke."

"Was he a football player in high school?" Through the barroom haze, he imagined the face in youth. It was him. That was certain. But those eyes. From kind and witty to that?

"Yeah. He joined the Marines, Green Beret in Nam. Came back with a smack habit, they say. Detoxed in town for a while, then took off, rode the rails, came back a few years later with a little woman and a son. They tried it in town for a while. Upset the neighbors. A bit addled maybe."

"My soul mate."

Clarissa looked at him with an expression that seemed to question the depth of his dementia. "We see him once every few months now. Comes in here and orders a bourbon, sits for an hour staring at the glass. When he's done, he picks up that eighty-pound packsack of supplies like it weighs nothing and walks out into the woods. Never says a word. One of the guys always buys his drink. He ain't got a dime. They say his family lives in a little cabin way out, hunts and traps for food. Sells pelts to buy ammo, salt and flour. Son is probably about sixteen now. Jacob. Thinks he's Chippewa. Whole thing is sad."

"Is he?"

"Chippewa?" She shrugged. "Well, mom and dad seem pretty white."

David wanted to tell her just how sad it could get, how easy it was to go nearly off your proverbial rocker, but didn't. Maybe another time. "He lived down the block when we were kids. We played together," he said.

David watched her eyes rise up and focus on something close and big. He turned.

"Tiny," Clarissa said. "What brings you over?"

"Gotta be a good host—even to ol' Davy here." He stuck out a broad hand. David straightened up and shook it. "Nice to see ya Chapman." He bent over, his face close to David's. "Not everybody thinks that. I know what happened out west. Very sorry, man. You did right coming here. Ain't gonna be easy. Wouldn't for any of us. This local shit'll blow over. Lay low a while."

"Anybody else know?" David whispered but got only a shake of the head. He studied the big man, looking for some motive but found none. Maybe face value was what you got here. A refreshing thought. "Thanks."

The lights flickered for last call. Tiny nodded, "Rumors become truth around here if they simmer long enough."

That meant something but what?

He slapped David on the back and walked away. Patrons filed out, in no real hurry, stopping briefly at the bartender. Clarissa slid off her stool and grabbed David's arm. They shuffled into the outpouring stream, through the only door.

"Why is everyone stopping at the bar?" he asked.

"Now they've seen you. Bet is you won't make February. I went against you. Might change it now."

Outside, the Miller sign went black leaving only a florescent streetlight shining. People milled around, still talking, in varying stages of drunkenness. David scanned the scene. His eyes locked on a big guy stuffed into a police uniform, gun belt strapped on, hanging low on the pistol side, hand resting on the butt, gazing at the faces, walking among the crowd.

"I'm starved," Clarissa said. "Let's get a pizza."

David nodded and stepped forward when a body slammed into him. He staggered back a step. A huge man scowled and stood his ground. "Get out of my town."

David recognized this guy. Running that deer was just a kid's game now. "Fuck you." he said and squared, planted his feet.

Clarissa stepped between them. "Beat it, Johnny," she snapped. "We barely put up with you. You're drunk. Go home."

He pushed up his sleeves. "She with you, pussy?" Voice loud. Fists clenched.

David saw it all in slow-motion. This wasn't his first time. There'd been other alleys, other thugs. He saw Johnny's roundhouse coming and swept Clarissa aside. Ducked. Then launched a wicked right hook into the man's jaw and waded in. A solid left, another devastating right and hard left uppercut. Impact rocked the man back, spun him around, face to face with the cop.

The officer grabbed his shoulders, straightened him up. "She's right. You're drunk. Now get home. Gimme them truck keys. You're walking," the cop said. Johnny stared, eyes treacherous. "Don't give me that look, boy. Get. Fore I lose my temper."

Johnny hesitated, then dropped his fists and staggered between two cars, cursing under his breath. Clarissa pulled David toward her car.

"Aw for pity sake, Clarissa. You can't be thinkin' bout driving. Give me a break here," the cop said.

"We're starving, Pete. Just out to the Hole-in-the-Wall?"

"You're gonna tell me you're sober enough to drive after you call out Johnny. And he takes his swings?" Pointing at David, "Do I look stupid? Have the damn pizza delivered. You're on foot, too."

David looked around, dazed. This was another world, some drunks getting into cars and driving off, others catching rides, and the cop refereeing the bizarre proceedings.

"They won't deliver at this hour."

"Bullshit. Use your charm. Russet's working."

"Fine," she said.

The cop nodded and touched the brim of his highway patrolman's hat. "Ain't like ya had a choice." He ambled away, searching faces, making choices.

"Got anything to drink?" she asked David.

"Case of gin from California." A rush of adrenaline pulsed through him fueling a rage that he tried to bring under control. He'd wanted to chop that chump down with his bare hands, bash him senseless for every bad break and misfortune suffered over the last thirty years, deliver a second pounding for the last two years, beat until his hands bled, beat until he felt cleansed, but the flash of confrontation was over. He feigned control as shame replaced rage.

"Your place it is." She grabbed his elbow and started the short trek across the street to the motel.

The cop watched David and Clarissa. "Where you going now?" he shouted to Clarissa.

"I'm on foot. What more do you want—Mom?"

An early autumn chill filled the night air. David shivered and rubbed the knuckles on his right hand. Clarissa ignored the cold. He noticed her stumble slightly under the weight of the whiskey, head up, admiring the sky. The motel parking lot held one car. His. In the room, they opened the drapes and the outside door. She got the ice. He got the gin, and poured two. She sat on the love seat. He chose the bed.

"Why you sitting way over there?" she said, sipped.

"How long before the food comes?"

She glanced at the digital clock beside the bed. "Well, twenty minutes to make it, five minutes for Russet to get outta the parking lot, and three minutes to here. Sit over here."

"No."

"Don't like me?"

She'd grown more beautiful with each drink until her teeth were straight. When he was her age the end of this evening would be a foregone conclusion. But not now. "Let's have some pizza, be friends. Evidently, I could use one." There were other things he could have said: she's too young, it's too fast, he's two years out-of-practice, too tipsy, the list was endless. He let it go. He saw her hide a thin smile with a tilt of her head. Her hand twisted at a red curl. That look, that gesture, he'd seen it somewhere before, but it flickered and fell away like flint sparking on steel.

"Kinda got me going with that he-man stuff."

He blushed. "That was stupid and embarrassing." Was her tone sensual or cynic?

She ran fingers through her hair, pulling it past the feigned pout. "If you're not going to sit by me, let's check out the stars?"

It was a cheap diversion and he went with it. In LA, ambient light pollution bathed the night sky, drowning out all but a couple token specks. The sight of boring celestial bodies gone so long ago no one remembered. Star meant something else there. Here, it was different, real. This sky awed him. He'd forgotten with the passage of time and now it came back unsullied, huge and vast. It fell down upon them, close, invading. He could almost touch it, a dome of sparkles that intensified as the blackness thickened, a flashing meteor here and there. A new moon. He remembered another moonless night here long ago. They watched in silence. Their bodies chilled. Clarissa moved to his lap. "Keep me warm," she whispered, snuggling close. Her aroma hinted expensive perfume, a whiff of booze. The air smelled fresh, scented with faint hints of pine, grass, creek mud, the sounds of crickets and frogs singing, not a voice nor a car nor a plane nor any discordant sound of man to spoil the music.

A twig cracked. A flashlight beam raked the silence. Russet with the food, right on schedule. David paid. Tipped twenty-five percent, like in LA, for karma. In the yellow light of the open door, he caught the glance, the pained expression on Russet's face. The guy was his age and somehow vaguely familiar. Was that hopeless love or something else, something related? One little gene and things could be so different. He remembered a girl in high school class with MS. She had a hard time walking and was damn smart but her face had changed to bitterness as the insults and harassments built. He'd never hurt her, but he'd never helped her either and now that felt shameful. Russet was probably the butt of cruel jokes too. David wanted to hug the guy, and hoped the girl had made a great life for herself.

They balanced the pizza box between the arms of their chairs and chewed quietly. The pizza crust thin and crisp, herb splashed sauce, fresh sausage and mushrooms, quality mozzarella cheese. It hit his stomach and dragged his eyelids down.

"Want me to take you home?" he asked in a whisper.

"You can't," she said. "Pete's ruling covers you, too. DUI if he sees you driving."

"Can't you take your car?"

"He takes inventory at five in the morning. Any cars gone, he writes up. Don't worry about me."

He nodded and creaked out of the chair. "Okay. I gotta get ready for bed." He had no idea what she would do. After his bathroom regiment, he slipped through the door. The room was dark. A faint green glow radiated from the clock. He saw the lump on the far side of the only bed in the room, red hair sprawling across the pillow and creeping out from under the covers. She curled on her side facing the wall. Now what? He listened. Only the sound of breathing, soft, regular. Too damn tired to care, he pulled off his shirt, and pulled gently on the covers, trying not to wake her. He lifted the sheet and glanced over. She lay naked. Sleeping. No inhibitions in that girl. He rolled away, asleep before his head hit the pillow.

Chapter Seven

Angie Thomson wouldn't admit, even to herself, that David's proximity weighed on her like that bear in her garbage dump last spring that wouldn't go away, out of sight but never out of mind. This morning she'd already turned her vegetable garden for winter, washed and put up the storm windows. Now, out on the back forty across the road from her cabin, she shut down the chain saw and set it aside. She had felled a big pine and a good-sized yellow birch, both in failing health, cut them to stove length, and piled the limbs. The sun was out and the temperature neared fifty, but she was sweating. She stripped off her flannel shirt, laid it on the limb pile, and fell back into it, gazing up at the puffy clouds floating by. The breeze on her bare skin felt soothing, good, then it started to happen. Her mind drifting like the clouds, off to a place she'd purposefully avoided for years, accosted by memories of the pizza that evening: thin crust, sausage, green olives, mozzarella, and the music: Led Zeppelin *Going to California*. She tried to fight off the recollections but could not, like a recurring nightmare:

They had driven to a one-lane dirt road deep into the labyrinth, up a hill and stopped at a slip of side road. David got out of the family Dodge wagon, flashlight in hand, and walked the narrow opening. Angie waited in the car, listening to the radio. He backed into the slip. She could hear the alder branches scratching against the car. She slid to his side.

"So, what's with the stealth?" he asked.

Angie smelled the chain saw exhaust rise from her shirt; saw the clouds passing. Why was she thinking of this right now—get up. Go get some lunch, something. But she didn't move, couldn't break out of the memory.

"My parents wanted me to go to some deer shack with them. I said no. They insisted, so I'm hiding." She said and thought of Bunny at home, hoped she was safe there.

"Take a search party a week to find us here. Think they left without you?"

"Pretty sure. I just . . . couldn't go." The truth bubbled to the tip of her tongue, but she held it there, in check, her mother's warning echoed. He smelled wonderful, the Brute intoxicating. She hugged him, hard and long and tipped her face toward him, kissed his lips, an electric zing tingling in her mouth, her stomach, her nipples. She slipped her tongue in his mouth, silencing temptation for the moment, then slid away and pulled off her sweatshirt, reached in the pocket of her cotton blouse and pulled out a joint.

"When . . . when did you start that stuff? I never knew." David said.

She thought back to that first Friday, stuck at the desolate lake cabin, the embarrassment, the degradation, the supplication and stealing the bag from that phony asshole after he denigrated her. Had he no conscience. She drew long and smooth on the joint. David tried to copy. Her eyes adjusted to the dim light. His face was red and she thought it was the most beautiful face she had ever seen, then realized she was high, and she loved him, and she'd loved him for a long time without telling him. Her eyes soften. "I love you, David."

No, Angie. Get out of this pile of branches. Go do something else—anything else.

He kissed her twice, butterfly kisses. "Say that again," he said.

"I love you, David. I have for a long time."

His elbow hit the steering wheel, jolted them apart. "I love you, too Angie."

Her heart was bursting. This is how it feels, she thought. God, this is so wonderful. She wanted to tell him everything, Stark, Barnet, all of it, right here, right now. But she couldn't hurt him, not when she knew the time was right, finally right. Northern lights rippled on the horizon, yellow, green, floating in space. They scrambled out the door and sat on the hood, arms around each other, watching the shimmering lights dance and waver in the sky, snuggling close, the idling engine warming them. Falling off into kiss after wondrous kiss, and back to the heavens and back into another kiss. She felt the wet spot widening in the crotch of her jeans, cool with the frigid air, and knew the time was drawing near. "David, please put the back seat down. I want to lay with you," she said in a voice just above a whisper. She clambered in headfirst and stretched out. He crawled in beside her, laid motionless. Her hand guided his.

"I've never done this," he said.

She wanted to reply in kind, but would not lie to him, not here, not now, even though she'd never done this either, exactly. Never made love. "We'll learn together," she whispered. And after, they melted together, spent, chests heaving in unison, fighting for breath. She never wanted to leave this comfort that was new and fresh, adult but colored with the innocence of youth. The scent of love filled the cramped space, like lilacs and roses. They stared at each other, not talking only smiling, satisfied to be in each other's arms and away from the world.

Angie was trembling by the time she regained her feet, sweating and breathless. "Damn it, woman, what is wrong with you? Have you no control at all?" She threw on her shirt, buttoned it, and started piling logs on the trailer as fast as she could. Maybe it was exhaustion, or just plain stupidity, but those thoughts needed censure, badly. Then it occurred to her that at least it was the one good part, the part that if she could wipe that entire period from her memory, that part she would want to keep.

How could it be so clear after so long? And finally she had to admit it, that night was a lifelong highlight. She wished it wasn't so, but that changed nothing.

Chapter Eight

David rolled over in bed. A chill filled the room and he pulled the covers over his eyes and pushed a leg slowly across the bed, feeling for her. Nothing. He looked over. She was gone. One problem solved for the moment.

He flopped his legs over the side of the bed and sat upright, tentative, skin tingling, foggy thoughts bubbling to the surface like so many dying fish, missing tails, dorsals, fins. The clock read nine. Six hours of sleep brought no renewal. First morning in town starting a bit rocky. He wanted coffee, badly. The fixings buried in his truck. He saw a note on the dresser beside the pizza box. The stale stench of greasy sauce invaded his nostrils. "Glasses?" He spotted them on the nightstand. The writing was a flowing cursive of curls and loops. *Fun Night, eh? See ya around town. Clarissa.* He wished he could remember the "fun," whatever that meant, and her persona certainly seemed to match the handwriting in his estimation, which was somewhat frightening.

Outside, the air was smogless, fresh, and damn cold, belying the bright sky and brilliant sunlight. He went back for a flannel shirt. On the short walk to the café, he filled his lungs with gulping breaths, trying to clear his head. The route took him through Tiny's Bar parking lot, a few cars left from "impound" the night before but not Clarissa's, past old city hall, now inexplicably empty, and into a field of ankle-high brown grass that grew in clumps. He could see cars and trucks filling the parking spaces around the single-story strip mall, and remembered the place as a teen, malts there with Angie then cruising the drag with her curled tight to his side.

He looked across the street at a bright-colored array of playground equipment, a winding walking trail of wood chips with benches planted in the shade of trees, none of which had been there thirty-three years ago. A useless field converted to a pretty park, another improvement, like the new baseball field he'd seen on the way in. The town looked better than when he'd left all those years ago. He ran a hand over the stubble on his chin, felt haggard and scraggly. The day, even the town looked scrubbed and clean. "Never underestimate these people."

He shuffled between parked cars to the sidewalk outside the café, saw people bent over plates and pulled the wooden screen door. The spring squeaked. He crossed the mudroom entry. Bacon and burnt toast aroma assaulted him. His stomach growled.

He stepped into the room. All eyes turned to him. No one smiled, like he was an alien or something worse. The men wore suits with white shirts and ties, hair combed slick if they had any, dark skirts with matching jackets for the women. Thirty-three years ago, there had been five churches, one bar, and three schools. He was Lutheran. Angie was Catholic. His parents had a problem with that. To this day, religion seemed like a twisted form of racism. His clothes, his beard, his very manner sent a twinge of guilt reverberating inside him. Was it missing church this morning? He nodded to the room in general, and heads turned back to food in unison, the clunk of cheap forks echoed on thick ceramic plates. Quick hushed conversations struck up between husbands and wives who probably hadn't talked in a long time. Couples stayed together here, divorce an unseemly option. Eyes glanced toward him from around the room. A walking meltdown. He recognized no one. Except wait, was that busboy the pizza delivery guy from last night, Russet? It was. He moved to the woman at the cash register.

"Can I get a table?" he asked.

She looked around without meeting his gaze, sorting through tickets. "Looks like it'll be awhile. Nine o'clock service just let out. Counter is all I got right now."

"That's fine." He moved past the tables, sensing eyes on his back and sat on a vinyl padded swivel seat that matched the gray-flecked linoleum counter. A distraught high-school girl screeched to halt in front of him. "Ready to order?" she said, scribbling on a green-lined pad. She had Dani's dark hair, that silhouette of womanhood, and when he didn't answer immediately, she looked down and gave a slight smile. The resemblance, though vague, made him feel like hugging her or crying and both sentiments made him feel foolish.

David glanced at the menu. "Sure, number two—with coffee."

"White or wheat?"

"Wheat," he said. "Do you have a paper here?"

She was already turning away, but whirled back. "Around the corner and halfway down there's a machine. Takes four quarters. Got 'em?" He shook his head, heard Dani's little-girl voice, "You never have change, Daddy" and reached for his money clip as four quarters clinked on the counter. He left her a bill.

Outside no cars were on the street, no people walking, no shops open including the grocery store. The notion of the Sabbath as a day of rest had grated on him in youth, but now it seemed antiquated, genteel. When his kitchen was finished, he would make his own breakfast on Sundays and give that nice girl one less person to serve.

He cradled the *Duluth News Tribune* under his arm and shuffled back to the café. He entered and again the heads flashed his way, but no one lingered this time. Old news already. On the stool beside his, red curls draped over a jean jacket, a menu floated in slender white fingers. She quartered, a stunning profile, beaming smile. "Knew I'd find you here," Clarissa said.

He wasn't ready. "Uh . . . right, hi. How'd you know?"

She gave a disparaging look that might've meant: do I look stupid but said, "Did you order?"

"Yes."

"I'm ready too. Last night was nice. Thanks."

He nodded, his mind searching a partially erased database. What had happened in the night? It was too embarrassing to ask, maybe later, when he knew her better. "I'm sort a foggy in places." His cheeks reddened.

"You were a gentleman. Ya gotta do better. My reputation's on the line here."

Now his ears turned crimson remembering the harlot part. He stuttered. She cut him off. "Probably never get another chance, though. I'll get to know you and—presto—romance incinerated. You'll be just another damn man."

Her jean jacket hung open and a tight white t-shirt stretched across her chest. "I'll live to regret that."

"Damn right. So let's cut the bull. What are you really doing here?" she asked.

His eyes darted from the pictures on the wall, to the pile of dirty plates visible behind the opening to the kitchen. Then back to her. "Thought it was safe. Guess that was wrong."

"Me?" Her eyelids butterfly wings. "You can take care of yourself." Then seriously. "But you're dodging. You can write anywhere."

How could he tell her he was near destitute, grief-soaked, and a failure at his chosen profession? He wanted to tell her it was about defeating fear, facing failure, about running away from his severed past, his dead daughter, ex-wife, the chaos of city life that exacerbated everything. But it was not the time or place and he couldn't—without sounding like a damn loser. He went with the next best thing, candor. "Obviously not. My last two books bombed."

"They weren't that bad." She looked him straight in the eyes, softly, flirtation gone for the moment. "But there's more."

Somehow, she made him feel better. He could feel a power pulling him in, something in her eyes, in her face. 'Resistance is futile' flashed in his head. "I hardly know you. Weren't those your words?"

She touched his hand. "We slept together. Doesn't that count for anything?" Then that damn smile. He watched her study his face. "You want to trust me," she said, and followed with silence and those doe eyes.

"It was actual sleeping." Just saying it made him feel old. "What do you want, more fodder for the gossip machine?"

"It's a leap of faith, David."

He imagined a useless deer leaping, gracefully, coming up just short of the other side, pawing to hang on before dropping into the abyss. He almost smiled. "A leap. Right." He wanted a cigarette, glanced around and saw no one else indulging. This wasn't like the bar. "Just got divorced after seventeen years."

She paused. "I'm sorry."

"Me too." He tried to hide it but was sure some leaked out.

"Well, that part is new."

He took three slow sips of coffee, watching her eyes. They invited him in. "And, I wanted a job change."

"Give me a break. You're a writer. What else can you do?"

"Ouch." He grabbed at his heart. "I used to teach."

She giggled. "Sorry. So that's the change, a return to academia?"

He didn't want to put his mouth on his next book, his real dream. Not yet. Not with anyone, but her magnet pulled. Was this an early stage inquisition? Candor was voluntary, not an obligation. "Sure."

She leaned in, staring at him like she was expecting exactly that response. "Sure. Fine. Daughter has clothes, wife has alimony. Like you said, novels don't sell much anyway, eh?"

He didn't want to think about Dani, much less talk about her. And he wasn't about to tell her that he was interviewing at the college, and he seriously needed that job. He sucked in a breath. "Yeah."

She raked curls from her face. "So, new dreams, eh? Kinda hot. Professors can bring it—not often but sometimes."

"You suck."

"You wish." She smirked.

His real wish was to take it all back, all he'd just said. "So, do you work?"

The subject changed and so did she. Was that a glare?

David felt a hand on his shoulder. He turned to a grinning Brad Sterling.

"How's it going?" he said.

"Hey, fine." David stood. "Those aren't church clothes." Brad wore a wool shirt and canvas pants.

"Nope, fishing. Took two clients out early. We filled. Three limits, big walleyes." He winked at Clarissa, and spoke softly. "Saw someone walking toward the impounds this morning, early. Clothes looked suspiciously familiar."

"Damn." Her cheeks reddened.

A glance at David. "First night back and scandal already. You *are* my hero." And to Clarissa, "Secrets are my business model, as you know." He clapped their backs. "You guys got some growin' up to do, here," he said and headed off to a table giggling. David tried to remember the last time he'd giggled happily without booze, like Brad.

Clarissa sighed. "Well, nobody knows where his fishing holes are."

"So where were we? That's right, your work."

She frowned. "Living here is my job."

"What about money?" She turned away, said nothing. "No reciprocal for old David."

More silence. An unmistakable gloom fell on her that was new to him. Some deep nerve skewered and twitching. He thought about all he hadn't told her, volumes really, about the slippery slope that landed him where he sat today, and it was easy to relent. Everyone had secrets.

"Food's coming." She was smiling again or faking it, sitting up straight again, watching, and in seconds it became real again. The glinting eyes. The puffed chest. Clarissa the indomitable spirit.

"You're something," he said.

"Damn right. And don't forget it. How's the food?"

His eggs swam in grease, the edges fried crisp, toast wet with butter, hashbrowns might have been deep-fried. "Like I remember," he said. This wasn't a café. It was a bar without booze, a gathering place only remotely linked to food.

He noticed a drop in the chatter and glanced at the door. A tall man in a brown suit stood near the cash register nodding around the room, half-smiling, pleasant, his gaze seemed to meet every eye in the room. As David watched, the gaze fell on him. The man started toward him, still nodding, touching a shoulder here, saying something there.

David looked at Clarissa, who now watched the progress, too. "Pretty good at what he does, eh?" she said.

The man stopped between their stools, bowed slightly, the smile practiced and perfect. "Clarissa," he nodded again. "And this must be the famous author."

David stood, quick, and met eyes that searched into his, not aggressively but not friendly by any stretch. He extended his hand. "David Chapman, sir. You're too kind. You ran the mine, right?"

The man shook hands, eyes never leaving David's. "Yes. The pleasure is all mine. Harry Barnet."

"Mayor Barnet," Clarissa said. "Slumming Daddy? Thought the Grand Hotel was your Sunday destination."

He ignored the comment and remained focused on David. "I'm sure your work here will reflect the character of the town. How long will you be staying?"

"Let's say, for the foreseeable future." He dropped the handshake and tried to figure that look, that subtle disconnect between the words and the eyes.

"Yes, well, we're lucky to have you. We all join in wishing you much success."

An impatient scowl flicked across Clarissa's face, then vanished. "Checking up on me, Daddy?"

Mayor Barnet sighed, the sound of an aggrieved parent. "Hardly. It's breakfast with Mr. Stark this morning. Ah, I see my table is ready. If you'll excuse me."

Just hearing that name sparked like a metal bowl in a microwave. David masked it as they watched Barnet start across the room before turning back to their plates. "Was there a message there?"

"Sure—'I run the joint and don't forget it.' Nothing new." That ended breakfast. "How about a drive?"

"Any chance for a rain check?"

"Too busy to see the place?"

"It's not that. Put off seeing the house yesterday. Emotional instability."

"No argument here."

He frowned. "Maybe we could meet here next Sunday, say at ten? Slip in before the second church crowd. Then that drive."

She eyed him. "Like a date?" He nodded. "Refreshing, eh. I'll be here." She spun around on the stool and popped up. "See ya round town then." The flirty smile, the bouncing steps, flaming red curls bobbing in rhythm. Out the door. Leaving him the bill.

David turned into his driveway on Elm Street and sat quietly looking at the house. A bit of Clarissa's indomitable spirit had somehow rubbed off on him, a faint ray of hope, a forgotten will to fight. But now, facing the house he grew up in, hope and will both faded. He surveyed the place, grief and failure pricking like so many tattoo needles, a damn big artwork. His wounds reopened. He wanted to fight through like Clarissa would, ignore the baggage and concentrate on the remodel, the quality of work, adherence to the plan, be objective. This was a serious expenditure of limited capital. This viewing couldn't be tainted by Mom or Sandy or Dani. It had nothing to do with Clarissa, though he wondered what she was really after. "Let's see it," he said it loud, his voice another needle.

The contractor had called back after his first inspection. "I can't touch one of the rooms until you see it yourself," he'd said. David had told him to just throw the stuff in garage and gut it. "I can have them walls moved and that floor in there by the time you get up here. Ain't touching that room, though."

Stubborn bastard. Well, now I'm here. The dumpster sat in the driveway.

The lot cradled the crook of a long arced street making a pie shaped front lawn. Beside the driveway a thirty-foot white birch displayed delicate leaves. He could hear his dad yelling: Yer gonna break that birch. Go climb the elm. And mom calling through the kitchen window: Get down. You'll break yer fool neck. The elm was still there, miraculously missed in the Dutch Elm plague. A healthy spruce set back from the sidewalk formed a tacit barrier between the western neighbors. Damn big Christmas tree, now. The grass needed mowing.

The prerequisite veranda protected the elevated front porch from rain and snow and a sidewalk ran behind the house to the back door. The house was smaller than his master bedroom in LA. He didn't need much space anyway. This place wasn't like the prison-home Dani endured in LA. This house was more a hub, a stop-over spot when his legs ran out of gas, hunger set in, advise or discipline required, otherwise he was out, riding, running, basketball, football, street hockey, hiking the forest trails, the beach. Freedom. Safe from all but his own devices. Dani never knew what she missed, but he sure did. The basement was a plus. He got out of his truck and walked to the backyard. No fences anywhere. Not in OZ anymore. Two large spruce trees and a white pine pinioned three corners of the yard shading the screened gazebo. His father had built it, hands good for more than just typing.

David's last summer here was a pinnacle, no premonition preceded defamation. Just a long string of warm nights, them sitting in the gazebo, away from mosquitoes, away from the parents. Angie's featherweight lounging on his lap, her voice whispering between kisses. The past passed. He looked around. The grass had gone to seed. Clover reigned now.

He walked to the front yard and up the concrete steps, solid under foot, his chest felt tight. A wooden screen door, not that cheap aluminum. It opened with a quiet squeak, always had. That was how Mom knew he was home. He slipped the key into the storm door and turned the lock. Another tattoo; needles pricked deeper. The prodigal son returneth, thirty-plus years hence.

The familiar hallway. The coat closet an empty reminder that he needed a parka, another expense. Hardwood flooring, complete as promised. Light colored, birch maybe, changed enough that it didn't quite feel like his childhood home. Freedom was gone regardless. He could see into the kitchen, spacious now, opening to the living room. A few careful steps brought him to the grand fireplace his father built and decorated with stone, the picture window overlooking the front yard. The openness made the room new, devoid of ageless apparitions.

It smelled good. Hope returned. Then memories. Gutting two houses in LA with Sandy, back when they were still in love. They'd planned and argued and laughed, dreamed and confronted budgets, together. The tiny house before Dani was born. The big one after his third book caught on and money was not a problem. The smell of sawdust and plaster filled the room, which always conjured Sandy. She was like Dad, good with her hands, afraid of no task. Until she left. He saw her cherub face, sculptured body, felt bruises on his knees from making love in an empty bedroom, on the floor.

He stepped into what used to be the dining room, where he and his parents had eaten thousands of sandwich lunches and meat-and-potatoes suppers, and turned toward the new French doors that led into the master bedroom. It smelled of new floor and fresh paint and didn't smell like mom or dad, but spirits lingered. Only so much you can change. None of what's inside and certainly not the past. Actions take on consequences of their own, unknown and unknowable.

But these weren't the rooms contractor Olson wouldn't touch. David went to the closed door at the far end of the hallway overlooking the driveway, his old room. He stopped, dawdled. Finally opened the door. "Oh God." He stood staring. The room had not changed since he walked out that door for school the last time. It wasn't neat, but it was clean. Some mystic deal with a cleaning lady? A pair of jeans hung over the back of his wooden chair. Beat up tennis shoes under it, with a pair of soiled socks squirming out like worms. He leaned hard against the doorframe, pushed the door wider. It hit the bed. His old single bed, the swale of wear, the crocheted bedspread, the old flat pillow. He lurched forward. Fell on it. The springs squeaked. He leaned against the wall and put his head in his hands. "What possessed her?" he said. Something churned inside him, something dark.

He swiped at his eyes, scanned the room. There was the window, the one Angie had tapped on that unforgettable night that they snuck away and finally made love. The tapping a result of the panic of not finding her sister Bunny at home. He still didn't understand that and maybe never would. He had gone because Angie had asked. She'd needed him and that was all he'd needed to know.

The writing desk. Shit, what was in there? He got off the bed, and pulled open the desk drawer. Ancient pencils with stone erasers, scraps of paper, fits and starts of assignments, math problems on graph paper. He dug under all that, thinking it couldn't possibly be there. Please no. Buried against the wooden bottom, he saw the blank piece of stationary. He pulled out the stack. A letter, an unfinished poem to Angie. 'In the night alone/ your spirit comes/ and I am home.' He read to the bottom of the page. No craft, no métier, just passion. Where is that, now? The purity of happiness, the simple clarity of young love came rushing back from the night he wrote it, the night of aurora borealis. Now, he floated through life like a zombie. All that was gone. Did he want it back or were the risks, the inherent price more than he could bear again?

He slipped the papers back to their resting place and stood and sucked for air, moved to the dresser. He opened the top drawer. It was full of underwear, t-shirts, and socks, jumbled together. How authentic was this place? He felt under the t-shirts at the back of the drawer. It was absolute. He pulled out the December 1970 *Playboy*. The busty blonde on the cover wearing only a Santa Claus cap resembled Clarissa, or was it his imagination?

On the wall behind the dresser hung his sports letter, purple with the year embroidered in white. On top of the dresser, a portrait of Mom and Dad, another photo of them all at a lake, smiling, arms around each other's shoulders. A strip of graduation picture proofs lay there, never selected or printed. Then the faded Polaroid, brown at the edges, framed. Angie at seventeen. She stood in the forest, the curly hair, tiny waist, nipples pushing at a tight t-shirt, low slung bell bottom jeans, and a smile that glowed. Even from the photo it sent out light that seemed to fill the room, and he hoped that she still had that inside her. Something that strong, that brilliant, that full of passion and life and happiness, should go on forever. He reached for his cell phone, still no damn coverage. He wanted to call Olson, tell him to preserve this room, just wire it to the max with electrical, phone, cable, and restore it to original. Instead, he wrote it out.

Maybe he could resurrect the remnants of youth's passion. Break out of the dead shell he inhabited. Maybe he could write again. Not another hate-filled memoir that had consumed the last year of his life. That was amateur therapy. But a real book.

He looked around the room again, a last glimpse until Olson could finish, and he felt it bubbling up again. It started with a harmless thought: Dani had a room like this. She decorated it with the things that made her life unique, special, pictures of herself with her friends pinned on the walls, posters that marked the eras of her youth: kitties, puppies, whales, Spears and Aguilera, dance trophies, dance letters. And he had sold it. He had fucking sold it, leaving only a tiny box of baubles, a few pictures, the letter, the dress. Then it came hard. He slumped on the bed, head in his hands, unable to fight it off. Time and memory floating away, meaningless. Hopeless. He stood. Out the door, down the driveway, into his Rover, and pulled the Walther .32, walked back into the room and sat on the bed, turning the gun in his hand. The weight. The time. Hemingway had it right.

He felt a hand on his shoulder, heard a soft voice. "Expectin' robbers?" He smelled her perfume. Weeping overwhelmed him. Felt the bed sink as she sat beside him. Felt an arm pulling him close. Still he couldn't look, and couldn't dodge the next wave as it swept over him. "I wanted to see your new place, eh? The door was open." Her pause seemed eternal. "Anything I can do?" One hand still covered his face, the other fingered the gun. He shook his head. "Thanks," he muttered, voice soft and soaked. He felt her get up, felt her presence leave the room. For a moment, he was thankful. Thankful she saved him. Thankful for her slim comfort. Thankful for her company that seemed to break the rhythm of the moment and bring him out of that sucking black hole. He pulled up his t-shirt and mopped at his face, didn't know how long he'd been there, like that, but knew this wasn't the end of it. He looked at the portrait of Mom and Dad and felt it returning, rising and curling and crashing as he held the pistol. He put the barrel in his mouth once. Maybe it was time.

"Crooks never did show up, eh," he heard Clarissa say. She touched his hand softly and drew away the pistol. "We'll just set this over on the dresser." He pivoted his head, watched her nonchalance. "Brought you something. You got nothing here. Had to run home." Her jean jacket was gone. The tight t-shirt that looked sexy at breakfast just looked clean now. There was a towel draped over her shoulder and a glass appeared in each hand. She stepped toward him and passed him one. "Take it," she said, quiet, sympathetic. "Ice water." He took it and sipped weakly. She handed him the towel. He set the glass on the floor and wiped his face, which hid under the fluffy cotton. "Want to talk about it?"

He shrugged, "Wouldn't know where to start."

She touched his free hand, slid the other glass into it, closed his fingers on it. He felt the smoothness of her palm, the delicate fingers gently pushing on his. "Bloody Mary, thought you could use it."

He uttered a wry chuckle. "Probably right."

She sat again on the bed, close beside him, pulled him close, and when he wiggled, she squeezed tighter instead of letting go. He felt shoulder muscles untangle and drank. A long pull. Finally, he looked into her eyes, seeing only comfort and mercy. He wanted to bawl again, but she said, "Water's on in the bathroom. Go on and clean up a little. Make you feel better. Always does for me anyway."

They were outside, now. The early afternoon air warmer, maybe sixty degrees, the sky a brilliant blue. Clarissa in her car. The windows down. David stood at the driver's window, stoic. "Thanks," he said. Clarissa frowned. He knew what that meant.

"Left my number by the sink. Call me, eh. If ya feel like talking."

He was about to respond when he noticed the black F-150 come around the corner, rolling slow like a surveillance run, windows down. Even with the passage of years, he recognized the driver, saw him slowing further. Stop at the mouth of the driveway. Clarissa's car door flew open. She was out and down the driveway before David knew what was happening. He followed. Another wave building inside him. This one different. The other side of grief. The adrenaline surged, firing like lightning bolts. He heard Clarissa's voice saying, "What in the world do you think yer doing here, Randy?" And the response sounded dim and far off, "Want to talk to Chapman, here." Clarissa's snarl quivered in his ears like Jimmy Page distortion. "Fuck you, Stark . . ." and that's where David stepped in.

"What's the problem?" David said, calm, removed. Stark was out of his truck now. David squared, his eyes narrowed.

"Told ya not to come back here, boy."

David's eyes never left Stark's. Clarissa shouted something that David ignored. He smiled. "Now you're gonna 'boy' me? Now you crooked old fuck are gonna try to 'boy' me." David took a step forward, and another. "Never fucking 'boy' me." And now he was within fist range. For both of them. "I don't give a fuck what you said back then. You got that old man?"

"Find another place to live. That ain't a request."

David bounced forward and slammed into him, chest on chest. Stark stumbled back. "Don't fuck with me," David said, deadly calm.

"Beat it, Randy," Clarissa said.

"Ain't the last of it," Stark said, his eyes never leaving David as he moved away. David said nothing, just stared him back into his truck. Glaring as it pulled away.

"Guess I don't know the whole story," Clarissa said, almost a whisper. "Care to tell me?"

David looked at her, wondering how much she knew but only as an afterthought. She looked like she wanted to hug him again, stepping closer, arms stretching, and he let her come. Felt her face against his shoulder. She probably knew about the planted marijuana. Hell, the whole town knew one side of that or another, but she couldn't know about that jail cell, the handcuffs, the perpetration of violation, an evil so twisted a man would never talk about it. Not then. Not now.

"No."

Chapter Nine

The sun was dropping behind the trees, squirrels gathering pinecones for winter, another day fading like so many predecessors. Usually, Angie drew a streaming bath after a hard day working in the woods, but today was not a usual day. She was afraid to slip into that hot water for fear more of that past might follow her from the back forty, might overwhelm her again as it had earlier in the pile of limbs. Instead, she fried up a slab of sirloin and a batch of carrots, and dined with a glass of red wine. Even a second glass didn't calm her nearly enough, and she decided to go for a canoe ride hoping the paddling would put her into that state of total exhaustion that would drown out all thoughts her undisciplined mind apparently had to think. At least a bit of the guilt had subsided over the years, which had been misplaced to begin with.

She shed the work boots in favor of a good pair of moccasins and put on a down vest that was easy to paddle in. The moon was up in a half phase and she took the Coleman lantern and a life vest and started down the path to the beach. The owl that lived on the back of the property hooted and by the lake, she saw the silhouette of a red fox silently hunting the shoreline. Nature in its incarnations. A welcome respite. She turned over the fiberglass canoe and placed the lantern and life vest on the floorboards and pushed off into the black water, a still mirror reflecting the moon, leaving a candle burning on the sand. A few strong J strokes had her headed along the shore toward the mouth of the river some two miles hence, and she thought that her life had been cordoned off into sections by riveting events. Certainly everyone shared that distinction if they examined their life at all. Hopefully not like hers.

Boulders and cedar trees shown in silhouette as she passed and she missed the sight of fireflies that would have been blinking there in early summer. They'd captured and released them as kids. Those early years were the happiest. She and younger sister Bunny roaming the back yard, which stretched on to the outdoor skating rink, three ball fields, and the expansive elementary school yard where they attended. Dad took them skating in the winter and to the beach in summer where they swam in the chilly water until their lips turned blue and he'd splashed in and taken a sister under each strong arm, bringing them ashore to warm up before setting them free again. She remembered one night when they packed a bucket and a flashlight and walked far down away from the public beach in the dark and shined crawfish along the shore. Bunny squealed with joy and fear as they learned to grab the little crustaceans far enough behind the pinchers to not get bit, although each girl had red pinches acquired in the learning curve. They had over a dozen in the bucket when dad said he would build a fire so they could cook and eat them, to which Bunny said nothing, and dumped the entire bucket out into the lake. Bunny always sided with the prey until she became it.

It was a glorious way to grow up with forests, lakes, and snowballs. However, growing and changing happened in utopia too, and one day when she was fourteen and Bunny was twelve, their mom sat them down for "the talk." Bunny was already more advanced physically than Angie, and the talk content was nothing new except for the part about mom being molested by her father at age sixteen. Mom assured them that their dad would never do such an awful thing. That she'd picked dad to marry her because he was strong, hard working, honest and simple. What Angie learned later was that her mother had been the great beauty of that county and could have had her choice of men, a blessing and a curse doomed to be repeated. The next demarcations happened quickly, life-quakes of extreme magnitude, meeting David, putting out for Stark, the death of mother, the birth of Clarissa, all in a period of months.

The canoe sliced through the glassy lake, the moon giving just enough light to navigate, and her shoulders beginning to burn with exertion. She let herself drift with each J stroke, Labor Day picnics, camping trips, birthday parties, all as a family, and avoided the dreadful parts, skimming ahead to repeating the same joys with Clarissa until that division and Bobby. Paddling tired her, as planned, and after a half hour she turned around and headed back, well short of the river. She roused some sleeping ducks in a bay that in her mind needed rousing if they were to make it south before the freeze, and finally the candlelight came into view, and she beached the canoe, pulled it up and turned it over to keep the rain out. The moonlight seemed all she needed, the lantern unused.

With the bath water running hot, she added just a pinch of fragrance and settled herself in with a glass of the Chardonnay perched beside the old claw-footed tub and the candle from the beach burning again. She was near nodding off when it happened, the ghost of happiness creeping up and she knew the ending all too well but could not stop it and blamed David again.

She saw herself waving as David pulled out of the high school parking lot, and dropping her head so her face hid behind two curtains of hair, smiling at her books, the ground, a fallen leaf, head rising, still smiling at the chill air, the crowd, at everything and nothing. She felt the spring in her legs that rivaled track season and she wanted to run home, run through the crowd leaving school, but that would be decidedly uncool, so she walked with strong, proud steps, hair bouncing, wearing that smile. Kids noticed and they smiled back. It was infectious, a perfect autumn day and a love to match. A few brown leaves showed on scattered trees, but the brilliant fall colors were still to come and she couldn't wait and remembered thinking she'd spend hours driving around deserted dirt roads with David, admiring the changing leaves and him. Maybe stopping to make love. Everything was fresh and new. The fading sun washed blue from a sky she thought so rich it must have been a paint-by-number mistake.

She could feel herself smiling at the plumes of smoke rising from chimneys unwavering in the chill, still air, and remembered envying the husbands and wives that sat together after the day shift, sharing coffee and conversation, a roast in the oven, a languid evening ahead.

Dazed, she took a long gulp of wine and sat up grabbing the sides of the tub, but it was like waking from another nightmare that wouldn't go away and defiantly pulled her back.

She remembered her heart swelling further thinking they had everything in common, love of learning, books, music, the outdoors, even hockey. As she strode past a healthy spruce tree, she'd decided that she would attend whatever college he selected, and they would be together there, too.

She couldn't stop it. It pulled her deeper.

There she was, prancing along the sidewalk behind the elementary school, cutting across the field and across her lawn, kicking leaves playfully, darting between the house and the garage to the porch. Their truck was gone and she thought she could finish her homework before supper and later, read while David worked.

But she knew the ending. It would not happen that way and she sucked for breath.

The storm door was halfway open, a trail of fine red drops led off the landing. The screen door stuck and creaked. No other sound. Then a soft, muffled noise. She rounded the corner. A lamp tipped on its side, the top of Bunny's head appeared, bent down, hair hanging, hiding her face. The soft mumbling. Her mother was prone on the floor, her head in Bunny's lap. Bunny stroked her face, smearing it with a blood-covered hand, the other hand twirling mother's hair, Bunny repeating, "Mommy, Mommy."

Damn it stop, she said, and stood in the cooling water into the cold room and grabbed her towel and buried her face in it. But it was not done yet and it wouldn't stop.

She saw herself leap to them, kneeling. Dried blood spotted the chest of Mom's gingham dress. Angie touched her chest, no breath, no heartbeat. She looked in Bunny's face. Bunny's eyes focused on her, glazed, no sign of recognition, her face melted, the color of oatmeal. "Mommy. Mommy." It was soft, so soft Angie could barely hear it. She stood, her head swimming. This can't be happening.

But it had happened. She sat on the toilet beside the tub, wrapped in her towel, tears streamed down her cheeks like they had many times before. It occurred to her that if she controlled her body no better than her mind, she'd be forced to wear diapers and would probably deserve her reputation after fucking anything with a dick. How could it be so hard? Back then she had wished David would come to her, would help her, but he never did, and now he had ushered these memories back to her. She wanted him and the damn memories gone.

Chapter Ten

On Monday, David's third day in town, the realization sunk in that this really *was* his home for the foreseeable future, which would be very different and might just be good. He hoped. This morning, sitting outside the motel drinking coffee, he marveled again at the freshness in the air, the blue of the morning sky, the silence broken only by the songs of birds and that brought a genuine smile. He'd had damn few of those in the last two years. Many more times he feared the gifts of laughter, of exhilaration, were lost in some green-gray smog. But sitting here this morning, something as minor as an unexpected smile cut through all that.

A flock of pigeons flew over. A hawk followed. He walked out onto the grass, watching predator stalk prey, which happened everywhere and humans were included, rural or city, it was the American way and those thoughts clouded his attitude, reminded him of LA. In reality, location changed nothing. He hadn't recognized grief as the problem because his problems seemed to start long before Dani's accident, especially for her. The caste system in LA high schools segregated mercilessly on money. Selling fewer books gouged his personal finances and the school social order dropped his little girl lower and lower. How did they know? He'd bought her every brand and trend she wanted. Yet he was so damn blind to the whole thing that he had to hear it in court, from the DA, and David didn't even remember anymore why it was germane at the time, but he couldn't forget the stab he felt for letting his daughter down and not even knowing it. He felt like an idiot still. Why would you raise a child in a place that values money above all else, where second place goes to superficial beauty, and third to giving away sex? What happened to inner beauty, compassion, helping your fellow man? All as antiquated now as the concept of a village gathering to build a home for a new family. That was the old America. This was the new. The last bastion of bigotry so firmly entrenched and widely accepted that it was like a VISA card—everywhere you want to be. But not everyone could be. After Dani, his ego had melted like molten lead and flowed away to nowhere. He knew it would rebuild. Egos always do. But to what? Another caste? Where the leftovers pair off and find some semblance of happiness in a trailer park or rural hamlet or wretched apartment in a broken city.

"Let it go," he said to the birds, and to his over-reaction yesterday. He should have just laughed at Stark, let him rant and laughed in his face. It's still America. He was a property owner and there wasn't a damn thing anyone could do about it. But that incident wasn't like the one in the bar parking lot with old Johnny, probably based on some imagined town-wide embarrassment from thirty-three years ago. No, there was something else going on with Stark, less emotional, more dangerous, at least that's what it felt like today.

None of this made the mundane tasks of settling-in any more appealing. The prospects of running errands grated on him. He needed to get to work. He needed to shine in the interview tomorrow and get that teaching job. His money was finite, the job would help, and work might be the only antidote for the crap that nearly overwhelmed him yesterday, that had many days in the past, and might again.

He almost got that early good feeling back as he dressed, started his truck and drove the few blocks to town, but fiascos at the power company, and the phone company stretched him taut. Security deposits? What the hell was that about? He waited less than patiently at the bank and actually complained about the time it took to arrange the wire transfer to which the banker said nothing and did not smile. He shuffled toward the door, head down, flipping through the packet of papers. He finally looked up.

There she was, coming through the automatic door, the young lady accompanying her a half step behind. Angie's athletic stride brought them abruptly together. If she recognized him, it didn't register. Her face hurried, distracted, looking past him. "Hi Angie," he said in the calmest tone he could muster. "Long time."

Her eyes were expressionless. She nodded, almost polite. "Mr. Chapman." Then pushed past him.

"Angie wait," he said.

She turned slightly. "I waited once." Her voice held no trace of anger or derisions, only a matter-of-fact statement as if it happened every day.

"You know what happened." It sounded pleading which was embarrassing. He looked at the teenage girl, a spitting image of Dani even this close. Her eyes were large and round, the conflict seemed to upset her. He noticed her odd attire, a white shirt overlarge and buttoned all the way up, tight to her neck. Old fashioned was the only term that came to mind. He turned to Angie once more.

"This is my granddaughter, Elsa." The girl nodded, shyly. "We must be going." She turned her granddaughter and walked into the bank and straight to a teller window.

He watched them, stuck in a state of awe and bewilderment. Angie was still slim, and tall as always. Her hair shined with flecks of silver, a leather jacket cut her at the waist and matched the autumn brown boots, both expensive, contrasted against tight blue jeans. It reminded him of all the miles he had run behind her in cross-country, not because he wanted to but because she was faster, a stronger runner, and those beautifully shaped buttocks had been his inspiration to finish. And at night his fantasy. The jeans made his throat catch today, that hadn't changed. What had changed was her carriage, dignity bordering on aloof like a fifty-year old ice princess. Maybe queen would be more apt and he wondered about its origination. And the teen wasn't her daughter, but that was all he knew. That and her evident disdain, which hurt.

He stood outside the bank for a moment, contemplating waiting for them to come out, for another less lame attempt at communication, but that efficient emasculation gave pause and he walked across the parking lot to the hardware store. He'd see her again and would be ready next time, he thought as he stood in the display window examining a riding lawn mower with a snow blower attachment. He heard a voice say, "Need any help?" When he looked up, a young man, maybe thirty, was staring out the window to where Angie and Elsa were leaving the bank. "Wow," he muttered and glanced back at David. "That's magnificent, eh."

David raised his eyebrows slightly. "You know her?"

"The Lady of the Lake?" he smiled and shook his head. "Don't think anybody really knows her that well. Not overly friendly, if ya know what I mean. Lives alone out there on the lake, has for many years. Comes in every couple weeks for supplies and mail. Postman says she gets a box a books from Amazon every time, then after she reads em donates most to the library. They got a section there—Lady of the Lake books. I tried a few but too damn tough for my little pea brain. Never know what ya might find, though. Interesting woman. Never looks none too happy to me."

David nodded, polite. He couldn't argue that point. "Ever get anything like this used?" he asked, pointing at the machine.

"Sometimes, not too often. Keep your eye on the want ads. If ya don't see nothing before about mid-October, probably won't be any till next winter." The guy smiled and clapped David on the back. "No worries though, we always got these in stock." The clerk saw someone at the register, and darted away. At least David could get out of this store without further damage. That was already done. Word travels fast in small towns. His transition to rural life was botched, and it was only lunchtime. He was starving and the café was a mere hundred feet away.

At the café window, he saw Barnet and Stark. Now the place felt tiny, claustrophobic, the whole town closing in on him like it did when he was a teenager, like it did pre-Angie when he asked Kathy out and she turned him down (she didn't turn any boy down) and the entire school knew about it, his failure, his obvious lack of manhood. Adolescent bullshit and here he was again, but hunger won out and in he went, past the cash register, straight to an empty seat at the counter. He ordered a burger and fries, and sipped at the brown water called coffee, not acknowledging anyone including Barnet and Stark.

The silky voice floated in from behind him. "How are you Mr. Chapman?" Mayor Barnet said.

David turned, looked past Stark and took in Barnet. "Fine thanks," David said.

"You've left quite the trail of new friends this morning." Barnet smiled that thin politician's smile, practiced and perfect, almost inviting, almost sincere.

David wanted to say, fuck off, but thought better. Stark moved forward and held out his hand. David ignored it.

"Hey, sorry about yesterday," Stark said. "I was out of line."

David squashed the impulse to stand and punch the bastard. He heard the plate clatter on the counter behind him. "Thanks for stopping," he said, and turned away to his food.

"Enjoy," the mayor said.

The burger actually tasted good or maybe it was his hunger, but he ate it with relish and dipped fries in catsup, good, crisp and salty. He felt a tug at his sleeve and turned. It was Mabel Ottoman of the boat trailer, smiling. "How you getting along?" she asked and he thought he saw her wink. Three women trailed out in front of her, all holding green tickets and money. One was the banker, none looked his way.

"Bumbling is probably the best description," he said, feeling the blush take over his face.

She patted his arm like his mother used to when he was a kid. "You'll be fine. This place takes a little getting used to. You'll get the hang of it."

As she moved away, he felt a strange affinity like he'd known her all his life and then he remembered her comments on his mother's funeral. The mish mash of thoughts and emotions already expended today seemed taxing, and incongruous, but compared to the last months in LA when he'd felt overwhelmed with anger and grief and pointlessly obsessed, this felt like a relief.

Seeing Mabel renewed the memories of his parents and he tried but couldn't remember the town he was in when Dad succumbed. It was somewhere in the Mid-west, somewhere in the book tour promoting his best-seller, back when he had money. He did remember his publisher saying the tour could be rescheduled and he did remember saying: No, it wasn't necessary, he'd pay his respects later. Which he never did. He did remember getting the call about Mom and the anguish of his decision to stay at the trial, the verdict stage, and miss her funeral and all of it, and now knew he'd made the wrong one. Hindsight is always perfect, and he wasn't, and isn't. It ate at him as it should.

Chapter Eleven

Angie had dropped Elsa at school after lunch and made her post office and grocery run, loaded up and took what she considered the good road home to the lake. Good was always a relative term for the roads here, and dodging frost heaves and pot holes made her think of men up here and that good was relative to them too. Maybe she shouldn't have been so curt with David in the bank, but damn it, those old feelings of abandonment had surfaced and seemed as fresh as yesterday. Then there was the other thing that seemed new and presented itself below her waist, which was embarrassing except that no one else knew and she certainly wouldn't let it out, and damn well didn't want to think about it herself. She'd tried dating a few times after divorcing Harry Barnet, but none of them went anywhere. She'd always blamed it on being raped so many times that trusting a man was impossible, but maybe it was more than that.

Daylight faded fast this time of year and she quickly unloaded a fifty-pound sack of birdseed, a heavy sack of apples, salt blocks for the deer, some staples that fit in her small refrigerator, and started repackaging the meat into single portions for the freezer. A single portion of steak for a single girl. No, it wasn't just the men. The women of the PTA treated her with deference when Clarissa started school, and in retrospect it probably had more to do with the amount of her donations than any real friendship. They turned on her quickly after she divorced Harry Barnet, who'd begun to believe the fallacy of a loving wife and started wanting intimacy in return for his monthly payments, which was never the deal and he knew damn well that was the case. Divorce left her a bit strapped. She should have made a better deal and had she known anything about money, she would have. But the so called friends sided against her and that hurt. The kids did the same to Clarissa and she never cried about it once, but it was there in her little girl eyes and Angie couldn't forget it to this day.

The evening was not cold, and she took a glass of wine to the dock and killed the Coleman lantern. The stars dim in the moonlight. After her divorce, she'd dated a restaurant owner from a neighboring town and a foreman at the mine for about two months each, until it got to the part where spilling her guts about the past should have happened along with a possible fall into something sexual. Each time she'd forced herself to examine what they had for a relationship and the answer came up wanting. Had there been an intellectual connection, some common interests, something more than polite courtship to hang on to she may have been tempted. That damn loneliness was a lot harder to deal with as a young woman, but she always came back to compromises already made and she could not force herself to make another when she knew it was wrong for her, for Clarissa, and the man would be the only one gaining in another obvious bargain. Or maybe not. The wry comments behind her back, "Bitch needs to get laid." had disappeared since the era of sexual harassment, but sometimes the look on people's faces said it without words and at times she sorely wished they lived in a big city instead of this mud puddle. Yet, with terrorists running loose out there maybe this little place was a better option. She'd driven into town to watch the news after hearing about 9/11 on the radio, but only made an hour before the gruesome repetition repulsed her. She had made another hour of Americans as storm troopers earlier in the year, but for her all that was just too far away to affect her in any way but compassion for the casualties. Her terrorists were where they'd always been. World history changed nothing for her. David Chapman did. The world she'd built now wobbled.

She heard tires scattering gravel on her driveway, a usually insignificant noise that tonight sounded like a bulldozer, and she lit the lantern and started for the cabin. Only Clarissa dropped by at night, which led her mind off to another life-changing incident. They seemed to revolve around her daughter who was always willful. At fifteen, Clarissa had been caught in the back seat of Bobby's car half dressed, by Stark, which put Angie over the edge, screaming obscenities and grounding her daughter, who packed a bag and ran away to Harry Barnet's house. Infuriated, Angie had it out with Harry, who defended Clarissa as a strong, smart girl, quite unlike her mother. Clarissa did not come to her defense, and Angie immediately bought the cabin and moved there. In less than a year, her daughter was pregnant, married, and Bobby had a job at the mine. They moved into Angie's old house, the mortgage paid by Harry out of obvious guilt although no apology to Angie was forthcoming. Then less than a year later, with Elsa sleeping in the room next door, Bobby caught Rod Turner in compromising attire in Clarissa's bedroom, pot smoke filling the air. Of course, Angie wore the bad label for rearing another Thomson whore and Harry brokered a deal that kept Bobby out of jail for the horrendous beating he gave Turner, which resulted in full custody of Elsa. Clarissa got a job with Harry's property management company and a rental to live in. Out of guilt or love, she browbeat her father over the stupid compromise until he agreed to double the money he gave Angie every month. That marked the beginning of Angie's fulltime residence at the lake and the end of any misplaced traces of compassion for Harry Barnet.

The lantern flooded the path as the headlights went out and Clarissa's voice broke the hissing sound of white gas burning. "That you Mom?" The car door slammed.

"How are you, dear? Like a glass of wine?"

Clarissa entered the lamplight looking elegant as always, which had nothing to do with her black jeans or cashmere sweater and everything to do with her bearing. "Probably shouldn't, but thanks. Headed to Duluth to catch up with Skye. Some parties, maybe a few men." She laughed to add satire, but Angie never doubted any hint of outrageous behavior. "Saw Daddy today. He had a check for you so I brought it out."

Angie pocketed the envelope without looking. "Come on, dear. I'm sitting the lake patio tonight. Have you talked to your daughter?"

"Bobby is such an ass. Incredible. Then she carped about boobs and I told her to buy bigger shirts. She said she could since she was rich now. How much did you give her for God sake?"

"Nothing really. And you met up with Harry? Whatever for?"

"Uh, he had a job for me. Checking up on David Chapman. What's that all about?"

Angie had never gone into all the details of her and David and wouldn't now, but just the fact that Harry was paying attention seemed disconcerting. "Who can ever know about Harry."

"Yeah, right. Did you see him yet, David? No wonder you were hot for that guy. He's got that broken waif thing going on, and jez, damn handsome still. You ought to be all over that." The chuckle was unnecessary.

Angie paused, thinking of him at the bank, and on the road home. "Ridiculous. A failed relationship from a failed time in life. I'd prefer to avoid him as much as possible. Any help you can give me on that would be much appreciated."

"Name your own poison," Clarissa said. "Pretty damn smoldering if ya ask me. One of those guys ya want to cuddle and nurse back to health." She pushed up her left breast provocatively and grinned.

"Oh please. He's old enough to be your father." And that's when it hit her. "None of those ideas are really any good, dear. Don't you have enough reputation issues?"

"Now that's a laugher. So are you claiming him or is it open season?"

"I won't even dignify that with a comment."

Clarissa's laughter echoed through the trees. "Well, guess I've had enough fun here. Best be getting along. It's dark enough now to see those shining eyes in the headlights. Maybe I can dodge all the damn deer." She moved close and pecked Angie on the cheek. "Think about it, eh? See ya next weekend. Love ya."

Oh, to be thirty-two again, Angie thought. She killed the lantern as Clarissa climbed into the car. Angie watched her taillights recede down the long driveway. Clarissa had always brought a whirlwind of something along with her like that cartoon character in Peanuts, or was it more like the Tasmanian Devil? Cacophonous chaos certainly covered it tonight. This delightful half-hour visit brought confirmation of her granddaughter's insecurity and her daughter's patent promiscuity, not to mention a refresher course in David's allure and Harry's conspiracy. The typical mundane evening decisions on which chores ranked highest for tomorrow's work were all preferential to the droppings left by Clarissa.

Those pellets all presented potential problems and all seemed to digress back to David in some way or another, but the most troubling was the possibility of Clarissa bedding David. Angie hadn't bothered to consider paternity in years. Maybe she just didn't want to face it, or thought it made little difference anymore, which until David showed up, was essentially true. Clarissa's comments changed everything. Angie couldn't really make a direct assault and tell Clarissa not to screw her father unless it was true and she didn't know that for sure. Back in the black time, it had been sex with Stark on Friday night, David the following Friday, and Harry Barnet on Tuesday. Any of them could be Clarissa's father. Until ten minutes ago, she didn't care to know. Now it became a necessity. She decided to find one of those DNA identification companies and ask what they needed, then supply it.

"Think about it, eh." Clarissa had said. About which part, for God sake? Angie went back into the cabin, refilled her wine glass, grabbed her portable CD player, and stood examining her CD's, looking for a particular one whose track played in her head right now, searching for some calm that may be hard to find tonight.

Are you sitting comfortably?
Let Merlin cast his spell.

Chapter Twelve

The contractor Olson finished ahead of schedule. His critical eye for detail made the work flawless, exceptional given the limited budget. He'd even returned the guns dad had left, a nice old Weatherby .308, Remington pump 12-gauge, and a beautiful short barrel .38 Smith & Wesson revolver. In LA, the job would still be going on and who knew what might have happened with the weapons, but this wasn't LA and for that he was grateful.

Today was his second morning in the house and David sleepwalked toward the kitchen. The fog of half-sleep made it confusing, like being a guest, not knowing where things were. Even the smells were new. It was Friday. His sixth day in town. His new life was officially underway, the trajectory too familiar. The coffeemaker beeped. He took a cup outside, lit a cigarette, and sat on the concrete steps, feeling the chill, smelling the air. Another beautiful day in the north. The interview with the college president had started well. He'd shined, glib, articulate, his old self at times. She should have asked if he could start next week.

She should not have asked about a thirty-something year old arrest, but she did. It didn't make sense. Like thirty-three years erased and he was there for a custodial position. She even had the reference letters in her hands, the publication list, letters from students and faculty. Sure, the question had come up at Cal State, but when he'd told his story, they'd hired him on the spot. "That's history. You teach English." Not yesterday. She'd said something about remorse and maybe it was past time to face up to mistakes, be an adult. A time-warp gone wrong. He'd resisted the urge to lash-out, quote literature. "It was all a mistake." certainly hadn't cut it. But today the why nagged him. Justice taking its perpetual pounding which never made sense except to brutal people in a brutal world. The Cal State people didn't know it was a kilo. That wasn't in the FBI file, that was local, that was Stark. Without the college job, he needed a new book, the gestation period long and his money short.

The refrigerator was empty and he was starving. He showered and tried to let his imagination wander, but it kept wandering to food. The clock read seven as he started his truck. He was impatient, needed to get some food and get to work. He gunned it around the curve, left on Main, another left on Central, the streets deserted, flying past the little houses. Up ahead, another car pulled onto Central. David slowed, followed. The car never sped up, speedometer locked on thirty. He seethed and trailed for another block before pulling into the left lane and gunning it, past the car, past Beech Boulevard, going sixty when he saw the patrol car at the next intersection. He braked. Too late. The spinning lights flashed. Suddenly, his heart was pounding, the past replaying itself back to the day thirty odd years ago when Stark had stopped him. David slowed and pulled over on the dirt curb, opened the window and waited. The patrol car pulled behind him, the lights went out. Policeman Pete scrambled out of the car and ran to David's window.

"Hey, hey, hey. What the hell was that back there? We don't do that here. Kids live in these houses. They ride bikes. For God sake, man, you're gonna kill somebody." He didn't look pissed off, or even sacrosanct like freeway cops. He looked scared, hurt, sincere for God's sake. "This ain't Los Angeles, man."

In the forty-degree chill, beads of sweat rose from David's forehead. "I'm . . . sorry. The road seemed so . . . empty . . . guess I was in hurry." It was lame.

"Roads are always empty." He was waving his arms now, waving the ticket book. "We don't never be in a hurry like that up here. You was doing sixty or better. These streets are all 25 zones. Ya gotta slow down if ya wanna be here. Randy Stark told me I better watch out fer you. Didn't think you'd run me down the first week."

"It won't happen again, officer."

"Well I damn sure hope not." He wrote on the ticket pad. "I'm writing you up for 38 in a 25 so your dad-gummed insurance don't go up, but we both know better. No break next time, Chapman. Now, let me have your license."

This whole event was out of sync, weird, David didn't know whether to laugh or kiss the guy, so he played it straight, handed over the license, and said nothing. Pete handed him the ticket and the license.

"Let's not you and me get off on the wrong foot again," Pete said. "I really don't want Stark to be right about you. He showed me your file, but I got confidence things is different now. Git that license changed to Minnesota and get back to what you was doing—but do it a damn site slower."

David nodded, solemn. "Slower. Yes sir." He paused. "Slower, I'll remember."

Pete nodded and walked back to his vehicle. David pulled out, still shaking a little, and kept it a level twenty-five the rest of the way to the grocery store.

Back home, he sat before the computer screen, typing nothing. After another cup of coffee, he worked steadily for two hours, then read what he'd written. Disgust grabbed him. It was drivel. The ghosts of Angie and Mom and Dad in the room with him didn't help. Another illusion. The rest of the day stretched before him, and nothing good was happening in this room. And that had to change in a hurry.

He put on a jean jacket and started walking. The café maybe, might be someone there to inspire him. Certainly, the bitter dregs of overheated Folgers couldn't possibly be the draw. He watched the frozen vapor escaping his lungs as he walked. An indigo sky and a palette of greens colored the hills rising behind the town, but left no impression. He noticed the browning dormant grass invading every yard and common area he passed. This wasn't Great Neck or West Egg with their ancient histories, their subtle intrigue. No, this was northern Minnesota, plenty of iron but lacking irony. Tiny, remote, a working-class place where no one had any money and no social strata existed that he could ascertain and you couldn't buy your way in and the circle of teepees kept the wolves out and women and children in. It might be America, but it was that of his childhood, a delusion of safe and innocent, not what he now knew the world to be.

An image of himself at twelve years old sprung up, on this very street, riding his chopped bicycle, banana seat and ape-hanger handlebars. A Saturday in the fall with the humidity gone and the bugs gone and the sun shining cool, like today, and he saw his brilliant smile, shirt snapping, riding with wild abandon, free, happiness impregnable, cutting left at full speed, ski-jumping out of ditches, in total control, invulnerable, showing off for the girl who trailed by a half block. He was the wind, the sky, strong, unstoppable, "Come on. Come with me." His spirit so infectious that the pre-Angie girl had to smile and she had to follow; some innate animal instinct telling them this was right and would always be right and they would have it forever. No sex, no money, just innocence and happiness.

It wasn't until a few years passed and her hormones moved too far ahead that they parted, still childlike. The tribe condoned these rights of passage. There would be more. Coupling was survival. Hope and happiness superseded pain. Until adolescence, until Angie was taken from his life, along with his parents, and friends, and truth, and safety, and the world became a dark, drug-addled place without hope or justice.

Maybe he could have just written better pulp fiction, more creative, more entertaining. Let the marketing machine do the work. Collect the money. Ignore the critics. Stay in the beautiful gilded box, like a good American. But it wasn't a manufacturing process.

The next morning David woke to a light, steady drizzle. He put on a slicker and started walking, coffee cup in hand. His legs ached to run but he refused. That was exercise not the reflection he required. A paved bike path extended two and a half miles to the public beach. He walked it, losing himself among the changing terrains. The scrub poplar trunks seafoam green, a color more delicate than ever he'd seen, muted dark on the rain-moistened side, carpeted all around by decayed leaves. Then into the tall red pines, thick trunks, spaced like a city park, like a landscape architect had planned it that way, but this was nature. Designed according to Darwinian theory or by some God. Then over a ridge and across a creek flowing full with root-beer-colored water and rocks and rapids, and further still, through the tree farm of white pine planted after the clear-cut, or so the sign said, and he imagined what this woodlot looked like before the harvest, not manufactured, not a farm. Not like his last book. The rain fell in drops so small they beaded on his jacket and in his hair and magnified his depth perception until he felt he was inside something from another time. Forests that grew out of an earth gouged and grinded by sheets of ice that drove everything south and finally retreated ten or fifteen thousand years ago leaving a latticework of lakes and ponds, soils and minerals from who knew where with flora and fauna following in the wake.

The silence inspired reverence, the smells pure and clean, even the decaying leaves smelled like a promise, new growth, and he smiled and tossed the coffee and put the crushed cup in his back pocket and walked on, energized but walking slower to take in each sight, sound, smell. A twig snapped and he sought out the sound. A ten-point white tail buck stood staring at him. David froze, studied the brown fur, so smooth it resembled skin, the gray creeping in around the nose and neck, the thick body, the thin legs. That old crap crashed inside but could not gain him in this setting. A vehicle passed slowing on the nearby road. A foreign sound. Ears perked straight up. A quick lunge. A big white tail flashed in his face. David muttered a profanity as the buck bounded away, but it was half-hearted, serenity had control.

The deer and the vehicle meant nothing now. They were outside his world. The path broke out of the forest into a clearing on a hill and below him the lake stretched as far as he could see both left and right, the dark gray sky reflected across it, soft waves glittering metallic and the distant shoreline faded into the horizon. A gust of breeze shot cold air into his open collar, sending a jolt, a shiver and a story seemed to fall out of the sky as if it had waited for him to get there. He smiled and turned for home and the more he thought about it, the faster he walked. This was it, what he'd been preparing for his whole life. Finally, a place to start.

Chapter Thirteen

Angie drove into town on Friday to pick up Elsa for a weekend visit. She'd planned nothing exciting. This was the break between seasons, with summer already gone, and autumn inching up but not quite there, the leaves drying but not turned yet, the bugs gone, and the promise, or was it threat, of winter waiting just around the corner. All the time Elsa spent at church seemed to soften the girl, and coming from a long line of Thomson women, and receiving the curse of beauty, Angie sometimes hauled her along on physical endeavors designed to build strength and character. Strength by work was the only plan. The church built one kind, Grandma another.

Friday night, they lit a bonfire and roasted hotdogs with s'mores for desert and drank hot chocolate. Angie asked how her week went but Elsa wasn't forthcoming. "Fine," she said, but not taking her eyes off the fire.

"That doesn't sound right," Angie said.

There was a long silence as Elsa fitted marshmallows on her stick and held them above the flames. "I don't know how to put it exactly."

"We're alone here, honey. I'm pretty understanding."

A blue flame ignited on the sugar and Elsa waved it gently to extinguish it. She turned to Angie with a sad face. "I bought a big shirt and a giant sweatshirt but it didn't help. The girls didn't say ten words to me. The older boys kept glancing at my chest, the younger ones just giggled. Why does it have to be like that, grandma?"

Angie moved her camp chair closer and took the girl's hand. They sighed in unison, which brought a tiny laugh from both. "I guess it's some strange part of God's plan, darling. Survival of the fittest maybe. Your mother's opinion would certainly be different. To her, it may be closer to *The Art of War*."

"She flaunts, that's for sure. But I don't."

"I know. And I can see it hurts you. We all have our little crosses, don't we? This probably won't help you now, but please believe me when I tell you that one day you will find a person that is more interested in your eyes, in what's inside you, than how God chose to adorn your body." She hoped Elsa didn't connect that comment with Angie's life. "That's why it's important to learn about yourself, what you believe besides religion, what you want out of life, what you like and what you love. Many people never examine themselves, never really know what's inside them, and those are the ones that let life and other people lead them around. I did that for a while and I can tell you, it's no way to live."

Elsa held the stick away from the fire, listening to Angie, and now touched the blackened puff balls with her fingers. Satisfied there was no unseen fire, she pressed them onto the graham cracker and chocolate squares that grandma held. She blew on it and took a bite. "It's very good," Angie said.

Elsa ate hers, too, then looked at grandma. "I believe you. Just doesn't make it easier right now. Gosh, it's like being a perverted center of attention. When did you follow the pack?"

Angie folded her hands, paused. Maybe she shouldn't have brought it up, or maybe a young lady this sequestered wasn't ready yet, but her body wasn't helping and didn't match her heart now, and that reminded her of her sister, Bunny. She had been just as beautiful and just as curved as Elsa, but Bunny simply refused to acknowledge that people were obsessed with her figure, with her looks, and kept her life ordinary, loving in every way she could, compassionate toward man and beast alike whether deserved or not—often not. "It was right after my mother died. I didn't know what to do or who to turn to, so I just sort of went along. It wasn't until a few years after your mom was born that I figured it out. That's when I started to ask myself those questions. What did I like? What did I love? Things started getting a bit better then. I hope they still are."

"Think I should embarrass those boys? I mean, they deserve it. I'm not an object."

Now Angie laughed. "Your mother's spirit. Which I happen to like. You do what you think is right, baby. I'll back you up. You don't need to even ask where your mom stands on that one."

Elsa laughed, too. "No."

On Saturday the sun came out and they tried fishing but with little luck so they decided to try finding the owl's nest, which took the rest of the afternoon. They took a trip to Ely and had supper out, then rented a movie, selecting Pretty Women in the name of Cinderella stories. Grandma told her the party was over, and Sunday would be a workday, to which Elsa quoted "Keep the Sabbath holy." Angie smiled and told her that going to church four times a week was certainly holy enough and if she wanted to visit in winter, they'd better build a bigger woodpile as it was always the granddaughter who wanted a hotter fire. Elsa nodded, knowing that to be true.

The next morning, after pancakes and link sausages, they rolled the wood splitter over by the pile. Angie let the girl drive the four-wheeler, parking two trailers behind the splitter, and they got down to it. Angie hefted the logs out of the trailer, laid them on the rack and said, "Clear." Elsa touched the button and the hydraulic piston pushed the blade until the log fell in half. When the ground around the splitter was littered with halve and quarter-rounds, they both worked loading up the woodpile. They talked and laughed through it all and got so giddy Elsa uncharacteristically started doing impersonations of the boys in her church group. Sarcastic and funny. Angie did one of Mayor Barnet. Elsa returned the volley with one of Angie herself, parroting her formal language. Angie said, "Hey, wait a minute. The only reason to have a TV out here is to lose that damn Minnesota accent."

"Well, you succeeded, Grandma. Just stay away from the locals, eh. Like me, eh."

"That's why I live here. And for you, girl," and Angie grabbed her. They both laughed and hugged, then wrestled together until they fell to the ground. They rolled, laughing, tickling, and when they stopped they saw a boy watching them from the edge of the forest. Elsa stood and turned to him. His eyes bulged, his face filled with dumbfounded awe. He had a shotgun slung over his muscular shoulder. Angie saw the sculptured bones of his cheeks, the greasy hair, oversized, tattered fatigue jacket. His expression didn't change. He looked wild, savage, but with gentle eyes and he glanced at her, then back to Elsa. She took a step toward him. "Who are you?" she asked.

He opened his mouth but nothing came out at first. "Uh . . . Jacob."

"That's from the Bible," she said. "I love that name. I'm Elsa."

Now, he looked downright scared. "P-p-pretty name. Uh . . . I got a go. Dad will be mad."

"Wait," Elsa said. "We were just going to have some lunch, weren't we grandma?"

His aroma wafted to Angie now, a mixture of dirty clothes and unwashed skin. "Yes, why don't you two sit at the picnic table."

Elsa pointed the way, Jacob followed at a distance, while Angie darted into the cabin and came out a short while later with three paper plates and a bag of fruit. She set a plate in front of each of them along with an apple, a peach, and a banana, with an extra sandwich in a Baggie for Jacob. "Uh . . . this is too much," he said, but Angie told him men needed their food, and what he couldn't eat, he could take with him. She asked where he lived, and he said about three miles from here, and pointed to the east, deep into the forest. His fingers were stained and he ate hesitatingly, watching Elsa's every move as if this was an entirely new ritual.

"Do you hunt around here often?" Elsa asked.

"I'm supposed to stay away from the cabins. Was trailing a grouse and ended up here. Sorry."

Angie smiled at him. "That's my land," she said, pointing. "You can hunt it anytime."

He chewed the last of his thick salami and cheese sandwich, and nodded to her. "Gotta get going." He got up from the table. "Thanks . . . uh, for the food."

"You're more than welcome," Angie said. "Please, take the rest of the fruit."

He nodded again, and gathered up the fruit and put it in the flap pockets and turned to go.

"Maybe we can talk next time," Elsa called behind him. He just kept walking.

They watched him. He had an athletic gait that smoothed further as he got farther way. "Now that's what I call a boy," Elsa said.

"What did he smell like to you?" Angie asked.

"The forest," Elsa replied and Angie knew it was already a lost cause.

On the way home from dropping off Elsa, something she volunteered for so Bobby wouldn't inhabit her kitchen for even a short time, she took the back road which always endeared her to nature. She never knew what she might see and earlier it had been a Canadian Lynx that she nearly ran over. And it wasn't the cat's fault. She'd been engrossed in her own lost cause, hoping Elsa's wouldn't turn out anything close to similar. Yes, she'd liked David and over a short time came to fall in love with him, but her lost cause moment happened in David's basement, on a couch.

Cross-country season had ended, hockey hadn't started, his father was working afternoons and his mother had gone to pick up groceries, and they were alone. Homework was finished, kissing had begun, and all she could think of was a wish to stay here, to never go home, never have to see or feel Randy Stark near her again. As time passed, she'd found the ability to block those dreadful nights from memory, but on that couch it was still a gaping wound, fresh from just three nights before, and she'd decided there, on that couch, that she would never do it again no matter what happened to anybody, including her.

As she drove past the large pond that marked halfway home, she had a difficult time reconciling that decision with what happened after it. Would her mother still be alive, her father, would Bunny be married with a family, would she have gone to college with David? Even if she could have known the eventual consequences, would she have made more concessions, let it string along further? It was impossible to say, just as it was impossible to know, and in her heart she couldn't imagine doing anything that might harm her parents, no matter how much she hated what they'd done to her. But she could hate Stark, and she did. To this very day. Behind her shield and her persona lay a streak of hatred deep and long and as she came to the county road, she hoped revenge would be served someday, someway. When the time came, she would do her part.

Chapter Fourteen

On Sunday morning, David sat in a window booth at the café waiting for his "date" with Clarissa. He'd arrived early and had now finished reading the Sunday *Duluth News Tribune.* It was ten o'clock when he started on the *Lone Pine Weekly*. She was late. He read the entire paper, from town council news, to bowling highlights, even the cribbage club news. The want ads were a highlight including possibly the best want ad he'd come across in all his years of reading the papers:

> WANTED: Looking for fishing
> buddy. I am a single, disabled
> "50ish" lady who loves to go
> fishing-just needs a little help
> getting in and out of boat or
> snowmobile. Only a real man
> need apply, preferably single or
> have a very understanding wife.
> Send note to "fishing lady"
> General Delivery, Lone Pine.
> Please include picture of boat,
> motor and ice house.

Something in that little ad made David want to respond. He had no boat, motor, ice house or any idea about fishing, which slowed him, but that vulnerability hit home. This place was full of "real" men and the ad would probably be gone by next week's edition. He admired the honesty, wondered if he might have known her in high school. He could use a friend and it was looking like his breakfast date was a no-show so he may have to scratch Clarissa off that list.

He'd sporadically watched Russet work, a methodical machine, limping but never behind, nodding but never talking, bussing dishes and filling cups and glasses. The third time he stopped at David's table, he filled the coffee cup and reached for a wadded napkin. David grabbed his wrist. "What's your name?" Russet glanced at David, then at his wrist, "R-r-r-usset." David studied the man's face, trying to imagine it years younger. It was familiar but he couldn't place it, yet. His eyes softened. He let go of his wrist "I mean your real name," David said. Silence and a confused look, like it was a trick question.

"R-r-russell Clairton."

"I know you, don't I?" David said. Russet shook his head no, and moved to the next table.

At ten twenty-five, the place teemed with people, the papers lay in a neat pile and David was ready to give up when she blew through the door wearing tight jeans, a blousy blue sweater. A long scarf encircled her neck accentuating pink cheeks, no make-up, red curls loose, wind-blown, exotic. All heads turned. Her eyes danced, she waved at David and flounced around the tables toward his booth, her smile impervious as she greeted diners by their names eliciting glances and whispers as she passed.

"Hey man," she said. "How'd you get this booth? This is old man Lockridge's. Gets to church early to get the front parking spot and takes the very back pew. All planned. He's over there." She nodded toward an elderly man who sat with his blue-haired wife and a younger couple, about David's age.

"Looks glum," David said. "I've been here since eight."

"Surprised Mrs. Thorson let you sit here. She obviously didn't think you'd keep it this long. He'll get over it, but probably not today. Too bad, he's such a sweet man. How was your week? Oh wait, I heard a little. You offended half the town, got a speeding ticket, mercifully went into hiding."

"That sums it up."

"Just can't leave you alone, can I? Ready to order?"

David shrugged. "What are you having?"

"Bagels and cream cheese, pickled herring, side of bacon. Eino butchered last week. Nothing like fresh smoked bacon."

"I'm going with the special, corned beef hash." Hunger beat at him. He'd compromise for expedience since nothing here registered on his culinary scale excepting the burger and fries. "Thought I'd see you around?" His voice cracked, a little tentative. Maybe she left town for a good roll in the hay with an unknown man in an unknown town. Not that it should matter to him.

She interrupted her room-gazing to check his expression. "It was a woman." She grinned, teasing. Paused to drive it home. "Old friend."

"Have fun?" It seemed innocuous.

"Got this sweater." She bulged her chest and extended an arm to him.

He felt the material. "Nice."

She smiled again, irresistible. "We met ten years ago. That's old."

"Talk about me?"

"Dreaming, are we?" She leaned forward and gazed at him, corners of her lips upturned.

He blushed. "Maybe." He had dreamed of her last night, the two of them picnicking on a rocky, tree studded island, no land is sight. He wondered what it meant.

"Common in men I date. Uh . . . not that I'm dating you. You're too old for me." His blush deepened. She shook her head. "Jez . . . got a get you out more, eh," she said.

Over breakfast, she flirted and cracked jokes, made him laugh twice. He played along, but didn't tell her that he'd started his new book.

"I should be settled in by Saturday. Come on over, I'll make you a great dinner."

"It's called supper, here."

"Right. Forgot."

"I brought wild rice from the reservation."

David rubbed his hands. "I love wild rice. Come early and we'll cook together."

She raised her brow. "A little forward, Mr. Chapman."

His eyes darted away. "Didn't mean it that way."

She smirked. "You're too easy to pick on. Come on. Let's go for that drive. You need to get out. Chaperoned obviously."

He followed her out and slipped a folded five spot into Russet's bus tray as he passed. He crawled into Clarissa's green Ford Focus. Mud splashed outside, grungy in and a bit cramped. They pulled out and turned on Main Street. She pointed and told him about the park built five years ago with redevelopment funds, the mining companies decimation by imported steel, the towns along with it, kids leaving for greener pastures. "The people that stay have pride. They want to live here. Make it home. Any new public works project is embraced. We get things like the park, the new baseball fields, you had to see it on the way in, boat landings, that stuff. Always outside funding. Mayor Dad's a pro at that."

She turned left on Hemlock and five blocks down, turned left on Central. "They combined all the grades into the high school. Remember this building?" she asked, pointing.

"Sure. The elementary school. Great gym."

"Now it's the municipal building. Council chambers, mayor's office, city clerk, post office, police station, the works. Dad's pet project."

"I'll have to see that."

"Oh, you will. Still got your remodeling permits to pay for, eh."

He watched her as she drove. Her face changed expression constantly. He saw the mixture of pride and doubt. No talk of her. At the edge of town, she turned right, away from the only highway leading out of town and toward the boreal forests and the labyrinth of logging roads that lead everywhere and nowhere depending on whether or not you had a map. Two miles later, they passed the public beach road and hit the dirt.

"Roads are all dirt now until the county road. That's miles. Got any plans for the day?" she asked.

"Do laundry."

"Be lonely." She shot him a disgusted look. "That's what I thought. Hand me my purse, please."

David passed the leather bag to her and she drove with one hand and searched with the other, slowing down, a dust cloud billowing up behind, the road bending, over railroad tracks, over a wooden bridge spanning another rust-colored creek, more dirt roads jutting off to the left and the right, and not a car anywhere. Some swamps and miles of forests, white pine, jack pine, birch and poplar, a gravel pit here, another creek there, nameless and leading to ponds where moose grazed, foxes and wolves hunted, grouse grew, and bears picked berries storing fat for the winter. He felt the purse push against him and looked at Clarissa. A hand-rolled joint dangled from her lips. She grinned. "Got a light?"

He glanced up the road and spotted it, head down gnawing on some grass, a doe, and he reached across and pushed the steering wheel. The car swerved left, straight at the deer. Toward a ditch. She knocked his hand away, and steered clear. "Ah, a little joke, eh," she said. His eyes were glassy. They passed the deer. She glanced and checked him cautiously. Pushed in the lighter. "You could use a little of this."

He eked out a smile, sardonic. "Joke, yeah." The cockpit filled with smoke. It tasted green in his mouth, choked him, he coughed, hacked. She handed him a water bottle. His eyes burned and dripped. He tried to clear his throat. She laughed.

"This is fun," he said.

"Great fun. Perfect Sunday afternoon. We'll go find some Bald Eagles." She cracked the windows, driving out the smoke, filling the cockpit with cool, forest-scented air pregnant with the faint whiff of winter. The road ran up and down in gentle flows, bending around glacial deposits of granite, boulders the size of warehouses, and after his third puff, the car felt like a hovercraft floating. He marveled at the illusion and gazed out the window, lapping up the sights and smells.

She crashed into his thoughts. "What did you do when you left here?"

He ignored it and after suitable silence, glanced her way. "Drugs won't make me talk." The road seemed to rise out of a large pond now and he wondered what happened to the road in a storm or the spring snowmelt. Then he saw it. "Hey, stop!"

She braked hard. The dust cloud caught them and settled. A moose stood across the pond, weeds dripping from broad antlers, chewing, watching them back. David got out of the car.

"Where're you going?" she said.

"For a closer look."

"You're stoned. Get back in the car. They will charge."

"Right," he said, motionless, admiring before climbing back in. "God, it smells incredible out there."

"Quit changing the subject."

She turned off on a side road that quickly narrowed to one lane and he lost the hovercraft effect. After a couple miles and another turn, he knew he could never find his way back. Scattered cedar trees lined the banks of sloughs, thickets of spindly scrub pines drowned out the light and poured a new scent into the open windows as the car crawled over ruts and washouts and exposed boulders, deeper into the labyrinth. "Talk or I'm leaving you here," she said.

He looked over. She appeared serious and in his current state of mind he couldn't see the harm if ever there was any. "Found a room, got a job, finished high school. No great shakes. Stumbled across Auto. We hit it off."

"Yeah, great guy."

He smiled at the thought. "He traded me a car for three months rent. That *was* great shakes. Sprung me out of that rat hole."

"Bitter?"

"Takes a village, right? Bullshit."

"They skipped that with you. But hey, left an arrest, no conviction."

"Which just cost me a job at the college." He wondered how she knew, but was too high to care.

"Well, that sucks. Maybe Daddy can help. He donates to the school." She fell silent, clearly expecting him to continue.

He stared out the window. So that was the connection. A meadow on the right flowed with dazzling yellow buttercups and a birch thicket, bark curling off the trees like rolls of white writing paper. A hill rose before them.

"Wandered a little. Florida, Arizona, finally settled in California. Waited tables and finished college. Started writing, met my wife, the rest is history." He refused to mention his pre-matrimony period, an endless string of drugged out nights with women of all shapes and sizes, the only prerequisite was that they looked nothing like Angie, fractured souls, virgins and whores and anything he could find or ingest to stamp out the absolute lack of anything solid and responsible, anything like a home. Every house just another house. Until he met wife-to-be Sandy. It could be anybody's story and he wouldn't tell it to her or anyone else. You had to be there. A little dignity never hurt.

They crested the hill and stopped in the shade of a stand of jack pines. Below them lay a small lake, shining flat and blue like nature's own mirror, tranquil, surrounded by forest and fed by a creek at the north end. "You can get out," she said.

His head snapped around, at her. "Hey, I talked."

"Yeah, yeah. I'm getting out, too. Summary—more bullshit." She got out of the car and went to the hatchback, opened it, and picked up a folded blanket. He got out and followed her. She threw the blanket at him. "Carry that," she said and picked up a bottle of cabernet and a pouch. She slung a pair of binoculars over her shoulder and started walking toward the trees. She glanced back. "You coming?"

He looked at the car parked squarely in the middle of the half-lane road, shrugged and followed. They hiked about a hundred yards to a spot where the ground sloped gently toward the lake, tall white pines surrounding them, the forest floor covered in a bed of brown needles. "Spread the blanket out here," she said, almost in a whisper, the binoculars sprouting from her eyes, scanning the area. "Eagles like this place. No people, big trees." He shooed away the butterflies and straightened the blanket. "Here," she said. "Take the binocs. Look over there on the other side of the lake, kinda to the left." She pointed. "See it? The clump on the top of that pine."

"Yeah, okay."

"That's a nest. And the brown crowns moving are the babies, almost fledglings now. "

"Wow. No shit?"

"Wow followed by No shit. And you're a writer?" He stood transfixed, gazing through the glasses. She sat on the blanket and opened the wine, took a slug out of the bottle and lay back, staring up at the sky. "See anything else?"

"Not really. Beauty."

"This is a good spot. Mom and Dad fly right by bringing food. Want some wine?"

She handed him the bottle and pulled out the rest of the joint. A flick and the smoke drifted upward. "Here." She passed and leaned back on her elbows, watching him. Exhaled. "You can sit, eh. The glasses work down here."

He sat as gracefully as possible. Pine needles made a soft cushion.

"What happened to your wife?"

He looked past her, at the trees in the distance, then back. Her eyes said compassion, still, he didn't want to remember, didn't want to go to that place, that place scared him. "Just another sad divorce in America. We grew apart. One day she packed and left."

"Kids?"

He felt the knife in his chest and he wanted to just say no, but it was a lie he couldn't sustain and he knew it would be worse down the road but maybe he could stomach it then. "No. How about you?" he said.

She nodded. "A daughter fifteen, going on twenty-five."

"Thought you said you were twenty-five?"

She laughed and threw her hair back. "You said that." Another smile, sly maybe? "My ex ascended to some fundamental God after we split. He got custody. I won't go into that. That's how he's trying to raise her. I got a stay around just to give her some alternative perspective. Give her a chance to grow up independent."

"Like you," he said. "Might be a mistake."

It didn't affect her. She rolled onto one elbow and faced him. "Speaking of mistakes, what do you think about making love?"

"To you?"

"To me."

"Theoretically?" She shook her head no. He paused, looked up at the tops of the trees that now swayed in a slight breeze. "Filled with risk. Why would you even consider this old fart?"

"Limited resources." She winked.

A nervous laugh slipped out. "Nice answer. Go fuck a tree branch."

"Ouch. No. Mine was as straight as yours. And hey, I like you. I don't get that either." She smiled slightly, face serious, eyes inviting. He turned away and peered through the binoculars again. "They screech on the way in," she said. "It's hard to miss."

"If it went well, it might be dangerously uplifting. A healthy boost to a flagging ego. If not, the cost may be unbearable. In either case, the question of going forward in some dignified manner rears its ugly head."

She sat up and took off her jean jacket. "Very literary." She stripped off her sweater and leaned back, bare-chested. "Antiseptic, even." He looked away. "You can look. Unlike your vagaries, the girls are real," she said.

She was unashamed. He felt like a voyeur. She leaned his way and smiled, showing unrestricted feminine beauty, youth at its peak power covering any deficiencies in knowledge or wisdom or tragedy. He wanted to feel that again, be that again. He wanted to touch them, but feared this was a close relative of driving at deer, of Hemingway, another insanity. Another thing he didn't understand, but he recognized it and did nothing, said nothing, looked away nervously.

She stretched, devastating beauty. "Maybe friends, maybe more. Maybe nothing. Who knows? Oddly enough, I feel comfortable with you. You're whole story sure isn't out yet and the girls are used to getting the whole story, without begging. Usually goes the other way." She smiled. Killer.

"It's hard to, uh."

She winked. "Yup. You in there?"

She came toward him in slow motion, jerky, another movie at the wrong speed, the hovercraft bumping. She pushed him softly. He fell onto his back, eyelids twitching. He felt her hand rubbing his chest. Launch time, the rocket ready to leave. Details succumbed to warping and waving, some vague, distant, unrecognizable, and others intact, intense, standing still in time.

He felt the tug on his jeans and stopped her. The soft skin above him, the weightless pressure of her rubbing against him felt hot against the chilled breeze on his arms as they lay flat on the blanket. He wanted to kiss her, all over, but something, an instinct maybe, shouted no! He floated above the lake, into the sky. "I can't," he whispered.

She pushed up, hands on his chest, watching his eyes, his mouth, fingers running in his hair. "You can?" she said. Her hair dripping, hips moving, eyelids falling, chin jutting up, cords in her neck stretching tight.

Recognition hit him: the jaw line, the cheekbones, all Angie's. An eagle screeched. "I couldn't."

Words formed slowly, foggy, floating up with the fish, not yet to the surface. She rolled off, to his side, and grabbed the blanket, pulling it over them. "That's never happened before—ever," she said and lay motionless, in silence, the breeze rustling pine needles aloft, down the hill poplars showing the silver underside of their leaves. Another eagle screeched. "Am I losing it? Hell, you had two chances," she said.

Only his lips moved. "There's things you're not telling me either."

Her voice was breathy, soft. "Coulda been incredible."

"That's not the topic."

"I like that topic."

"I'm sure you're damn good at that topic, but . . ."

"Shush. Listen."

He listened. The tree trunks groaned, leaves clapped together, all barely audible, a silence punctuated by a chirp, a falling twig, a running squirrel and his churning mind, knowing there was more time. It was maybe another hour back to town. He'd lost track of it coming here. He'd get it out of her. Patience, enjoy the silence. Enjoy this woman, this place, wherever it is. Another screech, like she knew it was coming.

She scrunched her knees up and snuggled closer. "Cold," she said. He could feel her pressing into his side. He cinched down on the blanket. The afternoon faded, her voice hushed, like the breeze. "This should feel really uncomfortable but it doesn't. At least to me. Seems I've known you for a long time."

"Been a damn long week," he said. He tried to come up with some clever lead-in but couldn't so he just blurted it out. "How's your mother?"

She sat bolt upright, stared at him, started pulling on her sweater. Not taking her eyes off him. "What kind of a question is that?"

"Appropriate at this point, I think."

She crossed her legs, Lotus style, facing him. Silent, watching. She lit the roach, puffed deeply, and passed it. Sipped from the wine bottle. "How'd you know?"

He held it, but handed it back. "The angle," he said.

"Angle?"

"Angle." He picked at a pine needle, not wanting to look too closely. "When you were . . . uh . . . above me, I saw her."

"What?" Her face looked distinctly unkind.

"The chin, the cheekbones." He studied her face, now. "Hard to spot from here. We were in love . . . in another time. You had to know." She took another long drag on the roach, staring at him all the time, saying nothing. Apparently, no comment was the response. "You don't look that much alike. She was beautiful. You're the classic American fantasy." He paused. Unkind was growing into something worse. "It was a compliment."

"Do I look stupid?"

"Hardly." He gazed skyward, seeing little. "When can I see her?"

She picked up the binoculars and focused on the tree. Daddy eagle perched on a thick limb beside the nest, white head shining. Two orange beaks showed above the pile of sticks, squawking, begging. "When the time is right. Another leap, David."

"They're endless," he said, shaking his head as if his neck lacked muscle.

Clarissa dropped him off at his car. It was dark now and cold. He drove home in a state that fluttered between pride and shame. Pride that just two years ago, before Dani was gone, he could not have resisted that woman. Pride that he had finally broke the ice and let a few demons out of the closet, that he had trusted someone, anyone, and had almost been honest. But shame that he still couldn't talk about Dani and resorted to lying. Shame that not indulging that gorgeous woman brought anxiety, another form of fear, and he thought he'd banished fear from his life completely. Did fear have a part in not pulling the trigger a few days ago? Or was it the backhand idea that folks would say he came here just for that, but who would care? The town blew him off thirty-three years ago. Did he care about that? Yes, he was beginning to. Eagle watching was a damn interesting experience, images that would probably haunt him, and the lineage revelation. Angie's daughter for God sake. It hit bone. He found a cocktail glass, filled it with gin, and made his way to the garage.

A bare bulb on the ceiling. The old refrigerator hum. He sat on the corner of Mom's old couch as the cold enveloped him. A branch tapping on the window revived Angie tapping at his bedroom those many years ago. Her image appeared, Angie at eighteen, sitting on the hood of the old Dodge station wagon, Northern Lights glowing behind her. Her face turned to him, filled with tenderness, half moon eyes, lips like soft, bruised peaches moving toward his . . . stop. He jumped off the couch, lit a cigarette, took a long pull of gin. Their separation had shattered him. Somewhere in the recesses of his soul he'd perfected a defense mechanism that never let him get into that position again, that degree of vulnerability that left him at the mercy of whoever or whatever it was that held the incredible power to provide happiness or despair. But that love story was ancient, not even a decent narrative. His had a few quirks but nothing compared to Tristan or Juliet or even Dani. So get over it finally or go ahead and pull the fucking trigger. Real men live here—remember that.

He closed the light and went outside. Sharp cold raked his fingers. In the kitchen, he refilled the gin glass. A new room, a new life. But it seemed to include Clarissa. He found no reason that a woman of her age and beauty should have any interest in a man like him. In LA, women like her dug for gold with wealthy oldsters or high-flying CEOs, but never a writer with precarious finances. He picked up the phone and dialed her number but aborted before the last digit. It would come out later, whenever that was.

He saw it out of the corner of his eye, the black F 150 rolling slowly past his house.

Chapter Fifteen

Two weeks had passed since Elsa's last visit and each Sunday Angie had seen the boy stop in the woods by her yard. She knew he was the Foulke boy and she'd imagined how they lived out there and hoped they were all right, had enough to eat, and could stay warm. It had been maybe five years since they abandoned town, which left her with a degree of confidence.

The weather had become unpredictable and much colder. Soon winter would make travel difficult and she would see less of Elsa until spring. It was a long run down the lake on her snowmobile although it did go eighty miles an hour. She always tried to make a couple granddaughter trips a month, but factors got dicey at times, with the snowplows, ice conditions, and blizzards, so she'd called and arranged this weekend trip. The barrel stove belched heat and Elsa sat across the table, studying her cards, trying in vain to beat grandma at Cribbage.

"Do you think Jacob will be by," she asked.

"Maybe." Angie wouldn't tell her of the weekly sightings as it might be taken wrong.

"How do they manage out there, grandma?"

"I don't know."

On Sunday it rained lightly and they did more wood splitting, and covered the green wood pile with tarps secured by stakes and rope. The rain blew past about noon and the sun came out for the first time in a week. They were packing Elsa's things when she squealed, "There he is," and ran out the door. Angie followed. The boy's pants were wet but the fatigue jacket appeared dry and he looked warm and a bit scared as if he had done something wrong. Angie could see the hapless eyes of both and see that these young people had some kind of attraction that seemed healthy and innocent. "I've got a few things to finish up in the garage," Angie said. "You kids could grab a snack and take a walk or something." Jacob looked completely shocked and had no idea what to say or do, but Elsa said, "Thanks Grandma. Come on Jacob."

Bobby would have gone ballistic for letting those two go off alone, but she never put much stock into that man's ability to think or reason, and besides he wasn't around so screw that sanctimonious asshole. It was actually refreshing to be around young people steeped in infatuation. It reminded her of the beginning of her relationship with David when everything was curious and new and they'd talked of their childhoods and dreams, just getting to know each other better, tests of compatibility and trust and finally love, before it was ruined. She liked thinking of the first part, and had gained the discipline to not dwell on the ending anymore, knowing she'd run into him again. With her discipline still a bit fragile, she hoped that wouldn't be until after winter with a few extra months under her belt, and maybe some distance, maybe some tranquility that hadn't yet arrived.

Two hours later, she heard them coming up the path from the lake, Elsa's arms flailing in animation, while the boy seemed taller and more at ease. Angie heated up a leftover stew and they all ate a bowl at the picnic table, before Jacob said it was time for him to get home and thanked them. Elsa's eyes looked sad as he disappeared into the forest. When he was gone, Angie asked what they'd done for so long and was not surprised to hear they'd discussed religion, but was taken aback to hear Elsa go on about how much Jacob knew about the Chippewa and native customs, their relationship with the land and their Gods. Angie didn't want to spoil it by reminding the girl that our country's leaders had forced Christianity down their throats, resulting in mass death and destruction of entire native cultures, figuring she was smart enough to realize that without help eventually. In any case, it felt good to see the girl excited and happy, and not insecure for the time being. Maybe this passion was doomed from the start, but nearly all are at this age, and it was normal and natural. The real surprise came on the ride back to town.

"Grandma, I kissed him," she said, about halfway through the trip.

"Took a while to come out with that, young lady."

"Uh, I know. Sorry. Guess I sort of forced myself on him. That's not right, is it?"

The girl blushed. Angie glanced over at her and smiled. "Probably not. He does seem very shy. Sometimes the woman has to take control. Actually, more times than I'd care to go into right now." She thought about the first time making love to David again. It didn't seem to want to go away. "This might not be the best story to share with your father. I know your mom would like to hear about it, though."

"I get that. Sure wish daddy wasn't such a prude sometimes."

The irony of her saying that almost brought out a belly laugh, but maybe some of that discipline was actually taking hold. The real test would be if she ran into David again. Could she figure out a way to balance her anger and abandonment against that place in her heart that seemed preserved at exactly the point her lips last touched his? The thought made her cheeks redden and she hoped Elsa hadn't noticed.

She dropped Elsa at her house, politely declining an invitation for coffee without mentioning that Bobby's coffee was cheap and weak, like he was, and she wasn't inclined to hear a lecture on the Sabbath for the second time today. Clouds had arrived again and rain mixed with sleet and snow started so she decided on the dirt road home in case it got colder. The gravel yielded better traction in freezing conditions. Half way home, the snow started in earnest and she couldn't help wondering why she'd never left this place. She and David had decided back then that they would leave, get educated, and do something to change the world. Ah, so grandiose the dreams of youth that may or may not come to pass. More importantly, how does one handle the consequences either way? She had obviously made concessions. When your entire sensibility was warped and wounded as her was at a young age, it could irreparably change you; allow an acceptance of failure that was unhealthy.

Maybe staying all these years was a self-confidence thing like the star small town athletes sometimes fall into in which they will always be stars in their quaint constellation and somewhere in the back of their minds doubted they would be the same at a bigger venue. There was a certain sadness in that, which she felt now. The snow began sticking along side the road and she thought she'd maybe taken that same tract as a mine president's wife, later the Mayor's wife, and while the attention was at times extremely negative, it was always attention and that thought made her ill. How shamefully self-absorbed. No, that couldn't be it. No. She liked it here even though she lived as a near hermit. She loved being close to her daughter and granddaughter. Yes, that was more like it. Harry's money made all their lives easier. Sure, that was a bit of laziness or lack of risk, but hadn't she taken enough risk in protecting her parents and the Barnets, in bedding that sleezeball Stark? Hell yes.

She turned off on the county road a short distance from home, the snow letting up a little and the rain increasing when it came back like a needle poked into her side. Why was Clarissa spying on David? What the hell did Harry care about anything David did or didn't do? It was like Harry knew something no one else did and thought David was a part of it, or influenced it some way. It couldn't be the swapping and sex from back in the day. If that were the case, he would have been watching her for years. Maybe he had been. Or maybe it was something she didn't know about. Another pebble in the shoe. And if Harry was hovering, Stark couldn't be too far behind.

Chapter Sixteen

The dinner with Clarissa required rescheduling twice, without animosity, just conflicts with her daughter's itinerary. On the first Friday of October, David awoke early, eager to start cooking, arranging things, preparing a worthy presentation. Something unsettling still lingered from eagle watching but he let it go as he laid out the necessary ingredients. Regardless, he liked her. The doorbell rang at three. A fire burned in the fireplace, wood piled beside it, the salad already prepared, a chocolate mousse cooling. He had even shaved. He paced himself as he went to the door, trying not to look overly enthusiastic.

The window framed her face, wind blew curls across it, a black beret, a matching scarf, mouth moving, talking to someone. She looked radiant. He opened the door, smiling. Beside her stood Elsa, hair pulled up in pig-tails, head shyly inclined. She wore a jacket that shouted 1950. In LA, guests didn't bring someone unannounced, but this wasn't LA and he'd not been promised an intimate evening. "Come on in," he said.

Clarissa pushed in. She grabbed David and hugged him, then unleashed another blazing smile, and hugged him again. "So good to see you," she said. "You look down right spiffy. This is my daughter, Elsa. We're happily thrown together today, hope you don't mind."

The girl looked up at him, reserved. "Hello again," tumbled out of her mouth almost automatically but that face cut him at the knees. She wasn't Dani's twin—she was Dani. Only dressed wrong. And younger, before the jaded eyes. She said something, but all he heard was Dani's voice, real or imagined. He wasn't sure. He wanted to hug her but that would definitely be inappropriate. Emotions pushed at him that could become tears or laughter but some long-lost real man inside said keep it together, staying in the moment. "Yes, of course, at the bank. Welcome," he sputtered. He stepped back. Clarissa ushered her past, looking at him. "Is something wrong, David," she said.

He shook his head and finally noticed their jackets. "Where are my manners. Please let me take your coats." He blushed as he stepped to Clarissa and helped her out of the pea coat. Elsa took hers off. It was new. Where could you buy that old style? She handed it to David. "No coats in LA. Sorry, didn't consider this." He glanced around and seeing no place to put them, scurried off and hung them in his office. The sweet sixteen picture of Dani shouted at him. He bent down and looked. It wasn't completely his imagination, the similarity was striking. He came back quickly and grabbed the corkscrew. "You both look wonderful," he said as he stripped the wine cap. "You flatter an old man."

Clarissa flashed a grin. Her alpaca cardigan, pure white, pearl buttons made him shudder. Under it, a tight blue Tommy Bahama t-shirt with stone washed jeans and demi-boots with heels that clicked on the wooden floor as they sauntered to the island bar. Elsa said nothing. David poured Mountain Dew for her, wine for Clarissa.

Clarissa sipped, smiled and licked her lips. "Good wine. So, what's for supper, Mr. Chef?"

"I found some beautiful rib-eye steaks at Zup's. Salad with goat cheese, olives and light vinaigrette, and twice-baked garlic potatoes. For dessert, chocolate mousse with fresh whipped cream, lattes and some Port wine, if anyone is interested in that."

"Glad I met you, David," Clarissa said. "This is the best restaurant in town."

"Let me rearrange the salads for three. Why don't you two sit in the living room and enjoy the fire. Put on a CD, maybe." he said. An unforced smile leaked out.

"Love what you've done to the place," Clarissa said.

David worked in the kitchen on the island that opened to the living room. He could glance up and see them, hear hushed murmurs, but focused on the salad.

The women sat tight together on the leather sofa. "What do you think?" Clarissa asked in a soft voice.

"Seems nice," Elsa said. She looked down.

"What aren't you saying?" Clarissa paused, waited.

"Daddy says he's a druggie. That he got kicked out of town because of drugs. That he should have stayed away. He's like all your men. Secular."

"Uh ha. An intellectual descriptor," Clarissa said. "You get teased at school for that stuff?" She made a quick flick of her finger intended to encompass the clothing.

"No. Other girls dress like this."

"Do they get teased?"

"Yes." Elsa looked away. "It isn't fair."

"All from that Baptist church, aren't they?" Clarissa waited, the girl nodded. "Time to start thinking for yourself, baby. He's wrong about David. And it's a crime the way he's raising you. Only reason I hang around is so he doesn't ruin you."

"You're preaching again."

"Did you tell him we're going to visit Grandma tomorrow morning?"

She nodded again. "He's not happy about David coming."

"He's not happy about anything, except you."

"Sometimes not even that," Elsa mumbled.

"What?"

"Nothing."

After dinner, he put another log on the fire and sat in the club chair pulled to the corner of the sofa. He and Clarissa nursed snifters of Port. Elsa had hot chocolate.

"That was delicious," Clarissa said. "You'll make a fine wife."

He chuckled. "Thanks. How is school, Elsa?"

She looked at him, maybe for the first time, maybe a little suspicious. "Fine. Good. Not too hard. I like Home Ec."

Clarissa glanced at David. He smiled, a little forced. "Her father is training her to be the wife he never had," Clarissa said.

Elsa sighed. "It's in the Bible, Mom."

"Or so he told you. I couldn't find it. We're taking you to see my mother tomorrow, David."

At the word mother, his body flinched. He sat up. "Angie?"

"She may not see you," Clarissa said. "She's unpredictable."

"As always," he uttered under his breath.

"We'll be here early, tomorrow. Mom's happier in the morning. Think it's the birds," Clarissa said. "We should leave by seven. Come on, kid. Time to go."

David retrieved their coats and resisted glancing at Dani's photo. As he handed the coats, he said, "I'll have breakfast ready at six thirty."

Clarissa gave him a chaste hug. "Yup, damn good wife."

And they were gone. He sat before the fire, lost in thought. The smell of wood smoke lingered, the crackle of the dying fire, the tiny incendiary flashes scattered along the log, every cell in his body tingled. What you don't deal with at the time stays there, waiting, smoldering, and tonight it felt like they'd been forced apart only yesterday. Like it had when he saw her in her car and at the bank, a wrinkle in time straight to that fountainhead. Thirty-plus year old issues pressed into the present. The past is not forgotten, but tomorrow would be another chance. God, what to say?

The next morning, no one discussed their exact destination. They exited town on the backside and entered the labyrinth. David could see Elsa's profile easily from the back seat and tried not to stare at the girl, but it was impossible so he asked her about her other classes. Her mouth moved, her eyes never left the road. Still that frightening resemblance.

Forty minutes later, they turned off the Tomahawk onto a wide dirt road that ambled between tall stands of pine and balsam, past a swampy marsh, and up a granite-laced hill speckled with mature second-growth spruce. Two-track roads sprouted on the right, tire ruts with grass between, some with gates blocking unwanted passage, most without tracks leading in, abandoned for the coming winter. To their left, miles of wilderness.

Ahead, David saw the back of a man walking at the side of the road, shotgun slung over his shoulder and wearing camouflage fatigues, head turning side to side, panning for game. He turned as the car approached and glared, eyes psychopathic, staring down the offending vehicle. As it passed, his gaze locked on David's eyes and sent a shiver down his spine. It was Nick Foulke, the vet from the bar, his old playmate. They had spent time as kids in the woods, playing war in the era of *Combat* on TV, and David had always been the captain and Nick always the grunt sergeant. They were a team that fought the rest of the kids on the block and no one could blend into the forest like Nick, disappearing and reappearing out of nowhere beside a foe, blazing away with a wooden submachine gun, taking out their entire squad and vanishing again into the glade for the next skirmish. He certainly had done the same in Vietnam. David wondered how many lives Nick had snuffed out and still lived with, but couldn't live with. Now just another vicious trained killer loose in a world where killing scared the living shit out of people and Nick couldn't hide the training or the Post Traumatic Stress Disorder that David saw clearly. Eyes that showed no hint of recognition, no trace of the self-satisfied smirk that glowered over Nick's face when he ambushed kids with his fake gun or later, when he won a swimming race, or as a brutal middle linebacker when he flattened a running back at the line of scrimmage, grinning as he helped the battered guy to his feet. That Nick was a casualty, a death that didn't make the stat sheets, out here in the backwoods struggling to keep some kind of life together, away from the citizens he scared, away from civilization all together, his tiny tribe living off the land, off his ability to kill, while his other family, the one he grew up with, was scattered to the four winds, no roots left, no one to help in times of trouble, only a shell-shocked wife and a teenage boy who thought he was Chippewa to fight the ravages of hunger and cold in a land of radical extremes. A land that splintered families with limited opportunity, wretched winters and sweltering summers, the dense air filled with the constant buzz of biting bugs. A land difficult to live with if one had an established support system and damn near impossible without it.

Nick shook his fist as they passed. Their car would scare any grouse off the road, into hiding, and away from his dinner table. This wasn't sport for him. This was survival and David knew it. The car compromised the chances for success on this piece of road, at prime time for hunting. David watched him duck under a low tree branch and disappear into the forest, wishing him success and hoping for no rip in the fabric of PTSD that would send him over the edge.

Farther down, Clarissa slowed. A ruffed grouse flushed off the road and disappeared into the brown ferns coated with a layer of dust. David cursed under his breath. Clarissa turned into a thin, dirt two-track. He watched her face, but saw only a focus on driving. His stomach churned. He took a deep breath and looked ahead. A canopy of maples and oaks closed above them, leaves glowing with intense reds and brilliant yellows like colored flecks of helium tethered by decaying stems waiting to float free and rise into the sky. A covey of grouse huddled on the other side of a split rail fence, frozen as the car passed. A few pine and spruce added shades of green to the background of leaves, the ground absent of bushes or ferns but emerging baby trees, stark and brittle in youth, were scattered in places that received sunlight, back off the road, where today the early October mist floated through canopy openings and the low gray sky winked above. He wiggled upright in his seat and looked over Elsa's shoulder. "Is this it?" he asked. Clarissa nodded, the car barely moving forward. Ahead, he saw a building emerge from the mist. Square cut log walls graying with age, large porches on two sides ringed in split rails, an empty rocking chair, a freshly painted red screen door that opened as he watched.

A woman emerged wearing a green hunting jacket that hung open, hiking boots and those lovely speckled curls fluffy on her shoulders. Her face smiled softly as she stepped onto the porch, a much more relaxed Lady of the Lake than the sculptured woman at the bank, like the essence of the girl that haunted his past. His scalp tingled.

Clarissa stopped in the dirt drive thirty feet away. "You stay here," she said to David. "Come on, kid. Grandma loves to see you." The cabin sat in a clearing of grass and pine needles, and behind it the lake shown as a silver ripple shrouded in the mist. He watched them mount the three stairs. Grandma went straight to granddaughter with a huge hug and kiss. Then she turned to Clarissa, her arms out, thin face weathered and tan. David saw Angie's mouth moving and the women parted, facing each other, talking, he thought he saw her shudder. He saw Angie staring, listening, mouth not moving. She did not look happy. Her head shook now, side-to-side. Then it was Elsa talking to Grandma. Clarissa walked down the steps and toward the car, expressionless. She opened the driver-side door and pushed her head in. Her face showed with a self-satisfied smile, like her plan had fallen perfectly into place. "She says it's too cold to sit out here. That you better come in."

And here he was—in her presence again. A circle completed, an avatar outside time. He struggled out of the car, his insides a swirling mess. He followed Clarissa and Elsa through the screen door. They shuffled past Angie. He glanced around the room. The open storm door blocked the tiny kitchen, three cupboards, an old single sink, a shrunken refrigerator, a small range, speckled linoleum counters, and all spotlessly clean. To his left in front of a picture window, a thick oak table sat surrounded by four ladder-back chairs, rag woven cushions adorned their seats. The window looked out over the porch toward the lake. A barrel stove belched heat. He could hear the muted crackling of the fire and smell the wood smoke scenting the house. His fingers fidgeted in his coat pockets. He stepped inside and looked at Angie.

She bit her lower lip and looked away and he wondered about her absent haughtiness but was glad it was elsewhere. "Uh . . . Bloody Mary . . . anyone?" she said and moved into the kitchen, her back turned away. But, he'd seen her face, seen her bite that lip as he had so many times when she was hurt or disturbed. He wanted to take away her pain. Through the tanned skin, through the hardened crystal eyes, he saw the girl he loved as if thirty-three years had vanished or never happened, and his stomach snapped into a tight knot. He took a tentative step into the kitchen behind her.

"Yes, Bloody Mary for me," he said. Then in a soft voice. "It's good to see you, Angie."

She didn't turn around but reached into a cupboard and pulled out two tall glasses. Ice tinkled. Her hands trembled. "Wish I could say the same," she said. She splashed vodka over the ice, added tomato juice from a can, a dash of Worcestershire and one of Tabasco, then some pepper and an olive. She put a spoon in his glass, turned and handed it to him. "You girls deaf? Forget it. Clarissa, you take care of it." She pushed by David, sat at the table, and gazed out the window, an ice queen in woods attire.

David took the seat to her left where she could look out the window and not have to see him. He sat on the edge of the chair, hunched forward, and took a drink. Very strong. He noticed the rows of shelving that dominated a wall, one-by-four inch pine, leveled and bevel cut, stained a dark cherry color, and each filled with thimbles. Many designs and materials, some porcelain painted in unique patterns of flowers, states, bridges, faces, some of copper, tin, zinc, silver, gold, intricately dimpled or etched. A fairy tale. "How have you been, Angie?"

She replied without looking. "Delightful, thanks. And you?"

Clarissa was in the kitchen pouring OJ for Elsa and coffee for herself. The room was small. Grandma's voice almost edgy. "Elsa, there's wood to stack outside. Would you mind terribly," Angie said. Elsa's eyes were large anyway but they grew bigger now and she grabbed the glass and bolted out the door.

David took another drink and looked out the window. "Seen Bunny?" He remembered her flitting around school this time of year in unfettered joy, barely tethered like the leaves.

"About every other month."

"How is she?"

"David," she said. Now turning to face him. "Bunny's a vegetable. She sits on a shelf and they water her daily. Hasn't said a word in thirty-three years. There is a reason I don't care to catch up on old times. Ghosts don't interest me. My granddaughter and Clarissa do."

Clarissa sat down holding her coffee. "I know it's hard, Mom? It's hard on all of us. Might try being civil with each other, eh."

"It's okay," David said. "We both went through hell then." He thought the blast of emotion was a step forward.

Angie nodded and pointed at Clarissa. "You're the one who's pushing this."

Clarissa stirred in sugar. "Tell him something nice, Mom. Thanks for coming, maybe. Thanks for caring about me. Or maybe a bit of truth, like you've loved him for years."

"That's out of line," David said.

Angie glared at her. "Must you always stir the pot? Where *do* you get your manners?"

"Daddy."

"Of course. Shameful really."

David looked from one to the other, breaking the tension seemed improbable but he tried. "How do you manage way out here?"

Angie's lips relaxed slightly. "My road gets plowed. Garage is heated, with electricity for the head bolt heater. Subaru has four-wheel drive. All else fails, I have an excellent snowmobile."

"Seems isolated," David said.

"I talk to her on the phone." She nodded toward Clarissa. "Last winter she even came out a few times. Before it got bad."

"You told me not to come."

"You're not famous for listening."

"Please, Mom."

"Maybe make it a little more this winter with a man to chaperone? If he's still around," Angie said.

She didn't look at David, but Clarissa's eyes darted to him. "Sure, I'll help," he said.

Angie's nose pointed up, her face ice again. Clarissa glanced at her, butted in quickly. "Thanks David." She nodded imperceptibly. "Mom, I think we've stayed too long. Probably shouldn't have, sorry." Clarissa stood in front of her chair. "We'll call it a day and let you get back to what you were doing."

Angie's eyes flashed around the table, taking in both faces. "Well . . . thank you for coming," she said.

David exhaled. He looked into Angie's eyes. "Thanks for having me."

Angie stood but said nothing. She walked to the door and opened it and stepped out on the porch, holding the screen door open. David stopped in front of her, but said nothing either, only nodded. She did not respond. David walked down the steps and caught a glimpse of what appeared to be a young man in a tattered field jacket hurrying off through the woods and wondered where Elsa was.

On the porch, Clarissa embraced her mother with both arms. "It was hard, I know. Thanks. See you next week."

"Please don't bring him."

"Maybe."

"Thank God for coming winter," Angie said. "Where's Elsa?"

Angie stood on the porch watching the car disappear down the driveway. Clarissa eyed her in the rearview mirror. "I'm eating with you tonight, David. What have you got?"

"I was going to make spaghetti."

"That's fine," Clarissa said. "We have some things to discuss."

They turned out of Angie's two-track drive and had traveled a short distance when they saw a hunter cross the road. David thought the silhouette bore a distinct resemblance to Nick Foulke, when Elsa said, "That's Jacob." She rolled down the window and yelled, "Bye Jacob." There was no evidence he heard it, no evidence of where he'd entered the woods, and David certainly could not see him navigating an unseen trail, nor hear him muttering, "Elsa . . . Elsa . . . Elsa."

Clarissa parked in front of Elsa's house. She was all smiling and chatty the entire way home, which was new. "Are we going to Grandma's next weekend?" she asked.

"Okay, what gives," Clarissa said, and glanced at David in the back seat.

Elsa paused. Then blurted it out. "It's that boy in the woods. He's cute."

"Did you talk to him?"

"Not much today. I think you scared him off."

Clarissa looked at her daughter. Elsa's eyes pleaded. "Okay, probably go next weekend." They walked to her door leaving David in suspended animation, wondering what the hell had happened.

After dinner, David made a latte for each of them. Clarissa sat on the sofa. A fire burned and he added a log. "What are we discussing?" he asked and plopped down on the other end.

Clarissa looked at him, sympathetic. "You."

"Me?"

"You. You need to get rid of some baggage."

David glanced away, at the fire. "Baggage?" Still, he avoided her eyes.

Clarissa started slowly, softly. "You left a life that took years to build."

"And a minute to destroy," he broke in.

"You've migrated from one failed relationship to another, including your own parents."

"What the hell does that have to do with anything?" His voice rose. "My life here was throttled by a red-neck cop. He's just like Nixon and his clan of crooks. Least they got caught."

"Right," she said.

"Right? There's nothing right about it. I got thrown out when Angie needed me the most. Look at her, will ya. Do you think she got a fair shake?" He stopped talking and glared at her, defiant.

Clarissa's expression didn't change. "No. In fact, David, she's just like you." His eyes grew wider. Clarissa mellowed her voice. "You're both trauma victims. It's affecting your life, David, and hers. How many pages have you written lately?"

"Plenty. None of your damn business."

"Okay. You don't have to talk to me. Maybe it would be better to talk to Angie."

"And what the hell happened to Bunny?"

"She was the one who found her mother shot to death. She cracked. Currently resides at the Brainerd regional treatment center. Grandpa died prematurely, a convict in a hospital for the criminally insane in Minneapolis."

"I come up here to hide and write and instead I get all this."

"Life goes on in small towns, too."

David grimaced. Clarissa stood, went to him, embraced him. "I'll see you soon," she added and kissed his cheek.

"Right. Really looking forward to it."

It took most of an hour to cool down and realize Clarissa was right. He had work to do. A good first step might involve someone other than himself—like a real man.

Chapter Seventeen

The day after David's visit turned clear and cold and Angie worked to her physical limits, first clearing a trail she'd neglected for a year, then an ardent run at the woodpile, and by the time she was through, only enough energy for a steak and wine remained. Even after eating and cleaning up there was an intransigent restlessness that left her tapping her fingers which annoyed her to the point that a walk was required. She poured a martini into a cup and started down the path to her dock with an anxious feeling that rudeness had no place in her life but she had been rude indeed yesterday with David. Yes, she had kept the words reasonably formal and people that didn't know her would have probably thought her polite, but she knew and most likely Clarissa knew, and she was sure David had been able to ferret out her real meaning from the façade. She took a drink and sat on the dock chair.

It was colder now and a moorish mist rose from the lake that reminded her of the haze inside her brain, like it had been sheared leaving two separate spheres from which synapses could not pass. One side containing the abrasions she'd inflicted on him yesterday and the other holding the sealed warmth from years ago. She deemed it a deteriorated mental state that those two could not be reconciled, and although it seemed ancient, this was the first time it occurred to her in this light which gave a dose of optimism. The first step in addressing a problem was recognition. She took another drink. Her hands were very cold now and her breath frosted as her eyes caught specks of a headlight twinkling in the blackness across the lake where the road dipped and passed behind the trees. She thought of Clarissa's part in the David meeting and her question: you claiming him or is it open season? The owl called softly and she shivered now and started slowly back to the cabin, thinking a hot brandy might finish off the night well, and knowing what she would do tomorrow.

The following morning she was up early. With winter coming and New York Times Notable book list for the year only a couple months away, she got out her book boxes and took coffee in front of her bookcase. Time to replenish the Lady of the Lake section and she bent to the task, loading books she hadn't cared for and ones she liked but would not want to read again. She saved Morrison's *Love* and Coetzee's *Elizabeth Costello,* and still couldn't part with McCarthy's border trilogy, but had two boxes filled anyway, parting sadly with Guterson's *Our Lady of the Forest* although mainly for the title. She carried them out to the porch, made two eggs and toast, and got down to the important business of going-to-town image. Coiffed and made up, hair brushed and pinned, she selected an Orvis suede pant and vest outfit with a maroon turtleneck sweater. A final check in the mirror only complete with an upturn of chin, a microfiber coat to match, and she was outside loading boxes into the car.

As she arrived in town the thought of seeing David sent a chill, and while she knew she must apologize, it couldn't be today. That disconnect recognized last night was not yet overcome although it had softened just a tad, but there was still a vague nervousness fluttering in her stomach, as she entered the library. The librarian made her usual fuss, sending a volunteer to lug the boxes, fawning over the titles, even making a cup of tea that Angie took at the most private computer terminal in the place, sipping as she typed DNA analysis+Minnesota into the Google search box. She found three that looked promising and wrote down the names and numbers, finally clearing the browser history before going to

Amazon to order more books. She couldn't remember whether she'd donated David's catalog and made a check of the shelves that revealed nothing, so she ordered each of his titles before logging off.

It was already eleven-thirty and she decided a good lunch at the Grand Hotel in Ely was in order. She stopped at Clarissa's house but no one was there, which gave her a twinge, and since Elsa had school she would dine alone. She almost forgot her mail and detoured to the post office, where Jack Lasiter greeted her with his familiar Mrs. Thomson refrain. She paid him a hundred dollars a year to sort the junk mail out of her box, leaving only the important items. It hadn't taken that long to train him, a few months of bringing back the things she didn't want anymore, ever, did the trick. And actually it wasn't paying him, it was more like a tip at Christmas which she would have done anyway, though they both understood. She wondered now if anyone else employed him. The mail was light with only a few books in the Amazon box. Sometimes it was hard to decide, even with the list she updated from various book reviews.

Last weeks storms had knocked most of the leaves down and even without snow, it now looked like winter as she made the half-hour drive. The Grand had autumn decorations in the lobby and the front desk person greeted her by name. The maitre d seated her at a two top overlooking the lake and as the menu arrived, she saw Harry Barnet and Randy Stark being seated at a warm table near the kitchen, which churned her stomach. Small town bad luck at its worst. It wasn't too busy and she knew they would see her and hoped they would keep to themselves, but Harry's eyes glanced her way, and as soon as the waiter left with their drink order, Harry got up and shuffled toward her. She averted her attention toward the lake that looked rust colored surrounded by skeletal trees, a hawk circled in the distance. She felt him without looking.

"Good day, Angie," he said, his politician smile seemed false as always and his breathing was labored. "How was the reunion with your old flame?"

Her chin rose higher, which was natural in a sitting-to-standing conversation, and her eyes remained cold. "Hello Harry. You do understand that I offer civilized politeness only by virtue of your monthly payments." She wondered if Clarissa tipped him off, or Elsa had told a friend, or maybe he had been spying on her for years and she didn't realize it until now. "Old flame is rather derogatory, wouldn't you say?"

He smiled again, practiced. "Maybe. That didn't occur to me. May I offer you a drink?"

Angie felt the idea more than thought it, and returned a thin smile of her own. "That does sound good, Harry. I'll have a glass of Moet Chandon White Star." The idea of a nice champagne struck her as just right, and she decided to stop on the way out of town and buy a bottle. "And where did you hear that Harry?"

He looked at his table and back to her. "Confidential. Mr. Stark sends his regards."

Angie saw Stark nod to her and all she could think of was the smell of his cheap Jade East cologne that gave her a headache to this day. Her mouth narrowed and she looked Harry straight in the eyes. "You know what to tell Mr. Stark. If you'll excuse me, it looks like the waiter is ready."

Harry bowed and moved off, quickly conferred with the waiter who took his place. "I have the drink order, Mrs. Thomson. What can I get you for lunch?"

Now Angie hauled out her real smile. "May I have a piece of smoked whitefish and a small Caesar salad. A glass of ice tea as well please."

Her lunch arrived and the salad was marginal but the smoked whitefish was worth the trip by itself. As she ate, gazing out across the lake, she wondered what the conversation with Harry really meant. He didn't go out of his way to ignore her, but also seldom went the other way, a greeting, a meeting, and everything meant something to Harry. He was smart and left nothing to chance in spite of age and shaky health. She paid the bill, put on her jacket, and left, glancing at the untouched champagne with a smirk. Whatever Harry meant, she had left a message, too: fuck you Harry.

Chapter Eighteen

By noon the next day, David abandoned the computer and drove to the flower shop fifteen miles away, bought a dozen roses. On the way to the cemetery, he saw the sign "Auto's Place," elegantly hand-lettered like many others in town, the work of a man now dead, and he thought about stopping as he had many times but he pushed on.

Twenty acres of graves greeted him in a place he had never been, seemingly deserted but could one really know. He wished his daughter's grave was nearby, too. He walked the rows until he found them. The two graves lay side by side, with simple matching headstones. Someone had left flowers recently, without a card, and sadness crept over him, recalling the family suppers, hunting with Dad, reading with Mom, the gentle love, the tough love and all the good they'd shared before that world was erased. He stood in the freezing air, over his parents' graves and carefully laid out the flowers. Mom and Dad were both the first generation born on American soil, afforded all the opportunities founded in this country. He pictured them in their youth, strapping immigrant children. Their parents were Swedes, but the children, his parents, were Americans. Their native Swedish whispered in the alleys, never spoken on the streets nor in their homes. They were raised outside a tiny Lake Superior shipping port, by hard working, God-fearing parents that economics and railroad labor finally beat down. Who died wishing for a last trip to the family farm across the Atlantic. So his father had said. But they'd spent their dreams in one fell swoop, placed on red as the Roulette wheel spun and hit and they came to America with their infant sons, their infant daughters, and found their way to this inhospitable land that looked strikingly like their homeland but without the legacy of family, alone then to watch children die of diseases without cures. No extended family around them. A few acquaintances to witness the thud of dirt clods on tiny caskets in frigid Northeasterly blows, then home to their hovel, silent with grief and despair, knowing now what their parents must have felt when infant mortality felled thirteen of sixteen children instead of two out of three. So maybe America wasn't that bad.

David's parents had been neighbors living on the rural fringes of the port town and worked large abutting gardens against the onslaught of deer and rabbits and birds and the disastrously short summer in hopes of harvesting vegetables to tide them through the winter. Talking across rows of leaf lettuce, carrots, potatoes, talking above strung up string beans and buttressed tomato plants, each bent over a hoe, sweating and smiling and watering and maturing until they wed at seventeen and moved to this new town, Lone Pine, with the new mine where they paid him to clean grease pits and sweep floors and stream clean engines and undercarriages of huge trucks in sweltering temperatures and in cold so dense that steam-frost formed on his clothes. At night knowing intimacy only from the other, cleaving only to each other, finally having their only child after fifteen years of trying only to see him exiled seventeen years later, the joy of their lives departed, and cleaving together to the last, in bitter grief, until only these gravestones remained. "Stronger than me," he said standing over the markers. "Sandy bailed right after the trial and look at me. Guess everything isn't inherited."

He stared at the gravestones until the cold cut through his jacket and he shivered without control. "I should have made it different," he muttered. He turned and started walking, but stopped, looked back, sighed. "You did your best. I won't forget. I'll try to forgive myself for the lousy way I treated you guys."

His parents had lived firmly rooted in the present, seldom discussing the past and talking only of one future—his. He knew only the love they showed him, the pride they showed in him. They were home now, together. He wondered whether the gravitational pull of rural life was genetic or just a useless yearning for a safety known only in childhood, as ephemeral as the summer garden, a greener pastoral syndrome dating to the sixteenth century that mankind will never outgrow, never overcome, even as the forces of economics beat away at country life, paving a future in which all that will remain are cities and snatches of wilderness and nothing between. A way of life squandered and left for dead.

On the way home, David detoured at the Auto's Place sign and pulled into a driveway littered with cars and boats in various states of repair, a triple-wide garage door was open and the whine of a outboard motor filled the country air. Auto's real name was Jim Murphy. He and David were classmates in high school, but weren't really friends until after graduation when they happened upon each other in the Twin Cities.

David got out of his truck. The noise stopped and a man swaggered out of the garage toward him, cigarette dangling. Slim and wiry, Auto had acquired that swagger with his driver's license or maybe with his motorcycle. Either way, David was happy he still had it. Things like that can get lost. Back then, Peter Fonda would have envied that motorcycle, the culmination of two years work, a chopper in the finest, chromest sense, rumbling low and loud so every head turned. The day after he got his DL, he parked it beside the principal's car in the front row, grinning, cigarette dangling from his mouth that he spit out, stomped on, and said nothing as he strutted into the school—on time for the first time.

"Wondered if you'd ever stop out," Auto said, grinning, wiping grease from his hands.

"Been meaning to."

Auto gave him the old locked-thumbs handshake, a man's embrace. "Look damn good for an old man, Davy."

"Shit, you don't age at all? How the hell you do that?"

"Clean livin'," he said. And popped a beer open. "Have one?" David shook his head and saw the black F-150 roll by the mouth of the driveway, slowing further. Auto flipped the guy off. "Asshole. Lives down the road a block or so, there. Don't say shit to me. We go way back, him and me. Harassed me for anything, and for what? To prove he was boss. He ain't no fucking boss a nothing. I see right through his new do-gooder bullshit. He screwed you and a lot a other folks. Can't change that with a new suit of clothes. Small town, Davy. Got a be careful if ya want a hang around."

"Apparently."

"Out for his nightly patrol." Auto laughed. "No car, no badge, no nothing and still on patrol. Been doing it for maybe couple months now. Crazy."

Couple months—since I got here, David thought. He ignored it for the moment. "What about you, man? Family?"

"Married Donna Palsson, remember her?"

"Yeah, I think so. Quiet. Kind of a petite girl?"

"Not so much anymore. She's inside. Wanna stay for supper?"

"Well . . . been out to the cemetery. Saw the folks. Was thinking I'd lay low tonight."

Auto slipped another cigarette between his lips and snapped open a well-worn Zippo. A cloud billowed out of his mouth. "Understand. Sad, man. Come on up and say hi to Donna." Auto turned toward the house, his head jerked that way and he grabbed David's arm. "Two kids, boy, Jimmy Jr. and girl, Stephanie. Both graduated." Auto smiled. "Jimmy's a pretty good mechanic. He's down in the Cities working at a dealership. She's in college down there. Got Donna's brains, not mine. Both say they're never coming back, Davy." Auto chuckled. "I remember saying that."

David kicked a stone off the driveway. "I said it three months ago."

"Place is dying, if ya ask me. Be a ghost town pretty damn quick. Taconite mine's shrinking. Company in town can only sell so many pool tables. Always some rumor of a new businesses coming. Just never happens. Could end in our lifetime, old boy."

"Hope not. Got to have someplace a person can live that's quiet. Away from the madness of modern life. A place that's just plain safe."

Auto glanced over and grinned, sucked a puff of smoke. "It ain't that safe. Shit, we lived in the city. Only difference here is less people to watch. Fuck that. What about you?"

David knew what he was asking. "All gone."

Auto stopped and turned. David could see that hurt him, his face was serious now, like at a funeral. All the swagger seemed to melt out of him. "I can listen."

"Not today." He dropped an arm around Auto's shoulder and turned him toward the house.

Auto nodded. He glanced at the Range Rover and shook his head. "Fine. Hey what ya doing driving that money pit?"

"Got me? Ego thing from LA mainly I guess." He knew that wasn't a secret.

"Going deer hunting?"

Just the words pissed him off. "Damn right."

Auto grinned. They stamped dirt off their shoes and went inside. Donna was sweet and perfect for old Auto. A half hour later, after promises of supper in the near future, he swung his truck around in the loop and stopped at the mouth of the drive. There it was, coming again. He waited for the black F-150 to pass in the fading afternoon light. David remembered the night in the jail and the words, "You're tighter than Angie." A scared kid then. Now he would get the grown up David. Maybe a real man. Fuck all that shit that no one will talk about.

David worked hard the next morning, beating the keys, falling into it like watching a movie and scrambling to keep up. About noon, exhausted and exhilarated, he made lunch, then headed to the hardware store, the Weatherby .308 in the back end. He bought a deer tag, three boxes of ammo and leaping deer targets. It was a short drive to the gun club. Everything was a short drive here. Four or five guys milled around, talking, not shooting. He put up a target at about fifty yards and sat at a bench. Beside it was a table with sandbags. His hands shook slightly. He'd never been much of a hunter. Dad took him out a few times. He'd read up on his rifle, Internet research. Carefully filling the magazine, he snapped the bolt locked, rested the stock on the sandbags, and zeroed the scope onto his target. The rifle wobbled in spite of the support. Exhale, squeeze. He had read that, too. The sound was deafening, the recoil harder than expected. He scanned the target but couldn't see a hole anywhere. He bolted in another round and tried again. Still no hole. Three more shots, not a single hit. Now he was pissed. As he came out of his trance to reload, he noticed a guy sitting on the next bench. It was Stark.

He peered through a spotting scope. "They're all high, right," he said. David thought he heard a trace of compassion in the voice. "Know how to sight that scope?"

David looked at the scope. He had no idea, hadn't read up on scopes, yet. "Sure. Couldn't see where they were hitting."

"Nice looking rifle," Stark said. "Old, solid." He stood up and reached in his pocket, came out with a dime and popped off the scope caps. "Let me help you out."

"You can 'help me out' by talking to the college president. Tell her the truth, that you planted that pot in my car." There he'd said it. Maybe that's how it works in small towns, trench warfare. Somehow it felt better than just shooting the bastard.

Stark didn't look up from his scope adjustments until he was finished. "Try that," he said and sat back down at his spotting scope. David loaded five more rounds, aimed and fired. "Must be just a freckle high and left. You hit it in the head."

"That's what I was aiming for."

Stark shook his head. "See the circles on the shoulder? Ya never aim at the head, always the shoulder. Never been hunting, have you?"

"Sure."

He looked straight into David' eyes, not menacingly, more as if he were looking for something and thinking. "Can't say that, but I could talk to her. Maybe make up something to help. Might have been wrong about you, Chapman."

David's eyes narrowed. He snapped another round into the chamber.

"Who ya hunting with? And don't say yourself. Dan'l Boone is dead."

"No plans, yet."

"About ten of us go out by Kawishawa. Why don't ya come with us? We'll show ya the ropes."

This was just too weird for words, but he remembered what an LA cop once told him: keep your enemies close. David shouldered the rifle, put the crosshairs on the circle, and squeezed. Stark looked into his scope. "Nice shot," he said.

The following day, David left at seven with a thermos of coffee, a stack of CDs, and a lunch. The drive to Brainerd was nearly four hours. When he pulled into the parking lot, another car was leaving. Sun glinted off the window, but he swore it looked like Russet driving. Can't be, he thought.

A nurse led him to a community room and seated him in a yellow upholstered chair. He looked out the window at the brown grass and bare trees. The temperature was stuck at thirty-eight degrees. A wind had blown away the last of the leaves and a cold snap hung in the offing. He saw the nurse enter with a woman on her arm and his heart dropped. Bunny's hair was a smoothed over nest of snarls. She wore a stained flowered robe and slippers. Her stooped shuffle broke his heart. She was obese, her face puffed and spotted with broken capillaries and eyes flat and remote. The nurse seated her beside David and walked across the room, sat at a table, watching.

"Bunny," David said softly. There was no hint that he'd even spoken. "Remember me, David Chapman? Angie's old boyfriend." David looked into her face, her eyes, for any sign of recognition but found none. "Came to sit with you. You can talk to me, but you don't have to. It's okay. We can just sit."

He turned in his chair so he could see her better and gazed into her face, searching. Somewhere inside there was the most beautiful girl in his high school, in town for that matter. The girl with the golden spirit who loved everybody and everybody loved her, the girl who protected the animals, and couldn't sit through biology dissections and had a hard time keeping up with academics. But she could feel you, your happiness and your pain. And right now, David felt great pain and great sadness at the devastated remnants of this lovely creature, and he had a hard time fighting back the tears, so he tried to smile, still silent.

"I've lived far away for years. But now I'll come and see you more." He turned away, gazed out the window, and tried to choke it back. It wasn't just Bunny now, but also Dani and Sandy and Angie. He felt a touch on his hand. It was Bunny's hand. He turned to her. There was still no sign of recognition and yet her hand rested on his. She had put it there and it seemed to suck away his pain and grief. Imagined or not, it didn't matter. He knew what mattered. She was in there.

He sat with her for another hour. Her hand never moved. He didn't care that the end of his drive home would be after dark or that a storm was coming. He felt a comfort that he couldn't explain. A nurse walked up and said it was time for Bunny's medication. David nodded, looked at Bunny. "I'll be back," he said.

The next morning, David made a thermos of lattes. Forty-five minutes later, he turned into Angie's driveway and drove it slowly. He stopped but saw no sign of her and walked toward the porch. A door creaked and she stepped out. "What do you think you're doing?" she asked, leaning her shotgun against the railing.

"Came to talk," he said, plaintive, certainly defensive.

"I thought I made myself clear."

He watched her. "I went to see Bunny, yesterday. It hurt me." Angie studied his face, his eyes. Stayed silent.

"You were right. She looks terrible. It's still Bunny, though. She touched my hand."

Angie's eyebrows rose. She stared at him. "I doubt that."

"Truth."

She hesitated, studied him for what seemed a long time. "Come in," she said.

His nerves tingled, but calmed a little when she set the shotgun in the corner. Her shoulders looked tight, face tense. She fumbled with the cups. White china with a pastel-flowered trim, more delicate than he expected. He poured their lattes in a forced, uncomfortable silence. "She told me I'm a mess," he said finally.

"Who?"

"Clarissa."

She didn't look at him and went back to the kitchen, returning with a loaf of bread, a cutting board and a knife. "Don't take it to heart. She's been telling me that for years."

He cut thick slices off the loaf and laid one on her plate. "She said I need to talk about it, maybe to you." She frowned. "Still read a lot?" he said.

"Of course," she said. "Read your stuff."

"And?"

"You can do better."

He cringed, glanced her way. She wasn't looking at him, eyes gazing out to the lake, taking a delicate bite.

"Uh. . .thanks, I think. Keep trying to improve."

She chewed, jaw barely moving, prim. Her swallow was imperceptible. "You don't seem to know much about women."

"What happened back then?" He couldn't believe his ears. That he'd just said that, asked that. His stomach tightened, ready for a fight.

She took another bite, still gazing out the window. "Thought you knew." He followed her eyes to the lake. It shimmered, reflecting an impossibly blue sky, faint puffs of condensation rose from the water, miniature clouds painted above a reflection.

"I got third-hand information, rumors. I wanted to go to you."

"But you didn't."

"It could have cost me twenty years in prison."

"She was already gone anyway."

"Wish I could have come." His eyes fell to the table.

"Thirty-some years later and we're still fighting it."

The words stuck in his head. That's what Clarissa was driving at.

"Coffee's good," she said, gazing out the window again.

"Yeah." He tried to smile but it came off poorly.

"So, you learn anything in LA?"

He paused. That was the voice of *his* Angie, the personal question, the intelligent tone searching for insight and it felt like nineteen-seventy-one again. The answer could be so many things. "You were lucky we didn't hook up." He wanted to tell her what happened in LA, but couldn't make himself do it, yet.

She turned and finally looked at him. "I needed you then, David. I didn't know what happened to you. Then it didn't matter. You weren't there. No one was there." Her words came out cool, lacking emotion, distant.

His chair creaked as he slid it back. She didn't move. He went to her and hugged her as she gazed again out the window, his face buried in her soft curls. "It killed me, too."

She couldn't see his tears, reliving a moment in his life that he had buried as deeply as he could dig the hole, and still not deep enough. A wave of embarrassment came over him, for not being there then, and for hugging this woman now, but she placed her hand on his and pressed it softly, confirming the idiosyncrasy of her and time itself. And it felt good. He stepped behind her and wiped at his eyes before returning to his chair.

"I read clips in the Minneapolis paper. Called some friends from the hockey team, but they hadn't seen you and didn't want to talk to me. I let them down, too." He paused. "How'd you get through it?"

Her gaze came back from the window to him. "Not sure I did. Barnets took me in the day of the murder. The doctor came, examined me, and drugged the shit out of me. They kept me out of school and away from people. At the time, I thought that was good, but in retrospect, maybe not. I lost it. I hated them. I hated you. I hated the world. When Joplin died I envied her."

He sat silently, absorbing, trying to piece together the anomaly of her words and the dearth of emotion in her voice, her delivery. "I can't imagine . . . ."

"I asked for you a hundred times. They finally told me. I knew it had to be a set-up." She paused, her head dropped, eyes looking at her finger idly tracing the flower pattern on her cup. "And I knew why." She didn't look up.

It was almost a whisper. He barely heard it. Still, it registered like a cymbal clash. The answer to the question that plagued him for all these years, right here, right now, in front of him. He struggled to remain calm. "And?"

She looked at him now with a face so sad and humiliated that it tore at him. He wanted to say, forget it. I don't need to know. I don't need to know anything that makes you look that way. But he couldn't get it out.

"Stark was in love with me."

He was astounded to the point of disbelief. "That's crazy."

"Yeah." She scraped at her cuticle with her thumbnail, eyes faking attention.

David watched her face, her fingers, felt something he couldn't place. She didn't look up. He waited. His eyes followed her gaze to the lake, again. The little clouds of condensation were thunderheads now. Finally, she turned to him, her eyes pleading, tears forming in the corners. "He was fucking me, David. I couldn't stop it. I was too weak."

Her hands folded onto her lap, head tilted, a lost soul withering before his eyes. The words hung in the air, echoing off the ancient propane lamp globes, the fake log lath. *He was fucking me.* He thought he was prepared, but not for this. He watched her liquefy before his eyes and felt himself melting, too. "I, uh, don't know what to say. Can't believe you had to live with it."

She held out her arms like a fragile doll, and he went to her. She buried her head in his shoulder and cried harder and he held her tighter. His mind spun back in time, and fought a childish jealousy. His face flushed, consumed in her curls. Time drifted, floated, like the condensation clouds. The convulsions subsided. A voice broke through his thoughts. "You were the first one I made love to, David." A long pause. "And the last." The voice broke through again. "There's more."

Chapter Nineteen

David lay in a two-man tent that he shared with a guy named Larry Johnson, who slept in the other cot, stinking of brandy and sweat and snoring so loudly he was probably scaring the deer for miles. But it didn't bother David. He had barely slept anyway. The Walther .32 rested under his pillow. It was Saturday, the opening morning of deer season. A voice came through the tent flap. "Breakfast is ready. Time to hit the woods." It might have been Stark but it was a stage whisper. He couldn't be sure. It didn't matter. He pulled on his gear and went to eat. Keeping enemies close was hungry business. It was cold out, felt like twenty degrees.

They assigned him to a stand, a board nailed to a stump really, that sat on a hogback overlooking a valley. With the leaves down, the view was good. Stark would be stationed on the other side of the next hill, hunting the next valley. Four men were to fan out at the camp and hunt toward them, driving any deer their way. David was uncertain whether he hated deer more than Stark, but he would kill something today. The revelations of Angie made him hope it would be Stark, but he wanted a deer for Dani, too. He was sure of that. A double would be incredibly lucky. It was still dark. He shouldered his rifle and scanned the area with the scope, which gathered the fragile light. He could make out the terrain which sloped downhill from his left to his right and fell away steeply in front of him, pock marked with aspen. Young balsam dotted the valley floor, the ground frosted and slippery with fallen leaves. He sat on the bench and rested his back on a thick poplar, rifle across his knees.

Daylight came slowly inhibited by low clouds. It smelled like snow. His eyes searched but always drifted back to his right, the direction from which the drive should push the deer. Every noise was magnified. A squirrel scampering sounded like a buck. The wind rustling dead leaves became a doe approaching. Even with Arctic-quality clothes, the thick down coat in blaze orange camouflage—three words that never belong together—he was still cold. He got up carefully and meandered silently around the bench and the tree, trying to get the blood moving a little anyway. After two hours, the sleepless night began to catch him. He fought to stay awake, thinking this was most boring thing he'd ever done. The chances of shooting Stark and making it look like an accident now seemed a lot like winning the lottery and if it wasn't for the chance to kill a fucking deer, he'd go back to camp, pack his truck, and leave. But that would entail knowing the way back to camp. Of that, he was less than certain, but the GPS in his pocket gave him a degree of confidence. He took it out, set a waypoint for where he was, and poured a cup of coffee from his thermos. He'd made it at home, the day before so it was slightly cold, but still thick and robust and tasted wonderful. He laid the thermos on the ground, set the cup beside him on the bench, and went back to hunting. A buzz crept up as he sipped.

He looked down the hill. Halfway across the little valley, he spotted a huge buck standing, as if placed there by some magic trick. His heart surged. A rush of adrenaline charged through him and he was up, his rifle shouldered, searching through the scope. An orange bump appeared, Stark. His chance. Vengeance. Rapist Stark or a murdering deer. He steadied for the shot, locked on Stark's chest who squatted now. His body trembled. The buck appeared in the crosshairs, blocking him. Fuck it, take the deer. He heard a report and a dull thwump behind his ear and the deer leaped out of his scope. "What the . . ." The buck bounded now, up the hill. David's scope followed, looking for any brown fur. He fired once, twice, three times. It angled to the left, flouncing away. He fired two more shots and clicked on an empty chamber. He could barely breathe as he reloaded. He looked up. Stark was waving toward him.

When David got there, Stark was down on his haunches, peering at the ground. "Didn't think you were going to shoot," he said. "I slipped just as I pulled off. Nicked him. See there. Hair and a trace of blood." He pointed. David squatted. Sure enough, some brown hair. He touched a dark patch on the ground and checked his finger. It was blood. Deer blood. "We'll follow the track and see how you did," Stark said, and they were off, up the hill. A hundred yards or so up, Stark stopped, frowning over a pool of dark liquid. "You hit him," he said. "Gut shot. That's like torture. Die eventually, but run a damn long way before that. He's got a good head start. We don't have to rush but steady wouldn't hurt. Only so many hours of daylight." David almost smiled. One down, Dani.

They found it after about three hours, down and breathing hard. David's eyes glazed over. He dropped his rifle and waded in, his KBAR knife out, grabbed an antler and slashed, slashed, slashed. The animal screamed and David's knife finally cut through the larynx. Stark radioed their position, instructed David in the dirty work of gutting. As he wiped off the knife, he remembered his thermos. "How do we get back?" he asked.

"Walk," Stark said. "Only room for the deer and the driver on the four-wheeler. I'll wait if you want to get going. Know the way?"

"No problem."

When he was out of sight, David produced his Garmin and turned it on. The deer must have zigged and zagged endlessly on its death run. David took the direct route, followed the GPS readings and an hour later had the thermos in his pouch pocket. It was then he saw it, looked like a bullet hole in the poplar tree. He dug in with his knife. It tapped against metal. He stood where he had for shooting. The bullet missed him by no more than six inches. "Slipped?" He walked down, found the hair on the ground, lined up with his tree stand and carefully followed the line until he came to a spent shell on the ground, found the footprints. And no sign of any slip.

Coleman gas lamps cast white light as the men strapped the deer onto David's hood. He walked over to Stark. "Did you talk to that college woman?" David said, barely able to contain his desire to pull out the Walther and murder the bastard where he stood. David could see the stripe of hair where Stark's bullet brushed it. It was in the hind quarter, nowhere near where a shooter as good as Stark would aim. "Yeah, but I didn't get anywhere. Guess you oughta go in there and own up."

Okay, so it's war now, and in damn close quarters.

***

The next morning he called the Tribune and placed an innocuous ad in the miscellaneous section of the Sunday Want Ads, and paid for four months. It read: *If you lost a kilo in 1971, call 310-356-8961. Possible reward.* It was his cell number, nobody would recognize that.

Chapter Twenty

Angie rocked slowly in the swing she'd built for Elsa. It creaked in the cold this morning. She wore a thick jacket and didn't give the temperature a second thought. Instead, she thought about the phone call last night from Clarissa. David will come eventually, soon probably. He had some things to work through. How could he not? Back then, she could have explained it, made him see he was the one, the real one. They could have nursed each other through, maybe saved each other. She couldn't comfort him now like she could have then. She understood the betrayal was new to him and he was on his own. They both were. Orbiting something, never touching.

The lake shimmered and when she turned away from it, she saw Jacob Foulke, standing frozen at the edge of forest. A makeshift red overshirt covered the fatigue jacket, rifle over his shoulder, eyes wide. "A little close to the cabins for hunting isn't it?" She said it softly.

He looked at his boots. "Yes, ma'am. When I'm tired I like to think by the lake." His eyes ran away.

Shy, she thought, *or is it troubled?* "Unload that thing and you're welcome to it." He nodded, emptied the rifle, and walked toward the lake. She watched. He sat against a tree at the shoreline.

She heard the crunch of tires on ice and saw David's truck coming down her driveway. She stood on the porch, waiting as he pulled in.

"I was outside. Heard someone coming," she said. "Invigorating today."

He had two thermoses in one arm and the bag in the other. "One word for it. Feel any better?" He glanced down looking for ice on the steps.

"Some. You?"

She opened the door for him and followed him in. A fire roared in the barrel stove and the house smelled of pinesap smoke. "Brought some blueberry muffins and latte."

"Do anything besides cook?"

"Write fiction," he said. He poured two cups. "Want to sit in the soft chairs?"

The drapes were open and a ring of frost framed the picture window. The lake reflected the partly cloudy sky, but the condensation clouds were gone. He sat in the chair facing the window. She saw him gaze at the lake. It was like having a magical painting that commanded attention and changed constantly. Today, she wondered if the absence of waves meant a layer of ice.

He sipped the latte. Foam stuck to his lip and he licked it off. "Where were we?"

She laughed, but her finger rubbed the cup rim in quick, short strokes. "I think we left off at the part where I was screwing Stark."

He glanced outside. "Glad I didn't know, then."

She ignored the lake and looked at him. "I never told anyone that."

"Maybe you should have."

"Who?"

"Clarissa maybe?"

"A mom tell her daughter that? No. She starts on one of her benders and it's God's guess what might come out of her mouth next." He was silent. Angie wondered about that look on his face, but took a deep breath and thought about slogging through deep drifts on snowshoes. She'd rehearsed this a hundred times in her head, but now the words wouldn't formulate. Maybe there were no right words. "Stark got me in exchange for his silence." David choked. His eyes widened, like he wanted to say something but couldn't. "They were wife swapping, David, and other things." Now part two was on the table. She wondered if he was connecting the dots. She doubted it and it didn't matter. She trudged on.

"So that search for Bunny was for fear of her taking your place?"

She nodded. He hung his head. "They promised it was about to end." She sighed. "You made it anyway. You're stronger."

"Made what? I'm back here broke and living with my parents. But they're ghosts. Shit, I'm teetering on the edge of sanity everyday."

She saw the disillusion and sadness in his face. "Least you can talk about it. That's something."

"Talk is cheap."

"Clarissa's friend Sky says to heal you must walk with your pain."

"You've never made love since that night with me?"

Angie blushed. When he said it like that, it sounded like such a wasteland of a life. "We were invincible then."

He looked out toward the lake, nodding. "Cruel trick." Then back to her, his eyes soft, compassionate. His voice almost a whisper. "When do we get to the part about Clarissa?"

Angie stared at him. There was silence. Around here, everyone knew. It was ancient history, forgotten, maybe forgiven. A chickadee flitted past the window, a squirrel perched on a branch chewing a pinecone. Angie pretended to watch. She didn't want to say it. "Harry Barnet was screwing Mom on Friday nights. He's the mayor now. Clarissa's father."

"That's so wrong."

"Barnets took me in. I had nowhere else to go. Deserved a seat next to Bunny's. They fed me Valium all day, Demerol at night. That second day, they let Stark in. He said he loved me, and fucked me again. They came in the next night. Raped me, both of them." She paused. "I was too drugged to resist. They were crying, calling me Susan. It was sick."

"Susan?"

"My mother's name. When you can't resist is it still . . . "

He shrugged, looked defeated. "I don't know," he said. "It should be."

"Two months later, they learned his wife had an aggressive breast cancer. They made me the deal. Keep quiet and have the baby before she died and he'd take care of me for life." She took a breath. The thing she always avoided closed in on her again. Three men in a week and she don't know for sure. She had tried to keep it factual, unemotional, but knew she slipped on "raped." She wondered what he was feeling. Ancient history was now headline news for David. She studied his face. It was sallow and taut. Now she had to know the truth. She'd start on that immediately.

"Time to get outside," he said.

"Cold for a California boy."

"Always hated California."

Chapter Twenty One

David followed her out the cabin door. As with their first conversation, the tone of her voice was practiced, distant, almost third person, like it happened to someone else. Maybe it was easier for her with the distance of time, but it didn't feel that way. Certainly not to him. It was all new to him. They started down the driveway, each walking slowly in a tire rut, dodging puddles layered with ice. Branches of the maple and oak clattered, emptied of sap, frozen, dormant, the noise of winter rattling with each gust of wind. They walked in silence the length of the driveway, watching winter birds flit their short flights and chipmunks thrashing around in the dead leaves under the split rails. Near the main road, he saw an ermine, pure white with a black-tipped tail, stark against the brown backdrop, tricked by some ancient error and totally vulnerable. Two miles down the main road, a few scattered snowflakes floated from the leaden sky and he looked at Angie. Was that a tear or a melted snowflake on her cheek? "You're running away," he said.

She didn't break stride and walked another fifty yards, absently kicking stones in her path. "And what are you doing?" she said.

He looked up in the trees and felt the snowflakes touch his cheeks. "Writing the Great American novel."

"How's it coming."

He picked up a rock and threw it at a tree. Missed.

She laughed. "We're a pair. Not even a dog to walk. Pathetic, David."

He nodded but didn't respond. They walked down a steep hill. At the bottom and off to their right, a beaver dam rose higher than the road, water at eye level. Leaks trickled through threatening to break it open. "Thought about making any changes?"

"About like you, probably," she said.

"I'm here, starting . . . uh trying. Sure don't want Grade C-Writer on my tombstone."

"Beats the usual dates."

"In the city, no one wanders by a grave and says, 'I remember ole David. Good guy.' There's a difference between anonymity and dignity." A raven squawked at the trespassers. David and Angie climbed the rise. A sliver of lake peeked through the trees. He watched her walk, her body trim, athletic, and wondered what it would be like again, after all the years, all the busted dams. "Thought about ending your recluse phase?"

"No."

"Could be time to let that wonderful woman out."

"I'm getting hungry. Let's start back."

They turned and headed down the slope toward the beaver dam, neither saying anything until they bottomed out and climbed the other side. "You were the smartest girl in school."

"I'm thinking. Quit selling it."

They sauntered along in silence again, but with this newfound communication, such as it was, his conscience worked overtime. It would come out, eventually. Waiting would make it worse. He almost whispered it, then stopped. Worse relative to what? To this woman he once loved opening her heart, as he was opening his. No this was not the right time to talk about Clarissa. "What if you had it to do over?" he said, knowing that although he might want to do things different, better, he had been powerless.

Her pace quickened. She didn't look at him and lengthened her stride, leaving him behind. He stopped. Fifty yards ahead, she stopped. "What the hell you doing back there," she yelled. It rattled through the forest.

"Couldn't keep up," he said. "Like high school cross-country."

"Wimp." As he got closer, he studied her face but couldn't see a hint into her thinking. He caught up and she walked again, matching his steps. "There's no do-overs," she said.

He paused. "That night in the station wagon with you was one of the best in my life. I'd take a do-over on that."

She blushed. Said nothing.

"Someday, I'd like to write well enough to do justice to that story," he said.

Her eyes began to mist as they searched his face, her ice facade gone, her body suspended in hesitation like she knew what she wanted to do, what she felt, but something wouldn't let her. Then it broke. She flung herself around him, squeezing him and pushing her head against him, not letting go. Then, she did let go, raced away again, without another word. He hurried to catch up. His calves burned now, glad her driveway was downhill and as they stamped the mud off their boots, she looked at him with a confidence he hadn't seen before. "I've got summer sausage and cheese, some onions. A little potato salad."

He smiled. "The lo-cal plate. Perfect." He followed her into the kitchen. "What about the future?"

She didn't look up from cutting the sausage. "It'll work itself out."

***

A week later, David drove the four hours to sit with Bunny again. That same red car was leaving. This time he was sure it was Russet and wondered who he visited here? He would ask next time he worked the café. Bunny sat alone in a corner when he arrived. He sat with her and talked, softly, gently. "It's tragic, like something sucked the meaning, the caring out of life. Left us in some existential void. Literally for you." Paused. "Maybe you're the lucky one." For a moment, he thought he saw a spark of recognition in her eyes, but it vanished, like confused imagination. A glimmer of hope. Flint lacking steel.

The days were so short now, he took a room overnight and stayed up late reading *You Can't Go Home Again.* The passage, "and the real things . . . have become just words. The substance has gone out of them." That passage made him think nothing had changed since the Depression. He flashed to an Emerson essay. It went back even further, skating on surfaces since the mid-nineteenth century. Status quo died hard. Historic events come and go, and still the artist was doomed to be an outcast, as Wolfe said, his inevitable fate in the hands of the tribe. "Remain hopeful," he told the dead writers and swore he heard them laughing.

The next afternoon, he entered his little town and drove Main Street toward home. A light layer of snow covered the ground, brown tufts of grass and weeds protruding, attesting to the staying power of autumn. A Subaru passed him. He looked in the rearview mirror. The car was stopping. Angie. He stopped, backed up, they came side to side, windows rolled down. " Hey," he tried for a smile. "What are you doing in town?"

The corners of her lips curled. It sparked the dimples in each of her cheeks and reminded him of Clarissa. "Shopping. Come out and see me sometime."

"Just got back from visiting Bunny. You were next."

"Good. This talking makes me feel better."

"Be out this weekend."

The change was obvious. He felt warm, even with the icy wind blowing in the cab. A car slowed behind him. He didn't move, and it pulled around him on the right, a wheel in the ditch. Angie waved and pulled away. "See ya then," she mouthed.

That night, he tried the Wolfe book again, but his mind was too cluttered already. The approaching holidays brought down a weight of grief. The first without Sandy, second without Dani. He didn't want to be alone. He dialed Angie.

"You looked great today," he said.

"Perpetual victim is dying, along with that old recluse."

"That's the spirit."

He didn't say anything else. "So, what's on your mind?" she asked finally.

"How about Thanksgiving dinner at my house? Thought I'd invite Clarissa and Bunny." He paused. This was the test.

"Umm . . . thanks. I'd love to come. No chance for Bunny. But nice of you to think of her." Now she paused. "Clarissa's her own women, as you well know. Ask her."

There was no derision in her voice. It sounded almost hopeful.

Clarissa was cool, said she had early visitation shift on Thanksgiving. He told her early dinner was fine. She implied acceptance but didn't actually say it. He hung up feeling bittersweet, not about her but his holiday mine field. Hoped he could get through this one better than the last, maybe the busyness of preparing the meal and the company would help.

The next morning, the computer screen taunted him. Outside, a light fluff of snow was falling, sticking in the spruce needles, and he decided to drive down to the beach, take Angie's secondhand advice: to walk with his pain, talk to it, let it know he was aware of it, and that a million other men have felt this way.

When he started, Dani walked with him, a young teen, beaming, letting flakes fall into her open mouth and stick in her eyelashes, absorbing her virgin winter experience, and his imagination claimed this as her version of heaven. As he turned onto the asphalt bike path, she floated up away and the snowflakes swallowed her, getting larger and softer, billowing down between the treetops, and sticking in his hair and on the arms and shoulders of his jacket. He stopped to study the huge flakes that landed on his cuff until they blurred in a mist of tears. "We're going until you're worn out," he said to it. "I'm not alone. I know you. Know your twisted power. Come on, maybe we'll run a little."

He didn't run for long. His legs burned and his lungs sucked for air. After an hour in the forest, he turned back. The snow covered his tracks, leaving only a blurry indentation on the once-black path and he walked faster. "You like it?" he said. The snowflakes fell tight together now, almost blinding and coming straight down in the windless day. Still sheltered by the tall pines, he approached the beach. "You're black and damn cruel. Wash yourself in this."

He broke out of the woods into a sparkling field of snow, brilliant and blinding, completely white. The lake panorama extended it further, a veil of flakes miles long that fell in a silent, constant blanket. The ice surface twinkled, a carpet of diamonds. Stunning whiteness everywhere and David smiled and walked into it. He reached the other side of the beach clearing, looked back and saw his tracks disappearing. Saw the cleansing whiteness, heard the soft, eerie silence. A soothing, smothering blanket that, maybe stupidly, felt almost like optimism.

Chapter Twenty Two

The day before Thanksgiving, David got out early and strung strands of red and white lights in each tree and around his house. Laborious work with countless trips up and down the ladder, but it felt good, natural, not like the ring-around-the-rosy of decorating palm trees in LA. At dark, around four thirty, he hit the switch for a test and walked out into the street to get that view. It looked cheery, festive, which seemed to brighten his mood. He saw old man Nelson, his neighbor, shuffling toward him and heard the shout, "Chapman, hey Chapman."

David waited, "Hi Nelson."

"Looks good. Didn't know ya had it in ya."

David shook his hand, and clapped him on the back. "Happy Thanksgiving, Nelson." As the man ambled off, David turned the lights off. The inauguration would be Thanksgiving evening, just before his guests were to arrive. He wanted them to feel something in the season with which he struggled.

The food was coming together and in the morning he would make the final push, make the Egg Nog, the turkey, the dressing, the mashed potatoes. Cranberry sauce from scratch was already in the refrigerator, along with the pumpkin pie. He would stay busy, think about his guests, not about himself, not about his daughter. This had never been her favorite holiday. He had claimed that title and now carried that burden. Elsa would be there tomorrow. She was not the ghost of his daughter and he'd gotten over the twin thing, down now to looking like distant sisters. For that alone, he should celebrate.

Angie was the first to arrive. He helped her with her overcoat and noticed the black knit dress. She set a bottle of champagne on the counter and hugged him. It seemed chaste but he felt her breasts push against him. She wore light makeup almost self-consciously, highlighting her cheekbones and lips. She beamed with warmth he could not have imagined a month ago. "I haven't felt like this during the holidays for . . . well, maybe since I was seventeen. Someone even waved at me."

"Did you wave back?" She nodded. "Something to drink?"

"Wine, I think. It smells incredible in here."

He smiled, caught up in her attitude. "Come on. I'll give you a tour."

She glanced outside. "Your neighbors haven't put up lights."

"In LA decorations go up Halloween night. Commercialism at its finest."

"Santa versus Jesus, the real war."

He saw a car turn into his driveway. "There's the girls,"

They arrived at the door with a bottle of wine. Clarissa handed her overcoat to David and pecked him on the cheek. "Season's here, eh." She hugged her mother. "Ya look great, Mom. Never saw that dress before."

Angie ignored her and went straight to Elsa, gave her a grandma-squeeze. "I swear you look more radiant with each passing week." Angie helped her out of the coat, revealing a silk blouse with a matching camisole top underneath and a short black wool skirt. Angie eyebrows fluttered. "Very flattering," she said. David turned away. The girl looked more like Dani than ever.

Elsa squirmed, uncomfortable. "Mom made me wear it."

"Sorry. I couldn't stand one more of your father's outfits. You look great, kid. And Mom's pretty hot there, too."

Angie blushed. Clarissa wore a mini skirt, and a red and green holiday sweater. "You look . . .uh . . . nice as well, Clarissa. Am I still staying the night?"

"Get as fuc . . . uh, messed up as you want. The sheets are even clean." She glanced guiltily at Elsa, who faced David and appeared not to hear.

Angie noticed it, zeroed in on her daughter's eyes. "Are you high?" she whispered.

"Not nearly enough."

David heard the hushed voices, not the words, and herded Elsa to them. He looked from face to face, now engrossed in his role of host, flattered and nervous to have this honor. In his mind, the compilation of the town's brains and beauty all stood in his kitchen. "Let's sit by the fire. Dinner is close."

"We'll open the champagne? Elsa might try a tiny taste," Angie said. The girl's face crunched into a 'yuk' look. Clarissa laughed.

David ushered them into the living room. A leather couch and two club chairs centered on the fireplace where three logs blazed, Christmas music played softly in the background. Clarissa sat beside her mother. There was something different about her, not just in attire, something in her eyes. "How's this one stacking up to those grand events from our murky past?" Clarissa asked, now studying, teasing out an answer. Angie gazed into the fire.

David stepped around the island and looked into the room, a white chef's apron covering his Polo sweater. He glanced at Angie and caught the milky blue eyes sparkling like that night years ago and his heart thump-thumped.

Their eyes met for a second. He broke it and there was Clarissa, watching. "Well, almost ready," he said.

Clarissa's eyes stalked him as he disappeared into the kitchen. Angie caught the stare. "He told me about the eagles," she whispered.

"I love eagles," Elsa said.

Clarissa blushed and looked away. "Uh . . . they got babies, eaglets. Kind a cute."

"He told me all of it."

Clarissa's ears turned crimson. David poked his head in again. Her red face grabbed his attention, flamethrower eyes. He didn't get it and wasn't about to ask, so just pushed forward. What else could he do? "Okay, we're ready. Let's sit down."

Clarissa snapped to her feet, went straight to the TV and found the on button, clicked to football. "Needed something manly in the house," she muttered to the now empty room. David set out the side dishes as the Detroit Lions game flickered soundless in the background. Angie and Elsa smirked at the notion of holiday football games. Clarissa glared, undaunted. "What's wrong with a little testosterone? We could damn well use some, even from a team nobody gives a shit about."

David heard the knife's edge tone. As he carried in the turkey, football drifted him to the waste of lavish events at acquaintance's homes around LA with everyone appropriately dressed down in chinos and starched button-downs, discussing the fortunes of USC or UCLA football as they feigned watching the "anemic" pro game and handed out business cards during commercials, networking for their next deal wearing fresh haircuts and hard tasseled loafers with expensively turned out wives, another office party in the City of Lights with something to gain or lose. He was lucky to break-even.

He set the bird in the center of the table. It looked like a picture from Martha Stewart Living. When he stuck the fork in the breast, juice sprang forth and trickled down the brown skin. He was poised with the knife, but suddenly not there again, drifting, fading out, not hearing the compliments now, instead flitting off to the first bird he cooked years ago for his wife: dry and shrunken and he butchered the carving and neither of them cared. A much different memory than three years ago when the bird was perfect and their marriage was the turkey, going through the motions for the sake of a daughter, still with magic and innocence in her eyes. Then to a year later, an empty cavity with her gone. The ole David-of-the-city, always part of the entertainment, the writer with the golf game they envied, who beat them out of pride and money at every opportunity and did it with dignity and sportsmanship. He should have spit in their faces.

He cut the first slice with practiced perfection and glanced at the faces gracing his table this year. The wave returned in force, sentiment this time. He felt a lump of gratitude in his throat for real people who wanted to be here and cared about him and each other, with not even the most remote thought of money or status and he was glad he worked so hard on this meal, for these people, and focused his concentration on the carving. To honor them with a standard higher than he'd ever achieved. His cultural divides collided, country against city, winter against fake winter with green smog and green grass, sickly palm trees and the background hum of the air conditioner. Real diamonds. Fake smiles. He breathed in the fragrance of rosemary and sage and smoke from the wood fire, welcomed for warmth, not decoration. He felt a gust of chill air from the cracked window and saw the snow on the spruce needles.

He reached for his third glass of wine and smiled, recalling only a single glass among acquaintances to preserve his ability to entertain, to navigate clogged freeways. Today, not a car on the streets except relatives on their way to dine with family. Outside his window, a clump of people walked off their early dinner, laughing and talking, trying to make room for pie and probably not five dollars cash in their combined pockets, caring only for each other. It was Jared Lamppa, a welder, a hunter, a happy man, his job simply a means to take care of wife and children.

David sliced the last of the breast and arranged it on a platter, a drumstick at each end, and passed it to Angie. Elsa said the prayer. A moment of hungry silence followed the serving platters around the table. Tastes finally met the smells. Angie thanked Clarissa for standing by her all these years and David for helping to draw her out of herself and Elsa for just being Elsa, the way any grandma would. David took his turn, "I'm grateful you could all be here."

Angie smiled and touched his hand. All eyes turned to Clarissa. "Me, I'm thankful for my daughter's health, for Mom's apparent happiness, and for turkeys that take their secrets to the grave."

She shot a glance at David. He looked confused. "I . . .uh . . .."

"I told her," Angie said. "No secrets around here. It's certainly nothing to ruin this beautiful day."

Clarissa chewed machine-like, methodic. She finally swallowed. It took forever. "Might have overreacted, eh. Sorry David." She cranked up her best holiday smile. "Food's great. Pass a little more dressing my way, would you please?"

He lurched for the bowl, a morbid effort to regain the host charade. Angie passed it on and said, "I made an offer on a house in town."

Clarissa whipped a scoop at her plate, scowling, not hiding it. "Great news."

"Yeah. I'm turning the page. David was right."

"A regular messiah among us," Clarissa said.

"Oh and I saw the boy in my yard last week," Angie said.

"Jacob," Elsa said. All eyes turned to her. She blushed.

Angie sighed. "See, we have much to be thankful for." She glanced at Clarissa.

After dinner, they bundled up to walk off the food and strolled arm in arm, four abreast in the road. David had Angie on one arm and Clarissa on the other. It was cold and clear and he felt the heat from the women. Food and wine muddled his mind. A cautious joy swamped all other emotions. Lights twinkled on his yard and the stars fell on them as they walked back up the driveway. "Have time for dessert?" he asked Clarissa.

"Got about a half hour until he's out of church. He bitches when we're late. Daddy's taking them to the Grand Hotel tonight. Elsa will be the star of that show, won't you baby?"

"Not in these clothes," she said.

"Right. Make mine to go."

David switched off the Christmas lights. The mouth of his driveway sat dark between the streetlights. Headlights sparkled off the layer of new snow, stark against the black asphalt, and they watched her taillights recede into the night. "I might try that Egg Nog, now," Angie said and blew into her hands. "Should feel good on the fingers." She looked at him. His face sad, distant. "Are you alright?" He shrugged and went into the kitchen. David worked on the Egg Nog in silence. Angie came to his side, put her hand on his back. "What's the matter?"

"Nothing."

She rubbed his back, gently. "It's something. You were here and now you're gone."

"I don't know. Guess it's the holidays."

"You miss her."

His head fell, arms holding him up. "She was just a baby."

It stopped her. "A baby?"

He'd not told her. He'd not told anyone in town, just horded his misery in quiet desperation. "I had a daughter, Dani. She died. She was sixteen—a baby." He turned to face her. There were no tears, only a resigned sadness.

Her face registered the shock, then compassion. She pulled him close in a soft embrace. "I'm so sorry."

He felt the comfort and melted into it. "Kid driving a Beemer drunk. Swerved to miss a deer, a fucking deer. A useless fucking deer. He walked away."

He doubled the brandy. She rubbed his shoulders as they sat on the couch, another log on the fire, and sipped the sweet, thick drinks, warm and nutmeg laced. She held him. It soothed them into a dreamy illusion that floated from present to past. Years gone, time jumbled, age a meaningless number neither considered. And they were lost. She snuggled at his side. His arm held her, feeling her against him soft and warm, her hair lilac-scented, soft curls that touched his cheek. "I remember walking home from school that day," she said. "I envied the married couples in their tiny houses, warming each other, cooking and caring for each other. All so faded fifties." She paused. "Maybe I should go."

He knew she was right. She should have gone. Afterwards, they fell asleep together. She lay naked beside him, curled in close, her leg crooked over his, breathing contentedly. He felt her breast against him. Some things crossed through the veil of time unscathed and exploded. But the veil had not let everything through and he lay with his eyes open and mourned the absence and cursed sentiment. His heart like the cactus in his old LA courtyard.

When he woke, she was gone. A note on the pillow said: *Had to get to Clarissa's. Talk Soon. Love, Angie.* The room felt cold. He put on the sweatshirt from last night. "Where's my skivvies?" He grabbed a clean pair.

***

David walked into the institutional waiting area and saw Russet and Bunny huddled together in the far corner of the day room, away from everyone and everything. They had two plastic chairs pulled close, their knees almost touching. Bunny faced the room and sat straight backed with her head tilted down. Russet faced her, bent over, his elbows resting on splayed knees. David didn't see them signing in rapid bursts. Bunny leaned forward, her hands hidden from view by Russet's body, signing back.

"David's here, don't look. We can trust him," she signed. "I can feel it."

"No, no, no," he signed back. "He hacked a deer to death with a hunting knife, had to be restrained. Stark tried to kill him. I heard him talking to the Mayor. Don't think Chapman knows anything. Doesn't even know they tried. They'll try again. It's too dangerous. You have to stay under a little longer."

"But, I want to be with you. We could run away."

Russet looked up at her. A thin smile crossed his face, then disappeared. "It's not time, yet. I'll think harder. We'll make a plan."

Her back straightened again. She signed. "David's coming toward us."

Russet only moved his hands. He took hers and gently covered them.

Bunny's eyes glazed over instantly, automatically. David stopped behind Russet. "Hi, Russell," he said softly. "I thought that was you in the red car. How is she?"

"Uh . . . n-n-never changes much." He looked at her and then at the floor.

"How long you been coming to visit?"

"A while n-n-now."

"It's great that people come for her," David said. "You're a good man, Russell."

"Yes, sir." He patted Bunny's hand. "I'll b-b-be going n-n-now," he said.

David took over when Russet left, talking absently, burdened and remote, glancing out the window more than looking at her, seeing the pristine white, feeling black and tainted from the holiday season without Sandy, without Dani, and a strange guilt about feelings for Angie which defied explanation. Bunny's eyes were dull with a hollow emptiness. Again, she reached for his hand. When it touched him that strange redemption washed over him. She sucked the blackness from him as easily as she sucked Mountain Dew from the straw in the paper cup beside her. He wanted to hug her and thank her. Her powers awed him, but he buried it behind the same mask of sadness that all the visitors wore in that dreary place until the nurse escorted her out.

He tried Wolfe again that night at the motel, but came to the line: ". . . to seek out the most forlorn and isolated hiding spot that he could find." He clapped the book shut. It cut too close.

He lay on his back watching the flash of red neon flicker across the motel room ceiling and wondering how the Thomson women got to him, Angie, Clarissa, and Bunny each differently, but all completely under his skin, possessing a power over him that he couldn't seem to control. They elevated his losses, brought them to consciousness where they couldn't be ignored.

He left early the next morning and picked up Angie at noon as planned. He pleaded exhaustion to cover his silence and played CDs from the past hoping to coax the rest of it through the veil. They fired up the snowmobile and she drove tight trails that he couldn't see to a field of Christmas trees. They shook snow off the trees, laughing as it covered them, and as he walked circles around each nominee, he warmed to the task and to her. Maybe Thanksgiving night rectification came by talking, sharing fun. Spending time together. But, after he dropped her off, he realized, sitting alone in his chair, that this was the same hollowness he felt with his ex-wife in the years before she left. He was not cured, nor fixed in any way. That prospect made him sad and alone and he sat in a chair, sipping gin and staring at the naked Christmas tree, doing nothing to decorate it.

A week went by and he finally decorated the tree. The newspaper ran frequent articles on 9/11 and every time David saw that date, he thought of crumbled lives, not towers. They represented more to him than the event, not just a chink in American armor, not just the loss of life, but the crumbling loss of his own complacence. The changes had engulfed him, first the attack on America, then on his daughter, then the rest of his life. He thought the mourning period was over, but it was not. There was backslide. Here. Now. Closure: who the hell made up that word, that concept? Just wishful thinking in the twisted mind of some fucking griefologist.

And he had lost love's ideal. Angie was real now, not imaginary nor on a pedestal. He had to deal with that, and deal with the conflicts presented by Clarissa and Elsa and Bunny. The finally-decorated Christmas tree sat in front of his picture window in the living room. He saw it when he came home from walking last night, a muted twinkling image that helped him, made him think of it as a home.

He ate at the café two nights in a row and met new people each time. The first night it was Toivo Tukenan, young, balding, pulp cutter, with hollow cheeks and tough eyes that hid a ninth-grade education, a crooked smile when he talked about spear fishing and ice houses. His wife was two years younger and had three children in diapers. He worked six days a week and ate at the café once a week to give his wife a break, he said. David was not sure from what, but that was their business and he seemed happy, so how could one knock that?

The second night, he met Inez Laramont, the woman who'd opened his bank account. She turned away when he sat down, but he apologized profusely until she relented. Inez was forty-two but prematurely gray making her look much older. The wrinkles had also come early, but her eyes were sharp and bright, her manner calm and reassuring. She ran the knitting club, widowed for five years, her husband dead of mesothelioma, a rare lung cancer freely distributed at the mine, no kids, no plans to move or remarry, church every Sunday, choir Wednesday, knitting Saturday, cards on Monday, bowling in the winter. Her league started after the holidays. He liked Toivo and Inez. Real people. Down here roaming a planet, getting by as well as they could and meeting them made him feel better, not so alone.

After dinner, he stopped at the bar, talked to Jerry for a few minutes about the ice on the lakes and ordered a gin on the rocks. He sat facing the tables but saw only a few guys huddled in small groups. He didn't remember any of them. He heard "Vikings" and "Packers" flit out of the muffled noise and he nursed his drink in solitude.

David raised his glass to dump down the rest, ready to leave. A hard jab hit his ribs spilled the drink on his jacket. He choked, turned, ready to growl.

"Drinking alone, eh?" she said. "Mom busy tonight?"

"Damn it, Clarissa, you spilled it all over me."

She glanced at his jacket. "Wasn't much left. Gonna buy me a drink?"

He waved at Jerry. She ordered a whiskey and when it came, twirled the cherry in her mouth. She stared into his eyes, and bit it. "So, what's going on with you two?"

He looked for an intimation. Found none. "We barely know each other anymore. I like her. I like you. I like Inez Laramont."

"Bet Inez was home on Thanksgiving night."

He felt his ears flushing red. "Best holiday I'd had in a damn long time."

"Had a good time, too. Not good as Mom."

"We were lovers long ago."

"Yeah, blah, blah. And now?"

"Too soon to tell."

"Not too soon to fuck?"

He said nothing and realized the mistake immediately. He had swallowed the bait.

She guzzled the rest of her drink. "Let's get stoned and hear some music. Your place, eh? You drive. Don't want my car decorating your driveway."

He seemed pulled by an unknown force. She understood her power perfectly. While he poured wine, she went straight to the master bathroom. He came out of the kitchen holding two glasses, not seeing her. "Clarissa?"

"I'm in here," came the muffled reply. He entered his room. Confluence. One holding glasses, the other naked. One crumbling. One confident. "I don't think this is right," David said, though it was far from forceful.

"I love Mom. So do you. Just not enough."

"Enough?"

"It's past, David. You both know it. Clinging to some perverted nostalgia. Maybe sympathy. Neither is good. Sure, both are dignified. But happiness? Do you care about her happiness?"

"Fuck you."

"That is the question." She leaned on the doorframe as if dressed in an evening gown. "We have some strange connection. You have that with Mom? You've both tried. I watched. I wouldn't be here now if I could see it. But I am. Yes, it's sad. Is that the future, sadness? Hey, I'll bail now if that's the case. Got plenty of that already."

"That's not it."

"Bullshit. I was there and I've been with her since. Look, why I feel this way is a total mystery to me, too. But it's a future not a past. You turned me down twice. I'm patient but there are limits." He stared, dumbfounded. She came toward him. He pushed her back, forceful now, and held her shoulders at arm's length.

"Test it, David. Test the limits."

"No. Not like this. I'm not like that. Sure, there's a million questions, a jillion confused emotions. But it can't be this way."

He heard a knock and jerked, heart pounding harder that it was already. "Ignore it," she said. It didn't go away. Three more times it came, rattling at his nerves. They both knew. He walked to the door, turned on the porch light. Her face came to life, the smile, bright eyes. His heart sank. He opened the door a crack.

"Hi David."

"Out late, Angie. What's happening?"

She pushed in. "Couldn't sleep. Out for a walk. Saw your light on." She pushed forward to kiss him. Stopped halfway.

"Oh, uh . . . I have a guest. Sorry." And he was sorry and wishing he was anywhere else in the world right now. He knew how it would look. Integrity mattered little in this situation.

Her smile dissolved, eyes iced over. "I'd know that perfume anywhere." She stepped back. He could see the hurt covering her face, her hands came up, quivering, pushing him away. "Stupid me. I thought it was something."

He stepped toward her. She retreated. "Come in. Let's talk. Nothing happened."

"Fuck talk, David. There were implications. A man would know that."

"Implications, Mom?" Clarissa said from behind them. "From what? From thirty-three years ago? Implications that make anything cool? I asked if you wanted him."

Angie darted by David. "And you'd deny me a little happiness. Standing there freshly fucked. Wearing his shirt. How dare you?"

"Don't talk about feelings Mom. I thought I had something, too. Until you stepped in. Or did you forget that part. He told you. You think I just go after men for fun? It ain't like that, not with me. It takes me a little longer. Not one orgasm and, bam, straight to love."

"I should have smacked you when you were sixteen." Her hand came up.

David stepped between them. "Stop, both of you. It's my fault. Sit down. We can talk. It doesn't have to be like this."

"Shut up, David. This isn't about you," Clarissa said.

Angie dropped her hand and spun around. "Damn right. I'm leaving—fuck you both." She slammed the door.

David stood there, feeling like he'd taken a shotgun blast in the belly.

Clarissa's eyes cut him. "Quit looking so fucking pathetic. Drive me to my car. Nobody could be worth all this."

Chapter Twenty Three

Angie sat with her hands supporting her head. Wait. Stop. This can't go on. Leave this dismal head space, now. She sat in her new house, in the kitchen which definitely needed some work. Ancient floor linoleum curling in the corners and more of that shit on the counters, "work" hardly covered it. She had a plan for that. She didn't have a plan for the mess de jour. Okay, maybe Clarissa was right. Maybe David was totally wrong when he told her, "Clarissa isn't like that, exactly." Maybe he loved her and wouldn't admit it. That would make some sense. What man wouldn't? Why her daughter would want a relationship with a fifty-something man was unfathomable. That's why Angie believed it was just sex. That's what she led you to believe, but that was not what she said.

The words still had bite, today. "One orgasm and bam, in love." That hurt. Sure, it was a damn nice orgasm. And Clarissa didn't know the wasteland of her "love" life. Maybe this was part of the victim syndrome, to go back in time and ignore the present in some lame attempt to escape. Or to beat down the devils that manipulated your thinking and controlled your life for all those years. Sure, it's easy to say, "I'm coming in," but what does that mean? Coming in to go back to 1971 and restart a relationship like it was a classic car that just needed a few parts replaced before it fired up again and roared on all eight cylinders, complete with rumbling carbs and stripped mufflers so all the world took notice.

Clarissa was right. It was embarrassing. As embarrassing as stealing his underwear for a DNA test. Or behaving like thirty-some years never happened, like the Friday night parties never happened, retreating to the bliss of romance that kept her sane when she was eighteen, thinking it might work again. Well, it didn't. She'd been blind to her daughter and blind to David.

And David. No wonder he gets, uh, erratic. She tried to imagine how she would have behaved had she lost her daughter at sixteen. She remembered that fragile time in her life when Clarissa was that age and shuddered. Probably would have given the old .12 gauge the ultimate blowjob. Hell, she'd thought about it plenty of times. It was always Clarissa's existence that stopped her. But that was then. David was certainly fucked-up-beyond-all-recognition, but somewhere in there was David. And somewhere inside her was that extraordinary girl that made straight A's, that ran the boys into the ground, that got accepted at top colleges, and damn it, she would find her. But she was afraid the only way to resurrect the essence of Angie, was to quit running away, quit being a victim, and take command. One failure doesn't mean quit. Identify reality and accept it or clean it up.

She took a deep breathe and looked out the window. Her hand trembled as it raised the coffee cup to her lips and still trembled as she picked up the phone and dialed, biting her lip, waiting.

"David, it's me, Angie. I . . ."

"Angie, God I am so sorry. I know it looked bad but it wasn't like you think."

She had scripted those exact words, the manifestation of the adolescence they both suffered under and she had to get past. "We'll both live. But you're dangerous to me right now. I can't see you anymore . . . for a while, don't know how long. We'll run into each other, but I won't talk. And doing Christmas is out. I'm sorry, David. I had to tell you myself."

The silence seemed to last an eternity. "You don't understand."

She wanted to shout, 'no, you do not understand,' but instead, in the calmest voice she could muster, she said, "But I do. See ya around." And hung up.

She sat with the phone in her hand, staring at it. In spite of the heartache, she felt horrible leaving him alone on Christmas, alone with his ghosts that she knew magnified and multiplied during holidays. But it had to be this way. She could not be distracted. The slate had to be wiped clean. How could a spark of passion leave her so miserable?

The DNA testing process was already started. The plastic Ziplock bag containing his soiled underwear lay at the bottom of the cedar chest in her bedroom, buried under spare blankets and sheets. And maybe it wasn't embarrassing. It was necessary.

When she found out that she was pregnant with Clarissa, and they stopped the flow of drugs for the sake of the baby, she first had to fight withdrawal, then the enormous pile of grief that the narcotics had allowed her to avoid. Then the helpless little soul that depended on her for everything sapped all her time and energy, and filled her with love, and it wasn't often she even considered the question of paternity. Harry claimed them. That was that.

She didn't want to think about it. It brought back a trauma that was unbearable. Unthinkable. When Clarissa hit her teens and certain behaviors reared up Angie couldn't stop the comparisons: That's way too much like Stark when she was cold and cruel to a young boy. Too much like Harry when she was manipulative. And too much like David when her genuine creativity oozed out. But she refused to dwell on it. Sure, Harry's trust fund for her was probably unbreakable and secure. Yet, he could afford lawyers and what could she do to make a living if it went badly? And my God, what if it was Stark? That would be the pinnacle of embarrassment.

She wandered into the living room, and now stood in front of a wall of pictures of Clarissa and Elsa. She studied each of them carefully, looking for a hint, a clue. She saw subtle parts of herself, the delicate jaw, the neck, but Clarissa favored her grandmother and Bunny more than anything, and she couldn't see any of those men in her. Maybe it was avoidance, a deluded blind eye. Her attention focuses on another photo, Clarissa at the lake, her hair tied back, no make-up and about the age when Stark was raping Angie. She conjured his face as a young man and stared at the picture. Nothing in her face aligned with Stark, but images of her old bedroom and him slamming it to her took center stage, and she felt denigration now as surely as she'd felt love for David.

There's nothing free about love. Then or now. If it turned out to be Stark, she may have to kill him. Not a court in the land would convict her. And she could damn well shoot, now. Another thought floated by and she laughed. Half the townsfolk have probably been doing this exact thing for years, gazing at that gorgeous daughter of hers and trying to figure it out. Probably, finally, settling for the Gospel-according-to-Harry. Then David showed up and fairyland vanished.

And what about him, shit. She had wished over the years in her dream of dreams that it *was* him and he would appear on a white horse and rescue them. When he does, what happens? Clarissa fucks the prince and kills the horse. And there you have it. All neat and tidy. Unless it really was David. Then neat and tidy go right out the window. Oh, it can't be. Somewhere inside each of them, they would know. Wouldn't they?

Angie climbed the three steps and walked under the expansive covered porch. Harry's door represented his home and his life in old age, solid, expensive, and understated. Nothing about him or his possessions could be called flamboyant, except his Mercedes, and even that he had bought second-hand, black and classic and in many cities would go completely unnoticed. It was noticed here, but almost expected. Harry carried little extra weight, bordering on emaciated lately, and his red hair was cropped and graying. If he wasn't the mayor, people would probably call him Senator or minimally distinguished. Angie called him many things, never any of those: snake, weasel, megalomaniac, undercover-slime, were a few of her favorites, but she still had a healthy respect for his cunning and power. The fear she felt in youth had metastasized into a combination of hate and manipulation. Yet, she would challenge him only to a point. She used the brass door-knocker.

"Hi Harry," she said breezily as he opened the door. "You're looking well," she lied. "Got a minute?"

"To what do I owe this great pleasure?" he said, ushering her inside with a sweep of his arm. "Do I owe you money?" He almost chuckled as he took her coat.

Angie caught his eyes giving her the once over. It was almost a leer and she wondered if he did the same with Clarissa. Incorrigible. Lecherous at every age. "I'm all moved in. Wanted to give you my new address."

"So I've heard. I believe I have it. How is Mr. Chapman getting along? Blending in well?"

He either had a sixth sense about where to stick the needle or damn good intelligence. She suspected the latter. "Can't say, really. My house is going to need some renovation. Ya know, to make it livable."

"And what do you hear from your poor little sister?"

It made her wonder if he knew something she didn't. "I haven't been over recently. No news from the medical staff, anyway." She thought of telling him that David had been there a few times, but thought he probably knew that, too. Then the irony hit her. She had to test it. "Chapman has visited her a few times. Says she's doing well. More perky, actually."

She watched closely. His eyebrows pinched together for a fleeting moment. It passed like a cloud in the wind. "How much do you want?" he asked.

"Twenty thousand should cover it."

There was the pinch again. He nodded and muttered, "Suborn."

"I'll take that as a yes. And thanks. Can I use your restroom, Harry?"

He nodded and ambled off toward the living room. She went around the corner, and instead of using the bathroom on that floor, headed up the stairs. She closed the door and locked it, went straight for the cabinet. The first drawer contained pill bottles. In the second was a brush, a comb, and an electric razor. She frowned, there was hardly any hair in the brush, but she pulled the Ziplock baggie from her purse, pushed the brush into it, and scraped at it with the comb. A few hairs fell into the bag. She opened the razor and dumped the sparse clipping in the bag as well. Not much there either. Damn neatnick. The shower? There, accumulated on the drain was what she was looking for and she refused to consider their origins. She pulled out a tweezers and plucked the damp hairs, squeezed the air out of the bag, and stashed it in her purse.

Downstairs, she detoured to Harry's chair. "Well, thanks again. Seems you could dispense with the archaic check writing. They do automatic transfers nowadays." She smiled—the one she'd learned from him.

"How was Chapman's deer hunting trip? Did he mention it?"

"He got one, alright. Had it butchered and gave it all to Toivo's family. That's about all I know." *I'm winning today,* she thought.

"Quite thoughtful."

"He hates venison."

She sighed as she put the car in drive and pulled away. Her next stop would make this one look like child's play and she knew it. It wasn't far, nothing was "far" in this town except an escape and although there were times she relished the thought, she couldn't tear herself away from her granddaughter. Something always told her that the girl would need her one day, and she had to be here for that. No one else could give her what she might need. Egotistical, or was it premonition? Who knew and who cared at this juncture. Focus on the task at hand. She knocked on the door.

The door opened. "Mom. Didn't expect to see you."

Angie bit her lower lip, looked down at her shoes. "Can I come in?"

"Suit yourself. Want a beer or something?"

"No thanks. I . . . uh . . . came to apologize. You were right. I was way out of line. Sorry." She could see the suspicion in Clarissa's eyes. "Really. I was insensitive, should have thought about your side of it—or at least asked you. Guess I was so caught up in my own fantasy that I . . .uh . . . just didn't consider it. Sure can't be fighting over a man with my own daughter. That's just too tragic."

"Gotta give ya that one. You know, he's never touched me. Unbelievable if ya ask me," Clarissa said, rolling her eyes. Was that disgust or pride Angie saw?

She paused. "Yes, it is. I called him and bowed out of Christmas. You can go if you want. It's okay—by me, anyway."

"Haven't thought that far ahead, yet. Still trying to swallow the bile of the present. But thanks."

"Maybe we could have our own little celebration. Be kind of primitive at my place. It needs a lot of work." She looked around at Clarissa's house. She had never been much of a homemaker. Today, three baskets of laundry littered the living room floor and drink glasses sat abandoned on each side table.

"I'd feel . . . I don't know, guilty I guess leaving David alone. But that might work," Clarissa said. "Let me figure out Elsa's Christmas schedule. Her father may have her sentenced to church for the week, eh."

"Did he tell you about his daughter?" Angie asked.

"Daughter?"

"She was sixteen. Killed in car wreck. Her date was drunk."

"Well, ya gotta say the guy can keep a secret, eh. Damn, that's a load. I found him bawling in his house the day after he got here, toying with a pistol. Didn't think it cut this deep. Now I feel really bad."

"Me too. But, we can't be fighting. We're all we've got. I don't know about you, but I've got to get some self-respect back. David helped, but the rest is on me."

"I don't want to fight, Mom. Apology accepted. But crap, he was the only guy I felt any connection to for a damn long time. I know it doesn't make sense—hell, it don't make sense to me. I guess I just ought a leave it alone for a while too. Try to figure it out."

Angie went to her and gave her a hug. She knew she should tell her daughter about her DNA testing, but what if it was really Harry? She couldn't bring herself to pollute her daughter's opinion without some proof. This was way past passing a rumor. "Think about it," Angie said. "No pressure from me. If the Christmas thing works, let me know."

"Sure. Thanks for coming over, Mom. At some level, I feel better."

"I do, too." Angie stood up. "Oh, can I use your bathroom?"

Chapter Twenty Four

Alone was different in the city. There David had comforted himself with the thought that millions of others were alone, too. Many by their own choosing, maybe he was one of them. There, if he didn't want to be alone, he could do something about it. Go out, find someone, maybe talk, maybe hook up. Here, when he looked around or went to the café or the bar, everybody was coupled up. Even when they were alone, they were still coupled, just the spouse was elsewhere for the moment. Sure, young single people would come in to visit parents and hit the town, but for the permanent residents it was Clarissa and Angie, and now they had both disappeared from his life. He missed them. He'd tried to do the right things and wound up wrong anyway.

Temptation was powerful, but perception trumped honesty every time. It always did. He'd seen it forever, from his life down through all of history. Not a surprise or how could gossip magazines be so profitable. And somehow, it seemed that everyone in town knew it, whether they did or not. Okay, some folks were friendly anyway, or was it pity?

He drank his coffee at the island bar, watching the sunrise, not even trying to write, looking out the window at the field of snow, his first white Christmas in thirty-some years. He wanted to blame the holidays, blame his unrealistic expectations that Thanksgiving had built, a connection with those women who meant something real to him. He desperately wanted to stretch that across this joyous time of year, but here he sat, alone. And no one to blame but himself. Break with one before starting another, even the potential appearance of another, stupid. Elementary school kids knew that one.

And worse, he didn't seem to know what he wanted anymore, with them, his career, his life. This had to be the classic symptom of depression. Maybe he should get rid of his guns. Logic said he wanted to rise above this madness, write a real book that would stand up, make him almost immortal. He wanted a home, honest relationships, but now it all seemed no closer than the day he left LA. He glanced at the final dissolution papers from Sandy that had arrived the day before, and tossed them in a corner.

It wasn't the holidays and he knew it. It was this insufferable loneliness assaulting his famous American independence. It was a smashing verification that his internal strength was not the pillar his deluded mind believed it to be. That he wanted it to be. That thought retched his belly. A man with no home, his family gone, his once-secure finances ruined because he couldn't look into those dark bolted doors of his mind with the honesty and professionalism necessary to write. Fuck writing, necessary to live, necessary to grasp that his independence was dependent on other people. He had fought against that for years, and all that time he had obviously been so wrong.

So here he sat, facing black demons but looking out over a beautiful field of white. Everyone else in town, with their modesty, with their limited education, living on the edge of poverty, were wrapping gifts that meant something, walking around smiling, joyous, filled with the spirit of the season. Now what was rich? Who was rich? It was like that first Christmas with twenty bucks in his pocket, in a musty overheated apartment, a man-child with no friends and no family. The love of his life gone. Now, thirty-some years later, he had a hand-me-down house and the same sad circumstances.

He was a fool. And he didn't suffer fools well. He thought about the loaded Walther in his bedroom.

On December 23rd, he arrived in Brainerd at two in the afternoon. The patient's lounge had a tree with plastic bulbs but no lights. He sat with the present in his lap and watched the nurse come across the floor. Bunny walked beside her, unaided. Her eyes widened when she saw the Christmas paper and the big red bows. She sat beside him, glancing at him but her eyes ran back to the box. A magnet, it seemed.

He looked at her, his eyes sad, half-open and alternately blinking and glancing around the room. "You look better, Bunny." She stared at the box. "I made a mess of things. Your sister won't talk to me." He wanted to say more, explain more, but her eyes kept flitting away. "Wanted to wish you Merry Christmas and bring you a little present. Here." He handed it to her. "Open it up."

She stared, not seeming to know what to do. He grabbed a corner of the paper and ripped it slightly. "Pull the paper off," he said. She looked serene, even loving. She had to be in there. The thought warmed him, brought him back to that day shortly after Thanksgiving when he had made that shopping trip for their presents. A day he was alone, but filled with those women, Angie, Clarissa, Elsa, Bunny. If he'd been wealthy as he once was, he would have gone to a jewelry store and they would all have diamonds of some kind. But wealth made him stupid and lazy. Finding just the right gift for each of these wonderful women was much harder and more personal. He'd handled thirty music boxes, none of them right, and finally saw the stuffed panda. It didn't have a sale tag on it, part of a display, and it looked so much like the one he remembered Bunny having in her room when she was sixteen that he knew she had to have it. "Been here a long time," the man said. "Quit trying to sell the poor old thing. Give me two bucks and she's yours."

She ripped the paper, revealing a shoebox, lifted the lid and the old stuffed panda appeared. Her eyes softened. She held it up and hugged it to her neck, then to her nose, almost sniffing, then bending her head to cover it, to shield it and rocked the little bear, glancing, moving only her eyes, to David. Her free arm snaked around his neck and she rocked him, too. His face cradled above the bear. He felt another part of his blackness sucked away into her, screaming as it left, and he relaxed and felt the pain releasing, tension flowing out of his shoulders. A faint hint of recognition appeared in her eyes and she hugged the bear tighter. A thin crease of an almost-smile appeared and she reached for him again, pulling him close, sucking more pain.

The nurse led her away, panda on her shoulder like her baby, turning back every few steps to look at David. He could see her lips moving. No sounds came forth.

He spent that night at the motel, ate a blasé turkey dinner at a diner, thoroughly enjoyed it, and was up early the following morning and at the hospital when visiting hours opened at ten. Bunny walked across the lounge leading the nurse, bear in one arm. He swore she looked younger but dismissed that thought. She sat beside him and gently laid the panda on her lap and touched his hand.

He arrived back at home before dark and put a pot of beef barley soup on the stove to simmer, turned on the tree lights and the outside decorations and looked at the presents under the tree. He selected them specifically for Angie, Clarissa and Elsa and they would have them. Damn the repercussions. He had to get out of here, anyway. The ghosts gathered around him, he could almost see them. Dad and Mom, Dani swooping, and Sandy faded nearly to white. He loaded the gifts into his truck and drove to Angie's house, rang the doorbell. Clarissa's car was parked outside. Angie's face appeared in the window. Curiosity quickly changed to something he didn't recognize, but it wasn't anger and for that he was happy. She turned on the porch light and stepped outside. A forest green sweater accentuated her skin and hair, and he thought she looked beautiful in cold-weather clothes. "Merry Christmas, David." She leaned forward and pecked him on the cheek. "I can't invite you in, sorry."

"I bought these for you guys before the . . ." He swung the bag off his shoulder and held it out to her.

"That was very thoughtful. Thank you."

"I hope it won't always be like this."

Angie took the bag. "Happy New Year, David. From all of us." Her eyes were soft on his and she turned away slowly, hesitantly, and went back inside.

And now it was just him and the ghosts. He drove aimlessly around town, looking at the Christmas lights. It was good to see all the passionate amateur displays instead of the citified professional jobs hired out back in LA, it gave him another reason to appreciate these people in this little part of the north woods. And he was one of them, always had been.

A few cars slowly rolled the street now and it surprised him. He turned a corner, the Walther loaded and under his seat, still wandering, looking for something or somewhere, and there was the church he attended as a boy, where he was christened, attended Bible School, took communion, people were filing in.

He knew the way. Minutes later, he found himself in a crowd, walking up the stairs to the sanctuary, nodding to some, being swept along. He took a seat in the back pew, away from the door where no one ever sat, a program in his shaking hands. The solid A-frame was as familiar as an old glove, the tree dripping with white symbols that he couldn't remember, and everywhere potted Poinsettias. The organ played softly. This is where they had the service for Dad and Mom. He should have been here. He should have brought Dani more often. He felt a spirit filling him and fought back tears.

He followed the service without the program, sang the Christmas hymns from memory and by the time he got back in his car, the seats ice cold now, he felt a peace that had escaped him for a long time.

He sat before the fire, nursing a cup of soup. A glass of gin on ice rested on the coffee table. When the soup was gone, he drank the gin in two swallows and refilled. The gift from his agent sat on the coffee table, too. It was obviously a book. Halfway into his second drink curiosity got the better of him and he opened it. Another copy of *You Can't Go Home Again.*

December 30, he drove to Brainerd again and sat in the lounge waiting for Bunny. When she came through the door, he hardly recognized her. The ancient flowered robe was gone, replaced by a hip-length cardigan sweater in a light delicate blue, straight cut with gold buttons. She wore loose fitting jeans and a white blouse buttoned to the top. Her hair was brushed. She clutched the panda in one arm as she walked to the chair beside him and sat down in a soft, ladylike fashion. "Happy New Year. You look wonderful," he said.

She glanced at him, then out the window. She held up the panda.

"You're welcome," he said. No response. He saw Russet coming into the room and thought he saw her eyes spark, but at second glance they were flat again, and he thought he imagined it, but he didn't imagine the new clothes or the brushed hair. Something was different. "Here comes our friend Russell. I guess I'll run along." He stood. Russet walked up in his normal head-down shuffle, affable and efficient. David put out his hand. Russet shook it without looking up. "Happy New Year," David said.

"H-h-happy New Year to you."

"She looks great, doesn't she?"

"Uh . . . yeah, g-g-g-reat."

David nodded to Bunny and turned to leave and as he walked, he abstractly counted the times he'd run into Russet here. Past coincidence, certainly, and it made him wonder what those two had going. It didn't resemble any relationship he'd experienced but the repetition had to mean something.

***

For the next month, he escaped into work. His home became a cocoon, leaving to visit Bunny and buy groceries. His only interruptions were paying the bills and the weekly e-mail from his agent, the bills a constant reminder of dwindling resources, the e-mails a nagging token of unfinished work. He wished it was the dark before the dawn, but had no way of knowing. When his eyes grew too tired to read any longer, his mind ran loose and out of control for far too long before work began again. Sleep came hard, evasive. He tried to tell himself it was creativity in positive moments, depression in others. He missed those women.

A January deep freeze hindered his walks, most days barely reaching zero. Manual labor remained his friend, shoveling the driveway after a snowstorm, chiseling ice off the blacktop, and below-zero air filling his nose, freezing his lungs. His office was another comfort where he was his work, though he knew that was probably not healthy, with only words and savage, stabbing work to face each dwindling day and endless night.

The first day of February dawned to a cold snap, the overnight temperature sinking to forty-five below zero. The window above his desk grew a thick layer of white frosted fuzz that moved out across the windowpane leaving an oblong hole of clear glass through which the world stood in an eerie silence. He set his coffee cup down beside the computer and checked his e-mail, the newest a note from his agent wishing him a happy February and hoping he was working well. David half-smiled. Since the Thomson women abandoned him, it was the only thing that went well. He delved deeper in thought, in pain, in truth, than he ever had. The pity party was over, and he was still in town in February. He'd won the bar bet.

That evening, he donned his warmest clothes and boots and went out to challenge the elements. Even the wolf-fur trim of his parka was no match for this artic assault. His cheeks burned, the feeling in his nose disappeared and he pulled the stocking cap down to his eyebrows and the scarf up to the bottom of his eyes and where the breathe blew through the scarf an ice shelf formed. The smoke from the chimneys didn't billow or roll, but looked painted in the night sky, a frozen exclamation point. The only sound was the creak of his boots on the packed snow and the occasional snap of a tree fighting the ice in its veins.

He remembered a night like this as a boy of twelve, boot-sliding home from the outdoor hockey rink, not realizing his cap had slipped up, exposing ear lobes to frostbite. Smoke painted in the sky that night, too. His skates dangled from the shaft of his broken stick, smashed by the older boys he played against, lacerated blade in one pocket, frozen puck in the other. Another night of shin-bruises and stick marks across his back, hurting from runs into the boards. Oh—but the ice. Ice so cold and fast and smooth it was worth the punishment. He'd scored a goal and didn't complain, knowing he'd get bigger. He'd make them pay. He'd never quit.

Tonight was frozen affirmation. Never quit, not now nor ever. Hemingway was wrong on that one. Another tree snapped and he boot-skated in the street like when he was a boy. His eyes watered from the stinging cold. And he loved it and laughed out loud. He rounded the last curve, his driveway in sight, his clothing— no, his spirit beating back the elements. Stamping his boots on the porch brought blood to his toes and he looked at the tin thermometer. It read fifty degrees below. A car turned into his driveway. Clarissa's car.

He stood on the porch, shuffling his feet and stuffing his mittens in the big pouch pockets of his parka. Angie got out on the passenger side and waved but did not smile. Clarissa got out of the driver's side. "Bunny made us," Clarissa said.

"Actually, it was Russet," Angie said.

She slipped on the snow bank bordering the driveway, but caught herself. Graceful even at that. He should be graceful, too. Take the moment and enjoy it. Give self-indulgence a little time off. For God's sake, quit thinking and feel something, anything. They were here, in the present, make the best of it. "Come in. I'll make coffee."

"Brandy for me," Clarissa said. A thick wool cap knit in bright colors, sky blue, mint green, and white snowflake trim covered her ears and the blaze of red curls flew up from her parka collar in an uncontrolled mass.

The new coat rack held all three parkas, coffee dripped, and David stoked the fire with two more logs. He drank a hot brandy with Clarissa, while Angie sipped coffee. They sat in the club chairs, closer to the fire, farther from David.

"Bunny is progressing," Angie said. "She's doing simple things for herself, showering, picking clothes, even tried a little make up. They doubt she'll talk again."

"What do they know," Clarissa said. "Damn sight easier for them to just dope her up and let her sit."

David had seen little of these women and had suffered for it, but for the first time in his life had faced ruin without running. The payoff came slowly, hard won and fragile and if this were part of it, he'd gladly accept it. Now he'd seen firsthand the definition of "snow bunnies." They looked gorgeous. "Why are you telling me this stuff? Not that I mind."

Clarissa rolled her eyes. "Forecast says a cold winter."

"Russet thought you should know," Angie said.

"I'll thank Russet next time I see him."

"He thinks we should keep this quiet," Angie said. "I pressed him, but he won't say why. Maybe you can get it out of him."

"Oddly enough, my charm doesn't work on him . . . either," Clarissa said, pushing hair back from her face with those long slender fingers. "Maybe yours will."

David watched her teasing. She was a pro and he'd missed that, too. "Sure, I'll talk to him tomorrow. If I can get my truck started."

Angie snickered. It was the first time he'd seen her smile since that night. "Hard when it gets this cold. Mine was cranky even with the head bolt heater on all night."

"Tomorrow might be better."

The next morning, a knock interrupted his work. Damn, and it was going so well, almost like transcribing. It died hard and he thought about ignoring the door, but someone was standing on his porch in sub-artic cold. It was Auto, parka hood up with a cigarette poking out, smoke rising.

"What the hell you doing out in this weather? Get in here," David said, smiling, extending his hand.

"Seen worse," Auto said, striping off his coat. "Got any coffee?"

"Sure."

"So I get a call last week from an old biker buddy of mine. Hadn't heard from him in years. And he said something about an ad in the Trib. Said he called the number and your name was on the message. Wanted to know if he could trust you." He eyed David, snuffed out the butt in the sink. "So, can he?"

David poured two cups. They sat at the bar. "Want a shot with that?" David asked.

"Might hit the spot." David grabbed a shot glass and the bottle of brandy. Filled the glass and slid it to Auto, who downed it. David told him the rest of the story.

"This is your guy," Auto said. "Doesn't remember the officer's name. Ya might need a picture."

David stood and paced behind the bar, thinking hard now. Auto watched, saying nothing. "I'll try to get a picture. If not, hell, the bluff might be enough."

Auto grinned, hand went to the shot glass instinctively. "I like it. I'll set up a meeting. Duluth, tomorrow, supper at Applebee's on Miller T, okay?"

The drive to Duluth crawled by, nerve-wracking, skating along sanded roads, rocks clattering on the undercarriage, salted spots bringing up blacktop patches, and finally dropping into town with the wind whistling off Lake Superior, grabbing for traction on iced hills. What will this prove? The odds of getting a picture are so remote it's almost not worth the effort. And what if he did get one, what then? The guy would look at it and say, "yup, that's the cop that took my kilo and didn't charge me with a crime." That would give him what? Nothing. The word of a now-confessed pot smuggler against that of a lawman with probably no blemishes on his record, and the "supposed" incident happened thirty-plus years ago, with no apparent relationship to David in even the slightest way, except the significance he was trying to hang on it. It's doubtful it would have any effect on that college president. With her, it'd be better to quit hanging on to some flimsy thread of justice. Think about it: justice for the poor in America, come on. The best line with her was to confess, add remorse, make it believable, and hope for the best. Hope it changed her mind before his money ran out completely.

No, the only reason to continue this little endeavor was to put the needle to Stark, hope it freaked him out, maybe pushed him to a mistake, to some desperate screw up that wouldn't end up with someone dead. Like David. It was damn close last time. He'd examined the carcass of his deer when it was roped to his hood. But back then he didn't want to revisit that blood-lust, that holy, or was it hellish, physical, mental and emotional release of hacking at that deer's throat with a KBAR until Stark had finally grabbed his arm and said, "I think it's dead now." The deflected bullet was meant for his head. What would Stark do now? Did David care? There is a point where there's nothing more to lose and you just say "fuck it" and go in guns blazing. He arrived at the county building housing the sheriff's department. The response was short. No picture. He checked into the Radisson hotel downtown on Superior Street, in full view of the Aerial Bridge, the Blatnik Bridge and the sea of ice below them, all of it muted in the blowing snow crystals whistling hard off Lake Superior.

He sat at the Applebee's on Miller Trunk Highway waiting, the décor familiar, the menu mass-produced, like anywhere in America, in California. His eyes scanned the room, a cornucopia of pictures and trinkets and he was in

California again, wondering why after all these years he didn't have friends there he could confide in, talk of his failures and frustrations, about the vast abyss between selling some books and being an unqualified success. He wanted to have friends, have relationships good and bad and as dangerous as literature, the kind he'd already formed up here. And he wanted to write books that after he read the final galley, a wave of satisfaction warmed him, books that added something real to the lexicon that would live after his ashes sailed on the winds and his marker sat next to Mom and Dad's, where people would leave flowers and wish another book existed. That was his abyss. It lived down there and he could find no ladder long enough to climb down and wrestle it out, nor a bridge long enough to span it, no way to reach the golden ring.

A comely college girl posing as a waitress set a cup of coffee before him, smiled and asked something, an order? He smiled back unconsciously and asked her to come back. He glanced outside at the field of snow and saw the wind whip the trees and the twinkle of lights spread out down the hill to the black bay and the two bridges and he imagined the people in the houses and homes, imagined people happy, without an abyss, people without the strain of erecting some creaky structure built foot by painful foot that would never be completed before they gasped their last breath. And after that, the remnants would stand for a single moment as a monument to folly before it crumbled, like its trillion predecessors, falling endlessly, timelessly into the graveyard of American dreams.

The voice startled him. "You Chapman?" The guy was extra-large with dark hair cut in a flat-top and wearing a long wool car-coat over a blue suit. Who dresses like that besides bankers?

Donald Carlson's story sounded familiar, except for the ending. Drugs, rehab followed by unqualified success. They loved a comeback-kid story and they loved Big D. He grabbed the check before the college girl waitress could get it to the table. "The date's crystal clear, November 4, 1971. I didn't know that sheriff then, but I did later. He's not a nice person. Why don't you move down here, to Duluth. I'm sure I can find a job for you."

The thought of reinventing himself another time held little appeal for David. And it would just skirt the issue of justice, no matter how far-fetched that might be. Then there was the recent reality that he liked more of the townsfolk than he cared to admit. His book was taking form, and his sanity—while far from stable, at least headed in the right direction in spite of all the ghosts. "Maybe a letter to the college would help," David said.

"I'll call. Don't really have time for a tussle with that dick, Stark. Not that it wouldn't be fun, but my fights are non-violent now. I got kids and all."

Ole Big D was damn near bullet proof, money hoarded and invested wisely, reputation clean and above reproach even in this sordid matter, and still arms length was as close as he wanted to get. "Look, you wanna say you found me, go ahead." He handed David a business card. "It ain't like I'm afraid of the guy."

***

Randy Stark's F-150 slowed as he rounded the curve in Elm Street. Moments later, his burly hulk stood on David's porch. The flight jacket exaggerated the bulk of his shoulders. The dangling scarf hid the girth of his neck and nothing hid the flat blood-shot eyes. A speckled gray beard covered the cop expression as he knocked on the door.

David opened the storm door and spoke through the screen. "Why are you here?"

"Hear you been asking about me at department headquarters. What ya want?"

The sour smell of bourbon reeked. Stark drank a few boilermakers at the deer camp but went to bed in pretty good shape, better than most of the troupe. David felt a chill in the pit of his stomach, that old adolescent fear. "A picture of you. Turns out I don't need one."

Stark's eyes didn't seem to focus well. He wavered on his feet. "You're starting to irritate me, now. Things ain't like they was back then. You had your little experience in rural America. Why don't ya head back to some city like a good boy."

David jammed the screen door, knocking the man back. "You scared the shit out of a seventeen-year-old kid. Not now." His arms jutted out. Struck Stark's chest. He tumbled off the porch. "I found the guy you stole the kilo from. He's willing to testify." Okay, a little lie. "Now, go bother someone else."

Stark struggled to his feet and dusted snow off his pants. He glared. His words slurred. "And what's that gonna get ya. Some lo . . . long-winded trial in another town. For what? Nothing. That ain't gonna change your life. You're stuck with what ya got."

That was solid to the solar plexus. Justice might be buried in boot hill, but after thirty-three years, David still carried the woe-is-me whine like some millstone around his neck. Maybe Mrs. College was right, give it up, confess to nothing just to get rid of it. If Stark could see it, damn. David wobbled, weakened inside and struck back with all he had right then. "Fuck you. You tried to kill me, asshole."

Stark's lips curled into that slap-happy drunk's grin they get when by some accident their muddled mind hits on a zinger. "Might again. Tell me this, who ya think was the only one visiting your Momma in her Alzheimer dreams? She called me Davy half the time, but did I care? Who keeps puttin' them flowers on their graves, while you out gallivanting the countryside." His eyes lit up, burning like a crazed man. "Yeah. Me."

This scene ran in all the wrong directions. He should jump down there and pound the crap out of him, take advantage of him drunk-on-his-ass, then file a police report and have his ass thrown in the can. Or maybe ask a few probing questions since he seems enthused about blabbing. Like: What really happened to Angie's Mom? Or: How does it feel to be a serial rapist? Lucidity hits at the strangest times, and David could see how Stark felt about being a reformed serial rapist, among other things. He faced it head on where it stood, in the bottom of a bourbon bottle, a florist for remorse. "Randy, you're drunk. Go on home. We'll try this another day and don't hit anybody."

"I ain't done wit you," he slurred, turned, and barreled through the snow toward his truck.

David watched the truck pull away. It could get interesting and real soon. His body shook with cold and pumping adrenaline. He went inside, slowed to grab a short glass of gin, and headed straight to his office. His nerves calmed waiting for the computer to boot up. He started the letter with "I respectfully request another appointment. There are items that in retrospect deserve further discussion. Thank you in advance for your consideration." Would Mrs. College give that consideration?

David dressed better this time. He hauled out the long black car coat he'd bought to wear for winter publisher meetings in NYC, having no need for it in Southern California, black gabardine slacks with cuffs, a crisp white

Oxford dress shirt with a yellow tie and his black cashmere jacket that he used to wear to desert dinners on cool evenings. The irony came to him while knotting the tie. Mrs. College would see it as an excellent attempt at professionalism. It was actually a funeral suit. For justice.

The leather seat crunched and complained with cold, the gabardine slacks thin and useless. He shivered. The Rover ground and finally fired and he turned the heater on full blast and went back into the house. Burning gas without moving always struck him as a waste, for wimps and pussies, which he felt like now. It wasn't like he never did it. Hell, it even happened in the desert, in the season of opposition, summer, where his skin burned through the shorts and sweat dripped instantly, but most times he fought it off until the A/C caught up. Here, it wasn't just that *he* needed warmth; the damn car needed to unfreeze, too. He grabbed a coffee and waited. Guilt ratcheted back a little, and when he returned, the seat was warm and the car ready to go. "Guess I'm ready, too," he mumbled, though it seemed like a trip to the gallows. The wimpy sissy he brought from California had started to toughen up, but it still took effort sometimes, some days, and today was one of them. Anger and bravado ignited quickly to protect what lurked in the shadows of grief and failure. Today, macho had to take a seat in one corner, wimp in another, so David could run the show.

School was in session and he had to park well away from her office. The cold bit at him as he crossed the parking lot, skating gracelessly in leather shoes, wishing he could have worn his green insulated boots stowed in the car for emergencies, but they wouldn't look good with this outfit. Shit, how California. Style over substance. The door handle was cold even through his designer gloves.

The secretary led him to her office, a quandary of concrete block mixed with wood paneling on three walls and a large window overlooking a snowscape of sidewalks meandering toward buildings housing higher education. Her desk quartered the window allowing her to observe the rhythms of her rule. Behind her, the wall filled with diplomas and awards and before her a solid oak desk as spotless as a new blanket of snow. She stood as he entered and nodded to him. "Good day, Mr. Chapman." Nothing followed, no outstretched hand or welcoming smile. "Please have a seat." She motioned toward a hard chair in front of her desk and pulled a file out of a drawer.

"Thanks." He pasted on the subservient smile of a job seeker, his eyes never leaving her face. Her thick graying hair was pulled back into some archaic style from the fifties, her suit brown and dowdy. "And thanks for seeing me again."

"It seems you have a new friend. Some ex-biker gentleman. Big D, is it?" He watched her eyes wander across his outfit and her subconscious nod pronounce it fit, which only served to make him want to ditch the jacket and roll up his sleeves, but that guy stood in the corner with macho. He needed this job and if he could get it, he'd outlast her at this little college. Hell, he might even take over her job.

"Possibly. May I get right to the point?" He paused, waiting for her eyes to catch his. He could only stomach saying this once and he didn't want her to miss any of it. She nodded and looked at him. "I got caught with my hand in the cookie jar. It was a serious error in judgment that I deeply regret. I admit glossing it over. Contrition is sometimes hard to come to grips with, but it has arrived." Almost unbelievably, he thought he saw a softening in her eyes that ignited a serious desire to stand up and either slap her or leave. If she talked to biker guy, she got the whole story and should have damn well just called and offered him the job, along with an apology. But that obviously didn't mean a thing in her world, and she ran that world. "I will do an excellent job. And teach anything."

"Of course," she said, noncommittal. "Mr. Biker Dude compared your life's trajectory favorably with his. I remain skeptical, but he did offer up a handsome donation."

"The school comes first," he said with a practiced sincerity. And there you have it. Down to money, something any college administrator can wrap her arms around and get comfortable with in very short order.

"He doesn't seem to have a high opinion of Mr. Stark. I called him, of course. He feels that you may be rehabilitated. He mentioned someone else that was rehabilitated . . . some female with an animal name I can't seem to recall."

He knew the name. The question was: how did Stark know and why would he tell her?

Then it came rushing in on him, his heart thump-thump-thumping. A message delivered like a three-rail bank shot that could only happen in a place this size and even here it was tricky. But it had worked and put him in a panic, probably meant to upset the flow of the interview, possibly not even true. Salvaging this interview, this job, was the main priority and distraction was the enemy. He wanted to say, "Rehabilitation is my middle name," or "What else did he say about Bunny?" but smartass and diversion would not be taken kindly by this woman, so he looked her straight in the eye and said, "I feel like I've made substantial progress." Simple, humble, subordinate. In character. God, the things one must do to get a job in America nowadays. Know the norm, be the norm. Nothing out of place. A bit part in A Brave New World.

"Quite," she said, looking down at the lone file on her desk, glancing over the rim of her glasses. She took out a form and scribbled something on it, handed it to him. "Run down and get this test taken. If you pass, I'll put you on the list for next year."

"Thank you," he said, standing, smearing on his best professorial smile, warmth, integrity, intelligence, all rolled into one, while his mind ran through multiple questions, not the least of which was: Is this a hair test or a urine test? But the big one was: What's up with Bunny and Stark?

In LA, the test would have been administered in a tiny lab that ran people through like cattle, but up here, everything revolved around the hospital, the small waiting room functioning like a triage. Oldsters sat on hard chairs or shuffled around trying to get the blood flowing to their legs again, and the expressions on their faces seemed consistent and universal, all worried. He wished there was something he could do for them, individually or collectively, but couldn't come up with what that might be besides a sympathetic smile, some empathy. He helped a lady with a cane find her bearings in a chair. Nurses and doctors sashayed through, picking their next, professionally scrubbed down to their manner and expression, all business, all medical science. Once their hands were on you, your body became their project. Saving souls was someone else's job.

Except up here, it took people of incredible focus and stability because they knew these patients, had lived with them, had seen them in the market and in church, and certainly carried some form of attachment to them, whether positive or negative, that had to be ignored, pushed aside for the sake of science, the sake of continued life. The doors to heaven and hell opened from here, and David swore he could hear the prayers rising from the floorboards, the walls, the ceiling, probably more immense in number and piousness than all the town's churches on Sunday.

Finally, a nurse ambled up to him, handed him a plastic cup and a couple sterile wipes. The eagles were over two months ago, so he knew he'd pass. Great news. The hair test would not have turned out the same. And he could get on with the next piece of business. Bunny.

It was a little after noon when he left the hospital and strangely warm for this time of year. He knew where he had to go. The problem was getting Russet aside, alone, away from his work. He slipped the truck into drive and wheeled out of the parking lot, down past the five blocks of eighty-year-old houses and onto the county road that wound back through the forests to Lone Pine. Within a half hour, he'd made The Hole-in-the-Wall, found Russet's ancient car in the lot, ordered the pizza, paid and received a blank, then annoyed look when he asked for delivery. No one ordered at the bar and asked for delivery, no one was that hurried.

He drove home to wait. Questions floated around by the hundreds and he knew if he asked too many, he'd scare Russet off. Selectivity was key. Try to get the important stuff first and hope he could get the rest out later. He made coffee and paced. The cloaked message from Stark seemed to say he wasn't planning anything violent or why would he bring Mrs. College into it where she could be a future witness? Maybe his plan was so good it didn't matter. God knows, there was no shortage of drugs in that institution that could knock down an elephant and let it die in its sleep. Maybe that was it.

But why would Stark care about Bunny in the first place. And why would he care about David or send that message. From Stark's side of the fence, he was just a guy who knew about stolen and planted contraband thirty-some years ago. It could never be proven, and he was already retired so who cared anymore. Except David, who should've let that go years past and *that* he now understood. He glanced out the window and saw Russet's car pull into the driveway. He waited for the knock.

David's face was serious when he answered the door. "Come in, Russell," he said, swinging the door wide. "Maybe put that on the table, there."

Russet barely glanced at him and set the box down. David closed the door and moved in front of it. Russet fingered the ticket, bending closer to read through the grease stains. "S-s-says it's . . . it's p-paid for already. W-weird."

David handed him a five spot. "I didn't want pizza. I wanted to talk to you. Stark sent me a message." He saw the jitter, saw what might be fear in Russet's eyes, but it vanished immediately and the lumpy, sad face looked at him impassively.

"W-what w-was it?" Russet asked, and his voice said it like, "who cares."

"Said you two were able to talk. She's never talked to me." It was a stretch. He watched the face, the cheeks twitching, the eyes heading for the floor and the fear lingered longer this time.

"Th-that's . . . c-c-c-razy," Russet stuttered. His stutter increased with his nervousness and it was obvious he was getting pretty darn nervous right now. But scaring him off could be counterproductive so the decision was easy, just wait it out, be calm. David painted on a look of eternal patience and moved to the table, sat on the edge, hands folded in his lap, inviting Russet to trust him, knowing he would have to trust someone pretty damn quick if this stuff were true. He saw Russet studying him, eyes furtive, thinking. "Ar-are you B-Bunny's friend?"

David nodded, then almost whispered, "That's why I go see her." He said nothing more, just watched Russet's face, his attention drifting around in deliberation, eyeballing

David every few seconds as the fear seemed to change into a grim determination.

"W-we got-ta get her . . . out . . . of . . . th-there. N-n-n . . . shit . . . s-soon." Russet's frustration commanded his face, lips twisting, eyes flashing. "S-she knows s-stuff." It was like he wanted to tell it all, say more because it was important, but the damn stutter was his enemy now as much as Stark.

"We can't get there in time to take her today. She'll be shut down in her room."

Russet nodded. His anxiety level seemed to drop slightly. The "we" must have registered, made him feel like he had an ally now. "T-to-morrow?"

David put his hand on Russet's shoulder. "Sure, tomorrow. Calm down a little. Come over after work, tell me the rest of it. I don't care about the stutter, we'll stay up all night if that's what it takes."

That seemed to release a little more tension. Russet exhaled, shuffled foot to foot. "R-r-right. L-later," he said and headed for the door.

Chapter Twenty Five

Angie set a cup of coffee in front of Clarissa and looked around the new kitchen, watching Clarissa's eye roving, analyzing the remodel. "Olson do this?" she asked. Angie nodded. "Damn fine job. Between you and your boyfriend, keep that guy in firewood all winter." Angie saw the glint, felt the dig gentle by comparison and just smiled and shook her head. "He does good work." The phone rang and Angie went to answer, greeted by the stricken voice of her granddaughter. "I couldn't get Mom. Can you come and get me? Now?"

Clarissa's car slid to a stop in front of the house. "Stay here," she said to Angie, who followed anyway. She watched Clarissa fly across the yard, up the porch, and straight in the door without knocking. Bobby sat glum, virtuous, in the living room, and stood when she came in. "What do you think you're doing here," he said, taking a step forward.

"What have you done to my daughter? Forget it, I'll find out myself." She barely slowed down long enough to get the words out, and immediately continued toward the bedroom. She opened the bedroom door. Elsa sat on the bed, her dowdy winter jacket already on, and when she saw her mother, a fresh rain of tears flowed. "What happened, baby? Tell me."

"Jacob came to see me. Walked all the way. Daddy called him an evil heathen."

"Where's the boy?"

"He left. It looked like he was stabbed."

Angie stood in the doorframe now, listening, staying calm. She knew this would come eventually. Whether from selective memory of Bible lessons or the remnants of a shattered relationship with Clarissa or that she just looked too much like her mom and he was taking it out on her, it didn't matter. Those were his problems. She had enough of her own, like a devastated granddaughter, that boy alone in the woods beaten down by the phony religious asshole. Elsa was off the bed and at the closet, her backpack shouldered. "Just get me out of here, please."

"Come on." Clarissa took her hand and led her out of the room. Angie watched. Bobby stood blocking the hallway, their exit. The same "blocking" he had done to Clarissa for years, since the incident, since he took custody and extracted his pound of flesh every time there was a visitation, a weekend, a trip, a holiday, any moment that she could beg to be with her daughter, and the panicky phone call, the look on her daughter's face now, brought it all back. Angie was pissed but obviously momma bear had had it.

"The Lord knows you're not going anywhere," he said, harsh, hard, pious, like some tent-show weirdo.

Clarissa slowed, like she might stop, but inched closer until she was in range, then fired a straight right to his face that landed full and solid. His hands went up. She kneed him hard in the nuts, and shouldered him back as he fell, holding his groin. "Fuck you, Bobby. And don't give me any of your God shit, eh. Ya wouldn't know God from a peat bog." They pushed past him, down the hall.

"I'll . . . have her . . . back in an hour," he managed to stutter out.

Angie wanted to kick his face, too, but enough damage had already been done. Clarissa couldn't resist and laid on a final blow, hard to the jaw. His eyeballs rolled back. Angie knew he'd have the cops after them as soon as he could get to a phone.

They didn't slow down, out the door, into the car, and off. The town now seemed even smaller, microscopic, with no place to hide, and no way to get out. "Did he touch you?" Clarissa asked. Elsa just shook her head no. "Okay, then how about an adventure, honey?" she said. "We can talk on the way."

Angie realized that yeah, okay, it's technically kidnapping and will result in a trip back before a judge, but she was too young last time to take a stand. It might be different now. Clarissa slammed the car into gear. In two minutes she was parked in her driveway, the car still running, Elsa ducking down in the seat. Angie ran inside with her. "What can I do?" she said.

"Ya probably shouldn't have even been there," she said, and grabbed a cordless phone and tossed it to Angie. "Can you call David for me? Tell him I need to trade vehicles and I need one of his parkas and a stocking cap."

She filled a gym bag as Angie waited for David to answer. "Hey, how was your interview," she asked and didn't have time for much in the way of detail so she pushed on. "Listen David, we've got a little situation going on right now, can you help me with a couple things?" His answer came back quick and unqualified. It reminded her of how much she liked him. He was a damn good man and friend, not just to her but to all his new acquaintances in this little town. She detailed Clarissa's request. "Great, thanks David. Can you pull it out on the street and wait in it. Leave the garage door open. We'll be there in like two minutes. We'll hide Clarissa's car in your garage."

"You kidnapped Elsa, didn't you?"

"Sort of. We're leaving now. Guess I'll be dropped off with you."

They pulled into David's driveway and into the garage. David followed her and parked close behind, just enough room for the garage door to close. Elsa and Clarissa jumped out, each with a bag, followed by Angie. David got out and closed the garage door as Clarissa and Elsa climbed into the Rover. The stocking cap lay on the seat. She pulled on the parka and began stuffing her hair up into the cap. "Where ya going?" David asked.

"Not sure. An impromptu vacation, right honey?" Elsa nodded, almost smiled.

David leaned in and whispered in her ear. "Listen, I caught up with Russet this morning. He's worried. Bunny and Russet communicate. He wants her out of there pronto. Stark knows."

She closed the door and flashed him a smile. "Then I guess my vacation runs through Brainerd. Wish me luck." Another smile, she pulled the parka hood up, hit reverse, and they were gone, with Elsa lying on the floorboards. Out of town. Angie and David saw them turn toward the labyrinth. They both sighed. "Guess I'll just walk home," Angie said. "What did you say to her." When David told her, she was torn between fear and sarcasm. "My daughter the criminal."

"Want some coffee, a drink maybe."

"Thanks but think I'll just head home. Wait for the phone to ring."

Chapter Twenty Six

David sighed as he watched Angie disappear around the corner. Extraordinary things happening to ordinary people, and he was one of them. He felt a strange degree of involvement, even though he had no personal stake in any of the day's events, except his interview. A runaway cum kidnapping, a veiled threat toward a mental patient, hell, what was extraordinary about that? Where he came from that constituted a slow news day. But here, there was this odd communality, this abstract feeling that even though there existed no personal stake, it was all personal. If it happened in the town sphere, it happened to you. John Dunn home to roost.

If it was always this way, no wonder half the town had a chip on its collective shoulder for the quasi-drug bust those thirty-three years ago. A black eye for each of them, shame at every supper table, a trusted relative who let them down and deserved to be banned. No wonder Stark fought to keep his secret and it was becoming obvious it wasn't just one secret or why would he send a message about Bunny. A diversion? Doubtful.

Regardless, Clarissa would spring her the minute visiting hours started. He had no doubts about that. Clarissa was brash, bold, she didn't have to contemplate a personal stake. It was all personal to her. Always had been. She would walk Bunny outside immediately, have Elsa distract anyone lingering or watching, stuff them both in his Rover and bolt. Probably stop to buy clothes somewhere safe and sixty miles or so removed from the mental joint, then who knew what she'd do. But he couldn't wait to find out.

Russet knocked on his door at close to midnight. With ample time to think about things and not knowing Clarissa was already dispatched, he appeared ramped up, wracked with fear, and stuttering so badly that staying up all night wouldn't have scratched the surface. When David told him that Clarissa would spring Bunny tomorrow morning, he sensed some relief. Russet even smiled slightly at the observation that Clarissa's regard for rules and conventions was so deeply flawed that she wouldn't think to ask for permission, but just grab the mute girl and go.

The relief was temporary. After an hour of patiently trying and the stutter only getting worse, David asked if he could type, at which Russet became re-energized and they reconvened in David's office at the computer. Russet, in fact, could *really* type, much faster than he could think. But the thoughts were clear, committed, from a simple man with simple values and a love deep and true that went back decades. Completely lacking in what might be good for him, centered solely on her safety and well-being. The hiding-in-plain-sight part struck David as both ingenious and horrifically tragic. Two people who felt so powerless, so completely overmatched in this drama that they would sacrifice years of freedom for minutes of togetherness because they could not calculate how to find justice, how to beat an obviously corrupt system.

Russet finally typed about taking her back to the scene of the crime. It was their almost absurd hope that the shock might retrieve Bunny's voice, maybe allow her to speak again. At that, David's passion passed the abstract and rooted itself firmly in the present. The sphere now belonged to him, too. He didn't know what difference her voice, her speech, might make to the world at large, and didn't care a tinker's damn about the world at large. All he cared about was the happiness of these two people, and if they thought it was important, that was good enough for him.

That they were both plenty scared raised the stakes for all. If she retreated into herself again, they would suffer the ultimate loss, their world so narrow and protected that no one else would even notice, and the fact that they would take that risk certainly spoke volumes to what they hoped would be their lives until death do they part. And who could say they were wrong? They'd squandered years in fear and silence, and if they were willing to risk it all for the sound of a voice in the truncated remnants of their lives so be it. He would help them in any possible way.

And the first way he could help them was to get Angie on board. He thought of calling her when Russet left, but it was three-thirty in the morning, and he suddenly had a distinct paranoia of telephones, akin to when he really was awash in drugs and denial and debauchery and thought every phone was bugged.

The stuff Russet had typed in answer to David's questions was downright frightening and definitely made him think more than once about picking up the phone and calling in the heat. But with an ex-cop, how could you ever be sure about the blindness of justice. Crap, now he was in the same boat as Russet and Bunny. That's how easy it was to fall into. People thought Russet was a dunce. Shit, he was probably smarter than all of them and hid that just as well as he hid Bunny and his immense love for her. No, this wasn't the time for cops and that wasn't his call anyway.

His call was to Angie, and who knew how pissed off she would be when she read what Russet had written, or what she might say or do. What she'd been through already with these guys made it a complete toss-up. She might pack a bag and never look back or load up that shotgun of hers and go postal. But he needed a few hours sleep. It was four in the morning. Angie would have to wait.

David didn't sleep long, awakened by Dani, sweating. The dreams had diminished since the screams of that deer as he slashed it. That made something change whether in him or in heaven or hell and most days he was thankful and somewhat remorseful but it didn't matter today. He didn't even try working. How could writing fiction match this? It was still too early to call Angie, so he headed off to the café for breakfast. Brad Sterling sat in a booth with a couple other guys he didn't recognize, clients obviously, back from a weekend of ice fishing in one of those warm, cushy ice houses with bunk beds and Coleman stoves, tons of food and booze, and an indoor outhouse, most likely had an emergency generator, and they probably caught so many walleyes they'd have to buy another freezer. Brad waved him over and introduced the strangers. David shook hands and wished them a safe journey, then took a seat at the counter and ordered.

On the way home, he decided the phone was a jinx, so he pulled into Angie's driveway, went up and knocked on the door. As he waited, the thought hit him that his small-town acclimation must be nearly complete now. In LA, the only time he would ever knock on a door unannounced was if he were shot and bleeding and then only if he couldn't make it to a pay phone. But here he was, knocking and waiting and thinking about Russet and Bunny and Clarissa and Elsa, and even with his newfound passions, there was still a distinct lack of action, because in reality it wasn't his problem. Sympathy, compassion, advice, bleeding-heart liberal enthusiasm, he felt all that now, but action was still someone else's bailiwick.

"Who's knocking at this hour," Angie yelled through the storm door. He felt guilty now and it was too late to feign injury, or death.

"It's me. David." The drapes parted, her face appeared, hands pushing at the billows of hair, then, amazingly, a half-smile and the snap of a lock clicking open.

"Come on in," she said, turning away shyly, one hand rubbing at her face, the other still pecking at her hair. "Just getting myself up. Coffee for you?"

"Coffee'd be great." She motioned to a birch table, sleek and modern, with thickly cushioned chairs. He glanced around the room. "Heck of a job on the kitchen," he said.

"Thanks. Harry's . . . uh . . . New Years present." She grinned, sly. "What drags you over here this early?"

There were times when he would look at her and age melted away. He looked away thinking his eyes might be giving away his thoughts. "News."

"I got a call last night. My criminal daughter." She smiled that coy in-the-know smile that made him think his thoughts were tattooed to his forehead or typed out on a sheet of paper and handed to her before his arrival. It was a little disconcerting. He'd changed completely over the years. How could she know him this well?

"I had a long talk with Russet last night," he said with authority, stumbling back to the present.

"That could cure insomnia." That damn smile again.

"This could create it."

Chapter Twenty Seven

Angie looked across the table at David and listened to his story, her tranquil face replaced by a stony expression. She heard the chilling account of her sister's life that no one knew about nor could have even guessed, excepting her God if she still had one. The only missing pieces a few critical seconds submerged in the vault of her mind that contained the answer to: Who killed Mom?

It was evident that Russet and Bunny were not taking any chances because those memories were still gone. If it were Stark then was Harry implicated too? He had to be. And the more she thought about it, the more she knew her dead father could no more kill the woman he loved than he could kill his own daughters. Yeah, he was a fool and had made horrible misjudgments in going along with his wife, her mother, but that was fear and ignorance and did that add up to the ability to take her life? No, no and triple no.

"Well, the plot sickens," she said. "Clarissa will be a double kidnapper."

"You think Bunny will remember her?"

"Who knows? And I just knew Bobby would go off the deep end one day. That boy Jacob was so nice, so polite. And handsome, my gosh."

Her voice calm and measured, keeping the subject a moving target, but she wanted to blow up here and now, to shout, to scream, to murder that SOB Stark herself. But that thought composed her further. Maybe she would do it. The no-court-in-the-land thing. Yes, eventually she'd have to face her Maker, but if He were a benevolent God as advertised, that would not be a problem either.

Still, she had to get that DNA paternity test back. For God sake, one can't kill the father of their daughter, no matter. Stick the fucker in jail for life, sure, but not hunt him down and finish him. No matter how good it would feel. And it would feel damn good. Even better if she could shove something hard and hollow up *his* ass and pull the trigger. She swore if he was not the father there would be nothing to stop her.

"You're taking this surprisingly well," David said.

"It's all such a jumbled mess. What can you do but wait it out?" She knew what she'd like to do. Go get into Stark's face to begin with. Case his place, put him on the defensive, let him know where things stood. The clock was ticking now. She primped her hair and shot him another off-hand smile. "I'm not that hot on dragging Bunny back to the scene, but it's their life. Count me in."

"The whole damn thing makes me jumpy. I could be hauled in as an accessory to any number of crimes." Now he smiled. Angie liked that, and couldn't help thinking how things could have turned out so differently, and he was still darn good looking, especially when he smiled, which now that she thought about, happened far too infrequently.

"So, call me if you hear from the outlaws," she said and reached across the table and touched the back of his hand, holding him with her eyes. "Think you'll get that job?"

He didn't move his hand. "Hell, I don't know. Hope so. Need money coming up, here. Although can't say I trust Mrs. College much farther than I can throw her."

"Like to see that," she said, deadpan. They both laughed. Secretly, she hoped he'd get the job, too. She was kind of getting used to having him around town, in a friend sort of way since he'd seemingly learned to keep his dick in his pants. But then, does a man ever really learn that? She doubted it. She'd remember that. Maybe it could work to her advantage again one day.

"You ever think about phone taps?" he asked.

"Never once."

He grinned and stood up. "Me neither. If you hear anything don't call, just drop over. I'll do the same."

She stood and punched him in the arm. "Paranoid old hippie. Get outta here."

When he closed the door behind him, she let the façade of calm fall away. Things were happening beyond her control and she had to figure how to get a little of it back. She wanted to inflict damage on Bobby and Stark. Russet and David both gave her a warm feeling of humanity, rosy and caring, rising above the fray. But how would Clarissa handle the mess with Elsa, even though she can certainly speak for herself at this age. And why would Bunny want to go back to the scene of the crime. If you could forget a mess like that, why wouldn't you. She wished she could.

About midnight her phone rang. It was David, the outlaws had arrived. She grabbed her coat and started walking, not knowing what to expect. When she arrived, Letterman was on, which Clarissa ignored and dialed Russet's number. Angie listened. Clarissa's orders were clear: no extra cars, walk. Packed two items, a toothbrush and a Gold MasterCard.

The following afternoon, Angie dropped Russet and Bunny at the bike trail that the kids had used to walk home from high school and waited. The unseasonable warmth of the day before climbed higher and the cirrus thickened and lowered and light rain dusted the snowfield. She watched them walk off surrounded by a nervous silence. It was windless and warm for February, already up to thirty degrees at two in the afternoon and still rising. She looked away, glanced at the western horizon and saw darker clouds. Weather this weird always meant something, rarely something good.

They took the narrow path past the old elementary school playground, now a park lying beneath two feet of packed snow. Angie started her car and drove toward the home they'd shared all those years ago. When she got there, she walked up the driveway and waited until she saw them between the house and garage. They broke out of the snowfield onto a narrow shoveled path. Bunny stopped, frozen, Russet at her side. Bunny's face was aghast, eyes wide with fear, lips trembling but set, determined. Her eyes glanced at the driveway and the house, quick, and darting.

"You w-w-ant to run?" She heard Russet say.

She nodded yes, then no, then yes again.

"R-r-r-remember it? L-last t-time you were here?"

Bunny slowly moved up the three porch steps and stood on the landing, looking at the door. Then her arms snapped straight, her mouth a mute scream, face turned to panic. Mittened hands covered her face and she tottered. Russet leaped to the landing, steadied her, helped her down the stairs. Tears streamed down her face, mascara dripping, lower lip quivering out of control. Her mittens dropped to the ground, hands spasmodically signing, "Yes. Oh God, Mommy." She whirled and grabbed Russet.

Angie darted to help, picked up the mittens. Russet whispered in her ear, a stage whisper above the sobbing. "A-angie's h-h-here. L-l-let's go. R-r-remember it, B-b-bunny. E-e-very det-t-tail."

Bunny said nothing, sobbing harder, sitting in the back seat with him. He rubbed her back, held her hand. Angie studied her eyes in the rear view mirror. They were vacant and black.

Chapter Twenty Eight

Clarissa lounged on the sofa in David's basement, smoking her third cigarette in the last twenty minutes. He watched her eyes blankly following images on the TV screen, expressionless. She tapped her foot. The three-eyed white sneakers looked ridiculous. The gingham dress and embroidery trimmed apron made her fidget, uncomfortably, and look like she had stepped out of time, a throwback wife cooking a pot roast and waiting for the old man to come home. David thought she looked, well, great in any attire.

He sat at the other end of the sofa, flipping through a Golf magazine and glancing at Clarissa between sections. Her hair was pulled back in a bun, around her face strands escaped and dangled down her cheeks, her ears, the nape of her neck. Fire-red strands with long looping curls. He thought she may be the most beautiful woman in the world, if you could just ignore her mother, her daughter, and her aunt who seemed oddly serene in the face of what was going down, maybe due to the sleeping in the same room with Russet the night before, which had to a first for both of them whether it went farther than sleep or not.

All had sat at his table for lunch and he had marveled at the genetic accidents procreated by Walt and Susan Thomson. God what a gene pool, besting all the budding magazine models, and pop stars, and aging queens of the runway, of screens big and small, and he felt old and embarrassed, lost in time and memory, flitting back and forth, second to unmarked second. First a Technicolor movie, then a black and white TV show and he thought if Susan Thomson ever looked that good it was no wonder Harry and Bea Barnet couldn't keep their hands off her. These women, the girl included, made him reverent, bowing at the alter of Helen where stood Clarissa in the absolute prime of womanhood with Elsa in waiting a few years hence.

Small wonder he got his ass handed to him for the Angie/Clarissa issue, and he deserved that. If only because he wasn't man enough to let them know how he felt, that he was battered by death and divorce and failure, was meek, afraid of risk, dreaded commitment, and was dipping his toe into the freezing water of love just to maybe test it out quickly, without pledge or promise. Formidable women these, who deserved more than that, which was mercifully past.

Still, as he sat here today, he couldn't help but feel like an outsider, like he'd rented out his house for this endeavor, like some play was about to unfold before him and he was neither audience nor actor. Not enjoying or participating, not invested in anyway—once again, battered and meek.

Clarissa sucked on a cigarette, her cheeks hollowed and drew his attention to her fine facial features and her eyes. She blew out smoke in a violent exhale and rapped the butt on the ashtray rim. "What's taking so fucking long?" she asked, staccato.

David synchronized with time again and he managed a thin smile. "Got another appointment?"

"Don't be fresh."

"Guess it depends on what happens out there."

She puffed hard and crushed out the butt. Her hand swept at loose hair. She nodded. Mumbled something.

David heard the kitchen door open. Clarissa sat bolt upright, glared at him, and dropped back in a chair. He glanced at her, heard the thud of feet coming down the wooden steps into the basement. He saw a boot appear, snow stuck around the sole and balled on the jean cuffs. Then another, a different boot, the steps hesitant, halting, and jerky. He heard the soft sobs and rose, turned to Clarissa, his face tense. She stared at the stairway, expressionless. "I don't like it," she whispered. Three figures clustered in the narrow passage, their faces not yet visible. Two cocooned around Bunny, arms wrapped, helping the slumping woman along.

David moved the coffee table well back from the sofa. The faces showed. Bunny's wretched, contorted, tears flowing. Angie and Russet grave. Angie glanced up and saw the pathway. Her eyes hit David's, then Clarissa's. David stepped back and made room for the cluster to pass. Bunny's head tilted down, blank, her feet shuffled following Russet's lead. David heard Angie's deep soft voice quivering at Bunny's ear, "Let's get your coat off darling. We'll all sit here a while." The procession stopped before the sofa and Russet pulled the thick zipper with deliberate care, like undressing a baby, slipped the parka off her shoulders. It fell to the floor. David grabbed the coat, felt the bulge in the pocket, and hung it on a nail against the wall. Russet and Angie let their parkas drop. David retrieved them while the other two cuddled close to Bunny, eased her to the couch and sat on either side of her, closer still, arms rubbing her back and shoulders and neck.

"Can you get her boots off, Clarissa?" Angie asked.

Clarissa knelt and unlaced the boots. Bunny's eyes rose slowly, red and watery, and saw Clarissa and signed. "Mommy?" Her head dropped again. Soft sounds escaped her lips, unintelligible. Clarissa pulled each boot off and set them out of the way. She remained kneeled in front of Bunny, sad eyes looking up at the desolate woman.

"S-s-she's f-fighting," Russet said in a whisper.

David went to Bunny's parka, found the bulge and grabbed it. He was back at the cocoon in a second, crowding in with the others and rubbing her back. Clarissa stood first, then Angie. Bunny's hands were folded in her lap like rose petals closing for the night. David set the panda on them. They open, the bear dropped to her palms, her hands closed gently. Her eyes rolled up to David, then back down. She pulled the panda to her heart, her head went down, nestling. Russet stayed, nestling her.

Upstairs, they closed the basement door quietly and stood in the kitchen, silent, shuffling, looking around, not knowing what to do or say. "I could make coffee," David whispered. Both women nodded. "Living room, maybe? I'll build a fire." He glanced out the window. The snow was starting.

A fire crackled in David's fireplace sending a glow over the antique yellow walls. Two stubby candles burned on the coffee table, the only light in a room heavy with anticipation, dread of the possible, the probable, the damn unknown. A designer version of a hospital waiting room. They sat on the edges of the furniture and sipped lattes. David offered refills and tended the fire, listening at the basement door but heard only muffled sounds. Angie alternately sat and paced, her face drawn and looking her full age, in contrast to earlier in the week when David saw her at the market and swore her new regime had knocked off ten years. She had appeared vibrant and fresh, skin gleaming. Now she paced into the kitchen bringing a cloud with her. Elsa sat silent, impassive but not impatient. Clarissa wrestled with her own demons as long as she could stand it, then donned David's parka, her boots and left.

Outside, the snow had begun an hour before and added a layer of bright soft white to the hard gloss of the winter shell. David stood at the window and watched the snowflakes stream through the streetlights, a conic veil that disappeared into crisp blackness, thick and silent, where Clarissa walked. She had pitched the gingham and the apron soon after they were upstairs, replaced by a ribbed wife-beater, a plaid flannel shirt and jeans. He watched her disappear into the night, wondering what was going on in her mind but he knew whatever it was, she was fully invested, daughter, mother, aunt. It wouldn't matter to her.

The kitchen door opened again at ten and David went to meet her. Clarissa hung his parka on the rack. She ripped the bun out of her hair, shaking the red curls, snowflakes flying, melting immediately, fingers fluffing the matted locks, and walked into the living room. "Kinda morgue-ish in here. What's happening?" She moved to Elsa and gave her a hug. "How you getting along, babygirl?"

Elsa looked up, half smiled. "Okay, Mom. Think they'll look for us here?"

"If they're looking at all. Pete's had Bobby pegged for years. My guess is there ain't a lot a looking going on at all right now. Stay outta sight and we're probably fine for the moment. I'll see my lawyer soon." Her eyes darted to Angie and David. "Any word from below?" Two heads shook in unison. Nothing.

David made sandwiches for everyone and brought two of them and two glasses of milk down the basement stairs. The sight was eerie, Bunny and Russet sitting, facing each other on the couch, their expressions grim, not a sound in the room, no motion except flying fingers. They both looked at him when the stairs creaked. "How's it going?" he said, lightly, nervously, feigning upbeat. "Brought ya some food."

"It's . . . o-o-kay . . . I-I guess," Russet said. "Sh-sh-she's not g-g-going back i-i-inside, n-n-now." He signed it as he said it, out of habit. Bunny faked a smile that David recognized. He'd seen her use it on the high school jocks trying to get into her pants. "Angie's getting ready to head home. Your room is ready. Clarissa and Elsa got a room in Ely. She wants to see her lawyer first thing."

Bunny nodded. "W-we're trying t-ta f-f-figure what t-to do," Russet said, his face pale and confused.

"Ask me, ya ought to get out of this town as soon as possible. Remember, I got that message. Don't trust Stark."

They both nodded, looking too exhausted to talk anymore. He set down the plates. "I'll send Angie down before she leaves. Snowing pretty good out there. Plows will be out early." He didn't say: you ought to be following them at dawn. Instead he just said goodnight.

David woke before first light and went into the living room. He turned on the porch light and saw a foot of new snow blanketing the driveway, the snow still falling unabated. He sighed and went to his office, his bedroom as a kid. No one was going anywhere without difficulty, and probably chains.

The screen door squeaked and closed, the newspaper wedged between the doors. He dressed and took a cup of coffee alone at the bar, scanning the papers with little interest in anything. The weatherman predicted more snow, followed by a cold snap. He slipped on his boots and parka and headed outside to shovel this first layer off the driveway. It felt good to tax his muscles and breathe the fresh air. The clean smell of new snow stuck in his hair and on his wool shirt. His parka lay draped over the porch railing. Too warm for that. He chiseled the packed footprints off the porch and swept it clean. Inside, he started bacon and fried potatoes and toast, thawed a tube of orange juice and stirred up a gallon.

Russet came out about nine, showered already, hungry, quiet. Bunny appeared a few minutes later. Angie knocked on the door. Inside, she hugged her sister. "Good to see you out of that place," she said. "Looks like David's whipped up a grand breakfast." Bunny nodded. Angie looked concerned.

David knew she'd give about anything to communicate with her sister, but absent the miracle of learning sign in the next thirty seconds, that was out of the question. Russet seemed calmer today, Bunny distracted. "W-we're g-g-going to t-take off today," Russet said slowly, controlling his voice.

"Pretty bad out there," David said, though he knew Russet had been braving weather like this for years on his trips to see Bunny. It wouldn't faze him. "Where you headed?"

"N-n-not sure. A-away f-f-from Stark," he said. Bunny took a deep breath.

"Call us when you get somewhere. We'll be worried," David said. God, just like a Mom. And now we're all running like a bunch of scared sheep. What a damn travesty.

Russet pushed his chair back and stood. "Th-thanks D-D-David. Got to g-get my c-car. T-t-talk to Mom, then I'll b-be back."

He gave Bunny a peck on the cheek and an LA hug. Was there trouble in paradise already? Probably just the stress of what? Going, not going, where to run, how to hide, will she talk. Christ, with them the list seemed endless and David almost wanted to volunteer something but he didn't know what or how beyond offering up home and hearth, food, safety of sorts, a little escape from the danger maybe. He started cleaning up the breakfast mess, prompting Angie into action, too. Bunny finished the last piece of bacon, and got up to leave, presumably headed for the bathroom. "Need any help?" Angie offered. Bunny blushed for some reason, and shook her head no. David remembered he hadn't put out any more clean towels. He darted to cut her off, but she was in her room, so he left a clean set at her door and got back to his chore. "I'm worried about them," Angie said, hand washing a pan.

"Me too. Wish I knew what was going on in those two heads."

"When I went down to say good night, they were signing like crazy. It looked aggressive to me, though I couldn't tell you why."

"That kiss before Russet left wasn't exactly Bogie and Bacal."

"It's got to be hard for them. Even I had high hopes yesterday. Thought something new might surface. 'Knows stuff' is pretty vague. Got a good mind to visit Mr. Stark."

David stopped drying a pan and looked at her. "That might wait until those two are safely tucked away."

Angie nodded. "You're probably right."

"Hey, how about a shower?" He shot her a sly smile. Way off base and he knew it, but it would change the course of this conversation, which needed changing. Abstract worries were a playground he wanted to avoid.

Her expression changed to feigned consideration. "You'd shit if I said yes."

She fingered a strand of hair, pulled it toward her mouth. He'd seen that often all those years ago and now realized how much he missed it.

"You don't know that," he said. But her expression told him she did. Bunny in the house made it a no-risk invitation. Right up his don't-get-too-involved-in-life alley. An alley he'd walked for quite a few years, stepped off a few months ago, got slapped, and retreated back into with unrepentant vigor. It had a few downsides, but he felt pretty safe here right now, sadly. He started another pot of coffee. "Shower would spruce my day right up," he lied. "Make yourself at home. This'll only take a minute."

She raised her eyebrows. He ignored the meaning, refused comment, and headed down the hallway. Slowing at the guest bathroom, he leaned close to the door to see if

Bunny had finished. No water ran, but there was a funny gurgling noise that he couldn't place. Almost like water trying to get down a half-plugged drain.

Russet and Bunny left a little before noon, giving the plows time to get ahead. Angie bailed at the same time. Just after they left, the snowplow socked in the mouth of David's driveway, so he shoveled that out, sweating from the exertion. Later, as darkness dropped its quick winter blanket, he sat alone in the chair, thinking of family, of Bunny's troubles, of Clarissa's troubles, of Angie.

Then things turned for the worse, to Dani, waiting for her to come home, and not coming, and finally the phone call, and she was gone. Even after two years, it still eviscerated him and brought tears. It can turn bad fast. He hoped it wouldn't for the Thomson girls. They'd had enough already, enough for a dozen people and a few lifetimes. The Wolfe book lay in his lap and he tried reading but couldn't get anywhere. He'd read about twenty other novels by the living masters during his slog through Wolfe and now thought he may be right, maybe home is just one of those quaint, romantic concepts that prove hollow and ephemeral in the end, though he didn't want to believe that.

He made a ham sandwich, poured a tumbler of gin, and retreated to his leather recliner. The house felt empty now, after teeming with people. He had liked it too much, the bustle, the feeling useful to others, his makeshift family, it was easy to get used to. Turned bitch when it was gone.

If he was absorbing a family, they came intact, including Elsa, and his grief was not her problem and he couldn't let it taint things. He would talk to her more, though he had no idea how or about what. He could never figure that out with his own daughter, but he'd try. She was a person, there had to be a way. She seemed complex and confused, and who wouldn't with the anti-Christ and

Clarissa for parents, the exact opposite of Bunny's simplicity whose happiness didn't hinge on success of some undefined and existentially worthless idea cooked up in the brain of an egotistical, over-analytical man who couldn't face his own reality, own mortality or any mortality for the matter.

He remembered talking with Bunny when she was sixteen, always about the simple things, walking in the woods, the wind in the trees, the change of seasons that, for her, weren't a symbol of anything but the existence of God and nature, the cycle of life, a cycle in which she loved the beginning and mourned the end and enjoyed every moment in between with the perpetual amazement of seeing it for the first time.

She didn't want a big house or a rich husband or genius children. She wasn't eternally questioning the meaning of life. No, she just wanted a simple shelter, food to eat, and a simple man to keep her warm at night and even the man was optional, although she didn't use that word. More like, "maybe a simple man." And maybe she had one, maybe she'd had him all along. But Russet aside, what had she received? None of it. Not a single portion of her humble desires and David prayed, though he seldom prayed anymore, that she might gain some small measure of the happiness she so deserved, that pedestrian happiness that should have been granted with ease and instead ended up being just as hard to win as the complicated, unachievable, evanescent Holy Grail that he spent his life seeking. The complete and utter unfairness of it made him realize why he didn't pray anymore. Then wonder if maybe that was the problem. And this was the result. Or was it the gin talking? No, it was the Thomson women.

A soft tapping knocked its way into his consciousness. He listened. It was real. He went to the kitchen door and cracked it. "You alone this time?" came Angie's voice.

He swung the door open. "Sure. Always. Come in."

"Not always." A slight your-forgiven-asshole smile on her face. "The snow made it a nice night for a walk, fresh and peaceful. I got a call from Russet." The snowflakes straightened and matted her hair and made a bonnet of fluff on her head that she tried to shake off. Most of it fell away, but sparkles tangled with the curls, and flakes fell on her cheeks and her skin radiated vigor.

"They landed?" he asked and tried not to stare, but her look said she noticed.

She smiled. "It was a long conversation. They made Two Harbors and checked into a ritzy hotel."

David grabbed her and hugged her. "That's great." She smelled like snow perfume. He didn't want to let go.

"He mentioned something about Canada, but frankly David, his stuttering was unintelligible. Worst I've ever heard him. Poor guy."

"But you should see him type. Want to come in? Have a drink maybe?"

It looked like she considered it for a fleeting moment that vanished like it never existed. "I should get on with my walk." She gave him a thanks-anyway smile and tightened her scarf. He stepped out on the porch with her. The snow had stopped as suddenly as it started and a thin crescent moon shown between waves of clouds in the black sky, appearing and disappearing like a bobbing cork. He could feel the temperature dropping as he stood there. Maybe they were all back in his life, which would be a bloody miracle. "Will you have dinner with me?" he asked.

"Clarissa and I?" It was not forgotten.

"Just you. We should talk."

"Could give it a try. Nothing elaborate."

"Promise. Tomorrow, then? About five."

She nodded, turned and waved a mitten over her shoulder.

He slouched in his chair with Angie on his mind and dinner and that night in the station wagon and that ephemeral novelty that explodes in first love, bombarding the senses with feelings never imagined, even though they had been imagined often in day dreams and real dreams and vicariously in books and magazines and poems and movies, and even the greatest geniuses in artistic history couldn't bring it to life the way it had been brought to life that night for him. He should be happy it happened at all, but now it was just another golden ring, another American Dream lying out of reach.

***

David felt he kept his promise. It was not an elaborate meal. He scanned the wine shelf for Chardonnay. None. Fish with no Chardonnay? He didn't know if it would matter to Angie, but she was his guest and it mattered to him. With two hours left before her arrival, his truck groaned and finally started in the subzero chill and he drove toward the liquor store.

A hundred yards from the corner, at the entry to the labyrinth, he saw a dim, snowy figure stab the back end of a snowshoe into a drift and bend down. The figure struggled upright. Over its shoulder balanced a long rigid object. David drove closer, arrived at the corner. He stopped at the sign and saw it clearly now, Nick Foulke. The object weighed on him, slung over his shoulder like a heavy mortar. My God, it looks like a frozen body. He swung the truck around the corner and abreast of the man. The body had a face but the top of its head was gone, the flesh blue, translucent and slashed with what looked like Native war paint. David wanted to vomit. He choked it back. Rolled down the window. "Nick, can I help, man?"

Foulke's head rotated slowly toward him, his eyes glazed, solemn, face a combat mask. "No. Almost there. Pvt. Jacob didn't make it. Gooks got him. Give him a decent burial at the base."

David glanced at the body, a boy, a fucking boy. Nick's son? Did Nick kill him? The man was obviously so deep in some trauma dream he didn't know it, or wouldn't accept it, and it didn't matter right now. He stopped the truck, jumped out and opened the tailgate. "Come on, Sergeant. Let me help. Here, put him in my Jeep. Give ya a ride to base."

Nick Foulke turned, faced him, looked him square in the eyes. "Right, Captain. Save time. Gotta get back to my unit. Gook patrol still out there." David folded the back end flat and Nick slid the frozen body in. David closed the gate. Glanced at Foulke. He walked to the passenger door and got in. David slid into his seat. Foulke stared straight ahead, eyes darting to the snow banks and treetops, head a slow moving turret. David drove to the infirmary a half-mile away and backed up to the emergency entry. A nurse appeared, his face quizzical. David vaulted out of the truck and opened the gate.

"Oh shit," the nurse muttered. "I'll get a gurney." Foulke didn't wait. He pulled on the boy's heels, hoisted him and walked through the open door, meeting the nurse, and gently placing the body on the cart. "Rest in peace," he said, no change in expression, and stepped back for the nurse to take over.

David stood there, numb, looking at the boy. He had Foulke's nose and cheekbones, juvenile whiskers, the frost melting now, droplets trickling, some clear, some red, some green. David glanced at the nurse. "Suicide," he said, pointing. "Through the mouth, out the head." David shivered. He looked up for Foulke's reaction. He was not there. David turned. Foulke was already out the door, walking across the snow-covered lawn, toward the woods, not rushing, just a determined slogging step after step. David grabbed the cart for support.

"You alright?" the nurse asked.

"Yeah. I guess. Not used to this. Little dazed."

The nurse watched him closely. "This is Foulke's kid. Treated him a few years back. Axe accident, lost a fingertip. There," he pointed. David saw the missing half of the boy's left forefinger. He gagged. The nurse said, "You're looking a little green around the gills."

David shook his head to clear it. "I'll leave my name and address on the desk."

The nurse nodded. "I'll deal with the authorities. You go home."

David stood at his bar and downed two shot glasses of brandy to calm his shaking hands, then poured some in a tumbler and shuffled to his chair. He sat, staring out the window, light snow again drifting down between the trees, his stomach calmer now, but his mind raced. He could see Nick Foulke stamp snow off his boots and push into some grungy cabin somewhere in the labyrinth and look at his wife thinking she was a nurse or something and tell her Pvt. Jacob didn't make it and see the shock, the grimace of unimaginable pain and grief spread across her face as the words sunk in, like it had happened with Sandy. He'd been there. That was a drunken, meaningless, moronically stupid accident with the same tragic result. A child gone.

What was this? Some twisted second-generation revenge on his boyhood buddy and the guy is so deep in PTSD he didn't even know, didn't even grasp the significance. And his poor wife. For God sake, how can this shit happen? Unending remnants of war right here in this safe little town in the middle of nowhere.

Nick Foulke, one of the smartest and toughest kids in his graduating class, went off to defend our country, defend freedom, life, liberty, the pursuit of happiness and came back to this for a life? Did anybody help him? And who was the enemy he so diligently and skillfully destroyed with his training? A bunch of peasants fighting to the death for the land they farmed with no goddamn interest in political theory or the world stage, just trying to save a rice paddy to feed their family in a jungle halfway around the world—and they got Nick. Or the government got Nick, or Nick got Nick, and because he's so damn smart, he understood his actions and couldn't live with them, but couldn't die either. He was too efficient, nobody could kill him, and he probably prayed everyday that someone would come along and finish the job that should have been finished in that jungle, but instead it's his own son, his own flesh and blood snuffing his own life out at sixteen.

David couldn't put the useless whys out of his head. Why Dani? Why Nick? Why his kid, Jacob? This thinking was pure and utter bullshit. No one could know, including Foulke. Hell, this might be it for him. He might never come out of the jungle now, never know he ever had a son, or if he did know, pull the trigger on himself. The depths of despair, the black-absence-of-hope-without-end can creep in on anyone, does creep in on everyone at times and fighting it can be damn hard. You can lose. And if you do, you can wind up frozen, over a shoulder, like a field-dressed deer, like Pvt. Jacob. "Like me—almost—in this house." His voice echoed, quivering in the silence.

David glanced at the clock. Pull it together. She'll be here any minute. You need to cook, to converse. It seemed so trivial now, but it wasn't trivial. Then it flashed. Elsa may have been the final straw, but the kid killed himself for the complete and utter lack of connection to the outside world, the same thing he, David, did every day.

He reached for his glass, his hand shaking again, picked it up, glared at it and slammed it down. He glanced out the window. Her Subaru turned into his driveway at precisely five o'clock. She got out of the car and came in, smiled, asked if this was a date. He assured her it was an official date. She blushed. Her makeup was natural and perfect. It brought out the new Angie. He noticed her blousy starched cotton shirt, pure white, oversized, two buttons open revealing a gold necklace, and khaki chinos that fit elegantly.

She obviously noticed something, too. "What's the matter, David?"

He set out the appetizer tray and opened a bottle of red wine, poured a glass for each. His hand trembling as he poured. He saw her spot it.

"You look gorgeous," he said.

"David, you're scaring me."

He sighed, glanced out the window. She'll hear it anyway. The macho cover is obviously transparent. "Saw Nick Foulke today. Helped him bring his dead son to the infirmary." He said it without emotion.

"Dead? My God, how?"

"Suicide. Kid blew his brains out."

"Oh my . . . No, no. That's beyond awful." She paused. He saw panic spreading across her face "And Elsa—oh poor thing. We have to call. She'll hear it on TV."

Angie shuffled through her wallet and came up with the scrap paper, the hotel and room number. David got the phone and hoped for the best, but what was that? He stood close beside her. She dialed and tilted the receiver, inviting him in, the desk rang the room. Elsa picked up.

"Hi Grandma. How are you?"

He rolled his eyes, God, was this another test? "Fine dear. How are you? Did you have supper yet?" Angie asked.

"Not yet. We're watching a movie—it's kind a boring."

He sighed, thankfully. "Can I talk to Mom?"

"Sure." The pause, Clarissa came on. "What's up Mom?"

"Don't turn to a news channel. We'll meet you in the bar in say forty minutes. Please don't ask questions. Just for one time in your life do as I've asked."

"Uh, okay. *Oceans* whatever ain't that good anyway. We'll grab some food."

"Perfect. See you soon."

She hung up and went to get her coat. As she put it on, she looked at David, standing there in the kitchen looking very lost. He had no idea where he fit in anymore. "Are you coming?" Angie said.

"Am I invited?"

"Get your parka. I'll drive."

The sky was clear again, stars thick and dropping like the temperature, which headed well below zero. The fitting end to a winter storm. The road was icy, plowed but snow packed, with a dusting of sand on the bad corners and they drove in dignified silence for the first few miles, getting the feel of the road, of each other. They came to a straight stretch, and finally David broke the stillness. "It can go so fast."

"Guess we all know that one," she said, brushing back her hair. The stars and snow gave her a cartoonish, luminous complexion, which he knew he wore too.

"I wanted to clear the air with you, tonight. Tell you I was sorry I hurt you. Really sorry." He paused to let her negotiate a sweeping curve that would have definitely commanded his attention. "I underestimated our relationship. It was a huge mistake. You know, I've never touched her in a sexual way. Which is no excuse. My mind can't make the same claim. Somehow, now it doesn't seem as heartfelt as I imagined it. Kinda trivialized in context."

He saw her glance at his face. She spoke softly. "Look, I accept your apology regardless of the circumstance. You're struggling. I can see it."

"No . . . yes. I'm not very good company. You should've left me home." He paused. "But thanks, I didn't want to be alone."

She navigated another sweeping turn. He could see her thinking. Another curve, a soft silence. "I could use the company, too. Who knows how Elsa will handle this. Maybe I'm making more of it than there is. Maybe she didn't know him that well or something. Teenage girls, how would anyone know?"

"I had Dani and still couldn't tell ya." A first quarter moon rose above the tree line now, the reflection off the snowfields so bright headlights were unnecessary. He could see her face clearly, see the strain in her cheeks, biting her lip. He spoke slowly, softly, like he didn't want to say it and he didn't—he dreaded it. "Uh, not sure how to say this right, but when you and I slept together . . .something was missing." He saw her wince. "No, no, Angie. Let me finish. Wonderful physically, but I, uh, thought some magic spell would make it the night in the station wagon." He stared at the moon. "But that's gone."

She shook her head, swiped at her hair. "I'm a fool too. Hoped for some . . . I don't know . . . rekindling maybe. It could never be the same, but I hoped for something just as good, mature maybe. A chance to build on a base of trust most people don't have."

"I killed that."

"Hey. One in a million shot. We took it. That says something."

He reached over and put his hand on her leg. They drove in silence. He pondered Jacob Foulke's thoughts in the moments before he pulled that trigger and realized that he, David, would die alone like everyone else, but he didn't have to live alone unless he chose to, as he had. That seemed a bad choice today. He felt empathy flowing in from Angie, and knew there were no new frontiers. He sighed. "I gotta get out more."

"Apparently tonight's a forced start."

"How will you handle this?"

She sighed. "Carefully. Separate them, tell Clarissa and ask her what we can do to help. I can't think of another way."

"The ultimate fuck-it-all."

"Can't say I haven't thought about it."

"Me too. Ask your daughter." He sputtered out a satiric chuckle. "We could give classes. Entice unsuspecting locals into our lair and fill their heads with revolution and anarchy. Make them miserable. Send them out to fight the tragic war, chase the impossible dream, change a world with no interest in change. Yes, rip them out of their cozy, complacent, happy lives so they can lie on their death bed and think they failed."

She frowned. "Or . . . we could learn something from them."

They entered town now, and he looked out the window at the rows of houses with muted orange or yellow lights glowing, probably some feeding children, some missing children grown and gone, but even doing that together. "Or that."

The infinite amount of knowledge and wisdom that existed and floated around from all corners of creation seemed to swoop down on him, swamping his mind. Every person big or small, complex or simple, genius or aboriginal, all contributing in some way, all could teach something if he would only listen, only hear.

"Where'd you go?" she asked. The streetlights turning her skin a glowing yellow.

"Acid flashback. Hell, I don't know tonight."

They pulled into the parking lot at the Grand Hotel, smoke rising gray and unwavering from the chimneys, the snow thick on the roof. They found a place in front, near the entry. Their boots crunched the packed snow and breath gushed out in clouds and when the door opened, he smelled chlorine from the indoor pool and winter was gone, his sphere of closeness with it.

They saw Clarissa and Elsa at a table, looking out the window at the frozen lake sprinkled with fish houses in the moonlight. Elsa wore an oversized red sweater, possibly Clarissa's, and jeans, a little rouge on her pale cheeks and a light lipstick to match. She had a cup of hot chocolate in front of her, a marshmallow bobbed. She smiled when she saw Grandma coming, jumped up and ran to hug her. "Thanks. This adventure is getting boring."

Angie put her face on the girl's shoulder, maybe to hide it. David knew she wouldn't thank her in a minute, but he smiled through it, and reached out his hand to shake hers. "We'll try to perk it up," Angie said, and David cringed inside. They waved to Clarissa and started toward the table. Her face wore a serious, impatient look, waiting to get to the bottom of this "thing" whatever it was, which David recognized before Angie could speak. "Elsa, I've forgotten my purse in the car," she said, holding up the keys. "Could you be a dear and get it for me? We're parked right in front."

The girl took the keys and started through the lobby. "Pretty good," David said.

Clarissa stood up, hand on hips. "What the hell is wrong now?"

"Sit please," Angie said. "Jacob Foulke committed suicide. I didn't want my granddaughter to see it on TV."

Clarissa's face turned hard, angry. "Bobby's big fucking pious mouth. I shoulda killed that bastard."

Angie grabbed Clarissa's hands, both of them, and shook them firmly. "He'll wait. Elsa is the priority here. How will you break it to her?"

"Break it? How the hell do you soft-soap suicide? I just got a tell her straight up."

"Right here?" Angie asked.

A hesitation. Elsa was coming in the door. "You're right. In the room," Clarissa said and stood up. They all watched Elsa walk toward them, her hips swaying, in no real hurry at all. "Save our table, David. Here's a room key, have a drink on me. And send mine down when it comes, might need it." Elsa handed the keys and the purse to Angie. "Come on," Clarissa said. "Grandma wants to talk to us in private."

"About what?"

"We'll talk in the room," Angie said.

David stood at the end of the bar, less than patiently waiting to order. They made a damn good Martini here, but with nearly every table overrun by snowmobilers and ice fishermen the service lacked a certain punch. Usually, his patience with cocktail waitresses matched that of Job. He had a deep respect for their critical function, the lubrication of social structure, but if his goal was inebriation he was better off at home. But after watching ice melt off wispy adolescent whiskers and drip down frozen azure skin with a Dad so batshit he didn't recognize his own son, his famous patience plummeted to zero in spite of the cocktail waitresses' cleavage. He gazed absently around the room while he waited his turn at the bar and after he studied all those faces, his attention turned to the dining room.

"What'll it be," the barkeep shouted above the din.

"Gin Martini up, extra dry with an olive," he said, and as the bartender moved to make the drink, David saw them in the dining room. Mayor Harry Barnet and Randy Stark. His heart did an immediate backflip and started pounding, a flock of vultures came home to roost, landing heavily on dead branches with blood dripping off bald, scaly heads, and David recognized each of these paragons of death as if they wore nametags.

The annoyance of an inefficient booze delivery system was no contest against the chickenshit way he'd let his life slide to fit in, though he'd always denied it, to work without distraction. All the low profile, under-the-radar bullshit that he'd done for the last few months sprouted wings, not big black ones like the buzzards, but little pigeon wings and flitted out the window. Jacob Foulke was dead and didn't have a second chance, and David was alive. Theoretically, he did. Denial for the sake of anything had to end no matter the cost. The bartender set the drink in front of him and it was goddamn beautiful, the glass frosted, a big fat green olive skewered with a sword.

David threw a ten on the bar, took that first incredibly cold smooth swig, and methodically walked back to his table. He took one more gulp, set the drink down, and meandered into the dining room wearing a smile as full and false as Ms. Cocktail's tits.

The dining room bustled with waiters and waitresses and bussers. The tables were filled, sounds and smells all chaotically ordered. In LA at this hour, quarter to six, you'd maybe see an Early Bird Special couple dining in the corner, the room empty until the real dinner hour unfolded about seven, but everything was different up here and nothing was different. He paused for a waiter carrying a heavy tray. This wasn't an epiphany that came in one of his stories, but a realization that came to him sluggishly like he was a dullard or something. It had been building unnoticed behind grief and loneliness and failure until those frozen blue lips whispered, "It's time, David." Still it didn't break through until the women left him alone and the service pissed him off and the bartender said, "What'll it be?" and he saw them.

He stood at their table, now. Harry had a tiramisu in front of him, his fork aloft, dressed as the kindly old man but his face didn't register kind. Randy had the look of a bouncer ready to throw someone out, David.

"Gentlemen," David said and let it drip with disdain. He pulled up a chair without waiting for an invitation. "Heard the news?" He paused, glanced man to man. Both looked a little deer-in-the-headlights but he had their attention. "Elsa's sweetheart blew his brains out. Tragic." Harry's eyes blinked. Surprise, guilt or maybe perception? David wasn't sure.

"What did Bobby say this time?" Harry asked, glum.

"Plenty." Now the man looked pained, gazed down, staring at his dessert. David watched him, saying nothing.

"Thanks," Stark said, as if that ended the conversation and David should leave now. But he had no intention of leaving and snared Stark's eyes and held them.

"Randy, Randy, Randy. All our history and now you want me to leave," David said calmly. "I got a couple things to say first, old boy." David dropped his voice an octave and spoke slowly, coolly. "Guess with my good behavior, you might think I forgot or forgave that 'history,' eh Randy. But no. I especially remember you cuffing me in that cell and sticking that little baby dick of yours up my ass."

"You can't prove that," Stark blurted out. David glanced at Harry, who looked like he was about to throw up. Starks eyes flashed, his face beet red.

"Probably can't. Make your life damn miserable, though. By the time the DA got done hearing my story, and that biker dude's you ripped off for that kilo of pot you planted on me. And Angie. God he'd love Angie's story. Wouldn't he Harry?" David glanced at him, then paused and stared Stark straight in the eyes, slowed down even more. "Conviction or not, you'd have a damn grand time."

Stark's fists were clenched now. He leaned forward, toward David. That's when he saw it, a cold calculated hatred, capable of anything. "I'll . . ." Stark started.

"Careful," David interrupted. He had him now, and looked at Harry again, his dessert untouched, face blanched. "Hey, you wanna have it out right here, fine with me. Just stand up." Now David leaned in, too. "Just stand up." Stark didn't move. "That's what I thought. Guys that can rape young girls and boys ain't really men anyway, are they, Randy?"

"You bastard," Stark growled.

David smiled again, phony as he could make it. "And ya know, I was ready to forget all that 'history,' until somebody fucked up a teaching job I had locked. Until somebody shot at me. But I'm biding my time, Randy. I think there's more. What do you think, Harry?" David riveted Harry's eyes. The man looked scared, beaten and embarrassed. David waited.

"I think it's time to go, Randy," Harry said.

David pushed his chair back and stood up. "Me too," he said and bowed slightly. "Gentlemen." He ambled off in no apparent hurry at all.

The women were back, seated at their table when he came out of the dining room. Clarissa had a half-full tumbler of brown liquid in front of her with a beer back, half empty, and her face said, "Talk. I dare you." If she had seen David, it didn't register.

Angie sipped what looked like a Manhattan by the cherry, and looked like she'd survived a close encounter with a two-by-four, but barely. A dazed sadness held her captive and multiplied each time she glanced at Elsa, who sat straight-backed, her head bowed slightly, eyes down, knees together, hands folded primly in her lap. Her gaze didn't waver. She'd changed into black jeans and a black sweatshirt.

David sucked in a breath. This was the greeting for a friendly face? He tried to imagine the scene if Bobby walked through the door. The image of a frozen, cerulean face returned, and he thought *if Jacob is up there watching, maybe he sees the profound impact he's had on all these lives.*

He passed the corner of the bar now, moving toward the table. It was a small room and he could see his ruined Martini on a coaster before an empty chair, and he wondered if there was anything he could say or do to make this better. Sometimes fewer words are best. He went to Elsa, knelt beside her and said, "My condolences."

He sat in the empty seat, picked up the stemmed glass, and softly said, "To Jacob." Then dumped it down. Angie lifted her glass, Clarissa her beer. Elsa reached across, grabbed Clarissa's tumbler and drained it, set it down and went back to staring at her hands, again folded in her lap.

David saw Harry and Randy coming out of the dining room, toward him, Harry leading. Randy hanging back. Harry had his overcoat on, gloves cinched in one hand, and a solemn expression. He focused on Elsa to the exclusion of the rest. When he got to her, he put a hand on her shoulder. She didn't move, nor look up.

"I'm so sorry to hear of your loss, my darling." His head tipped toward her. "I'll help if I can." He didn't move. She didn't either. Her hair cascaded, covering her face.

"It was my father's fault," Elsa said from behind the hair.

"I'm sure the boy had other issues, too," Harry said, softly.

Clarissa could not contain herself a second longer. "You can help by telling that freak-show fundamentalist fuck-up that I'll be over to get her stuff. He can keep the crap he thinks are clothes." She knocked back the beer, turned and raised her arm. The waitress saw her and she made a helicopter twirl with her hand.

Angie heard the sniffle behind the hair, leaned over, and wrapped an arm around Elsa. Angie obviously took this as her charge tonight, refusing to acknowledge Harry or Randy or their version of history, focusing on the present, her granddaughter, probably remembering the desultory blackness grief extracts from youth that she and David had discussed, something familiar and ugly that David knew all about, too. He glanced at Randy. Contrition replaced the murderous eyes now and David wondered where it went, what happened so quickly? Was it a reprimand by Harry or a self-made decision arrived upon, finalized, and prepared for execution. In a McCarthy novel, one of them would be dead already, but this story was real life and still unfolding and he felt oddly calm as if the cards he held he would play to the end win or lose.

He watched the scene with a strange detachment for the moment, Elsa rudely ignoring Harry, him taking it, Angie mothering, Clarissa seething, Stark in the background lurking, the surreal quality of it all amid the jovial, booze-addled bar patrons made him feel displaced as if they'd all been dropped here from another planet by accident. The waitress served fresh drinks and he sipped his, his expression constant, confident, which was easy when you're a stranger and he was a stranger to himself right now. He heard Harry say: We'll pray for his soul on Sunday. And Elsa say: Without me. And Harry say: We need to have you there. He saw Elsa turn away. And Clarissa say: She'll go if and when she's ready and not a damn minute before. The anti-Christ ain't calling the shots anymore, ever. He watched Harry scowl, recover, take his leave and drag Stark with him, and as they walked away, they seemed to take away an aura of menace with them. David missed it. The hostess came to their table and said Harry had bought dinner for everyone, and she could seat them in the dining room, to which Angie nodded and Clarissa snarled out an expletive. He came out of it when Clarissa said, "I'm sick of this party. Let's get really expensive room service. You two can bunk up in our room tonight. We can all cram in."

Angie seemed to consider it. "But it'll be twenty below by morning. The car won't start unless it's plugged in. We should go. What do you think, David? David?"

What he was thinking was how strangeness can get out of hand, how weird he'd feel waking up in a room filled with Thomson women, and would it be the floor for him or a bed with Angie and who would choose? The veiled glare Stark threw as he left was another example. Even a few days ago, it would have plucked a chord of foreboding but not tonight. There was something cleansing about throwing caution to the wind, walking into that dining room, and facing his tormenters, actually saying the word "rape" in their presence and humiliating his rapist in front of the man's obvious best friend. The toast, "To Jacob," may have meant different things to each of them at that table, to David it meant the beginning of a freedom he had scratched and fought for and never truly achieved in thirty-plus years—*so prayers for your eternal life, Jacob, and thanks for the gift you left me*. Strange maybe, but it felt damn good and he didn't want to tarnish it with questionable sleeping arrangements. "We should probably go."

***

David's eyes snapped open at four-thirty the next morning, a solid three hours before first light. The tired, groggy lethargy that greeted him most mornings since he'd arrived in his little house gave way to a sharp clarity, a quick lucidity, and he jumped out of bed, threw on some clothes, and made for the kitchen. As he ground coffee beans, he thought of his conversation with Angie on their way home. Her sympathy when he told her about the confrontation with Harry and Randy, and the I-don't-give-a-shit-anymore look on her moonlight illuminated face when she almost casually told him that back in the dark time, Randy nursed an affinity for the wrong entrance and "took me that way more times than I care to remember." The callous comment, "tighter than Angie" made sense now, and in the transparency of morning, it pissed him off even more, but last night it was more like a war wound he and Angie had suffered together that brought them closer, a bond so perverse yet so solid it shined like a diamond extracted by the dead, and soothed them, making the slow, slippery drive vanish in an instant.

As the coffee brewed, David booted up his laptop and opened the file containing his new book. Drudgery and skepticism evaporated and his fingers flashed as he typed notes in the trepidation that he might forget, or worse, never be granted this incredible state again. He wished he had a picture of Jacob to post for inspiration, but only the image of frozen flesh remained and the juxtaposition of running away and running toward elicited a moment of sadness. He heard the coffee pot chirp and fetched the entire carafe and a cup, poured up, and went straight to work. Three hours later at eight o'clock, a knock on the door interrupted the scene playing in his mind that he typed like crazy trying to keep up, not knowing or caring if it was good or bad, just getting it down on the page. The knock came again, and he emerged from his trance, heart thumping, exhausted, and ready for a break. He stood, stretched, and glanced at the page number. Twenty pages added this morning, many times his normal output. He smiled and headed to the door.

Angie knocked a third time just he got there. He saw her face through the window and almost smiled again until the thought hit him that something might be wrong to be at his door so early. "Everything all right?" He gestured for her to come in.

"I got a call from Russet—it took a half hour. They're moving around. There's hundreds of motels on Lake Superior, seems they intend to sample a bunch of them. He wants us to meet them today. At Cove Point Lodge."

"Where's that?"

"Beaver Bay. It's ritzy. I reserved a room for each of us. Avoid the bed question." She smiled now, the radiant smile of the old Angie that he'd been hopelessly in love with. He hadn't seen that smile in person since the night in the station wagon, and it looked so good on her that the urge to hug her overpowered him, but he beat it.

He laughed instead. "How're you feeling?"

She paused. "Ya know, pretty good I think." Then the smile again. "We can catch lunch if we hurry." A reference to him standing there in his pajamas and bathrobe that inferred get a move on. A long comfortable drive, lunch, and an overnighter for reasons unknown, how could he turn that down?

"I can be ready in half an hour. Let me drive, we'll leave your car in your driveway for Stark to ponder. No question he'll be roving every night now."

The shortcut through the labyrinth wasn't plowed yet, so they took County Road 21 north, the same road they traveled the night before, and immediately settled into an easy peace until the sweeping corner where they turned off on the Blueberry Cutoff that took them east, then north to meet up with Highway 1, which meandered south and east through dense forests and frozen swamps, rivers and lakes.

With the recent snowfall, it was a fairyland. Plows had thrown splatters of snow that stuck high up on the sides of pine trees, white against the dark brown bark, the snow banks seemed to envelope them, and the farther they drove, the more complete the escape from their lives, their pasts, their present, their problems melted away in the sunny sparkle and they talked effortlessly about anything and nothing, animals and birds and trees, then houses as they came through Finland, and turned on Lake County Road 4, past the State Park, past Lax Lake, down the escarpment to the stop sign at Highway 61. "Should we sing it?" Angie asked, grinning.

"God said to Abraham, kill me a son," he sang, off key and horrible, which made her laugh louder.

"Down on Highway 61. Take a right here," she giggled.

They wound down the long driveway to the big log building hard on the lake. The snow banks were high, lake effect maybe, as he dragged their suitcases out of the back end, the frigid cold biting at his face, but inside the great room spread before them to a huge rock fireplace against the lake-side wall where logs crackled and he saw Bunny sitting on a sofa by the fire. Angie dealt with registration. He set the cases down and walked across the room toward the fire. Bunny wore a bright colored sweater with a matching beret and didn't hear him approach until he stood beside her and said, "Hi Bunny. How ya doing?"

She looked up at him. "P-pretty d-darn good. Th-thanks."

He sat down beside her, stunned, not expecting that in any way. "When did this all start?"

"After your house. I-I'm not v-very good yet. Stutter a-a-alot. Like Russell."

He leaned close and hugged her. "Guess this is what the trip was for."

Her face clouded over. "Not ex-exactly."

Angie arrived, smiling, holding two room keys and went to her sister and hugged her long and tight. David said nothing. He didn't want to ruin the surprise. Bunny's head rested on Angie's shoulder, facing David. He thought he saw her wink and heard the scratchy voice, "H-hi, A-angie." Angie pushed back, held her sister by the shoulders and stared. "Do that again," she said.

Bunny grinned. "Hi, s-sis. R-ready for l-lunch?"

"You bet. Here David," Angie said, handing him the two keys. "Take whichever room you want, but drag my bags along, too. I'm going to actually talk to my sister again."

The comment "not exactly" gave him cause for concern and broke the spell he'd been under since they left. He saw Russet outside on the patio, stamping and brooming snow off his boots and pants, which looked like might take a little time, so he grabbed the suitcases and headed off to find the rooms. They were two adjoining rooms actually, one no different from the other, just the mirror image, with tiny kitchenettes, a queen bed, a fireplace and a window overlooking the vast expanse of Lake Superior. He left Angie's things in one and brought his to the other. He hung up his parka and found the wool shirt to wear indoors.

Then, pulled out his laptop and plugged it in. He originally thought he might get a little writing time in the morning before anyone else woke up, but the "not exactly" meant something else.

They ate a traditional lunch with a selection of casseroles, meatballs, lingonberry jam, smoked whitefish, pickled herring and boiled potatoes served smorgasbord style with strong coffee and light conversation. The tough stuff would come soon enough. "So, why are we here again, Russet?" Angie asked, and glanced from his face to her sister's. The cloud David saw cross Bunny's expression earlier returned. Russet wore its twin. "It . . .it's com . . . plicat . . . ed, c-c-complicated" Russet stammered and signed something to Bunny, fingers flying.

David nodded. "I'll get the computer," he said and clapped Russet lightly on the back. He nodded back, signing and stuttering, "Y-y-yes . . . g-good i-i-dea."

They commandeered a window table in the corner, away from everything, and gathered around the screen. Bunny started signing and Russet staccato typing, David and Angie watched the words appear. Bunny's recollection started at an LSD party, Stark attacking her, Dad freaking, screaming, hiding, Bea naked and wanton, Mom and Bea kissing, touching, Mom and Harry fighting over Bea, about their future, which proved short. Safe, small town innocence gone in one night. David watched Bunny, the pain coming in waves and he wished he could freeze it like the lake outside the window, but he was powerless. The only comic relief was the fight Bunny and Russet had over him running away and leaving her on the stairs as the shooting began. Bunny was so angry with him that it took half a day to calm her down enough to make her believe he had run when he saw Stark pointing the pistol, but at the first shot, ran back and hauled Bunny off the porch and into hiding around the back of the house. It might have saved her that day, but what about today? Today was the question. Bunny wrung her hands, trying to act calm and failing miserably, looking from David to Angie and back with a befuddled expression that said: help us, we have no idea what to do now. "Th-they w-watched me in the h-hospital."

"Glad Clarissa isn't here," Angie said.

David caught Angie's battered eyes and slashed his own throat with a finger. "Let's take a quick break," he said and motioned for Angie to follow. "Type on if you want. We'll catch up." He touched Angie's elbow and gently led her away. When they got to the hallway leading to their rooms, she spoke first.

"It's gut-wrenching. I had no idea."

"Yes," he said, and moved his arm from her elbow to around her waist. "I don't know about you, but the emotion was drowning me. That won't help. They need us strong and objective."

With Bunny's revelations piled on top of his own crap, objectivity fled faster than patrons in a burning bar, and he knew it. They arrived at the rooms. He slipped the key into Angie's lock, opened the door, and handed her the key. "Grab your coat. Let's walk a little."

She surveyed the room. "Adjoining rooms?" The parka slipped over her shoulders, her arm reached out, snapped open the interior lock. "But let's walk anyway."

When they got back, Russet scrolled down to the place he marked when they left. "The e-ending is w-worse," he said, and pulled Bunny close. David put a hand on each of their shoulders, thinking how lucky they were to have each other—still. David and Angie read in silence, their agreement to rise above it, pretend to be lawyers, remained in tact, but traces of that fear that left him so completely yesterday crept back and he found himself praying again at the alter of the cerulean face, searching for strength. He couldn't tell what Angie drew upon, but she seemed to hold steady too. They finally came to the end. Harry was in this up to his elbows, but Stark was the loose cannon. David caught Angie's attention and arched his brow. She rolled her eyes, their war wound bond solid. He looked at Russet and Bunny, their fear factor preparing to launch. "You were right to run," David said in a measured tone. "I think we should print those pages, have Bunny sign it, and bring it to the DA. You two should head south. Minneapolis or maybe Des Moines. Far away."

Bunny's face crinkled, she turned to Angie. "I'm scared," she said. Angie nodded.

David lay in bed, in the dark, thinking of Russet and Bunny holding hands, comforting each other as they'd done for years only now they weren't hiding for the moment. Okay, they were, but not from friends and family anymore, and a few allies were better than none. And he'd fight like it was his own war—because it was. He was a victim, too. Albeit one with light wounds compared to the others. He should be thankful, but in fact, he was ready for this war. A faint sound broke in, a tapping he remembered from the dark times, at his bedroom window. It came from the interior door. He crawled out of bed and went to it, listened. It came again. He turned the lock, cracked the door. "David?"

"Yes."

"Are you decent?"

"Yes."

"Can I come in?"

"Yes."

She pushed through the door and wrapped her arms around him. "I'm scared."

"Me too. But ready."

He woke in the dark. She slept close, spooned to his back, and he remembered not kissing her, not caressing her nor she him, just two friends, real friends now, that needed each other and *were* there for each other. A thought of intimacy pushed in, only human, but dispatched, then the urge to write, to write this, all of it, in detail, complete with hopes and fears and faults and frailties, dreams, monumental aspirations—until Jacob came to him. He snuggled closer, took her limp hand, and closed his eyes again. Daylight would come soon enough and there was much to do.

Chapter Twenty Nine

David finally sat in his own leather recliner. The one with the padded arms, where he could spread his legs, relax completely without some slab of wood stabbing into his thighs, which he did for the first time in three days. Three unread newspapers lay in his lap. He undid that paperboy's fold and smiled. It was the old way, the way papers used to be folded before the advent of cheap rubberbands, with one side tucked securely into the other, another reminder of where he lived. And that he liked it. But tonight it was all toxic and had been since the drive with Angie from Virginia. He had spent so much time over these last days with Angie that he had to admit, if only to himself, that he missed her company. Maybe the attraction with romantic love was overrated, and this stuff, this friendship led to mature satisfaction without the baggage carried along with romance. But history can be turbulent and the wheels of justice turned slowly if at all. Jacob had started out whispering, but had shouted since he watched Russet and Bunny's taillights recede into the night headed south looking for safety, the cell phone Angie bought them tucked between them. The whole ordeal another bond. It takes a while to get a pot really boiling but critical mass seemed achieved.

It now rested in the hands of professionals, purported to know what they were doing. Could he trust that? The drive home seemed inhabited by a third party, much silence, much thought. Too much history. Too much injustice. His pistol was loaded and laid beside the papers. Was it time? Would Angie feel it, too? He hoped not.

He opened the first paper and scanned the headlines, flipped through the sections still skimming. A diversion from the inevitable, from Jacob, from the deer slayer, from the madman churning inside him. We The People hadn't had a good war in a while, except Afghanistan and that didn't seem to film very well, too brown, too mountainous, not enough speed, not enough shock and awe, for God sake what were they thinking. We The People liked the last Iraq war, long on bombs bursting in air and short on casualties. It filmed well and had a nice clean, tidy feel going for it here in America. Sure, he felt befuddled after 9/11 like everyone else, and look where his life had evolved to since then. Damn history. We The People were still on edge, and buying into this terrorist thing like land in Florida, and putting pressure on We The Congress who folded like a cheap suitcase.

Around here things were pretty cut and dried. He knew who the terrorists were. The same as they'd been for thirty-plus years, Harry and Randy, and someone delivering a little reality check and a warrant wasn't going to change that one damn bit. He doubted he could trust the sheriff's department to do this right any more than he could trust Stark. Sure, he hoped he could, but it occurred to him that he wanted to be there. He had to be there. His thoughts clarified, sharp and cold like the air outside. In fact, he dearly wanted to kill Stark himself. He stood. Picked up the pistol, Dad's Smith & Wesson revolver. Time to get this done.

David drove out of town toward Auto's Place. He'd rethought his choice of weapons, deciding on the semi-automatic Walther .32 with its nine shot clip and plenty of stopping power. Faster, more reliable, and he'd gone through over a thousand rounds at the range with it. The pistol was loaded and tucked under his seat, an extra clip in his parka pocket, and a strange sense of calm for which he couldn't account. Maybe is was Jacob's inspiration or possibly the years of hate metastasized into this moment which had started upon reading Bunny's narrative, festered at the DA's office in Virginia, and reached its head an hour ago. That wasn't important. Focus was important. Calm was important. He would call the bastard out, make him shoot first. Then blaze away and hope for the best.

It was ten o'clock when he saw Auto's Place and cut the headlights and turned on the road, driving slowly in moonlight off the snow. He didn't see Auto standing in his garage ready to light a joint, but Auto saw him, without headlights.

The temperature hovered at twenty below now, and David stopped in Starks driveway, eyeing the house. He saw houselights start to go dark until it was completely black. Angie's Subaru pulled beside him, lights out too. The field of snow between him and Stark's porch illuminated by the fluorescent streetlight, the moonlight, and that porch too far away for a confident shot. He got out of his Rover and held the Walther pistol in his right hand, tucked in the parka pocket, his other hand on the clip in the other pocket, and motioned for Angie to roll down her window. "Get out of here," he said.

"Not on your life, David. I earned it." Her voice fatally flat. Her shotgun lay stock up in the passenger seat and she reached for it and slowly opened her door, slid out, and stood behind it.

"Please," he said.

"Forget it."

"Then stay down." He walked toward Stark's porch, across the vast car-park and stood some hundred feet away, the pistol out, dangling beside his leg. "They're coming for you Stark," he shouted. "Murder one. You killed Sue Thomson." He paused and the sound echoed off the surrounding trees. "Not to mention the rest of it. Might as well come out now."

The door opened and Stark darted onto the porch. David saw a pistol in each hand, one rose and fired. He felt a hot flash in his thigh, ducked, rolled, and fired prone five quick shots. All misses.

He rose to his knees. Stark came down the steps, and David aimed and fired four more. He saw Stark recoil. A hit. Then Stark's arm came up, and *pop, pop*. David felt the pain shoot through his chest. His shooting arm went numb. He pulled the clip from his other pocket and clumsily grabbed the Walther with his left hand.

He saw a movement in the shadow as he tried to eject the spent clip and jam a full one in. Stark's good arm was coming up again. David heard a blast, then darkness, the tinkle of glass raining on the snow. The streetlight went out.

Only moonlight remained. He glanced toward the sound and saw Auto running toward him. The whole sordid scene in slow motion now. Stark coming at him, arm up, outstretched, pointing, aiming. David rolled away, toward his truck, ignoring pain with each revolution. He heard a *pop,* then he shot again. Stark was close.

He glanced left and saw Angie shouldered her weapon, saw Stark turned toward her, *pop, pop, pop*. He heard bullets hitting metal, and saw Stark turn again, pointing down at him. He shot two quick ones. Stark stumbled. Maybe a leg hit. Stark's other arm straightened, gun aimed. A flashlight beam hit him.

David heard a shotgun blast from his left, saw Stark recoil, a belly hit. His face a grimace as he pointed a weapon at David. "Now you die," Stark said.

David heard shotgun blasts from the right and the left. Part of Stark's face disappeared. David rolled again and managed to get up on his good knee. He saw Angie behind her car door, shotgun smoking, aiming, waiting. Stark bleeding, still breathing. Auto ran up to him, shotgun trained on Stark.

"What the fuck are you two doing?" Auto shouted. "You fucking nuts?"

Red and blue lights swirled now, coming up the road, sliding to a stop, doors opening. An officer shouting, "Everybody drop your weapons—now." Squad cars maneuvered headlights toward the scene. David saw Auto slip off the flashlight clip and drop the shotgun, holding the flashlight, slipping the clip in his parka pocket.

Cops rushed in, surrounded everyone, guns shouldered. They moved closer, slowly now. David saw a leg kick out twice. Stark's pistols kicked away. He saw an officer bend over and touch the body, heard him say, "Call an ambulance."

The crackle of voices smeared with radio static echoed through the trees. David thought it quiet but for the radio chatter. Amazingly nothing hurt yet.

***

Two days later, David sat at his bar, bandaged, numb with Vicoden, a gin in front of him. The events sank in slowly, becoming part of him, dual edged. On one edge, he felt elation, justice served with a swift and final blow, people liberated from a specter that hung over their lives even after the real threat dissipated, and the beauty of the final irony. The ones most wounded. He was glad he'd been there, at the scene, gun in hand.

He thought back to his years of youth in the wilderness, hunger, agony, and pain. The stained reputation his parents endured until their final breath escaped their lips. The desolate loneliness Angie suffered. The thirty-some years of life stolen from Bunny, beautiful children she could never carry, a love to give more pure and bright than anything on this earth, and that was only a small part of it, only the part he could wrap his mind around right now.

He heard the faint knock and yelled, "It's open." Angie entered. Glum, sorrowful. He haunts her even in death, David thought. He wanted to count coup, scalp Stark with a wicked slice, a depraved rip, and dance and sing on the bastard's grave. He wanted to shake Angie and yell, we're free, be happy, he's gone and can never come back, but then realized it was still there in him, too. No one left to blame but himself.

The hatred that was central in his life, the focus of years of wandering, wondering what would have been different without that watershed event, but knowing that every life has volcanic events at every stage. That in youth they blew harder and higher, knocking off more than the top of the cone but the entire side of the mountain, the death of innocence, the demise of naiveté, filling Spirit Lake, and remaking the landscape into a moonscape unidentifiable. And yes, it was a wasted thought, a foolish, childish exercise in blame-laying and back-looking that real men shouldn't do, but he did it anyway.

Angie sat beside him. He saw her mournful glance and knew they had to make this a beginning, bury the ghosts and hatred, locate a new center to nurture them both.

He put his hand on hers. "Want to talk a little?" He dumped a splash of gin in her glass. Her feet dropped from their perch, limp.

"Thanks," she said. He put an arm around her shoulders. Her eyes were sad, a thinking, feeling sadness that spanned some unknown spectrum of emotions. "I guess it hurts because he's dead and the town won't know Dad was innocent or Harry's part. Just doesn't seem fair."

"The town shouldn't matter." He pulled her closer and rubbed her arm. "But it will know. Clarissa will make sure of that. You and I—all of us, need to let go, get on with our lives. We've made progress. We'll make more. Big leaps."

She looked straight ahead at nothing. A clipped sarcastic chuckle. "That's the crap they feed the troops, David."

"Yeah, I know."

"The excuses are gone. Don't know how I'll handle it."

He sighed. "We'll worry tomorrow. Tonight we drink, celebration or not."

David awoke in his chair. A couple hours had passed since Angie left and the knocked-out sleep revived him enough that he didn't feel ready for bed. He sat there, reading the Wolfe book again. The end was near and Webber was reinventing himself, hacking away the past, time and memory. David pondered that wisdom. Metamorphosis for what? To move on to something else, something new and unknown. Is that the American way? Never look back, never go home again, careening forward at any cost: physical, emotional, spiritual, chasing your tail inside your little box until your heart explodes?

Chapter Thirty

It was still very cold. Angie had started her car in David's driveway and came back in to let it warm a little but more to be with him, make sure he would be all right. David was stretched out in his club chair, obviously a bit uncomfortable and dozing when she came back inside.

"You okay?" she'd asked and his eyes popped open, glassy and bloodshot.

"Sure. Fine."

"I could stay," she said and considering the pain medications and the gin he drank against doctor's orders and his lapse into unconsciousness, that was probably the right thing to do though he had insisted she sleep in her own bed tonight. That had made her wonder but he was a man and they all had some weird streak that originated genetically requiring a cave when wounded which she would never understand. Tonight she was too wounded and tired herself to argue. His eyelids dropped again and she waited and watched but his breathing seemed regular and strong, and with a surgical nurse living just a few blocks away, leaving seemed safe enough. She was too drunk to drive or to argue. A short trip to his room and she returned with a blanket and covered him. He muttered, "Thanks," without opening his eyes.

Another trip to his bedroom took longer having to search for a second blanket and seeing his room again reminded her of Thanksgiving in his bed. It seemed like someone else or years removed. All they had been through together since then had formed bonds not based on an ancient romance but on themselves, in the present, and that thought warmed her. She wondered if he felt it too. This room also reminded her of stealing his underwear for the

DNA test and she still felt guilty about it but nothing could be done about that now. She found a blanket, went back to the living room, then out to her car and turned it off hoping it would start when she decided to leave.

Maybe these bonds she felt were not shared. He hadn't mentioned anything like that, but as she curled up in the other club chair beside him and wrapped herself in the blanket, she realized they hadn't had time for that sort of conversation. And after the Stark day and night, and a day and a half at the hospital, that winter wonderland ride to Cove Point Inn where the world had disappeared leaving them in some fantasy together seemed like a long time ago. But what a great day and a great night. Would it go anywhere? She didn't know and doubted he did either. Her wound shot a sharp pain.

She looked over at him. His breathing was strong and regular though she could smell a whiff of gin. The doctor said he was lucky. One bullet grazed his chest but missed the organs, the other a flesh wound in his calf, no bones hit. It could have gone another way if Auto hadn't appeared. In the ambulance, David had said they were lovers not fighters. A fond thought. Other thoughts weren't.

As she had driven toward Stark's place that night, all she could remember was the hatred. He had killed her mother and degraded her body and she could almost feel his hands on her hips, holding her, and kneading her breasts, her thighs, and had wanted to kill him then. Then thinking that was wrong but that blood lust would not dissipate until he came out of his house holding a pistol in each hand and firing at David. She had remained calm, knowing the shot was too long for her shotgun, waiting, until David was hit and Stark turned and blew out her door window. Then it had changed to fear, thinking they'd come all this way and now David would be dead and none of it would matter.

Seeing Auto appear under Stark's streetlight, aiming and blowing it to blackness as Stark was aiming at David, and when Auto's flashlight beam hit Stark, she had aimed at his dick, missing twice, and in near panic, found the sighting bead and filled his belly with number four shot.

Without Auto, they would both be dead now. Stark had shot her in the leg, a nick above her knee, and she hoped it would scar and decided she would buy some short skirts to show it off, finally show off her runner's legs. It throbbed. Nothing like David's she was sure. In the chaotic aftermath, the wild intensity of emotions bled out leaving nothing but numb shock.

As the fire burned down to coals, it took some of her emotion with it. Since that night, she had felt guilty about feeling happy. But damn it, she was glad he was dead and remembered telling David, "It's strange, like I feel free for the first time in my adult life. Maybe feeling guilty about being happy, but damn it, David, I am happy. Or maybe at ease. Don't know yet, too new. My mind keeps going back to all those times he fucked me. He knew I hated it and did it anyway." Some angry bile welled up inside her and she knew she'd shoot the son of a bitch again if she had the chance.

"What are you doing," David said, his eyes open, obviously surprised.

"Nothing. A little too drunk to drive is all." It was like he had invaded her space.

"Okay. Good night." He rolled his head and was out again.

In the city, he would still be in the hospital but up here they were more interested in collecting the bill than making it larger, and stopping by a house to check on a patient was technically long gone, but in reality, it happened when necessary. She had vacationed in cities a few times, and knew why she stayed up here. Without Stark it would get even better, of that she was sure. Harry still presented problems. She could see his face melt when she and Clarissa had stopped to deliver the news. She maintained a hatred for him, but nothing compared to what Clarissa had developed. The scene played in her head like it was happening right now:

She'd watched Clarissa's car stop in front of Harry Barnet's home, and parked behind her. Clarissa boot-skated up the slick driveway, leaped onto the veranda, and rang the bell ten times. She beat on the door. Angie limped, the painkiller wearing off. It was getting light, another cold morning. Harry was probably up already. Before there was an answer, Angie stood beside her. "I'm not as wild as you. But I might catch up."

"Just here to protect David's bet, eh? You ain't fooling me."

"We're friends."

"Sure. There, he's coming. Now, let me do the talking," Clarissa said.

His face appeared behind the curtain, the lock clicked. The door opened. "Clarissa? Uh, oh, Angie. What's the occasion?"

Clarissa barged in. "Hear about Stark?" She paused, stared at him, waiting for an answer. "He shot David and Angie before somebody blew his brains out. I figure that's pretty damn good news for you, eh? No one left now to rat out your part in this little tragedy."

He didn't smile. His hands covered his face, then dropped. Angie saw the tears.

"You're alone in that sentiment," Clarissa said. "Listen, I'm heading down to the café, then the bar. Defend my honor, eh. I feel like talking. Wanna come? Give you a chance to defend yourself."

"Say what you will." He looked even older, sad and defeated.

"Whatever. The town ain't stupid. I know the truth now. You and your puppet are responsible for the destruction of five lives, not counting mine. I've lived as the third-generation town whore since I was old enough to know what it meant. That makes six. Six lives you've twisted for some goddamn reason. We're a little leper colony, while you ran the town and Stark lived in luxury." She paused, glared at him, enunciated clearly. "I am done with you. I see through your lies. I want no part of you, none of your time, and none of your cries for help or sympathy. I don't want you around my daughter. Just your goddamn money—that's all I want. When you die, I'll spit on your grave. Fuck you, Harry. And fuck the curse you put on the Thomson women. I hope you rot in hell."

His face reddened. He looked at Angie. "My sympathies for your loss," she said.

"You turned her against me."

This pause was long, a sadness falling over Angie, too. "No Harry. You did that yourself. I'm sorry," she said and limped away.

Clarissa stared at him, her hands on her hips, saying nothing. When he didn't speak either, she smiled. "Well, it's been real."

Nights like that should be reserved for nations at war, she thought. Angie checked David again, touching his forehead which did not feel feverish, and hearing his breath still strong, finally nodded off herself.

She awoke, chilly, a little after two am, and gently placed her blanket over him and slipped out the door. Her head was heavy and her bed beckoned, she crawled in, but sleep was halting and elusive, her mind filled with competing thoughts and emotions that should have been easy to reconcile, but were not. She laid there and wished she could be more like her daughter with that black-and-white character, definitions of right and wrong that defied convention but stood completely clear to her. She should be like Clarissa, able to hate Harry as much as she hated Stark. The grounds seemed endless and indisputable, and she'd had years of practice, but watching his face crumble that night when hit with the news of Randy Stark made her gloomy and sympathetic.

She couldn't exonerate him, but human decency demanded better than hate. Maybe the prospect of Bunny's safety prompted it, or hate focused so fully on Stark there wasn't enough left to distribute. Harry was indeed old and sick, seemed to look worse with each passing day and using hate against him, as a wedge to separate him from his beloved granddaughter could only be categorized as cruel. More cruel than public degradation, though that had a few spikes too, but in the pool of public opinion Harry always seemed to escape drowning some way.

She'd have to talk to Clarissa and Elsa. He was flawed and the list of grievances was as long as it was creative, but this was wrong. No, people had forgiven a multitude of Clarissa's indiscretions and most of hers as well, no matter the misunderstanding, and Clarissa needed to buck up. And so did Elsa. The town was tiny and they all had to live here.

Her circular thinking whirled around Bunny too, then Russet, then them as a couple, and even David and where that might be going until sometime past three in the morning all the circles collapsed and she mercifully fell asleep.

At ten the next morning, Angie waited for the coffee to brew while sleepily sorting through days of mail, junk, ads, bills, solicitations. Then, there it was. An adrenaline spike blew away grogginess. She was wide awake now. The

VeriLabs logo on the return address. Her desire to spare herself exactly this emotional conundrum during the holidays had inspired waiting until February 1st to send the package out. She froze. Her heart suddenly rapping like a hard rain on a tin roof. Just as suddenly, she regretted sending out those samples at all, regretted the subterfuge, regretted even entertaining the question instead of leaving well-enough alone, although well-enough was not the true state. When that envelop was opened something or things would forever change. The box could not be closed. This was irreversible.

She shuffled the bills into one pile, the junk mail into another, leaving the envelope unopened in front of her chair. The coffee pot gurgled. She grabbed the bills and put them away, stuffed the junk into recycling, and poured a cup of coffee. Anything to not confront it. It stared at her from the table, taking on a life already, and she considered burning it unopened. Lives would be affected, certainly hers, not Stark's in death, maybe Harry's, David's, Clarissa's, Elsa's, but surely hers. She felt she could handle her part. Maybe nothing would change except a concrete certainty. Or. The "or" made her want to start the fire. Then again, she was a proven expert at keeping secrets if necessary, and she had to admit curiosity was killing her right now. But the lab kept her file for six months, so even if she burned it now, the answer was accessible and a moment of weakness later would land her right back in this place.

The table wasn't dirty, but she wiped it down anyway, set her cup down, and picked up the envelope. The flap opened like it came pre-opened but she picked at it anyway, slowly, as if intent to save the wrapping, exquisite torture. Finally she pulled it out and flipped it open, read it. "Oh my God. Why did I do that? Why the FUCK did I do that?" She got up and built a fire.

Chapter Thirty One

David put on his suit and a tie. This was one of the downsides of small towns, the funerals. His nemesis would be prayed over today by people that liked him and those that didn't because he was a fellow citizen and that's the way it was done. Like selling a car—all the parking tickets disappear. Brutus was wrong. So he would put on his good suit, go to a strange church, Baptist, listen to the service which might do him some good, certainly wouldn't hurt, and endure the eulogy without standing and yelling, "That's bullshit," even if it was.

The word had leaked out, shouted out by Clarissa was more accurate, of the damage Stark had inflicted on David's life but that was past and this was present and he would show he was a man and do the right thing in front of God and everyone. He wondered if Angie and Clarissa would do the same. He wouldn't blame them if they chose otherwise, especially Angie, but she had faced him down in life, in death he was sure it would be easier.

He wondered about Bunny and Russet, too. They had reason to stay away. The man had tormented them for years on the strength of his threatening nature alone, and David thought it would be good for them to attend, to get some closure—although after his daughter he felt that word was so much hogwash. Hell, he didn't have "closure" on her yet. There were still days he couldn't get her off his mind, blue days of sadness that time just couldn't erase, or hadn't yet. Yeah, most of the time he was pretty good, and even sometimes he actually felt truly thankful for the time they'd spent together, but most of the time he felt cheated out of knowing her as an adult that would talk to him on an adult level, and be a friend as well as progeny. But maybe he'd eventually have that chance with Elsa, or maybe not. She hadn't been talking to anyone much lately if you believed Clarissa. And her new wardrobe was pure Goth.

Death of friends affects young people differently, some glide through the grief and come out unchanged. There are the others that will never be the same, that something inside them died, too, and they don't know what or how to get it back, and some never did. He hoped Elsa would bounce back in time. Jacob probably was her first big love, and David knew what it was like to be torn away from that, which infused him with great empathy for Elsa. And for the selfish part within him, the Goth attire made her look less like Dani, who was always tan and dressed in bright colors.

The funeral went by quickly. He maintained a solemn composure, and nodded to all the people he knew in town, which seemed to grow weekly. Angie and Clarissa came together, and joined David near the end of a pew in back. Elsa didn't show, saying she'd die herself before she saw her Dad again and besides, she didn't know Stark. Angie wore a tasteful black dress, probably wool, and displayed an appropriate attitude, although she whispered to David that when they dragged that casket out of cold storage and come spring buried it in the now-frozen ground, she'd be there to spit on his grave in private, which would be her "closure." Clarissa looked like the Happy Hooker's sister and contained herself as well as could be expected, meaning she didn't stand up and yell "bullshit" either. But she did slip out the side door to avoid seeing Harry at the front of the receiving line on the way out of the church. "Call that philandering son of a bitch a father?"

Harry wore a bespoke suit that obviously had once fit perfectly but now dripped over him, black wingtips, and an expression that told the town his best friend was gone forever. It touched David, and made him wonder who, besides the townsfolk, would be there to mourn when his time came? Maybe his friends in Minneapolis, he hoped, but he hadn't seen them since he arrived and only talked to them a few times, which is how it is in the modern world where everyone is spread out, working their own asses off, caring for their own families, and if there is a goddamn minute to spare they probably slip in a Springsteen CD and turn it up—just to get away. As he waited to get out through the line, he saw Harry go to his overcoat pocket twice, producing a handheld oxygen dispenser, and sucking on it. His skin looked gray and pasty, and when David shook his hand, it was limp and weak and left an odor David couldn't place.

Russet came with his mother, helping her in and out of the car. Bunny refused to attend for any reason, regardless of local tradition, and had told Russet if he did, he'd be sleeping alone for the foreseeable future. Poor Russet could not win, torn between mother and girlfriend, and probably messed up royally giving in to Mom, but her argument that the man had tipped him well for twenty years, and converted to the church, so if God would forgive his sins, Russell better darn well do the same. That didn't work on Bunny, even for a minute.

By the time the line subsided, Harry had to shuffle inside and rest in a pew before he could leave. David saw him and followed to the door, watched as he sucked up oxygen and as two of the ushers helped him to his car. He looked like hell. Apparently, his Mercedes knew its own way home, or a divine intervention beamed out a guiding light.

David stopped at Tiny's Bar after the funeral to dump down a quick one with Angie and Clarissa. Just about the time he finished and was ready to head home, Dick Peterson, one of the ushers, stopped at their table to say he was worried about Harry. Dick had followed him home and helped him into his house, and the worry now centered around food sources. He suggested maybe Clarissa could drop by and check on him.

"Sure Pete," she said.

She called everyone named Peterson by "Pete," there were plenty of them in this part of the country and the way she said it, must have satisfied him because he went back to a table of five other good Baptists and blasted a shot and a beer. His concern passed along, mission completed.

"Well," Clarissa said when Pete was gone. "Ought a get home. Elsa's bitching that I never feed her. Told her I serve a figure friendly menu. She isn't buying it, eh."

David asked if she was really going to make a quick stop at Harry's? She just laid a sly smile on him. "Public image statement, David. To hell with Harry."

David looked to Angie. She had been uncharacteristically quiet the last couple days, and hadn't said much so far today except the grave spitting, and now she raised her arms and shrugged. "Saw him already today. Once is enough."

So when they all herded out to their cars, David drove to Harry's himself. He had no idea what he'd say, but when he got there, Russet's car was parked, idling in front, an obvious pizza delivery, and with that inherited responsibility checked off he went home to his Crock Pot of cheap beef hot dish that had been simmering all day. Harry had food tonight.

David finished eating, cleaned up, and poured a glass of wine. He sat in the leather recliner and read Wolfe for an hour. The Nazis were taking over Germany, the writing excellent and frightening. It made him think about the

Taliban and the Baath Party, two things he didn't want to think about. He closed the book, thought for a bit and dialed Angie.

"Anything the matter?" he asked. "You've been pretty quiet lately."

"Uh, no, no David. It's all good. All those days got me behind in school—a little preoccupied trying to catch up."

He knew that was complete and utter bullshit. Angie had enrolled in high school just after Thanksgiving, under the guise that a GED was not the same as a diploma, and she deserved a diploma. The deal struck with the school, based on her performance back in the dark days, said that she would take all tests, turn in all homework, and attend classes only as necessary for parts one and two, which turned out to be about twice a week, both times a subtle embarrassment. Her intellect slashed through the curriculum, so the notion of getting behind could only be classified as a little white one, but covering what? David said, "Work must be getting a lot harder." To which she responded, "That can happen toward the end of senior year." In his experience, it seemed that toward the end of senior year the administrators, teachers and students all threw in the towel and coasted to a robed walk. Some secret had surfaced that evidently wasn't coming out tonight, and he let it go for now.

"I'm always here if you want to talk," he told her before they hung up. She responded, "I know. Might take you up on it someday." Meaning not today. He thought about running this by Clarissa, but it was getting late and maybe it would either blow over or come out. Maybe she didn't want to admit that Stark's death affected her more than she thought it should, but if that was the case, she could've said that. That would have made sense.

In spite of or because of the turmoil, David's writing soared. The clarity of that morning after Jacob continued each time he sat down to work, and that was whenever the next crisis wasn't occupying him. He had sent a few test pages to his old agent, Felicia, and she'd written encouraging responses. Yesterday, he got a call from Mrs. College saying he'd passed the drug test, which tempted him to call Auto, and that Harry had called her to revise his thoughts regarding employment. Something sounded odd about that part. It just didn't feel quite right, but David was so happy to hear that he was considered the top candidate now, and that they thought his history of publication could only help their little school. Also, if there were substitute opportunities before Fall Term started they would think of him first. All that revelry relegated the sensation of something being slightly off to a place in the corner.

Friday afternoon, near quitting time, David was hammering out what he thought to be about the second to the last chapter when a knock on the door interrupted him. He made his usual yellow highlight, saved, and headed out his office door where he crashed head on with Angie.

"Oh sorry," she said, obviously shaken. "I knocked but when you didn't come, I let myself in." David started to say no problem, but she cut him off. "I just got a call from Harry. He fell and can't get up. His speech is a little off. Said he fell two other times today, but this time he can't make it up."

"Why did he call you?"

She scowled, impatient. "Because Stark's dead I guess. Get your coat. I can't lift him myself."

Harry's door was locked, but Angie retrieved a hidden key from a nail on the porch railing. They found him just fifteen feet from his ejecto-chair, one leg splayed out at a weird angle, the oxygen hose still attached to his head. Amazingly, he hadn't fallen on the hose. The room was hot and stuffy and smelled like a wet dog, and when they tried to roll him over his skin was cold but wet with sour perspiration.

Ten minutes later, the ambulance arrived. David recognized the nurse from his delivery of Jacob and the faces of the other three men looked familiar, but he couldn't put names to them. "We're bringing him to Ely. Who's coming with?"

Angie's face changed to a hard expression David associated with a charge nurse. "I'll go," she said. And to David, "Get Clarissa."

David could follow directions. Clarissa let him in, a quizzical look on her face, her hair rumpled. She wore no makeup, a gray sweat suit, a glass of Coke in hand. "What's up?" she asked.

He glanced around. Dirty dishes filled the kitchen sink, pans littered the stove, the floor needed sweeping, none of which seemed to bother her at all, comfortable in her skin, no matter. "It's Harry. He fell, a few times in fact. The last time he couldn't get up. The ambulance is taking him to the hospital."

She stared at him, her eyebrows pinched together, lips tighten. "Why is this of interest?"

He wanted to shout, he's your damn father, but resisted. "Angie asked me to tell you. Guess she thought you'd go see him."

"Doubt it. The more interesting question is What's going on with you and Mom?" She gave him a teasing smile.

He blushed. How did they get from a hospital visit to her Mom in the space of two sentences? "We're friends, something like that. It's not a defined topic with us."

She tossed her hair back, eyes serious. "I'll get more specific then. Can you screw me if you want?"

Okay, guess you can always count on her to cut to the chase. This was delicate country that had not crossed his mind in months. What man wouldn't be attracted to a woman with her intelligence, sensuality, and that goddamn body, but this path was fraught with land mines, many unseen until it's too late, and this is what ruined him before. He smiled, acting flattered, which he was. "Where's Elsa?"

"At a friend's. Studying supposedly." Her smile became flirtatious now.

There were so many things he could say, some workable if he didn't care, which he did, and some that would make a currently good situation flounder impossibly. He liked the Thomson women and didn't want to screw that up. "I'd feel better discussing it with Angie first, really. I value each of you and don't want to fuck that up." He smiled, a little chagrinned. "Again."

"Get rid of that antiquated Faith, Hope and Charity image you carry around. We're women. That's it. We live. We love. We fuck up. We cry. Big deal. That's life. That's living, David. You should try it."

The knifing words jabbed him. "I feel plenty."

"Right. Truth rings out from the king of denial. You can't even get it right in your books. It's pathetic. You got some kind of an Everybody has to Love David Syndrome. They don't. It ain't gonna happen. Get over it. Say what you think. Take a fucking risk, David. Here," she ripped off her sweatshirt. "Take a risk with these."

He'd forgotten and blushed again, but stayed locked on her eyes. "No."

She swayed gently to some unheard music. "Come on. Have a fucking emotion, David. I'm Charity. She's not one of the virgins. She fucks." She moved toward him, undulating like willows in the wind. "Ditch the fear. Ditch the guilt.

Ditch the 'I'm old' crap. You're young. You've got life in front of you."

He took a step back and smiled again. "Most guys would kill for this," he said. "But I'm not most guys anymore. You—go to the hospital, visit your Dad. That's where I'm going and right now." He turned and ran to the door. She ran after him, but he was out and gone.

She stuck her head out and yelled, "I'm not done with you Chapman."

Chapter Thirty Two

Angie paced the hospital lobby for no reason other than a lack of anything better to do. She had already glanced at the magazines, *who picks these anyway,* talked to the ER nurse, yes they were admitting him and they knew next to nothing yet, except his hip was probably broken, and rest assured a battery of tests would be taken, starting with a hip and a chest X-Ray already in progress.

As she paced, Angie had a hard time distinguishing her emotions. Like with Stark, she had a long history of hating Harry and blaming most of the tawdry events that tarnished her life on him, right or wrong, probably partially wrong at least. But seeing him lying there on the floor and twitching brought out a realization that life had finite boundaries and he may be reaching his. And if so, she was getting closer on hers, too. The power hungry, well connected, aggressive, and horny executive defined more than just his work, it defined his life, now reduced to frailty, sickness, and infirmity. A broken hip would leave him hospitalized for God knows how long, eating institutional food, which may kill him by itself.

Relying on the care of strangers would be another wound to his intense pride. She found herself feeling sorry for him, which bothered her and would irk him to no end if he knew, and even more amazingly, made her feel like she had some kind of inherent responsibility to him, if only that he had no other family, though she was want to subscribe to that role. His money had made her, Clarissa's, and Elsa's lives easier than most of the hard working people in town, but when she thought of the price they'd paid, it came out about even and made her feel stupid to sympathize for such a sorry son of a bitch.

But those damn VeriLab results. He was not Clarissa's father, nor Elsa's grandfather, but how could Angie break his heart with that kind of news while he was that sick, injured, and sentenced to hospital food. She couldn't. It just wasn't right in any way. Period. Any confused emotional responses to sickness and injury did not affect her feelings about telling him one iota. That was final and absolute. As far as she was concerned, he could go to his grave, whenever that turned out to be, and never know.

It had nothing to do with money. Their trust funds were perfectly adequate to provide a decent life for each of them, and they were irrevocable and not based on paternity. She knew it was David coming to town and Clarissa making passes at him that made her do it. It had nothing to do with money or Harry. She saw the ER nurse walking toward her. "He's in his room now, resting. The hip was broken. There was a shadow on his chest that might be pneumonia. We need a couple more tests to confirm. He's in room 124. You can see him now. Are you the daughter?"

The nurse was not kidding. "I'm the ex," Angie said. "But thanks, that made my day."

"Ex, eh. That's different actually. There's legal papers to sign. The steroids perked him up a little, so now might be good time. Any questions?"

Angie shook her head. And where is that daughter of mine, Angie thought as she walked to Harry's room. It would be just like her to draw lines in the sand.

She opened the door to a spacious private room which would be what she expected had she thought about it. Machines hummed and pumped and beeped. Harry lay propped up on pillows with the bed slightly inclined. He wore his glasses, reading the papers. "Thank you for helping Angie. This is all quite embarrassing. Are Clarissa and Elsa here?" Angie shook her head.

"Just as well," he said. "I hope to feel better and be out of here very soon. I can see them then. Now, these papers. I would like you named to make medical decisions if I can't. Lord knows, Clarissa would probably say 'just kill him.'" He frowned. "I've checked the box on this form that says Do Not Revive. I believe in dignity, as you well know, and that extends to death. Perish the thought."

Angie had a pained expression in the face of this much reality. "Of course, Harry. I'll do it."

"Good, sign right here," he said pointing.

As she came closer to sign, it was apparent the orderlies had cleaned him up. The noxious odor was gone, replaced by an antiseptic soap smell, not good but immeasurable better. She signed the forms. "You look tired," she said.

"I am. They say they are feeding me soon. That should be interesting. By tomorrow I'll be calling the Grand Hotel for take-out." He gave her a smirk, and she thought if anybody could pull that off it would be Harry.

David walked in. Harry nodded to him. "You're to blame for me being here?" Harry asked, another smirk.

"Me and those damn paramedics."

Harry's smirk disappeared. "I appreciate the assistance, son. Thanks for coming. It makes an old man feel good."

Angie wondered about all this appreciation, but chalked it up to gallows humor. An orderly wheeled in a tray of food, with those brown plastic covers. He cranked Harry's bed up and made a grand production of presenting poached chicken, white rice, broccoli and a funny, jiggling looking thing for dessert. Harry studied the food. His eyes went to David and Angie. "Will you excuse me," he said. "I prefer to be alone when I regurgitate."

Clarissa refused to make the trip to see Harry, thus cutting out Elsa, too. Angie and David visited briefly the next two days, riding together. David asked her if she thought it was okay to fuck Clarissa, a question in which Angie found little humor. "What is it with you two?" she said. "Guess I can't stop ya, but No, no, no, no and no." What a tangled goddamn web. The crass wish that Harry might kick off soon flitted by but she wasn't going tell David anything about paternity anyway.

"You love me or something?" he said.

"If any Thomson chick is getting any, I ought a be the first in line."

David stared ahead at the road home saying nothing and she thought maybe that had scared him. It came out convincing because damn it, it was the way she felt. Love? Who the hell knew what that was even? But last time was pretty damn special to her, and comparing Clarissa's lifetime orgasms to hers was no comparison at all. All other reasons be damned, she could use a little catching up.

Two days later, David dropped her at home after their visit. The afternoon sky flamed red as the sun dropped and she put a pasty in the oven for supper and sat at the kitchen table watching the sunset. She hadn't seen Clarissa since before the crisis at Harry's house and that irked her. She thought she should just drive over to her house and give her the lecture on responsibility toward the sick, but knew it would do no good. The phone rang. "It's social services," the lady's voice said. "Can you talk to Harry Barnet?"

"Sure," Angie said, confused. Why didn't Harry just call?

"Angie," Harry said, his voice sounded weak and far away and her antenna shot up. "I am going to die." His voice trailed off.

"We all are Harry," she stuttered.

"There's a growth in my lung. It's malignant. They are transferring me to hospice tomorrow."

"God, I'm so sorry," she said.

"Don't rush over here, please. I don't want to see anyone tonight but the minister. Heaven's probably a long shot for me, but we'll plead our case." His voice tapered off to nothing.

She sat at the table, stunned, guilty for the sooner-rather-than thought and overcome by clouds of conflicting emotions. The day she'd prayed for in youth had nearly arrived. Hospice meant no time and no chance. Determination beat through the clouds. She replayed her Clarissa lecture on herself, and while it seemed hypocritical to forgive all manner of fuck-ups in the hour of death, it was the Midwestern way and she was that girl, in that town, and she'd follow that tradition. She could renew hatred later, but it would not start until he was gone. She took the pasty out of the oven, covered it with tin foil and left for Clarissa's.

Angie stood on the porch and took a breath before she knocked. The walk was shoveled and the porch swept, both uncharacteristic. A few years ago, she would have wondered if amphetamines were involved, but today it didn't seem to matter. Everything had taken on an insignificant quality, except this conversation, which loomed large and fraught with hazard. She knocked and heard Clarissa shout, "It's open." Standard fare in their corner of the world.

She opened it and noticed the clean, swept floor. A glance around revealed a clean kitchen and not a single laundry basket in the living room, where Clarissa and Elsa sat watching Emeril on Food TV.

"Come on in, Mom. He's making pulled pork poor boys with coleslaw. Looks fantastic," Clarissa said, and finally looked at Angie. "Okay, what's wrong," she said. Elsa looked up from a schoolbook on her lap. Angie sat on one side of her, Clarissa on the other.

"Okay. Grandpa is going to the hospice tomorrow. He will die there."

Angie looked at Clarissa with eyes that said "careful what you say." Elsa misted up at the word "die." Until the incident with Jacob and her Dad, Elsa and Harry had a special bond together and Angie knew it had frayed on what the girl considered an inordinate amount of influence Harry had over her father. She never mentioned it, but then she hadn't said a word about Jacob either. As for her father, she adamantly refused to see him or talk to him, though he called every day.

"What's hospice," Elsa whispered.

"Honey, their job is to make dying people as comfortable as they can," Angie said. "Sometimes there's a lot of pain. The people need medication."

Elsa nodded. Clarissa sighed. "So, I guess I'm supposed to forgive all and go see him? Is that your thinking?"

Angie nodded now and did not start her prepared responsibility speech, for the moment. It was good that Elsa was here, listening. It kept Clarissa in check.

"I want to see him, Grandma." Her eyes dripped now.

"Yup," Clarissa said, clearly outnumbered. "We'll go tomorrow."

Angie stood. "Why don't I pick you up at about eleven? If he's not settled in yet, we can have lunch." Elsa looked up with sad, glazed eyes. Angie's heart cracked to see her that way, and she sat again, closer now, and gave the girl a tight, loving embrace. "Say prayers for him," Angie whispered. And didn't say: he'll need them.

"Walk out with me?" Angie asked Clarissa, and at the car she said, "I had a talk with David . . . about you."

"He can be such a wimp," she said, wrapping her arms around herself.

"I told him I can't stop him, but I'm not in favor of it. You know what I mean. If anybody's getting some, it should be me." She smiled at her daughter.

Clarissa shivered and kicked at the snow. "I saw him first, in this iteration. We have something in common, neither of us commit. Works perfect." Angie said nothing, just looked into Clarissa's eyes, not exactly pleading nor condemning, but hoping. "Fine," Clarissa said. "He's too old anyway. Can I go in now? You froze me into submission."

Chapter Thirty Three

Three mornings later, David pulled to a stop in front of Clarissa's house. Angie occupied the passenger seat and volunteered to go roust the girls. Harry had been fading fast the last two days and the drugs were getting heavier, a timed-release morphine started yesterday that apparently helped the pain but knocked him out.

David wondered if he were in Harry's position, would he suffer the pain to know his last hours on earth or just surrender and go blotto until the final hour arrived. He liked to think he'd stay awake to see it off, but pain varied in degrees like the difference between losing your wife to divorce and your daughter to death and if it got like that, the cancer eating at your marrow, what did a few extra hours mean in the scope of things. Maybe not that much.

They pulled up in front of the hospice and David let the girls out and went to park. Walking into the place, he thought it looked no different from the other big, old houses on the street, gabled, from the early twentieth century, in good repair with a cheerful ochre paint job. Only the gurney ramp distinguished it if you didn't notice the double doors in front.

He hadn't visited Harry since the transfer here, for no reason other than he wasn't invited, but last night Angie called to say Harry wanted to see him. A death-bed request to a Midwestern boy so here he was. Inside, the place was warm, too warm, and most of the doors to the five rooms closed. Angie and Clarissa stood beside one of them, and he joined them.

Angie was solemn. "Dr. Death says he's going now. Only one person in the room at a time. Elsa cried when she heard that. She wanted to go first."

David sucked for breath and glanced around. "Guess I should be happy Dani went instantly," he said. "I don't have to go in, you know."

Angie dismissed that with a cynical nod. David sauntered down the hall, examined the kitchen where they offered coffee and soda, then went back when he saw Elsa clinging to Angie. Clarissa was gone. She emerged from the room minutes later. "He came up, asking for drugs. The nurse is coming." She looked at Angie. "I told him I forgave everything. Maybe it's true. He croaked out the word 'David'."

Hearing that gave his heart a shudder. He'd never experienced anything remotely close to this and he certainly wasn't comfortable. Who would be? He didn't like it. "Now?" Clarissa jerked her thumb toward the door.

He walked in. Harry's eyes were closed. One small lamp glowed with a dim yellow light, the drapes were drawn, and an odor lingered in the over-warm room like nothing David had ever smelled. Was it stale linens, old carpet, unwashed hair, poison leaking, or the scent of death? Harry's chest heaved slowly, the iron lung pumped oxygen, and his mouth formed a perfect O. "Harry?" The eyes fluttered.

The nurse entered silently with a bottle and an eyedropper. She squirted it under his tongue. She said, "He'll be able to hear you." David thought that might be a blessing and sat at the edge of Harry's bed and placed a hand on his. "Harry, it's David Chapman."

Harry's eyes fluttered again but this time opened. They were glazed and milky, pointing toward him though focus seemed nebulous. Harry gave a weak tug on his arm, pulling David closer. A halting sound came out fighting labored breaths. "You are . . . Clarissa's father," he croaked. "I know . . . this for a fact."

His focus seemed to firm for a moment as if to add emphasis, then faded. The eyes closed again and the O grew larger, fighting for air. David understood the words, but dismissed the meaning out of compassion, sympathy for the hallucinations of a man out of his mind with pain and drugs and death.

"Rest in Peace, Harry." He patted Harry's arm and gave it a gentle squeeze. As he got up to leave, the minister came in and prayed loudly into Harry's ear. David went out quickly. "Better hurry," he said to Angie.

It seemed she was in there a long time, but the wall clock said only fifteen minutes had passed. She came out somber, silent. Elsa ran to her and she held the girl. "It's over baby. He went peacefully." She looked at Clarissa and David, said nothing, herding them with her eyes. "I'll get the car," David said. The aura of death, any death, carried a power of change.

Silence carried a power, too, and in that void four people made the trip back to their homes. David could not help wondering about transcendence, the passage to what and where and selections for kingdoms, of God or gods, hell or nothingness, and his years of Lutheran-ness that he had leaned on after Dani, and still believed, weighed heavy on him. But with Harry he had trouble. The man had been misguided, arrogant, certainly criminal at times, yet respected by many and vilified by others, including all in this vehicle. A contradiction of the highest magnitude.

David wanted to hate him but without Stark and Harry on the earth, it was clear hate had been too much a part of his life. He remembered hearing or reading somewhere that hate eats the soul. He didn't believe it then like a junkie doesn't believe heroine is bad for him. Now, in this altered circumstance, he hoped some soul remained. Maybe just being there with that dying man, and in spite of those delusional words, feeling compassion for him proved a remnant lived and if so, maybe with luck, it would grow over time, maybe become healthy. If coming here provided him that, then the world could get along without another book and he could brave blizzards to teach English and be happy, if that's what it all came down to.

Elsa said nothing but a murmured "thank you" from the time they left until David dropped them at Clarissa's house. "Guess we'll be making another public appearance, eh." Clarissa said and opened the Rover door. A cold blast blew in. She pulled her coat closed. "Again," Angie said.

Clarissa's eyes softened. "Hopefully the last for a while."

David pulled away and glanced at the house, a light glowed now from the picture window and he was ready for the same at his home, put the feet up, bowl of soup, glass of gin, some reflection. Maybe if he went to three gins tonight it would take him as far as, Why am I here? Ambivalence usually reigned over that exhaustive topic, maybe tonight would be different.

"Strange feeling isn't it?" Angie said, her first words since "Let's get out of here." outside the hospice.

"Yeah. I was just thinking that nobody is all good or all bad. Just shades of gray. People doing what they think they need to do to get along." His head was foggy, thoughts flitting here and there, skittish after meeting death head-on. My God, Clarissa silent?

"It's different than with Stark. I can't place it yet," she said.

David waited for more, but she looked up at the moon that shone bright as a neon scimitar and said nothing more. It seemed to him that if Harry had told anyone else what he told him, it would have been mentioned by now, which seemed to confirm his delusional theory, so he let it go.

There was certainly enough to think about without that. "You want to get a drink, or something?"

She looked at him now. He saw the tired sadness in her eyes. "Some time alone is about all I can handle."

***

Harry's funeral was planned as one to remember for years, a small town version of a head of state event. The flag at city hall flew at half-mast, the Baptist church overflowed with flowers, and a stretch limo hearse waited outside. Harry's attorney, Larry Zagget, meticulously arranged for everything based on detailed instructions. Nothing left to chance, meaning to most folks, he knew about this for a lot longer than he let on.

To David, it seemed the entire town turned out. Mayor Pro Tem Hanson delivered a eulogy long on accomplishments and Minister Barlow said the welcome gates of heaven opened and accepted a saint. With the amount of money Harry donated to the church, why wouldn't he say that. David knew Bunny and Russet didn't agree with the "saint" part by the way they squirmed in the back pew where he sat with them. Clarissa, Angie, and Elsa occupied the front pew as honored family and David couldn't see them squirm but doubted they bought it either.

The Thomson women were seated in the grieving family pew. Zagget had called Angie to set that up, saying it was in Harry's instructions, and they would head the receiving line as surviving family, which angered Clarissa but how can you fight a dead man. When the receiving line finished and the "food and fellowship" in the city hall gymnasium began, David couldn't help remembering playing dodge ball as a kid and seeing his first rock band in Bye Bye Birdie. This was the only place in town large enough to accommodate the crowd and his mind acted like it had the night of Harry's death, a confusing conglomeration of muck, and the best thing he hoped for was the strength to get through this. Clarissa looked like a whore in church, and when the caterers finally began removing the food she found David and asked, "How much booze ya got at home?"

"Plenty."

She put her hand on his shoulder and rolled her eyes. "Good. I gotta get drunk and that goddamn bar is gonna be full of 'wonderful this and great that' and I might just flip. Let's go."

They gathered up the troupe. On the way out, lawyer Zagget cornered them and requested, well actually demanded their presence in his Virginia office at 1:00pm three days hence. David pointed at himself inquisitively but Zagget just nodded without interrupting his thank-you-for-coming speech, probably also written by Harry.

It was fast drinking and slow talking at David's house. It seemed no one had much to offer. They had all lived through the damage and it seemed unkind to discuss that, but also strange to discuss compassion or eternal anything, so not knowing what to say, they said little. Just drank. Bottles and an ice bucket sat on the bar. They helped themselves. A somber and pathetic ritual. More Irish than Midwestern. All got roaring drunk, except Elsa, who had to drive home although she had no license nor even a learner's permit but could see the road.

The hangover pushed clarity to the sidelines the following morning, but after lunch it was back and in a twelve-hour sprint, he finished the book. He e-mailed it to Felicia with a request not to respond for at least two weeks, which in his personal experience was the minimum time he needed to wait for a re-read. He had to let it age.

It was almost midnight when he walked out of his little office that had been his bedroom in youth. Before he turned out the light, he looked at the pictures, the old ghosts, mom and dad, Angie as a girl, Dani an innocent, and nodded as a gesture of gratitude and respect. He remembered asking Dani, when she was fifteen, what her friends talked to their fathers about and she'd told him they didn't even like their fathers, much less talk about anything important except money for their next trip to the mall. He wished he could have talked to her more about something besides grades, or boys, college or becoming another cog in an economic machine. He hoped some of that got into the book the way he meant it to and by some magic it might reach her spirit. He sighed and snapped off the light. Opportunity was here, then gone. He went into the kitchen to get ice for a drink, maybe a few drinks. The thermometer outside read twenty-five degrees, a light dusting of snowflakes reflected the streetlights and fluttered against the window. It seemed to close some hidden curtain on lucidity, temporarily he hoped.

The second gin worked its spell and he descended another level to where his life seemed to play like a soiled DVD, stuttering and blurred. But with the book done, and Stark gone and Harry gone, David's entire existence seemed altered.

A wolf appeared with a bloody muzzle standing over a dead deer and he saw the hard eyes and heard the growl. The wolf didn't hate that deer or any deer. It guarded its dinner. It had no room for emotions that interfered with survival and it struck David that he shouldn't either—but he had—for his entire adult life. Even as a boy. He remembered the stupid city boy versus country boy prejudice that included occasional fights and thinking back to that now, it seemed that humans were the antithesis of wolves. There had to be something to hate and if nothing obvious presented itself, we would conjure something out of nothing.

He had spent two years hating deer until he slashed one past death with his own hands, the deer was just a legal substitute for the driver that murdered his daughter. He wanted to kill him, too. He had hated Stark for over thirty-three years, which had seemed justified by banishment and rape. When he learned of Harry's leadership in the tawdry affairs, it was easy to add him to the list.

Adding was easy, it was subtraction that was tough. It had crept into him innocuously in boyhood, and festered and grew until it became a part of him that he didn't even recognize as destructive. It played its subversive role in alienating his ex-wife, impeding his writing, warping his understanding of a world which played right into it. Hate everywhere, nations, religions, terror and war.

The void he felt was the absence of hate for Stark and Harry. How he filled that void would dictate many things. Sure, he could turn off the news, quit watching war as a spectator sport, quit following poison politics, quit flipping off drivers on the freeway, but what about his home, his consciousness, his corrupted soul? He went to the bar for another drink, but looked outside. The snow had stopped and his lawn sparkled.

"Here I am in one of nature's treasure troves and I wonder what can fill the void? Am I stupid?" He donned his parka and boots, started the Rover, and drove the streets until the county road, then turned right into the labyrinth. He drove slowly down the beach road, identifiable only by the white space between snow banks, and cracked the window and sucked in the purity of the air, the smell of new fallen snow.

A pair of eyes shined and he slowed further until he saw the buck and watched it bound over the bank effortlessly. His heart ached at the grace, the beauty, like Dani's dancing, the ambient light receding, the Milky Way descending upon him, the new moon black.

At the beach, he parked on the hill and gazed over the frozen miles of white and above him the first flicker caught his eye and grew and spread across the sky, wavering and flashing in green, purple, and orange, the Northern Lights dazzling. The question of filling the void dripped away.

They sat around a conference table in lawyer Zagget's office that afternoon. "This ought a be interesting," Clarissa had said on the way into the building. And in David's opinion, so it was. Zagget cleared his throat and began reading in a reverent tone. "There are four life insurance policies of one hundred thousand each to Angie, Bobby, Clarissa, and Elsa." At which point David wondered why he was there. "The balance of the estate shall be divided evenly four ways." David saw a glint in Bobby's eyes. "Between Angie, Clarissa, Elsa, and David Chapman."

A bullet to the brain of both men. Bobby glared and stomped out. David sat there numb. He looked at Angie who averted her eyes, Clarissa shrugged, her face said I-don't-get-it-but-damn-good-luck. Elsa seemed to register nothing except a subtle delight that her father had left in a huff.

Hearing his name in this context melted his bones. Clarissa and Elsa didn't seem to get it, but Angie did. Harry's deathbed words were true and David shuddered. He had nearly screwed his own daughter and now offered up a prayer for the vast dumb luck. My God, it could have easily happened, maybe he had some angel on his shoulder, guiding him away from a heinous decision he would now live with in horror. It was apparent to him that Angie knew, but when had she known and why hadn't she told him, or obviously anyone else. His mind reeled.

The rules the lawyer blathered on about went in one ear and out the other as his eyes flitted from face to face. They were listening intently, even Elsa. He heard Zagget say something million dollars but the context evaded David, replaced by the passing thought that maybe this was something other than a dagger Harry threw from the grave. A strange vengeance delivered in a golden sheath.

Clarissa was his daughter. He'd seen her naked more times than he cared to remember and now even those thoughts made him sick to his stomach. He knew his face must be flushed and red, but he masked it as well as he could until the presentation ended.

Outside, Clarissa beep bopped on the sidewalk in front of the old stone building. "You're a lucky bast . . .uh . . . bugger, David. You kissing ass when we weren't looking? Come on, Elsa. Let's go to Duluth and do some shopping, eat at a fancy restaurant, get a nice hotel room, spend some of Daddy's money. You coming, Angie?"

David was afraid she might explain it right there, or go with them and explain it on the drive, but the expression on her face erased those thoughts. She wasn't going to tell anyone now. Maybe ever. "Thanks. I'm not in the mood to shop. Maybe I'll just ride home with David."

Elsa was already in the car and Clarissa was getting in, too. "Suit yourself. Sounds like there'll be plenty of time to shop, eh. Ta ta." She waved, shut the door and pulled away fast.

Angie studied a dirty snow pile. Turned to him. It looked like she might cry. "I should have told you," she said, and looked down again.

"Harry did. I thought he was delusional. How I dodged seduction is really beyond me right now. Blind, dumb luck."

He tried to make light of it, but the guilt burrowed deep. Men had pillaged daughters since the beginning of time but that didn't make a lick of difference right now, and the fact that she had tried and failed to seduce him was meaningless as well. His thoughts were not as pure as his actions. Thank God for the actions.

"You and Harry had the same blood type," she said, aiming for explanation. "I didn't know until just recently." She looked at David as if she expected him to say something, but nothing came out. He couldn't cry, shout, swear, or blame, which was what he felt like doing. Instead, he said nothing. That seemed to wound her further. "Take me to the Grand for dinner?" she asked. Plaintive, what could he say?

David's arrival back in September had changed things. Had he not returned, it may have altered this outcome radically. Bunny might still be undercover and Stark still alive. Angie's face was sad and guilty, begging forgiveness without words, biting her lower lip like when they were kids, and a feeling of resignation swept over him. This couldn't be changed. Only lived with somehow. Maybe one day forgiven. Can one be forgiven for thoughts? Jimmy Carter confessed to lust in his mind—but it wasn't for his own daughter. He clicked the Rover key and the lights flashed, the locks popped. "I feel like lobster. You're buying," he said.

Chapter Thirty Four

Angie knew she should have told him when the lab results showed up and she couldn't fathom how Harry found out. He had to know or he wouldn't have made that sweeping estate change, but to think he could be man enough to not make a big deal out of it, not cut them all out and instead provide for her family made tears come to her eyes that she felt guilty about not crying before. He had infuriated her throughout her life and honored her in death. She understood why God claimed vengeance for Himself.

"Anything I can do?" David asked, glancing over and quickly back to snowpacked road.

"Not now," she said, turning her face away.

The drive was only an hour or so, but took longer today with the road only partly sanded and slick in places, you just didn't know where. The swamps were white and only the spindly bare tamarack announced them, and farther along the silvery green spruce mixed with bright green balsam, dark green jack pine, and now and then a big white pine missed during the timber holocaust. She apologized many times until he asked her to please stop. It wasn't until they were entering town near the Grand that she said, "Dani is gone and can never be replaced," she said softly, almost carefully. "Maybe another daughter and granddaughter will ease some pain."

The road was salted now and black in places. "Take some getting used to," he said, then paused. "Who would have thought blood could make that much difference?"

His tone suggested to her a cool breeze refreshing a hot day and made her feel better, settled her churning stomach. He was a good man at heart, she'd known that for many years, but you can never tell how a shock like this will affect a person, good or bad. His face said gathering acceptance, growing understanding, covered by an attitude of responsibility that she found admirable. But she still hadn't told him about the curse. "I'll talk to Clarissa tomorrow. I didn't want to say anything in front of Elsa for fear of what might pop out of her mom's mouth. I hope they'll both be okay," she said and looked over at the passing railroad yard. She sighed. "I feel like such a slut."

"What?" he said. "You were there. Shall I refresh your memory?"

That wasn't necessary. That night came back as fresh as if it had happened yesterday and wasn't the reason for the slut comment. It was how the town would perceive it. Harry knew that, which was why he had them in the front at his funeral without David or Bunny. To quiet the controversy he knew was coming. But in the end, it certainly wasn't the first hullabaloo surrounding the Thomson women and most probably wouldn't be the last. Clarissa still had wild oats stored in her saddlebags and Elsa was just getting started. Bobby would take it the worst, but Angie had always questioned his pious streak and his commitment to Elsa's limited education, and when she got right down to it, she was still pissed he took that girl away from Clarissa, so in the end, fuck Bobby. He could fend for himself among his fellow fundamentalists and see how that worked out for him.

"Bunny wasn't included," David said.

"She will be. I'm going to offer them Harry's house. It doesn't come with baggage for them. It's bigger, more room for Russet's Mom." She smiled at that thought and looked at David. "And my memory is fine."

He smiled back, the first time since his name came up in the lawyer's office. "Maybe we should get a room. Get drunk. Throw caution to the wind."

"Drive faster," was all she said.

By the time the waiter served David's lobster, and Angie's Filet Minion wrapped in a bacon slice, they were into their second martini and giggled as the waiter poured wine. "This seems sacrilegious," Angie said, thinking about the twisted fates, and that she could have told each of them when screwing-each-other came up last time, only days ago.

He carved a bite of lobster, dipped it in butter. "I can't yet get my mind around thinking of her as my daughter."

"Or me as your concubine?"

"You don't live with me," he said.

The "not yet" that jumped into her mind was too forward even for alcohol-drenched joking and she let it go. "Maybe this is the celebration of our daughter we never had thirty-some years ago." She tried to consider how different their lives would have evolved if they'd know back then, but with a booze wash, it made her confused and a little sad at the thought that her life would probably be more mentally stable, more educated, but not necessarily happier. She wouldn't consider that right now. It brought on sudden thoughts of rapacious affairs with lovely college girls destined to blow them apart. Or of her daughter trying to seduce her father. Those thoughts slapped at her sensibility. *Damn girl, you've got sex on the brain,* she thought and took a bite of the Filet, which melted in her mouth.

"Then cheers," he said, lifting his wine glass. "Here's to sexy Grandmas."

She clinked glasses, the wine lowered her eyelids, the comment inflicted damage. Clarissa had most of the fun up until today and that was about to change. "Bring the leftovers down to the room, along with a piece of cheesecake."

She made a quick stop at the gift shop, grabbing toiletries, some rather nice perfume, and two Grand Hotel t-shirts, before racing to the room. When she came out of the shower, dried, powdered and perfumed, he sat in the easy chair, the TV on a music station, looking out at the lake. She walked to him, dropped the robe, and curled up on his lap. "Whacha think—time to get comfortable yet?"

It went too fast, but she was surprised to find herself repetitively orgasmic, and she dozed off more satisfied than she'd ever been, thinking if this is what you get with age, she'd take it. She woke in the night and found David sitting in the easy chair smoking a cigarette. She watched for a few minutes, then whispered, "Where does all this leave us?"

She saw the red glow burn brighter and his silhouette unchanged, still comfortably slouched in the chair. "That's what I'm trying to figure out—Mom." The Mom part sounded good, a kind of gentle music she understood. She didn't have him before and may not after, but she had him tonight and that was enough for now. She closed her eyes and let him go on thinking undisturbed. Whatever it was.

The ride home was subdued. When he didn't come back to bed, she had gotten up with him and opened the bottle of champagne they hadn't touched, and drank it dry, talking about old times from high school. She confessed the grief that hiding the Friday sex parties from him had caused and his forgiveness sounded complete and true. They had slept late, lay in each others arms and finally showered together, got breakfast, and hit the road. Hangovers crept in on the drive and the silence was strange and anxious.

"After Sandy left me, I swore that was the last time for me," he said out of nowhere.

She turned from her thoughts and studied his face. "There's something I haven't told you." He glanced over as if to say now-would-be-a-good-time. And she started the whole sordid generational tale, fathers fucking Thomson daughters back to the 1800's. "Guess technically it stopped when I got Stark. Doesn't feel like it though. I told Clarissa early so she could watch out for Harry."

"Technically and finally a generation skipped. In the flesh. Should we ship Elsa to a nunnery?" He tried to smile but it came off sad.

She turned her gaze to passing scenery. "I'm going to bulldoze my cabin and build a new one. That piece of land deserves much better."

He smiled. "So do you."

Chapter Thirty Five

Angie called Clarissa that afternoon and asked her to come to David's place, alone, for a quick drink. He set up martinis in frosted glasses and when Angie was finished talking, Clarissa laughed out loud.

"Now that's a father-daughter relationship after my own heart," she said. "Kind a takes 'town whore' to a whole new level. And the curse is dead, eh. Thanks. You were smarter than you looked." Her eyelashes fluttered. "Or a goddamn coward. Which was it? Hey, I could cut Bobby's pecker off. Hear his fundamentalist buddy's aren't as forgiving as their God."

She laughed, then paused. Her face turned serious. "Elsa will struggle with this." She stared at David. "It's kind a yucky when you think about it, eh? And damn, I gave it my best shot. Seemed like I was always naked in front of you. Ever think about that, Dad?"

His face turned blood red. The first time she called him Dad and it had to be in that context. It had to be angels. Redemption also had a price. "Wouldn't it be pretty to think so—Jake Barnes said. Thanks, daughter."

"Is that true, Mom?"

"You're incorrigible, for God sake."

Clarissa laughed harder. "Never really did quite understand your appeal. Freudian, eh. I get it now." She was obviously enjoying her new Daddy thing and had no intention of letting him off easily. She sashayed around the bar and gave him a hug. "Okay, serious. I'm glad it's you. Past is past. You just be a good Grandpa and we'll be fine." She smiled, like she was ready to fire again, but stopped. "Okay?"

David pushed a swirling red curl away from her face, and studied it. He couldn't see a bit of himself in her, but he was never any good at stuff like that. And he would have to forget the image of her stripping off her sweatshirt the other day, but that was another woman, not his daughter. He would drill that into his head no matter how long it took. "I had a lot of hate in me when I got here," he said. "It seems to be dissipating." He looked at Clarissa, then Angie, and didn't say I Love You, but he was thinking it and would try it out when he thought the time was right. "How about I call Brad Sterling and book one of those fancy fish house weekends for all of us?" He knew Angie hated ice fishing, fancy house or not.

"Great idea, David," Angie said.

***

The ice house trip forced David to upgrade his wardrobe, including boots, to a super-warm version. He packed his gear along with Angie's, Clarissa's and Elsa's into his truck, the embarrassing LA Rover gone now, traded in for a used dependable Chevy Tahoe with four-wheel drive that started on cold days.

He'd learned that Brad Sterling's icehouse was one of three he owned and rented in various places that changed year to year. The locations garnering more than passing interest from the fishing community. His acquired intuition was a combination of art and science that he discussed only in nebulous terms, but his locations were precise, selected in autumn, GPS coordinates recorded, and the houses placed as soon as the ice was deemed safe. John Radecki always put his out first, and over the years he'd lost two trucks to thin ice and now wore a wet suit in an old Ford truck as he dragged his castle out. Evidently, he didn't like his wife. If the weather was cold, Brad went a week after him. This year twenty-two houses surrounded his, which was always the case, spread out over a five or six hundred yard radius. David's grapevine reported they'd all done well this season.

They got there Friday night and caught fish in the first hour. The wood stove steaming, warm in the bunk beds, and walleyes hitting for two days. David fried up filets with butter and capers topped with lemon juice and delighted at spending time with Elsa. Her sadness over Jacob seemed to be passing along with her anger at her father. She was intense every time her bobber went down and she set the hook on that short ice pole. She screamed with delight as she fought it in, which made David feel like a damn good, and young, grandfather. On Saturday, Brad took Clarissa and Angie to a small party on the other side of the icehouse village where a guy had a keg and a bon fire and David volunteered to stay with Elsa.

She jigged her lure, staring at the hole, trying to get her tenth walleye of the day, although seven were small enough to throw back. "My Dad says you're going to hell for being my Grandpa," she said, not taking her eyes off the bobber.

David studied her face. It seemed tight and nervous. "He means for relations outside marriage?" She nodded. "Right. Well . . . I hope not. I was deeply in love with your Grandma then. That has to count for something. You talk to him much now?"

"Mom makes me talk once a week. She gave me a book list, too. Said my education is lacking. It's Brave New World this week. She says it's a religious metaphor."

An interesting concept David thought. "I was pretty religious as a boy. You probably didn't know that."

"I don't know much about you, for a Grandpa. Newly ordained and all."

David detected sarcasm. "I had a daughter a year older than you."

"I heard. Sorry. She's probably dating Jacob now."

"Do they date there?"

"I don't know. Don't know much of anything anymore."

He saw a sadness in her eyes that he used to see in Dani's. "Maybe we should go with Grandpa C. I can't replace your Grandpa Barnet. Don't want to. He loved you very much. This whole thing is a surprise for me, too. I'm okay with however you want to think about me."

Her bobber wiggled and grabbed her attention. Then it stopped. "You don't go to church now?"

That seemed like a loaded question, given her break from Daddy and her long devout history so there was no point in attempting spin, which he disliked anyway. "Not much. I could never quite reconcile the preaching to what I read in the Bible. The exclusivity bugged me too. Can we be the only religion? Maybe He sent Jesus to us, and Mohammad to some and Buddha to others because He knew that's best. I can't claim to know the thoughts of God. So, I don't judge. Like He said." He smiled but saw she wasn't looking. The bobber wiggled again. This time it went under. Her thumb jammed the line spool and she jerked the pole.

"Haaaa," she said. "Got him."

The moment passed in the fever of an eight pound Walleye thrashing on her line and finally on the floor of the icehouse. They worked it as a team and at the end she didn't want to kill that magnificent fish but wouldn't throw it back and asked David to end its life mercifully, which he did. They took pictures with her new digital camera and celebrated with cranberry juice over chipped lake ice.

When her line was back in the water and the house was again quiet, she said, "Tell me about Dani."

In the dim light, Elsa's wide-set eyes glowed softly like pale moons and David felt tears rising and a lump in his throat. He pulled a short stool in front of his own fishing hole, facing her, his bobber mirroring hers. In his head, he heard lyrics: *may lie a reason you were alive/ but you'll never know.* "She was a dancer," he choked out.

They talked but mostly he talked and she listened for two hours until the girls came crashing in from their party. David and Elsa donned parkas and took a walk on the windswept ice field. "I feel like I know her," Elsa said, her face down against the frigid blowing ice.

"That's good," was all he could say.

When they left the next day, his two-year-old Tahoe complained a little but started right up and Elsa rode in the passenger seat, beside him, and he caught her glancing at him as they all talked and joked and laughed. Clarissa was impatient about the money from Harry for her grandiose plans, but it only sneaked out a couple times in sharp chides that were greeted with a snide, "Please, Mom." by Elsa.

They were all hungry for something besides fish, and as the early dusk collapsed around the truck, they stopped in Ely for supper. It was so pleasant that Angie announced they needed to make it a tradition, their first family tradition, to get together for Sunday dinners whenever possible, which she would organize. "Whenever possible" clearly meant every week to her, and David thought he wouldn't get neurotic about it but this felt good, this new family, this time, and he would enjoy as much of it as he could for as long as it lasted. He'd get used to the Daddy jokes Clarissa was now fond of, some not altogether asexual, and cherish the time with Elsa. He knew how fast that could vanish.

Back at his house that night, sitting in his chair with a hot brandy laced with cinnamon and lemon, a yearning for Dani struck him that brought tears. Maybe it was a wish for her to know these women, her family, that could not be, or another of the grief attacks that had been so prevalent for more than two years after, that had subsided for a while, but maybe would never go completely away, and maybe shouldn't. Whatever it was, it was with him now, and real. He thought about her with an odd mix of joy and despair and kept glancing at her picture, the junior class portrait that hung above his mantle. He got out a piece of stationary and an envelope, addressed it to Sandy Chapman in care of her lawyer, the agreed upon way spelled out in the dissolution papers, and wrote:

Dear Sandy,

I pray you have found some peace wherever you are. Your smile always radiated such joy. It should do that again. I'm trying. Might be getting closer. I'm hopeful anyway. I wondered what you thought of the idea of moving Dani closer to one of us? I feel like she's lonely. Please call or write. Either way, I'll understand.

Love Always,

David

He wrote it longhand, with a cheap Bic pen, placed an American flag stamp on it, and walked out into winter, to his mailbox. Whatever would happen would happen.

David soon found out that Harry's skill at running life and death again proved genius. His entire estate neatly folded into a Living Trust that avoided probate and taxes with Angie as trustee reporting to Board of Directors made up of David, Clarissa, and Elsa, all with equal votes. Elsa's share went into a separate trust which she gained full control over at age twenty-five if she'd graduated from college by then, or thirty without a degree. Angie administered both, making it obvious what Harry thought of Clarissa's money management. When that was explained to her by the lawyer, she said nothing but raised a middle finger toward heaven.

David came away with more than a little awe at the responsibility of money, something he'd successfully avoided in his own life, with consequences, and decided it would be different this time, but as close to the same as he could make it. For that, he hired help. He was not finished being a writer and changed little in his habits, but quickly came to appreciate escaping the financial pressure inherent in his craft.

He worked from five in the morning to two thirty on weekdays, taking lunch at his desk, a brisk trip on the treadmill after writing and a walk or a drive, depending on the weather, to somewhere soothing that let him appreciate his surroundings. It could be the frozen beach, a stretch of labyrinth road, a bar or café in Lone Pine or Ely. He looked forward to longer days that would allow him to extend his post-work world. He made a concerted effort on these petit trips to talk with people, new people from kids to seniors, fascinated by what kept folks up here in the north woods where opportunity sometimes seemed as scarce as warm winter days.

He had come here broke and broken but obstacles that had seemed insurmountable now seemed like grist to polish a life. A life that meant something to others, not just to himself. That made him *want* to stop at the café for coffee or an early dinner and a chat with whomever may be there, or buy a round at Tiny 's or the Hole-in-the-Wall and find out what occupied people's minds, how the fishing, hunting, trapping, snowmobiling might be going, or how the council was getting along without Harry.

He inadvertently found out about backstabbing, hockey, basketball, affairs, and poaching to name a few. All of it made the weave thicker and more textured. People beautiful in their virtue and frailty like flawed gemstones glittering in the snow, and he respected them more in this tiny fishbowl where everything seemed magnified. Celebrities all, their lives played out in a media faster than cable news, slicker than People Magazine, flashier than Entertainment Weekly with a delivery system to rival the Internet. Chet's affair with Lou's wife, all three of them on again off again lovers since high school; Bobby with the organ player from the Catholic church; Carey's daughter sexually active at thirteen, just like she was; a councilman so drunk at his home that he pissed on the street as Clarissa drove by, who honked and yelled, "I'll never be that horny."

Clarissa was a gossip unit all her own and would be on the cover six months out of the year if this were a magazine. It shocked David the first time one of the guys at the bar elbowed him and whispered, not that softly, "So what's it like banging a daughter that gorgeous?" Something inside him wanted to beat the guy bloody, but in an instant of clarity he realized that would only propagate the rumor, so he went with the truth, grinned and said, "Damn, wish I knew."

The rumor of the Will hit the street featuring Clarissa, and played a few times a night to the point that David stopped at her house twice to ask if she was spreading it. "What ya didn't like it?" she pouted, not giving him an inch. But it had mercifully tapered off as time passed and David took it with stoicism.

He'd come from LA and understood the celebrity part, nothing sacred ever, especially Angie's car parked overnight at his place occasionally. That one even got back to Elsa. Clarissa told her to ignore it, Bunny said good for them, and Angie said it was her prerogative as a woman.

When Elsa point-blank asked David, he sat her down and tried to explain that relationships in older people were difficult to understand, especially for the folks involved. They respected each other, had known each other for years, and might be trying to figure out if the love they felt was something that could fit in the context of the independent people they had become.

Elsa looked confused and asked what his God might think of that. David answered, "Can't say for sure. I hope He approves."

***

David thrashed at the final draft of his book, taking some of his agent Felicia's suggestions. Three months ago, he'd hated it, another hate list addition, but the characters had revealed themselves, the concepts had congealed and now it excited him. A hate list deletion. Felicia deemed the first draft excellent with reservations. "I feel like I'm there. And I know why you are." He wanted excellent. No reservations. Going home was a worthy subject. Wolfe was not wrong, nothing could be wrong in literature but bad writing and false thinking and Wolfe was a fine writer and a solid thinker. But David saw post-9/11 life differently, with hope and fear proportionally changed, human nature in America edgy, wary, like cornered wolves making desperate decisions that lacked compassion. Greater good was another casualty of war.

Today he was nearly finished. After work, he sweated on his treadmill and weight machine, beating down a runaway passion that didn't exist when he came to this town but nowadays visited in various forms. He couldn't escape the image of Jacob Foulke's frozen corpse or the sins of the father inflicted on Nick, the dazed, glazed look on his face as he had stood on the periphery, dragged to the funeral by his broken wife like a character in one of David's novels. Two more wars made him wonder how many of those boys in camouflage would end up like Nick.

And he thought the blended family withers sometimes in the face of perceptions from the past, histories and memories that never should have occurred but did and even with Clarissa's acceptance and gallows humor the guilt was difficult to swallow and the tough job of relationship-building suffered in its wake. The alarm on the treadmill dinged, thirty minutes finished, and he grabbed the towel, wiping sweat as he cooled down, thinking he'd get there with Clarissa no matter how much time or torture it took.

He read Jim Harrison that night, a drink on the side table, soothing poetic words on the page. The phone rang. He didn't recognize the number and picked up.

"Uh . . . hi David," the voice as familiar as his face in the mirror. "I got your letter."

His heartbeat jumped and thud-thudded in his ears. "Hi Sandy. How are you doing?" *Oh come on,* he thought, *that's the best you can come up with?*

"Fine. Sort of. I guess. I've got a life going on up here. It's a good life." She sounded halting but determined. "I re-married. It's different up here, real orgasms, fake diamonds." She chuckled at their favorite LA joke. "I miss her."

"Me too."

"I'll never go back to that God-forsaken place again. If you want to move her, it's fine. My attorney sent some forms. I'll sign them and get them off to you."

He wasn't sure if it was the voice or the content but he felt tears forming and a lump growing in his throat. "You could visit anytime—with the new Mr."

"Thanks. Maybe someday. Got a go now. All the best, baby." He heard the cradle click and the dial tone buzz in his ear. He was almost thankful. He had no idea what to say next. Maybe she knew that and saved him. It wouldn't be the first time. He clicked off the phone, wished he had a profound thought but all he had was more lost-child grief that he lived with, magnified now, and he knew it would never go away completely and he didn't want it to. Her portrait stared at him, frozen in time, and he smiled at it and said, "It's time, my girl."

***

April Fools' Day started warm, in the forties. He glanced out his office window at dawn and saw the overnight snow melt. The pure white field in his yard now took on a dirty sheen as all the layers of rubbish, tree scraps, and blowing road sand dropped out of their ice suspension and gathered on top of the remaining snow, and fell further as the temperature rose. This was his fourth full day of re-working the ending and at noon, after eight hours of labor, he typed: The End and meant it, truly as in fully complete, not as in tired and quitting. He tried to eat, but had no appetite, threw on a light jacket and went for a walk.

He didn't know how it would go over, how it would be interpreted, or whether it would find an audience, and he didn't think about that. He was struck with a satisfied sort of grief and anxiety that would pass, just not immediately. Maybe he was just another writer that took longer than anticipated to coax out his next book. An hour later, he walked up his driveway hardly realizing the presence of snowflakes, huge and wet, the Spring storm everyone talked about, and strode through the kitchen without slowing and to his office. He attached the manuscript to an e-mail addressed to his agent. He hesitated at the cover words and then typed: "Here's the final draft. Call me. David." Paused again, and pushed send. It disappeared.

It had a life of its own now. He stared at the screen, and couldn't shake thoughts of what it would be like when his granddaughter left to enter the world, an often cold, certainly merciless, sometimes cruel world, to have a life of her own. He felt sick and hollow inside. A book had never felt like this before, never felt so personal, so close, so much like a family member leaving.

The knock on the door startled him. Angie stood on the porch, puffy flakes crowning her hair, the shoulders of her nylon jacket. It hung open revealing a form fitting cotton top with a low cut neckline that looked wonderful on her. He greeted her with a hug, poured her coffee. He tried to explain his muddle of feelings. He jabbered about what he had tried to do and how he had tried to do it, yammering now just to get it outside of him. Angie was patient. The coffee was good.

"Just a blubbering pile of egocentric hope," he told her as he walked her home through the snow.

Then it was dusk. He was alone, gazing out the window at nothing, not wanting to exercise, and swilling gin against a gathering sadness that no amount of substance abuse could fight. He thought of the dangers of literature, the quest for knowledge, the Golden Ring, the damnable American Dream, and the shit he had tried to bury in this tiny town, but couldn't seem to. He had money now, and a book wouldn't make a damn bit of difference. Why did he even put himself through it? But he knew why. He didn't want to be seen as the guy that got lucky, the guy whose sperm hit the right spot at the right time. He wanted to garner a reputation as a writer and a good one and hoped if this book was published and it did anything at all, it would change his attitude about himself, allow him to forgive that vow to himself after Sandy left, and give him a shot of confidence that may help him to open up. He loved Angie, not in any conventional way, but he might someday, he hoped he could. He loved these people. He loved this place and knew he would be here for a long time, living his way, a way that many here would not understand. The price may be a deep personal loneliness. Special people that had happiness would try to bring it to him. Could they break through the crusted lining around his heart? A lining he hated and tore at, but it wouldn't give, wouldn't tear, wouldn't allow that final connection through.

***

Finally, his agent called. "Okay, I like it. How shall we sell literary fiction about a lost guy in rural America?" Felicia asked.

He wanted to say something snide but stayed calm. "How did they sell Ford or Harrison?"

"That's fast company." She paused. "We need a little face time, David."

An unusual request coming from her, but he had the papers from Sandy, his plot purchased, the only thing missing was the plane ticket that he'd been avoiding. Maybe this was the push he needed. "Do you think it's out there? People craving home, slowing down, wanting a simpler life?"

"Guess we'll see." They made a luncheon appointment in Los Angeles for the coming week. He thought of what he was, what he always would be, a working-class man who became categorized, marketed into a neat little box that didn't even look like a gilded cage until you wanted to get out and that's when you find out that getting out is next to impossible, the cost of freedom so wildly, patriotically bantered about, is so high that nobody can afford it. And they have you right where they want you. There is no escape without penitence so great that few can bear it. The American flag on one side and the dollar sign on the other, in between lies the abyss. His nemesis had opened the cage door. That irony was not lost. "I hope so," he said.

In the days leading up to the meeting, David read the new book again. Felicia seemed skeptical and that made him feel like someone had squashed his child. He packed the truck for the drive to Minneapolis, the flight to LA. She booked him in at a Ritz close to her office, reserved him an upgraded rental car, as if he were important, which he wasn't. The meeting would be whatever it would be. She'd probably want a few more changes and she was damn good and would probably be right, but in the end, either she could sell the book or not. It wasn't his main concern. He'd already let the book go. It's what he couldn't seem to let go of that caused undo friction. That damn cage around his heart.

He left home a little after ten o'clock the next morning and cruised up Main at thirty miles an hour, the street deserted at usual. Ahead, a car pulled out of the municipal building and headed toward him. As it grew closer, he saw it was Angie's new Subaru. He waved as it passed, and glanced in the rearview mirror. Brake lights flashed. He stopped too, and backed up, pulling beside her. They both rolled down their windows. Bunny waved from the passenger seat.

"Headed for LA?" Angie asked, something odd in her voice.

"Yeah. Kind of dreading it, you know."

She frowned. "Be gone long?"

"A week. Be back late Saturday."

This brought a smile. God he loved that smile. "Then you'll make Sunday supper. Great. My house."

It made him want to drive back from Minneapolis as soon as the plane landed, which would get him in at about midnight. Maybe he would and surprise Angie. He was scheduled to stay that night with his buddy in the city, but with men nothing is cast in stone. "Count on it."

The smile flashed again, like the one in the photo in his office when they were kids and she'd worn the t-shirt and jeans. "Okay, safe trip then." And with a car waiting behind her, she pulled away.

He stopped at the gas station at the edge of town and started the pump. It was chilly, high cirrus clouds approached from the west. As the tank filled, he thought about Angie, and passion, life and literature, and mourned lives based on sound bites from talking heads, reading headlines but never the whole story, skating on surfaces. Emerson again: The lords of life passing in a flash. He smelled the gas fumes rising from the pump in the brisk air, scanned the houses, the budding spring trees. He washed the windshield and paid the bill, felt the butterflies gathering in his gut. Clarissa pulled up to the pump across from him and jumped out of her car, beautiful as ever. "So you're seeing that agent of yours, eh?" she said as she unscrewed her gas cap. "Give her hell for me."

David smiled. He couldn't help smiling at this woman. "Thought you didn't like my work."

Her hair danced in the breeze. "You inferred that. I can criticize, but nobody else can. It's a father-daughter thing."

"Okay," he said, sitting in his driver seat now, the engine running, knowing as well as she did that was not quite right, yet. "See ya soon."

"Get going. You'll miss the plane."

The skies and the road were clear and he kept it at the speed limit as he drove past the baseball field, and the potato field, and the golf course, and around Dead Man's Curve to the straight away where he jacked it up to eighty. He slowed five miles out and waved at Auto's house, then back up to eighty-five. Dani appeared in the passenger seat. It startled him. They passed the cemetery. He glanced toward it.

"Aren't you gonna stop?"

"We'll be back."

"We won't make it back."

He dropped down a hill and onto the flat and glanced at her. "Our life is here."

A deer appeared out of nowhere. He saw it. Too late. He squeezed the steering wheel and cut hard left. The passenger-side front tire splashed into a hole and smacked a frost heave, flying off it like a ski jump. The truck landed, bouncing, spinning. Back tires throwing up gravel and ice. He cut the wheel hard right and held on. The truck spun two doughnuts down the middle of the road. Squealing tires, blue smoke, burning rubber, rocked to a stop facing back toward town, straddling the centerline. It happened in an instant. He had watched, a bystander. Now his heart pounded, his body trembled. He glanced at the passenger seat. She was gone. He opened his door. Slid out, slow. The silence, the acrid burnt smell. Weak knees barely supporting him. Big pine trees on both sides of the road closed in. It didn't roll over. They always roll. He saw the deer in the trees, fat, pregnant. He looked south, away from town at the vacant road disappearing into the swamp. His head swiveled. He looked north. "This isn't about literature," he said to the sky, and climbed back into the driver's seat. Still trembling. A deep breath. Another glance. He backed up to the edge of the road, cranked the wheel, hit the gas, and headed south toward the airport.

***

David sat on a barstool, staring at it, resting on his kitchen island, a crate two feet square and two and a half feet deep that weighed seventy pounds, but a ton to him. He couldn't move, couldn't cry, only stare. The tanned face from a week in the LA sun bore a chiseled grimace. He would never return to LA for any reason including promoting his book. A vague wondering swirled inside him. What would she have been like growing up here, would she still be alive, would he have missed seeing the grace and beauty of her dancing, or would she have found a way to dance anyway, something in her blood not to be denied no matter the place? Does place really matter anyway? It seemed to matter for him, to a degree, for now. It certainly mattered to the folks that spent their whole lives here, but was that place or family? Or friends, or a seemingly safe environment, at least now, where dangers are known, seen, acknowledged without fear but with respect, without random violence, faceless strangers, millions of cars and people crowded on top of each other until the tiniest spark sets off a raging inferno of death and destruction. Place was rural Oregon for Sandy. Was it death of a child or death of innocence or the slaughter of patience that pushed them to their remote new worlds? He had come here wounded, complacent, a failed shell thrown into a place littered with ghosts, extreme weather and wilderness, and he had survived. Someday he might even thrive. Not today. The crate took care of that. He thought grief had passed into mourning but now he wasn't so sure.

The doorknob turned and Clarissa walked in, eyeing him first, then the crate. She went to him and held out her hand, which he took. She lifted upward slightly and it brought him off the stool, standing full height, shoulders slumped, and she wrapped her arms around him and pulled him tight to her, her face settling against his shoulder. He felt only the comfort, the love.

"Let's let my sister rest in the basement," Clarissa said. "She's had a long trip."

The cemetery opened the first week of May with the usual bustle of loved ones planting flowers, laying out wreaths and bouquets. This year started with the interment of Stark and Mayor Barnet, which they attended out of community respect. That event, yesterday, under clear skies and warm temperatures attracted a crowd, but today low clouds had moved in and rain was inevitable and six of them stood around the exquisitely honed hole, the gravestone already in place, the crate inside, covered by plastic turf tacked to a square of plywood. The Lutheran pastor said a prayer. Bunny snuggled close to Russet, five hands entwined, faces solemn. Clarissa's head bowed, and he saw tears rolling down her cheeks. Angie bit her lower lip, her eyes misting too as they huddled with Elsa between them.

He removed the turf-covered board, kneeled in the damp brown grass, and extracted the top and sides of the crate. LA dirt mixed with cremation ashes in a Minnesota hole. He took the shovel in hand, heavy as a sledgehammer today, and gently filled the sides, finally covering her. The cemetery crew would lay the real sod. David pulled fake-turf over the plot and they covered it completely with roses, carnations, lilacs, and many lilies. The site would one day hold everyone that now waved tiny good-byes, and as he looked at his family and at the grave, a bit of grief flitted away, replaced by a strange and sad contentment. If grief could last like this, how long will mourning go on? He didn't know and for now, didn't care. It was enough that he'd done what was necessary. He could feel the grief losing its grip, the lies of closure in a single year long past, and he thought he might mourn until they put him beside her, and if so, that was fine with him.

"I wish I'd known her," Elsa said softly.

"I do, too," he said, his voice shaky. And he wished *he* had known her too, but she was young and didn't know herself, though God knows she had tried, like he had tried and even with the advantage of years, he felt no closer than she'd been. The eternal questions still lacked answers, nebulous, floating in some vast time memory ether. The only things solid were the earth beneath his feet, the sky above, the people turning and walking silently toward their cars, each wrapped in their own questions. They didn't need a place to go. Neither did he.

Sorry Mr. Wolfe. We're all home now.

The End

Acknowledgements:

Sincere Thanks to the many people and professors that helped with this work and my education. I will not name them here as their standards are very high. None the less, their insights were invaluable, as were those of my early readers—you know who you are including Amy Lindahl and Melanie Ahlquist. Thanks to Lauri Holman for the cover art. She didn't want credit but deserves it. Special thanks Darla Bruno for editing concepts and guidance, and to Colleen Graves and Barbara Cary Hall for copy editing.

Quotes:
From: Helpless by Neil Young
From: Are You Sitting Comfortably
by The Moody Blues
From: For a Dancer by Jackson Browne
From: You Can't Go Home Again
by Thomas Wolfe
From: Down on Highway 61 by Bob Dylan

Mentions: While they are not quoted, a few writers that I hold in high esteem are mentioned: Earnest Hemingway, Jim Harrison, and Cormac McCarthy.

also by **Ken Waxlax**

The Earth Abides Forever
ISBN 978-1530691616
Available on Amazon, Kindle
or write ken.waxlax@verizon.net

Author Bio:

Ken Waxlax grew up in northern Minnesota, graduated from high school, and attended college. After moving to Oregon, he traveled the Pacific Northwest extensively. He currently works and writes in the Southern California desert.